Michael Mewshaw's

WAKING SLOW

"Mewshaw is a writer of great scope and imagination."
The New Haven Register

"A real achievement . . . What really sustains the book is a continuous and unobtrusive yet most effective strain of comic insight which somehow nicely ventilates the pervading seriousness."

William Styron

"Mewshaw is sadly, curiously, gently involved with the predicament of the drop-out generation . . ."
Kirkus Reviews

WAKING SLOW

MICHAEL MEWSHAW

AVON
PUBLISHERS OF BARD, CAMELOT, DISCUS, EQUINOX AND FLARE BOOKS

Grateful acknowledgment is extended to the following for permission to quote copyrighted material:

Alfred A. Knopf, Inc.: Lines from "Esthètique du Mal" from *The Collected Poems of Wallace Stevens,* by Wallace Stevens (1954).

Doubleday & Company, Inc.: Lines from "The Waking" from *The Collected Poems of Theodore Roethke,* by Theodore Roethke. Copyright 1945 by Theodore Roethke.

AVON BOOKS
A division of
The Hearst Corporation
959 Eighth Avenue
New York, New York 10019

ISBN: 0-380-00804-1

First Avon Printing, October, 1976

To Elaine G. Mewshaw
and
Linda

The greatest poverty is not to live
In a physical world, to feel that one's desire
Is too difficult to tell from despair.

"Esthètique du Mal"
WALLACE STEVENS

This shaking keeps me steady. I should know.
What falls away is always. And is near.
I wake to sleep, and take my waking slow.
I learn by going where I have to go.

"Waking"
THEODORE ROETHKE

Chapter I

1

Late in his junior year at college, Carter White's parents drove their Pontiac through the guard rail on Chain Bridge and plunged into the Potomac River. Because traffic had tied up the rescue squad, it was an hour before divers attached great hooks to the chassis and hauled it out. Inside the automobile, as if in a diving bell, the Whites were buckled to their seats, blue, cold, and dead.

Although by the time Carter was told, a bus would have served as well, a gusty wind in Harrisburg whispered for him to hurry and he thought the emergency dictated an airplane. Yet once on board, soothed by Muzak and attended by a tall stewardess, he couldn't believe what he'd heard. Death seemed improbable, as the smiling girl cupped a yellow rubber mask to her mouth and instructed him how to breathe. She and the watered drink he sipped acted as guarantees against turbulence. If, as he had read somewhere, a styrene glass would last many lifetimes, how could his parents pass away so quickly and completely? He had just seen them . . . When?

Memory managed to do what the long-distance call from Washington had not—sear into him a sense of his loss. The argument at Christmas had been foolish. When asked by his mother what he planned for the future, he had spoken vaguely of a career which would let him express himself. His father had interrupted to suggest he set his sights lower. It was hard enough just to find a job. And who knew what lay ahead?

Like most of their conversations, this one had ended with cruel words Carter wouldn't forget. "Maybe you two have given up and are dead from the neck down, but I'm not. There's nothing between us any more. I have more in common with people in my dorm." Now, before he'd had a chance to apologize, they were entirely dead.

9

Carter asked for another drink, and a steady hand carried it to his lips. Off to the right the silver wing looked insubstantial, as precarious as his emotions. But his dark eyes didn't show the turmoil he felt when he wondered whether death was the end. Although his parents were Catholic, they had lived outside the sacraments, and this troubled Carter. If pressed, he would admit he had prayed for them until his freshman year, when he'd begun to see religion as a peculiar atavism, much like a domesticated dog's circling as it settled for the night. Afterward he had retreated into books and into the fortress of his body, refusing to pray, attend Mass, or take communion.

For the last two years, if he believed in anything, it had been in his youth, his meticulously trained intellect, his carefully cultivated strength. Weight-lifting had fleshed him out and raised him from ungainly adolescence to a muscular grace. In family photographs, he stood apart—or so it seemed to him. High cheekbones, a dark close-shaven beard, and a somewhat wooden expression explained the nickname—Indian—which he didn't like and wouldn't answer to. Death played no part in this life he had fashioned for himself.

Yet now, as the plane descended—touching the macadam the giant tires screamed—he feared his mother and father were damned. Or, if not damned, then lost completely. Their plunge from the bridge through fathoms of water had released them from a circumscribed life into a vast darkness for which he knew their quiet pessimism was inadequate.

As the airport limousine crossed the Potomac, he turned away from the river and watched the willows along the shore. Around the Tidal Basin cherry blossoms blazed in a banked fire, consuming themselves, casting off livid petals like live coals.

Far up Wisconsin Avenue he got out at a rowhouse where the front walk was canopied by a green and white awning, and a neon sign said Harahan's Funeral Home. Ray Quigley, his brother-in-law, met him in the hall, then guided him by an elbow back outside. When they had gone the length of the awning, Carter demanded, "How did it happen? I don't understand. I . . ."

"Calm down." Ray placed his hand on Carter's shoulder. "Bill was driving. He might have fallen asleep at the wheel or had a heart attack. Witnesses say the car veered

10

sharply. The brake lights never came on." After a pause, he murmured, "There's no sign that they suffered long."

Carter tried to speak, and when he couldn't, he hung onto a metal pole that supported the awning.

"Get a grip on yourself. The doctor has Marion under sedation. I'll need your help to pull her through. If anyone asks how Bill was feeling—whether he was depressed —say he was happy and in good health. The damned insurance company is already snooping around. I'm sure they'll ask a lot of questions."

"You don't think it was suicide? Be honest, Ray. Was it?"

"I really don't think he'd do it when May was with him."

Carter nodded. "Is there anything I can do?"

"No. I've made the arrangements. They'll be buried in Rockville."

"And the funeral?"

"Right here."

"No Requiem Mass?"

"You know that's impossible. One last thing. The caskets are closed. They were pretty banged up when I identified them at the morgue. If you want a last look, I'll ..."

"No. Let's go in."

Six somber rooms opened onto the corridor, each with a knot of mourners, the murmur of voices, and a bright spray of flowers. In the last one, Marion sat beside the sealed coffins, which looked cold and gray as the stone slabs on which the bodies must have lain at the morgue. Her hands, palms up, rested in her lap, as if she were studying her fortune and was sadly astonished by it. Carter put his arm around her, whispering, "I'm here," then when she began to sob, said, "It's going to be all right. I'll take care of everything." Patting her moist palms, he moved closer to the caskets, almost as though there were something to see.

For three days he stayed in that desolate room, greeting relatives and family friends. Fortunately, the visitors' list was lengthened by students from Mr. White's biology classes who shuffled in to offer condolences to Carter and Ray and to the crown of Marion's bowed head. Still the gathering seemed grimly quiet compared to the one across the hall where Alexander O'Reilly lay in state. After reciting the rosary—Carter had seen ranks of men and

11

women each evening, down on one knee to answer the consoling strophe of a priest—these light-hearted mourners chided their children and laughed as they spilled out into the corridor, trailing cigarette smoke and the smell of liquor. Ray muttered about "the goddamn Micks," but Carter, restless at his vigil, envied their vitality. Was it faith that allowed them to face death so casually?

One morning, before the others arrived, Carter crossed over to pay his private respects to the stranger who rested in a forest of flowers redolent of damp earth. His coarse flesh looked robust, still full of blood, and white hair alone revealed his age. Above his head burned two candles whose flames flickered on the glass beads wound around his fingers, and illuminated the holy pictures, Mass cards, and novena lists pinned to the silk liner of the casket lid. He seemed as well fixed for eternity as he must have been in life.

Back next to the metal boxes, Carter shivered and couldn't control the frightening, secret resentment he felt toward his parents. Despite his shock, his genuine sorrow, it was just like them to die and be buried this way.

The day of the funeral the weather went from spring to winter and back again at each scudding cloud, and the damp grass at the cemetery sucked the mourners' feet as they ascended the path in a silent line. Marion hung on Ray's arm, black and straight as a furled umbrella, numbed by three days of heavy sedation. Carter followed with the Unitarian minister whom Ray had hired to mumble over the bodies. There were only a few other people who gathered at the caskets before they were lowered into unconsecrated ground.

As they retreated to the limousines, a shower was falling and Marion broke down. Her legs wouldn't work right and she sobbed hysterically, so that Ray had to carry her to the car.

Her harsh moans remained with Carter at college, and for weeks he couldn't study, concentrate, or sleep. Cursed by recurring dreams of his parents' death, he began to keep himself awake at night, worrying about the deadliness of their lives. What he rememberd most was their chronic fatigue, the characteristic passivity which had deposited his father in an armchair by the window and set his mother pacing, flexing her fingers, rapping her nails on any solid surface. Though always

12

restlessly in motion, she could never escape the arid moderation of her husband's voice, which when something went wrong, assured her it wasn't as bad as it seemed, and in rare moments of good fortune, reminded her that nothing, especially not happiness, endured.

Mr. White seemed to have made a life's work of waiting for nothing. By the time he was fifty, he looked eighty, his lean frame folded over compactly as a bolt of cloth neglected on a shelf, and no matter what he wore, he looked gray, as though he were perpetually powdered with ashes or were being transformed into stone. His eyes alone had color—watery-blue, like the dyed cells he studied under a microscope in the biology lab.

To Carter, he had described his indifference to disappointment and to life as reason or realism or maturity—never despair. Perhaps the word was too dramatic for his taste. Yet nothing simpler could have induced this early deadening.

Carter soon came to care less whether his father had taken his own life than how large an inheritance of dryness and timidity lived on in him. At least suicide was a choice, an act of the will, whereas accidents happened to the strong as well as the weak, the bright and the dull. Before this fact, he felt particularly vulnerable.

By May the well-tuned machinery of his body no longer meshed, and he experienced continuing bouts of insomnia, headaches, and breathlessness. He tried to make love once, but found himself frustratingly incapable. Finally, when Ray called to say Marion had suffered a nervous breakdown and was under the care of a psychiatrist, Carter collapsed into an armchair for the remainder of the semester.

Images of death appeared everywhere. Each morning the newspaper was mad, accusing, and apocalyptic, and each evening the war was on television. One night after watching a brigade of waterlogged bodies stream down the Mekong River—they seemed to sink with the tasteless dinner to the sick ache of his belly—he switched off TV for good and fled in self-defense to slick science fiction, which promised to keep him in the dark a few hours longer. He preferred stories about amnesiacs—characters who, after a blow to the head, woke up changed. Unable to understand why anyone would fear to forget, Carter would have beat at his own skull if he could have convinced himself it was that simple. But he submitted himself to something much more painful. That summer he enlisted in the army, entered officers' candidate school, and volunteered for Vietnam.

2

By June, a year later, he was back in Washington, waiting on tables at a night club named La Grenouille. Although he walked with a painful limp and didn't like the people or the work, he preferred this pointless job to returning to college. He never considered a permanent career. The salary and tips, supplemented by a small disability allowance, were barely enough to pay for his room at Mrs. Vaughan's boarding house, but because he had committed himself to nothing, he believed he could do anything once he made up his mind.

The night club, located on M Street up three flights of stairs, was owned by a Frenchman who, against all logic, called it a *cave*. Plaster of Paris had been smeared on the the walls and ceiling, sculpted into tiny stalactites, then sprinkled with glittering slivers of glass. Obscurely lit by candles and dimmed further by cigarette smoke, the place did look a bit like a basement in which packing boxes had been covered by checkered tablecloths.

When, surprisingly, the club became as successful as he had hoped, the owner raised prices, intent on taking outrageous profits before times changed and the clientele moved on. Ambassadors came with their girl friends; socialites, barhopping after embassy dinners, arrived in formal dress; and students who could afford it picked off strays. Always the place teemed with women.

Yet that night in June, Carter noticed her at once. It was nine o'clock. His leg had ached all evening, and he'd had one eye on his watch. Slim, dark-haired, and wearing a navy-blue pants suit, she sat in a corner with a stout man twice her age. His hair commenced at the crown of his head and fell straight back, as if a weight hung from the gray wisps at his neck. They drank gin-and-tonics, Carter remembered, and while she talked, the man listened patiently, stifling several broad yawns. Despite his polite refusals, she insisted they dance every tune and kept him there until closing time, when his face looked like a punctured balloon.

The following night she was accompanied by a man

14

her own age, a big smiling fellow with sandy hair and a drooping red mustache. Hailed loudly by friends, he seemed not to want to sit in a corner with her, but she turned and left him standing in the center of the dance floor. After an unsteady instant, he joined her.

They ordered quickly, the argued. Or, rather, the man did—his gruff voice carrying through the smoke and music as far as the bar, where Carter had stationed himself. The girl didn't answer. Wearing a short white dress cut low on her tanned bosom, she looked away from him, apparently bored by his face.

At last he got up and danced with someone from another table, then staggered into the men's room. When he'd been gone ten minutes, the girl called Carter, who felt he had dipped into a trove of scent as he leaned over to listen. Up close her face was younger than he'd expected, her mouth wide and supple, her forehead broad and clear. She had dark brown eyes, basically the same color as his, yet hers appeared warm, receptive, and alive, while his flat eyes trapped on their surface everything they saw.

"Will you do me a favor?" she asked. "See if my date has slipped and broken his neck in the bathroom." She was smiling, but seemed upset.

Her date had indeed slipped, and was unconscious under the urinal. Carter shook him awake, pulled him to his feet, and helped him into the hall, where the girl was waiting.

"Thank you. We're leaving."

"I don't think he'll make it down the stairs."

"Course I will."

Pulling free, the man promptly collapsed, and Carter caught him before he crumpled to the floor again.

"Here, let me have him. He needs fresh air."

She opened her arms, and strangely, her willingness made Carter hesitate.

"He's heavy. Take one side and I'll get the other."

Their arms crossed behind his back, and Carter's hand brushed her bare shoulder. The fellow hung as a dead weight between them, his feet useless on the stairs. He giggled once, then was quiet as they labored at the banisters as though at life lines. A party of three met them coming up, but had to turn back, for there was no room to pass. At each step a stab of pain shot through Carter's leg.

"Have you hurt yourself?" the girl asked around the man's rolling head.

"No. I have a bad knee."

A crowd at the street entrance applauded as they emerged. The drunk was still wedged between Carter and the girl in the white dress as they walked west toward Key Bridge, breathing heavily.

"This is silly," she panted. "We sound like a locomotive."

"Want to rest?" He swung him against a wall, and they too leaned their shoulders to it. "I trust your friend has other virtues."

"Usually he can hold more."

"Jesus, that would make him heavier."

"Maybe I should call a taxi."

"No. If it's not too much farther, I think we'll make it."

Tightening his grip, Carter trapped her arm under his, but she said nothing until they reached a green Thunderbird convertible. "This is it." With her free hand she dug awkwardly into her purse, while Carter propped the fellow against a fender. He could stand on his own now.

"I can't thank you enough." Her hair, which was wound on top of her head, had started to uncoil in dark tendrils at her neck. She blew them back and continued poking around in her purse. "I didn't leave you a tip and I want . . ."

"Forget it. Let Big Red take care of that another night."

Looking up at him, she somehow seemed fragile and sturdy, lean and voluptuous at the same time. Though her arms and legs were slender, she had rounded hips and breasts which were taut even without a brassiere. Her nipples had tensed. "Are you sure?"

"Yes. Now let's pour your friend in. I have to get back."

She waved as she drove off. Then Carter limped up M Street to La Grenouille.

Late the next night she came alone to claim the corner table. In blue hip-huggers and a red-and-white-striped pullover, with her hair down and her cheeks tanned a deeper brown, she looked as though she had stepped off a yacht. Leaning over to ask for her order, Carter again smelled perfume. Or perhaps she had simply carried in the scent of the summer. Since it was a slow hour, he mixed a gin and tonic himself and brought it to her. "How was your friend this morning?"

"I wouldn't know." Clearly she wanted to put that behind her, and insisted he accept a tip. Because it seemed to matter to her, he agreed, then introduced himself. Her name was Elaine Yost.

"Do you go to Georgetown?" she asked.

"No. I may be the only waiter here who doesn't. How about you?"

"I went to school out of town."

"Look, I'm off in an hour. Why don't we go somewhere and eat?"

"Fine. I'm starving. I haven't regained my strength from last night."

"I'll mix you another drink while you're waiting."

"No, I'm not through with this one. I'll come back to meet you."

The moment Elaine left, he had a premonition she wouldn't return, and even if she did, he wasn't sure where they would go, since he didn't have a car. But when he had finished sweeping the floor and had toiled down the three flights of stairs, she was out front at the wheel of the Thunderbird.

"You drive," she said, climbing across the console that separated the bucket seats.

Coming to the driver's side, he trailed his fingers over the cool fender and tried not to limp. As he slid in behind the wheel, soft leather shaped itself to his back, easing the ache in his leg. "Is the car yours?"

"Of course. Do you think I stole it? It was a graduation gift." She buckled the seat belt at her slender waist. "Where are we going?"

"I know a place that has crummy people, but good food."

On Wisconsin Avenue they stopped at Britt's Cafeteria, where Carter often ate breakfast. The crowd semed the underside of the group at La Grenouille, the authentic, slightly seedy original which wealthier people found it amusing to imitate. There were exuberantly drunk students, bearded boys on the nod, frizzy-haired girls in fringed leather jerkins and Indian beads, and middle-aged men in pastel shirts who limply held cigarettes which stained their fingers brown. A young policeman paced the aisles, clutching a night stick in both hands. He must

17

have been new to the job, for behind his stern professional mask lay a look of purest bewilderment.

Elaine and Carter picked up plastic trays and silverware, still warm from the dishwasher, and ordered eggs, sausage, fried potatoes, and coffee. As they ate, both of them appeared dazed by the fluorescent lights, the noise, the late hour. Her eyes avoided his until, after nibbling her lower lip, she mumbled, "You must think I'm crazy, or worse, the way I conned you into buying breakfast. We should start over. I was raised to know better." Squaring her shoulders, she put out a hand and with a smile of amazing falseness announced as though they had met in a receiving line, "Elaine Barton Yost."

When the smile disappeared, he let go the hand, but said nothing.

"And you're Carter White. A good name. It sounds wealthy and substantial, like the gentlemen farmers who live in Virginia near my grandmother. Are you wealthy and substantial?"

"Wrong on both counts," he said, annoyed at her performance. He didn't enjoy being put on.

"You don't have to be wealthy to be a gentleman. At least you look like one in the little jacket and black bow tie you wear at La Grenouille."

"Company rules. What do you do, anyway?"

"Nothing." Pulling a pack of Parliaments from her purse, she leaned forward for a light.

"Where did you graduate?"

"Smith." She crossed her legs, then dabbed a finger at her lip.

He would have thought her beautiful if it hadn't been for the protective brittleness that broke over her face when he least expected it. It did something unpleasant to her—or to him—and he wanted to cut through it. "I've never known anyone who went there. Tell me about it."

"There's not much to tell. All the girls who just graduated are in the same predicament—panicky now that the four years are over. I've been looking for a job, but everything's such a let-down."

"What do you mean?"

"It's hard to say without sounding spoiled. I enjoyed school. I had a sense that I was growing. And at the same time I was anxious to get out and use what I'd learned. It's embarrassing to remember how eager and naïve we were." She smiled at him through the cigarette smoke. "There was this girl on my hall who had a habit of saying, 'Have a good weekend.' As a freshman she'd say it to you on Friday afternoon, but each year it got earlier and earlier, until by the time she was a senior, she'd babble on Tuesday, 'Have a good weekend. Have a nice weekend.' She couldn't wait. She seemed certain something great was coming. At graduation I almost expected her to go from girl to girl, shouting, 'Have a good life.' But then . . . then we were out, and it was like college had ruined us for anything else. Do you understand? It's a shame all that studying and energy and exhilaration leads nowhere except a dreary routine. The alternatives are horrible—sleeping in the park with the hippies and catching hepatitis, or living in Levittown."

"Can't you find a job?"

"I could, but I'll be damned if I intend to spend the rest of my life in some grimy government office."

"The rest of your life? Come on," he tried to cheer her. "With good behavior you'd probably be out in a few years."

"Sooner than that. I'm making my break now. I plan to say the hell with work, and take one long, last vacation to read and think and get a good tan." Crushing her cigarette in an ashtray, she let Carter light another. Her words had poured forth in a torrent, but didn't appear to have provided much relief. Instead they had swirled back behind a dam inside her and begun to stew again. "I'm talking an awful lot about myself. What about you?"

"I guess I could use a tan, too, but . . ."

"What are your plans?"

He shrugged. "I might go back to college someday. I need about thirty credits to graduate."

"It would be a shame not to finish."

"Oh, I don't know. With a degree I might decide I deserved a better job than being a waiter. Then I'd be in the same fix as you—unemployed and unhappy. I wouldn't want to risk my career at La Grenouille."

Rather than smile, she bit her lower lip—a habitual gesture which denied the generosity of her large mouth. Delicate features and cheeks as lean as his left her subject to quick changes of expression which should have revealed, but didn't, what she was thinking. "No plans?" she asked.

"None."

He thought he had lost her and was ready for the brittle smile, but she nodded. "I'm glad to hear someone

19

tell the truth. Everyone else says he knows exactly what he's doing. He's going to be rich and famous and happy. He has it mapped out from now until he retires to Tampa."

"Who's *he?*"

"What?" Her eyes swam into focus. "No one in particular. Just, you know, everyone. Who'd want a life like that? I don't care whether I'm happy. I simply don't want to be bored."

"I wouldn't be so quick to put down happiness."

"It's easy enough to be happy. Better finish your eggs before they get cold." But she pushed her plate aside. "Why did you leave school?"

"I was in the army."

"Drafted?" She was prepared to grimace.

"No, I joined."

"No kidding?" She couldn't contain her astonishment. "Why?"

"No reason." Now he shoved aside his plate and refused the cigarette she offered. "I don't smoke."

"I should give it up myself." She stuffed the pack into her purse. "How long were you in the service?"

"Nine months. I know. Don't say it. I should have gotten an abortion and saved myself the trouble."

She smiled, but didn't seem to think this was funny, and it hadn't thrown her off the track. "Aren't most men in for two or three years?"

"I had a medical discharge."

"Your leg? You weren't in Vietnam, were you?"

Yes, for a grand total of two days." He spoke rapidly, "as if he'd repeated this many times and wasn't anxious to run through it again. "I fell off a truck and tore the cartilage and ligaments in my right knee."

"That must have been terrible."

"It was no fun, especially when I was at Walter Reed. I felt foolish in a hospital full of guys who were really hurt. Each day I'd . . ." As his voice trailed off, he toyed with the silverware.

"What do you think about the war?"

"The same as everybody else. I wish to hell it would end." His voice was full of a weariness he hadn't intended.

"Are you in the Movement or anything?"

"No. I've been in one army. I don't see how it would help to join another."

"Don't you think you should do something, get involved?"

He couldn't be sure she was sincere about this. It sounded almost as if she were testing him.

"What could I do? It's easy to say you should be involved—as if anyone had a way of staying completely out of it—but does that help? I think it only gives the illusion that you're in control. From what I've seen, things just happen and always go wrong."

"Stupid people make them happen. Silly mistakes make things go wrong."

"Do they?"

"Of course! Though some people do act like they're determined to destroy their lives. My God, that's not for me."

Carter was smiling. "I can believe it. At least not until you have a good tan."

By the time they left Britt's it was growing light and a gray cloud of mist rode over the Whitehurst Freeway, wrapping the handrails and arc lights in spools of gauze. From a bakery along the riverbank rose the yeasty scent of fresh bread, and as they walked to the car Elaine asked, "Could I be hungry again?"

"You didn't eat much. Where do you live?"

"In Arlington. And you?"

"On P Street. I'll walk."

"No. Let me drop you off. You drive." Handing him the keys, she folded her arms against the cool air.

"We'll have to continue our debate another time," he said as the car rounded the corner of Wisconsin and P.

"Of course. Maybe daylight will help." She patted her palm over a silent yawn.

"I'll call you." He stopped the Thunderbird at Mrs. Vaughan's. "Meanwhile keep working on your tan."

"You can count on it." Then, suddenly slipping her hand behind his neck, she drew him close to kiss his mouth.

3

In San Francisco, the night before he flew to Vietnam, Carter had met an Oriental whore and slept with all Asia beneath him. Pleading fatigue, she lay still as he moved his hand over her hairless skin. Small in the hips

21

and breasts, she bore a blue scar beneath her navel, and the muscles there gave in easily to his fingers. Wordlessly she accepted his weight, let him do what he wanted, and was more asleep than awake when he withdrew. He abandoned her in that hired bed, seemingly untouched, her sleek yellow body yielding a scent of incense and the East.

In a way this was the closest he came to Asia, and his impressions of forty-eight hours in Saigon were less distinct than those he recalled from TV. He remembered little save that it didn't lend itself to fear so much as to confusion. The people had swarmed by him, over him, their hands moist and demanding, their voices clipped, monotonous. Then at dusk, on a balcony above the streets, he heard the clatter of birds dispersing and bats beginning to stir, of Vietnamese bent toward home on bikes, pedicabs, and motorscooters.

Billeted with another officer in an airless hotel ten blocks from the American embassy, he ate cheeseburgers and French fries that first night, his only night, and washed them down with lukewarm bottles of Budweiser. They sat on the balcony for the breeze, whose stronger gusts blew riffs of transistorized soul music up from the street.

In the morning, as he climbed aboard an army van which was to transport him to a briefing, Carter noticed on each soldier's face the identical bewildered expression he had seen on his own as he shaved. But if it reassured him to know his dislocation wasn't unique, the relief proved short-lived, for as the truck pounded through a narrow street, a boy on a bicycle tossed a green hand-sized object onto the flatbed. Someone shouted, they all stood at once, and before the word "grenade" could take shape in Carter's brain, much less on his lips, he was pushed from behind and tumbled over the tailgate. There was a muffled explosion, then a burst of pain through the deep inner flashing of his eyes.

Consciousness surfaced slowly; minutes slipped by while the sky pieced itself back together. He was on the sidewalk, convinced he'd lost his legs. But in the circle of faces above him, no one else had been hurt. A captain held up a Coke bottle. "It wasn't a grenade after all. Your foot got tangled and you took a bad spill."

"Here, give me a hand." Carter reached up for help.

22

"You'd better stay where you are."

"I'm all right."

But he wasn't. The instant he planted his foot, pain jutted from the sole of his shoe to the crown of his head, and only by a dry grating sound, like loose pebbles, could he locate in his right knee the hub from which the aching spokes exploded. This was before he blacked out again.

He came to briefly in the hospital as a medic slit the seam of his trousers and probed the bruise, which had ballooned to the blue limits of its skin. "Noncombat casualty," whispered disembodied lips, and someone needled an ampule of anesthetic into his arm. He tried to stay awake, but couldn't fight the drug, which affected his eyes first, then his hearing. Lying uncomfortably on his back, he listened to what he thought was laughter growing louder.

After the operation, recuperating at Walter Reed, he passed the days in disbelief, playing out punishing dramas in his mind. Even his good fortune—his "million-dollar wound," as the medics called it—seemed absurd, subtly threatening, and he imagined it made him an object of derision to the other patients. Sometimes at night when he heard them scream, he thought it was at him. But they were groping for lost limbs, thrashing against the metal bars of their beds.

During the day, while he rested in a wheelchair draining the incision on his knee, Carter avoided their accusing eyes, avoided the sight of their tortured flesh lacquered with scars. Then at visiting hours, near despair himself, he listened to them swallow self-pity and confidently discuss plans. They seemed to assume a statute of limitations on suffering, and after one tragedy, couldn't imagine another. All but the hopeless cases—those who never spoke, who having seen their mangled bodies no longer cared—looked with childlike hope to the future. Now they would do what they had always wanted, they repeated incessantly, as if Vietnam were a precondition for any venture. Not even the incurable cripples admitted that what they wanted had been forced cruelly into line with what they could do.

Only Carter, who, the doctors assured, could soon do whatever he pleased, had no plans. He knew better.

Because of his odd hours at La Grenouille, he seldom saw the morning sun that spring after his dis-

charge, and he spent his afternoons in a rushbottom
chair by the window, staring at the cobblestones of P
Street, his right leg elevated on a hassock to relieve the
pain. Buds had burst out on the trees in a systematic
pointillism which dazzled his eyes and filled his head
with pollen. Opposite Mrs. Vaughan's, three dogwoods
bloomed like trees of money. Coin-sized blossoms were
scattered in spend-thrift abundance on the patio.

But Carter thought of his bankruptcy, of his parents
dead a year. On the desk, in an old photograph, they
stood half in sunlight, half in shade, their mouths parted
in puzzled smiles, their eyes, like his, dazed. Enlarged
from a candid snapshot, the picture left them looking porous, already images of death.

Once he went to the gymnasium at Georgetown to follow a regimen of exercises the doctor had prescribed, but
haunting echoes resounded in his chest. The heat and
ripe smells were those of hothouse cultivation, the air too
thick to breathe. Everywhere he sensed empty spaces at
his back.

That summer he stayed in front of an ancient rotating
fan, whose rusty blades creaked like Mrs. Vaughan's
rocking chair on the porch below. A breeze blew along
P Street, rank-smelling from the river, but did little except rattle the parched leaves, ruffle the window shade,
and send spears of heat into the pavement. In that fur-
nace of a room, it was difficult to resist the natural reflex
of his character—the inclination to despair. Yet when the
idea of suicide sifted once through his reserves, he re-
coiled, angry and a bit ashamed.

Evenings he held an ear to the still air, which imprisoned the sound of talk and laughter with the softness of
a child's hand cupping fireflies. This seemed to promise a
life he might recover, if he were lucky. But then in the
earliest hours of dawn, as he limped home from work, he
occasionally saw a thin rind of moon sail overhead, a re-
minder of the crescent-shaped scar, bright as lipstick,
cool as a goodbye kiss, on his knee. He knew how far he
was from where he wanted to be, how ill-equipped he
was to travel the distance.

Not wanting to rush Elaine Yost or himself,
Carter waited four days before calling to ask her to a
rock concert at the Carter Barron Amphitheatre. He had

intended to borrow a car, but she insisted they use the Thunderbird. It had to be broken in, she explained.

For the rest of June and July they rode in her car through the heat mirages in Washington. Conversation seemed to come easier with the top down, for the words which might have fallen between them ripped away on the wind, offering an illusion that he and Elaine had worked beyond another disagreement. Still they disagreed a great deal. She said, so far as she cared, she was happy, yet she acted nervous and agitated, while Carter kept calm even when admitting he was far from pleased with his life. Elaine claimed it was simple to change that, if he wanted—in response to which he laughed.

Their points of agreement, though unstated, were simpler than the change she suggested. The most obvious lay at the surface of their skin, but curiously, neither pushed this at first. They seemed more amazed at what was deeper—a realization that they were alone, isolated by an antagonism toward the life around them. Something was wrong, and though they didn't agree on how, or whether, it could be corrected, each recognized it was rare to meet another who thought as they did.

After half a dozen drives, all lacking in destination, she suggested they picnic on her grandmother's property in Warrenton, which had a pond where they could swim. The day glinted like buffed aluminum, hot and silver-streaked, the sun glowing behind hazy, high-flying clouds. Leaving the city in light traffic, Carter cruised over Key Bridge, onto George Washington Parkway, into the shade of tall trees, and back out into bright heat. As they sped from one zone to another, the road roared in their ears, quieted, then roared again, as if they were traveling through a series of tunnels.

Beyond the palisades on the far side of the river, the spires of Georgetown University loomed in weightless suspension above billowing green foliage. Set against this background, the severity of Elaine's hair, wound into a bun, emphasized the clean lines of her face. Her chin was lifted, her head had a confident tilt. Small flat ears, seldom exposed to the sun, shone like tinted petals, the same color as her one-piece pink cotton jumpsuit. Sleeveless and short in the legs, its zipper was lowered to the crease of her bosom.

Farther south, on the Beltway, the forest had been butchered and chained behind a link fence, and as the sun burned through the haze, they felt its fire on their foreheads. While Elaine gloried in the warmth, Carter was grateful when they quit the highway for a state road, where tar bubbles popped beneath the tires, releasing a pungent odor. In the shade, the leaves appeared to be dripping green, as if they'd melted together to form a single tree with thousands of trunks.

"Careful, or you'll miss it," said Elaine. "The road is beyond that huge sycamore."

"Where?"

"There." She pointed.

"I'll do this on faith," said Carter, passing through a tiny fissure in the wall of foliage.

They rattled up an unpaved road, no more than a path, wavering and indistinct, overhung with blossomless wisteria vines and scented by crushed clover. Then emerging from the woods, they crossed a field of deer grass. "This can't be the way to your grandmother's house," he said.

"No, it's the back road to the pond. There wasn't time to call her, and I don't like to barge in. Grandmother's the type to give us a lecture out of Emily Post."

Cresting a hill, they coasted to a stand of cedars and pines which shaded a small pond. Carter cut the motor, but some tireless engine continued revving.

"Listen," whispered Elaine. "Locusts. The last time they came I was four, and the ugly shells they left behind frightened me. My grandfather explained what they were and when they'd return. It seemed so long. Now he's dead."

Reaching around to the back seat, she picked up a plaid blanket and a picnic basket. Carter carried a newspaper and his bathing suit rolled in a red towel. Pools of silence preceded them as they strode over pine needles to a grassy clearing that had a few charred bricks, like a black eye, in its center. While they spread the blanket, the soft wool billowed and slipped from Carter's grasp. Kneeling to smooth the wrinkles, he dropped the *Washington Post,* which landed with a loud smack.

"You shouldn't have brought that. I'm sick of news." From the basket, Elaine handed him a bottle of white wine. "Why don't you put this in the pond to cool?"

She acted almost angry, but he didn't answer. Walking down to the water's edge, he balanced the bottle on a mossy rock just beneath the surface, then covered it with moist ferns. Long and glowing green, it looked like a fish on a platter. A water bug rowed over, then skated off.

Back at the blanket, Elaine had unpacked the food and was lying on her side. The brown skin, drawn taut across her thigh, had a sheen lightly downed with copper-colored hairs. Holding his leg straight, Carter lowered himself next to her, but the paper was between them.

"The *Post* divides us," she said, smiling now.

"Should I have bought the *Star?*"

"It wouldn't make any difference. I told you, I hate news."

"Even good news?"

"It doesn't exist. Good news is bad news. That's the policy of papers in this country."

"Seems to me I've heard this before. You must be a Spiro Agnew fan."

"Yes." She laughed. "And Nixon too. I'm mad for jowly men. Which eliminates you for a few years." She drew a finger along his fleshless jaw. "Maybe forever."

"About this newspaper . . ."

"Not so fast." She stopped his hand before he could move it. "Tell me why you read it. Nothing ever happens."

"Wrong! Everything happens. Horrible things happen."

"So do good things."

"Maybe you could start a paper that publishes good news. Stories about airplanes that don't crash, couples reunited after decades of separation, pets found, safety records set, money . . ."

"Don't joke, Carter. I'm serious. I can't figure out who they're talking about when I read those articles about how much I'm supposed to think, drink, smoke, make love, and spend. It's enough to cause schizophrenia. So I've simply decided to forget the news. It's nothing but hysteria and exaggeration. Things aren't as bad as they seem."

"You're right. They're worse. I'd be glad to forget them if I could."

"You can. Just don't read the lousy newspaper."

"You mean it, don't you?"

"Yes. I don't want to hear another word about riots, Vietnam, Israel, ecology, or racism for the rest of the summer."

"I won't mention them, but they won't disappear."

"That's okay. We'll disappear. We'll *eschew* the news."

27

"We'll eschew it and spit it out," he said, unwilling to believe she was serious.

"Ugh! Let's eat."

The wine was still warm, and since Elaine had forgotten the corkscrew, they used a fork to clear the neck of the bottle, then drank from Dixie cups. Despite the slivers of cork and wax, both swore it tasted fine.

"I wish we had another bottle," said Carter, refilling her cup.

"Oh no. That would ruin me. I'm already dizzy."

"Lie back and look up at the trees." He stretched out on the blanket. "They form a steeple that tilts one direction or the other, depending on which eye you close."

"What if you close them both?"

"The blanket spins."

"It spins even when my eyes are open," she said, lying back beside him.

"You're ahead of me."

"Maybe it's the heat."

"A likely excuse."

"I feel a little drunk whenever I'm here. If you visit a place over the years, the perspective is always wrong. The pond seems smaller, out of focus."

"It's not very big."

"Don't you like it?" Her hand reached beyond the blanket and idly rooted up grass.

"Yes. It's lovely."

"The water's very deep. I've never touched bottom."

"Have you tried?"

"Not really. It's murky and I don't like to dive." Eyes shut, Elaine yawned, rolling over to face him. The jumpsuit showed the soft shape of her breasts, and the pink cotton suggested their color. "I love it here. When I was a little girl I used to pick blackberries in the field, then swim to wash the chiggers from my legs."

"Did you live with your grandmother?" Carter's voice, too, was drowsy, mesmeric. Dragonflies, like points of fire, darted and dipped across the pond, whose surface was stippled with sunlight.

"Yes, from time to time. I was out of the country a lot with my parents, but I always thought of the farm as home."

"Where are your parents now?" He struggled to keep the conversation alive and his eyes open.

28

"Costa Rica. Daddy's in the foreign Service. And your parents?"

"They're dead."

After a false, flickering start, her lips parted, and she propped her head in her palm. "When did they die?"

"About a year ago in an automobile accident."

"I'm sorry. We won't talk about it any more." She sat up, drawing her legs close to support her chin on one knee.

Bewildered and a bit irritated by her abruptness, he couldn't tell what was wrong with her. After a moment's silence, he asked, "Do you want to swim?"

"I forgot my suit," she answered tonelessly, staring at the water, her eyes wide to the glare.

"Well, I'm going in." He picked up the red towel.

Elaine didn't answer, but as he started for the car, there was a soft rasping sound, and he shot back a surprised glance. Standing, she slipped the jumpsuit from her shoulders, pushed it down her hips, and folded it on the blanket. In sandals and pink nylon briefs, she strolled toward the pond.

At the water, she kicked loose the sandals and thrust her thumbs under the elastic band of her bikini underpants as if to remove them, then left them on. She must have sensed he was watching, for she turned from the waist so that he saw in silhouette one firm breast, uplifted to its nipple, before she marched into the pond. She didn't dive, didn't lunge, simply waded in up to her chest and began to breast-stroke. Above her the dragonflies fluttered like a silk scarf, then resettled.

She was on the far side, staggering through the shallows, when he unbuttoned his shirt and felt sunlight on his chest. Prying loose his shoes, he unzipped his trousers, let them fall, and hesitated with his underwear before pulling it off. As he stepped in, the icy water wrapped tight steel bands around his legs, and he plunged in over his head, swam to the center of the pond, and dived into a deeper darkness, through a more profound cold, which closed over him like a metal lid. While he kicked to row himself lower, his lips expelled a chain of bubbles, blue and hard as greased ballbearings.

Was this how it had been for them? Leaden water, viselike, impenetrable. Their skin itself a body sheath, scorched armor crushing a bloated corpse. The panicked blood beating against their eyes and ears. Or, improbable

29

as it seemed, had they sat dry and upright, patient as he remembered them in life, suffocating in the padded capsule of their car?

Touching bottom, he tried to shove off and lunge to the surface, but his hand sank in six inches of muck, and he tasted slime. Lungs burning, he fought his panic down and pulled himself up, hand over hand, like a man climbing a rope ladder. At last air roared in his ears, exploded in his chest. Bicycling in place, he treaded water while his breathing subsided.

"Did you make it?" asked Elaine from nearby, her breasts buoyed by the water.

He nodded.

"I don't believe it."

He resented her taunting smile and disappeared with a splashing kick of his foot. This time it was easier, as if on his first descent he had hollowed out a tube to the bottom of the pond. When he felt the muck, he made a fist and squeezed up a handful, but surfacing, sensed its slow seepage, a steady oozing loss, and feared he would have nothing to show. Relaxing his grip, he seemed to lose less, and by the time he reached Elaine there remained a greenish lump, which she accepted reluctantly.

"You did it." Frowning, she rinsed the mud from her fingers as she climbed ashore in a bright shower of beads. Rivulets streamed down her back, plastering the panties to her behind. She removed them, yet except for the slim crease of her buttocks, might still have had them on. After twisting the panties dry, she spread them on the grass, pink and transparent as sherbet slowly melting.

At a distance Carter stood slapping the water from his arms and legs. He was unsteady, his breathing harsh and hurried, and the blows his own hands dealt roused in him a dull anger toward Elaine, who appeared not to notice. Oblivious to her own, and his, nudity, she fumbled with her hair, which unfurled in a dark rope over her shoulder. As she shook her head, the rope untangled, then split into wet strings and threads that snapped at her face, so that she had to shut her eyes. Her breasts swayed, while the muscles in her belly tensed and relaxed and tightened again. The sun was on her in spots, shifting as she twisted, dappling the skin light and dark, like the leaves above or the rippling pond below.

Stealing closer, Carter seized Elaine's hair, then released it when her eyes opened.

"I wish we had brought more . . ." She stopped talking and seemed not to know where to look.

On her left breast was a scar, long, thin, and startlingly white. Carter's finger traced its curve, as if it were a silk thread he could brush away. "How did this happen?"

"When I was a little girl I fell out of an apple tree and scratched myself. It wasn't much of a scratch, but as I grew, the scar grew." Shivering, she pressed her breasts together with her arms. "Don't look. It's ugly."

"No, it's not." His hand cupped the breast, and he kissed it. Then, as a rash of gooseflesh rose on her shoulders, he brought her close to kiss her mouth. Her cool fingers were clasped to the small of his back, but when he put his hand between her legs, Elaine whispered, "No. Don't."

He didn't stop.

"Please, don't."

"Why?" Though she lightly held his wrist, her eyes invited him on.

"I'm not on the pill."

"Are you sure we can't?" Uncertain what to make of her expression, he hadn't moved his hand.

"I don't want to take the chance. I don't think we should."

Neither stepped back, but the distance widened between them. A black thread of hair now intersected the scar on her breast.

"We could do something else," she said.

He shook his head no.

"Yes. Come back to the blanket." Leaning down, she retrieved her panties, and gently guided him up the grassy embankment.

"Are you telling the truth?"

She didn't answer. After hastily clearing away the food, she pulled Carter onto the blanket and pressed herself, cool and wet, against him. Above them the screen of cedar branches dimmed, then darkened altogether, as he closed his eyes, feeling her fingers flutter over him. Though she was still close beside him, he was conscious only of his own body and of that deft, disembodied hand whose slight strength had somehow begun to raise him off the ground. His back was arched, his breathing labored. Then there was a sudden, shocking, frigid sensation when she switched to the hand that held her panties, and he came into the sleek folds of nylon, convulsed in the release of which he had dreamed, a delirious ache of opening, cracking, turning inside out.

They stayed until dark, when the stars emerged along with the fireflies, and as they stared up into the depthless sky, it was often difficult to tell which was which. Though the shrill whir of the locust had ceased, crickets and frogs had commenced a hoarse, chanting chorus, in cadence with Carter's heart and with the pulse that beat everywhere he touched on her skin. When something splashed in the pond, the blood quickened beneath his fingers. "What's that?" she asked.
"A fish."
But they scrambled to their feet, and dressed quickly, close enough to hear each other breathing. In total darkness they folded the blanket before groping about in the damp grass for the picnic basket. Their hands collided, retreated like frightened spiders, met again and remained together.
As they drove to Washington, Elaine stretched across the console, her head in his lap, his knee cupped by her cool hand. Carter, too distracted to regret or be grateful for the quiet, thought of things he wanted to say, but he believed there was time, an entire summer. While heat and darkness canopied the uncrowded highway, he stroked her cheek, experiencing a delicious sense of suspension, for all the bad memories had taken leave of his mind and body.

Chapter II

1

They skimmed along at the crest of the summer, their course effortless and uncharted, and though Carter never quite comprehended the momentum which carried them, he asked no questions. Elaine possessed a grace which made everything seem natural. In fact, he never saw her do anything awkward. Her smallest gestures were beautiful triumphs, which defined her character more precisely than elaborate assertions might have. The way she smoked a cigarette, put on a sweater, took off her clothes, or lifted a glass called attention, not to itself, but to such intangibles as her confidence and tenderness.

Every day they came to the sundeck of her parents' apartment in Arlington and spent hours talking, dozing, and sipping the gin-and-tonics she mixed for them. His job was to massage her with tanning oil in a ritualized fashion, smoothing it over her shoulders, under the scant halter strap of her bikini, over her fragile ribs, and onto the cinnamon-colored down at the small of her back. The floral scent of the lotion, the hot silk of her skin, her deep tan, together they seemed a distillation of the summer's essence, which he could almost capture as his hands followed the glazed swells of her body.

Sometimes there was what sounded like gunfire out on the Potomac, thundering above Washington, heralding a storm that threatened, yet never broke. Elaine said it was probably a starter's pistol at the boat club, but one afternoon, bothered by the noise, Carter got up and limped across the creosoted boards to the edge of the deck.

Ten stories below and beyond the crowded boulevard, Arlington Cemetery simmered under a net of smog. The grass had dried a uniform brown and the leaves were curled on splintery branches. A few of them had already fallen, not as they would in autumn on a rush of cold air, but in slow spirals, like the birds which swooped from the trees to the ground, searching for shade. Next to a mound of red clay, a group of mourners fought the heat and their grief with stiff backs. After another salute had rattled over the river, echoing as static off the cobblestones of Georgetown, the pallbearers folded a flag into a triangle and handed it to a woman in black. Carter returned to tell Elaine it was a military funeral.

For weeks in that unflagging heat he was woozy from lack of sleep as well as the cocktails, and imagined Elaine and himself inhabiting a bright gauzy vacuum, like one of their highball glasses inverted on a table top, the silver beads of gin curtaining them from the world outside. This sensation of total, private beatitude persisted until the moment of re-entry, as they called it, when she would cross Key Bridge and drop him at La Grenouille. There in the smoky *cave* the vacuum would crack.

What Elaine did during his absence, he never knew. Although curious, he had no desire to pin her down, for he was with her whenever he wanted, and this accounted for all his free time. He presumed she had other friends, but believed he was the only one she dated.

Tuesday, his night off, they usually felt compelled to go out, return early, and reaffirm that it was better to be alone, savoring their hours together. Twice they attended twi-night double headers at D.C. Stadium, and he dutifully explained baseball until it began to bore even him. For a rare performance of Thelonius Monk, they ventured into the black ghetto and were robbed at gunpoint by a man who made good his getaway in a taxi that had patiently waited. At a restaurant in Bethesda, Elaine persuaded Carter to sample Korean cooking, which consisted of stinging slivers of beef and pungent dishes of aged cabbage and seaweed. After devouring what was placed before them, they laughed over Alka-Seltzer at their senseless gluttony. Another night, at the Theater Lobby, they sat on folding chairs in the appalling heat to watch two Pinter plays that put their feet fast asleep and left them agonizingly unable to flee.

Still they insisted on these evenings out, convinced that they didn't need to be entertained so much as tantalizingly delayed. The diversion doubled the pleasure of undressing afterward, stretching out on her cool bed, and

34

luxuriating in the certainty that there were no more courses, acts, curtain calls, or innings to endure.

At the start one minor detail postponed their lovemaking. Elaine refused to take the pill or be fitted for a diaphragm. The former she rejected on medical grounds —recent reports had frightened her—and the latter for admittedly squeamish reasons. She didn't care to visit a gynecologist.

In view of her other attitudes, this puzzled him—she pointed out the inconsistency herself, but wouldn't budge —yet Carter concealed his irritation. Familiar with the fastidiousness that often affected girls her age—the lingering commitment to a romantic spontaneity, the reluctance to calculate—he also realized that cautious planning demanded closeness and allowed for claims which curiously exceeded the act of love. He was unwilling to mention these before she did, and so when Elaine said she thought contraception was the man's responsibility, he didn't argue. He assumed it, and found her a tenderly passionate partner in bed.

June and July were serene. After an explosive spring, Washington nested in a profound somnolence which stirred very little at old alarms from the Middle and Far East. Each morning as Carter hurried out to meet Elaine, he stepped over the newspaper at his door, never troubling to look down. When he came back, it was gone, no doubt discarded by Mrs. Vaughan, a compulsive cleaner. Yet, content as he was with their isolation, he sensed that there were matters he would have to confront sooner or later. They might as well have been stacked in rows all around him, like the papers piled in Mrs. Vaughan's cellar, no less threatening for having gone unread. Despite the soothing lethargy of this summer, he couldn't bring himself to believe life had changed for him, especially since he knew that what attracted Elaine was what he least liked about himself—his aimlessness, his absence of ambition, his unclear future. For the moment they corresponded to her mood of whimsical impatience and studied irresponsibility, since she had forgotten, or decided to ignore, that they approached ideas from opposite directions and drew opposing conclusions.

Once, while slightly drunk, she said, "I like you because you don't bore me, and we have fun even when I'm depressed. You're not filled with your own importance,

35

always chattering about companies that are dying to make you rich. What a waste of time!" But it occurred to Carter she was speaking to herself or to the memory of someone else, not to him, and as the weeks passed, she seemed to address this absent party more often, until he finally crashed the globed perfection of their privacy, suffusing it with an insufferable tension.

By late August they were both angling for elbow room. Their humor, customarily good-natured, had grown barbed and belittling, and the silences lengthened as the days became shorter. Carter felt he was motioned on at one minute, held at arm's reach the next, for while Elaine never refused him, she had begun to act bored, or, at least, distracted. One night when he told her he loved her, she answered, "I'm not anxious to get married," to which he could only reply, "Neither am I." For all he knew, his words were more candid, since minutes later she was in his arms, whispering in a low, intense voice, as though afraid she might be overheard, "I love you too."

Angry, Carter wished she would make up her mind, but then realized she might reach the wrong conclusion. Much as it hurt his pride to admit it, the link between Elaine and him, no matter how tenuous, was more than he'd had in the last year. So he clung to it, as she, for her own reasons, did to him.

The last Tuesday of the month, Elaine's grandmother invited them to Warrenton for dinner. Elaine laughingly said her parents didn't trust her letters and wanted a second, thoroughly subjective, opinion about Carter.

"Don't expect too much," she warned him. "Grandmother's a terrible snob and never likes anyone."

"I'm fairly particular myself."

"Oh, Carter, please don't act defensive. I want her to like you."

At four-thirty, after a few hours on the sundeck, they descended in an air-conditioned elevator to the Yosts' apartment. A large gloomy flat of three bdrooms, two baths, and a library and living room littered with elegant, mismatched furniture, it reminded him of an import shop. Arranged haphazardly were a peruvian wall tapestry, a Florentine chest, a Persian carpet, a Chinese screen, and wood carvings from Haiti. Elaine explained that each item was a souvenir of their travels, and had an anecdote

36

attached to it. Carter's favorite—the story as much as the *objet*—was a mahogany bar given to Mr. Yost by Juan Perón. Behind it in racks rested bottles of wine, awaiting infrequent visitors. The Yosts hadn't been home in two years, and before Elaine's graduation, the apartment had been closed up.

Carter thought it nonsense to keep an unoccupied apartment, but Elaine said it was because of taxes. Her father, a member of the U.S. legation to Costa Rica—a second-rate post in a fourth-rate country, she admitted, and assured him it wasn't anything the family took seriously—liked to maintain an address in the States.

Carter showered in Mr. Yost's bathroom, which was nearly the size of his cubicle at Mrs. Vaughan's. The walls were finished in pink tile and the bath fixture shaped like a gold duck. When he twisted the wings, water splashed out of the bird's startled beak.

Afterward he shaved, put on a new blue suit that had slightly flared trousers, and went into the kitchen to wash down two aspirin with a glass of tomato juice. He had a thudding headache.

"Will you fix this? The catch is broken." Elaine came in, wearing a short yellow slip, and handed him a necklace. "Shall I leave my hair up or let it down?"

"Down."

"No." She prodded her chignon. "I'd better keep it up or Grandmother will raise hell."

"Do you think she'll approve of the rest of your outfit?"

"Don't you?" She performed a passable pirouette, her thighs flexing nicely.

"Yes. It's a shame she won't see it."

"Is the suit new?" She picked a loose thread from the sleeve.

"No. I've just never worn it around you."

"You should have." She seemed surprised, which pleased him. "It's more becoming than your others."

"You don't like them?" His voice was distant, as he concentrated on the broken catch.

"Well, in that tight green one you do look a little like a truck driver."

"Truth wins out in the end." He jingled the necklace. "Fixed? Good. Hook it, will you please?"

She turned her soft brown back, its bones delicately warm under his fingers. After fastening the necklace, he kissed the curve of her neck and pressed his palms to the

37

nylon over her breasts. In the circle of his arms, she twisted around and raised her lips to his.

He eased inside her panties, then halted. He knew the one place they could go from here. Her bed. But today this seemed a frustrating limit, not nearly enough to put him in touch with her. Eventually he intended to break through this confusion, but there wasn't time now.

As he pulled back, she caught his face between her hands, and an amazing expression of tenderness clouded her eyes. Tilting her head to stop two perfect tears from flowing, she said, "Promise never to get disgusted and leave me."

His arms fell to his sides. "What do you mean?"

"Just don't leave."

"You know I wouldn't." Then he asked the question which invariably preyed upon him when things went right, "Is anything wrong?"

"No." She tried to smile. "I'm being silly."

"I know something's wrong," he said, searching the shadow of her eyes. "I've known it for . . ."

"Let me dress. We'll talk about it on the way."

2

As Carter steered the Thunderbird through rush-hour traffic on Rosslyn Circle, fading sunlight reflected from the new glass and chrome high-rises, and the air tasted stale and tepid. Neither of them spoke. Amid the din of horns, car radios, and idling engines, it would have been hard to hear. Yet he moved to the inside lane, waiting for her to tell him what was the matter. He knew something was wrong—had been wrong for weeks—for Elaine had been more unpredictable than usual, her mood as unstable today as the sun was steady. When she'd held his face in her hands and implored him not to leave, a voice inside him had whispered *Go*. She wants you to go.

Crossing the stream of cars flowing south over Key Bridge, he accelerated onto George Washington Parkway, the ornate hood of the Thunderbird carving cool swirls of air. Soon tall trees fenced off the sun, the city, and the hillside houses, and it seemed they were far out in the country. A scent of honeysuckle stole through the exhaust fumes from a few withered flowers which had survived the heat.

Her face devoid of emotion, Elaine was smoking and watching the river, oblivious to him and to the question he'd asked forty-five minutes ago.

"What's wrong?" he pressed her.

"Nothing. Let's not ruin the evening."

"If it's nothing, how could it ruin the evening?"

"Carter, you're impossible. You have such a mania for defining things."

"Why not talk about it? Maybe I can help. Does it affect us?"

After a last drag on her cigarette, she stabbed it into the ashtray. "Yes."

Immediately he swerved from the pavement, bumped along the shoulder, and pulled in at an observation point high on the palisades.

"Carter, what are you doing?"

Beside a beige Buick with Ohio plates and an Airstream trailer in tow, an old couple sat on aluminum chairs, eating fried chicken and gazing at the Potomac, green as a garden snake, which glistened below. Carter coasted to the opposite corner before switching off the ignition.

"If we're late, Grandmother will be furious," said Elaine, who already was.

"We're not moving until you tell me what's the matter."

Knotting her arms, she bit her lower lip and studied the leafy patterns on the windshield.

"I'm not kidding. If it concerns us, I have a right to know." He sounded angry, but felt almost relieved, at last on the brink of discovery, confirmed in the suspicions he'd harbored that she wanted to break off the relationship. "I'm waiting."

In her lap Elaine's hands coupled, as though one were giving comfort to the other. She started to look up, thought better of it, and lowered her eyes. "I'm pregnant."

Carter kept very still, carful not to blink, not to swallow, not to reveal any emotion. "How?" he asked quietly. "I mean I always . . ." There was no sense continuing. Putting a hand on her knee, he struck a light tone to mask his inner turmoil. "Don't look so sad. It's not a fatal disease. We'll get married."

She shifted her leg so that he lost touch. "It's not that

39

easy. The awful thing is, you see"—as she faced him, the dismay in her eyes appeared depthless—"it's not yours."

For some reason, before speaking, he peered into the rear-view mirror and saw two blank dots, his eyes opaque as chips of slate. "Whose is it?"

"You wouldn't know him."

"How can you be sure it's his?"

"I'm sure," she said tersely.

"But how can you be? I might have slipped up."

"Don't blame yourself, if that's what you're doing. The doctor said I'm more than three months pregnant. We haven't been sleeping together that long."

He didn't know whether to regret or be grateful that he wasn't the father, for among the emotions which contended for his mind, one was still an unreasonable guilt, while another was a sense of total exclusion. He was drawn in many directions—responsible, saddened; sympathetic, incensed. "Look, you have to tell me how this happened."

"What good will it do? It was so stupid of me. So stupid." She shook her head in disbelief, annoyed, rather than sorry or upset, that she had been involved in this messy incident.

"Why were you this long finding out? You should have known . . ."

"Before I slept with you. Before I met you. Is that what you're saying?" Crossing her legs, she tried to compose herself, and spoke in short bursts. "This spring in Massachusetts, I stopped taking the pill. When I didn't have my period, the doctor said that wasn't unusual. I came to Washington, intending to have a checkup, but . . . I kept putting it off. First I was busy looking for a job. Then I met you and . . . Honest, I meant to break with you and go away, at least until I found out for certain, but last week after the doctor told me, I couldn't do that."

"What will you do? Are you going to get married?"

"No. I don't love him. I love you." Seeing him slump beneath the weight of this, she quickly added, "But I won't hold you to your promise. If you want to take me home, I'll . . ."

"What promise?"

"Forget that you said you wouldn't leave me."

"You don't see me going, do you? If you love me, we'll . . ."

"I'm sorry I said that. You'll think it was to trap you, and that's not true."

Carter extended his hand, wavered, and brought it to rest on the back of the seat. "If you love me, that's enough. We'll get married and keep the baby." But he spoke in resignation, as if only a drastic sacrifice by him could save the situation.

"I couldn't do that to you."

"You wouldn't be doing anything to me."

"No, marriage is out of the question. It would cause more problems than it would solve."

"It's up to you."

"It would be difficult enough if it were your baby, but this way it's impossible."

"Maybe you're right. Still, I'd like to help." Though he managed to clasp her shoulder, he had no confidence this would close the distance between them.

She was looking down at her lap again, fussing over the wrinkles in her dress, using a well-manicured nail to flick aside specks of dust. "I've arranged to go to New York for an abortion. I should have done it earlier, but . . ." Her voice trailed off, and it appeared she was incapable of comprehending her own indecision, this aversion to do what seemed sensible.

Yet Carter saw her silence as indifference, and believed his offer of help must have sounded ridiculous. "Why did you decide to do that?"

"What else could I do?"

"There are other ways. You could have the baby and put it up for adoption."

"No, I couldn't. Don't you see?" She seized his arm. "That wouldn't be fair to anyone, and there's no sense making this more difficult than it has to be."

"You think an abortion would be easy?"

"I didn't say that. It would be *easier*."

"I'm sorry. If you want an abortion, you won't need me."

Disconcerted, she cocked her head. "Is it because you're a Catholic?"

"That has nothing to do with it. You don't have to be a Catholic—especially not a bad one like me—to be against abortion."

"You actually are against it? In all cases?"

"This isn't all cases. We're discussing yours. And

mine. Do you actually believe you could have an abortion, come back, and find our relationship unchanged?"

"A baby would change it, too."

"Okay, but it wouldn't kill it."

"Carter, be reasonable. You sound like a preacher. A priest."

At last, unable to restrain his anger, he grabbed her face in one large hand. "Don't do that. Don't make fun of me. If you want an abortion, that's your business. But count me out."

Poised in the palm of his hand, flawless as a cut glass, her face was twisted by conflicting emotions. It reddened, then drained of color. She appeared angry, frightened, and finally very sad, as guttural sobs were wrenched from her throat.

When the first tear fell, he released her, leaned back, and closed his eyes. The hot lids stung, but it was better to keep them shut. As he felt now, he could have left her, and for a moment he was tempted to do it—bolt from the car and hike back to Georgetown. But after that, what? Return to Mrs. Vaughan's and resume the absurd repetition of his afternoons at the window? The thought chilled the perspiration on his neck. He didn't like to imagine his life without Elaine, and cared less to recall what it had been before he met her.

Yet whether he stayed or left, he believed there would be no escape from pain. It was a matter of lonely sorrow if he abandoned her, anguished recollection if he remained. So he sat there, hoping she would explain what had happened.

And as he waited, the issued assumed a frightening and familiar inevitability which, he suspected, could never be explained. He loved Elaine, but she was pregnant by another man. She was pregnant by another man, but said she loved him. Regardless of how he revolved it in his mind, he was not surprised. He should have known things would turn out like this.

The questions he might have asked struck him as futile. One would only lead to another, like a deck of trick cards which all bore the same face. Or no face at all. He would learn far too much or not enough, and in either case, there was no sense starting unless he intended to play out his hand and accept the possibility of leaving.

But then Elaine stifled her sobs and said, "Carter, you're right. I think I should have the baby."

42

Opening his eyes, he wondered how certain she could have been about an abortion. Would she have told him in the first place if she had made up her mind?

"I'll have to go away," she said. "I can't stay in Washington."

"Will you tell your parents?"

"No, I couldn't do that."

"Don't cry. I'm with you."

"I have to leave Washington," she repeated.

"Yes. I'll help any way I can."

"And when I go . . ."

"We could go away together, if you like."

She didn't say yes, yet didn't refuse him either. Straightening, she dried her cheeks with a Kleenex. "I got a lot of money for graduation, and some more—I don't know how much—for my twenty-first birthday. But I don't want to use it. I'd rather do this on my own. No one else should pay for my mistake. I'll get a job and . . ."

"No, you can't work while you're pregnant. I'll take care of that."

Minutes later they departed, leaving behind the old couple in their camp chairs with chicken bones on their laps. Ghostly columns of mist rose from the river, and as darkness began to brood over the highway, Carter and Elaine seemed to ride at the eye of a silent storm. Though no rain fell, stars streaked through the sky, their fire extinguished in soundless spurts, and bolts of heat lightning spread silver corrosion on the night. Too upset to think straight, the two of them talked on anyway, revived by the rushing air.

Elaine said they should go to San Francisco, but Carter, steeped in a tension which recalled that city immured in perpetual autumn, preferred Los Angeles. It was bigger, more impersonal, and while she couldn't conceive of what it would be like to live there, he reminded her of its obvious advantages. No one would find them, and like a six-month extension on the summer, all of Southern California would serve as their bell jar, globing them in its warm, anonymous light.

Telling her friends and family she had chosen to work on the West Coast, she would leave at once, before she began to show. Although he would have to explain nothing to anyone, Carter would come by bus two weeks later. This would give them time to think, perhaps reconsider. Elaine said she wanted him to be positive he knew what he was doing. She sounded sure that she did, but suspecting she would never admit half her doubts, he agreed, looking upon the separation as a test of his nerves and of her . . . He refused to put a name on it.

In Warrenton she fell silent for the first time in an hour, then murmured, "I can't face Grandmother."

They stopped at a gas station, where she called from a pay booth beneath a fluorescent arc lamp to say she was sick. Through the cone of light, a blizzard of moths eddied back and forth, blundering into the glass panels with powdery wings. Elaine looked as innocent and vulnerable as a doll in a clear plastic box. Yet in her womb swam a wormlike fetus, which he imagined not as the work of a man he would never know, but as one more product of his life's aimless and terrifying drift.

Chapter III

1

The Greyhound Bus Terminal in Washington smelled of fried chicken in wicker baskets, hot cotton and cheap cigars, old ground-in dirt and newly sprayed-on disinfectant, and mostly of diesel fumes acrid as soft tar. Through frayed speakers, the public-address system competed feebly with grumbling motors, the metallic ack-ack of pinball machines, and the squalling of portable radios tuned to various stations. Facing one another across the aisles, people sat in uncomfortable plastic chairs, staring blankly through the eye sockets opposite them. At the magazine rack a Negro boy, his head shaved, filigreed with ringworm and encased in a sheer stocking cap, pressed a transistor to his ear and danced alone in his private canister of sound. Soldiers, sailors, and marines roved past, chewing gum, prowling for girls, buying postcards and pornography, while nearby an immense old woman who had purchased a blue bandanna bearing a likeness of President Kennedy admired herself in the mirror-front of a candy dispenser.

Carter was propped against a pillar, resting his weight on his left leg, hectically whispering, When I get there I'll . . . When I get there I'll . . . But he couldn't complete the thought. After two weeks of acute loneliness it was difficult to complete any thought, and when he tried to force himself to concentrate, his mind flickered off into darkness, like a film clip that had slipped loose from its spool. The lone fact he knew for certain was how impossible it would have been to remain separated from Elaine.

Yet they had written few letters, and both seemed determined to act as if nothing were wrong and their breezy notes about the weather and other banalities could satisfy the craving for communication. Carter had matched

45

her, casual remark for casual remark, quip for quip, silence for silence, until finally last night, sick of the pretense, he had phoned long distance. Though she sounded happy to hear from him, her voice, like her letters, was sketchy, elliptical, punctuated by dashes and witty inflections, a childlike lip song. She failed to ask how he'd been, when or whether he would arrive, and didn't mention if she had reconsidered. There was nothing sad about what she said, but he asked, "Is anything wrong?"

"I'm tired," she admitted. "And I miss you."

"I miss you, too. I wish I were flying."

"No, we'll need the money. Call before you get here."

Her grasp of the practical, the shallow carelessness of her voice—surely it was a protective device—puzzled Carter, and he wanted to call her back, yet knew it wouldn't help.

He boarded the bus late that afternoon, and as it lumbered onto New York Avenue, then crawled up Sixteenth Street, men in shirt sleeves were walking home from work, bearing sweat stains and leafy shadows on their backs. They looked sunstruck, washed out rather than tanned, and winter would make it worse. He was glad he would be in California.

The air conditioner rushed on, rustling a few gum wrappers and swirling the stale smell of cigarettes. Clicking his seat back to a reclining position, Carter noticed a newspaper crumpled on the floor at his feet, but he refused to look at it. He knew the news. Vince Lombardi was dead. Much as that burly little tyrant must have trained against it—transforming his body into a steel barrel, his smile into glinting metal—death had stolen in and eaten out his strength.

Beyond the city line, they built speed through the suburbs and raced the long evening shadows toward night. In the foot-hills of western Maryland, the air became brisk, autumnal, and the high-speed whine of tires on the concrete reminded Carter of the locusts that had chattered through the summer. He wanted to sleep, but found himself thinking of his father, as he had so often.

Students came in dread to Mr. White's evil-smelling class-room and left in fathomless boredom, feeling oily, malodorous, and unclean. Carter, who had taken the course, recalled an over-ripe scent of formaldehyde, which was wafted from his father's hands—hands as precise as his voice, yet clammy as the reptiles he dissected.

Once, during a lecture about the nervous system, he had taken up a toad, and as webbed feet flapped between his fingers, spoken of the cerebrum, cerebellum, medulla oblongata—elongated fuzzy words which caterpillared through Carter's brain.

"In lower forms of life, the nervous system isn't centered in the cranial cavity. It may extend the length of the spine. You'll notice when I cut off the frog's head"—he flattened the toad in a glass dish, and the scalpel descended swiftly, just behind the ears—"it retains its basic motor ability." As he released what was left of the toad, it hopped about haphazardly. "This isn't a death spasm or a muscular reflex. The animal is alive." At a touch from the scalpel, the toad leaped again, landing on the tiny triangle of its head. "If we could nourish it and prevent it from losing blood, the frog might live indefinitely, since, to repeat, its vital functions are controlled not by the cranium, but by less localized ganglia. Thus when I put pressure on the vertebrae, the frog quivers, and when I press harder"—with a deft twist of the wrist, he severed the spinal cord "—its vital functions cease altogether. Now let us review . . ." Wiping his hands on a paper towel, Mr. White droned on, while for one of very few times the class was silent and transfixed.

At the semester's end, in a fit of sophomoric pique, he had accused his father of lacking the capacity to feel or to express his feelings deeply. He was a man who made his living mutilating animals. Secretly Carter had feared even then the desolate kinship between them, and sensed they were both like the toad, blindly awaiting a last stroke of the knife, all the while dead to life. Now he desperately wanted to bolt from under the blade, and believed he saw a way. He would help Elaine have her baby.

The bus lurched through cities and lunged out onto the plains, labored over mountains and inched through narrow defiles. During the day the air conditioner thrummed futilely; at night Carter froze, his face filmed with grime which no amount of scrubbing at rest stops could clean. Sleep came and went of its own accord, oblivious to clock, sun, or moon. Gnawing always at the tattered fringes of his consciousness, it would sweep over him suddenly, then just as swiftly recede. Once as he scanned the horizon for Amarillo, it fell in full day-light like an ax, and he woke hours afterward with a dull ache in his neck at the spot the blade had struck. Another time, in Arizona, during the dead of night, his eyes snapped wide and he saw a sheet of desert where cactus spread crippled shadows on the sand. The wind had clamped a strong hand on the bus and was dealing it a ghostly shake.

From San Bernardino he called Elaine, then returned to his seat and surveyed the distant suburbs of Los Angeles. On the window above his head a smudge from someone's greasy hair floated like a personal rain cloud. Outside, the sun was a swirl of color, swathed in smog, shading from orange to purple like a massive bruise, beautiful but diseased, while beneath it, as if beneath an endless arcade, the city possessed the seething life of a Bedouin village. Carter couldn't imagine how he would find a place here, and glumly speculated that they should have gone to San Francisco after all.

2

In a blue jersey and denim bell-bottoms, Elaine waited on a bench against the far wall, reading a paper-back and nibbling her lower lip. Her hair, knotted by a ribbon into a ponytail, swung over her left shoulder, and she rubbed the loose black ends. He saw she had gained weight, but wouldn't have said she was pregnant. A smile played at the corners of her mouth, and she looked comfortable, self-assured, even in that crowd of listless sailors, red-eyed Negroes with processed hair, and old couples who carried their meager belongings in canvas bags.

Carter wanted to shout and, after his anguished isolation, enter into an immediate, more intense contact with her. But feeling himself seedy and graceless by comparison, he hesitated to interrupt Elaine. Once she looked up, his responsibility would begin. So he paused a moment, trying to bring her into perspective, to picture the part she would play in his life. He wondered if these last steps would bring him any closer to her. Then, faintly annoyed —mostly at himself—Carter pushed forward, calling her name.

She finished a sentence and unhurriedly dog-eared the page before raising her eyes. She was still smiling. "Have you read this? It's so horrible, it's funny." She showed him the cover of *Love Story*. "It must have been a bad trip. You look awful."

"I feel awful." Putting his arms around her, he got no response, and when he went to kiss her, she turned a cheek.

"Not here. This place gives me the creeps." She guided him toward the parking lot, digging in her purse for the keys. "You drive."

"No. I have a headache." Brusquely he strode, as best he could, to the other side of the car.

Carter did have a headache, a raw sore where his half-thoughts spat hot grease. He resented Elaine, resented Los Angeles. Behind him, beside him, in front of him, rush-hour traffic crawled along ponderously, spewing smoke like a slow-moving freight train. The racket reached a deafening crescendo at intersections, as horns blasted pedestrians, brakes shrieked, and the pedestrians shouted back obscenities. On the sidewalks people shoul-dered one another into the trash-heaped gutters, and somehow the trash and the people looked the same—rumpled, dirty, and discarded. Overhead, in the narrow slot between buildings, the sky glinted dully, giving the glaring windows the appearance of blank eyes.

"Isn't it awful?" Elaine asked cheerfully.

"Look, if something's wrong . . ."

"There's not. It's just that after . . . How long has it been? Ten days?"

"Two weeks."

"I've spent so much time alone, straightening myself out, I suddenly feel I don't know you."

"What the hell!"

"Don't be angry. I'll be better in a minute. Let me get my bearings. How have you been?"

"Great."

"Did you have a hard time leaving?"

"Leaving what?"

"Mrs. Vaughan's? Your job?"

"Mrs. Vaughan was happy to see me go. She wanted to raise the rent. The people at La Grenouille couldn't have cared less."

"I'm glad you didn't have any trouble. That's the Civic Center." She nodded to a building on the right. Carter ignored it. "We'll be on the freeway soon. You'll like it in Hollywood. The apartment is bright and . . ."

"How much does it cost?"

"Two hundred a month, including . . ."

"Jesus, no wonder you said we'll need money."

"Wait until you see it. It's half a block from Sunset Strip."

"How will we pay for it? Don't you . . ." He stopped abruptly. His voice had soared above the noise, but he didn't know why he was shouting, and although Elaine looked calm, the hand that fumbled in her purse for a cigarette was trembling.

Despite himself, Carter did like the apartment, whose white-washed walls suggested the inside of an eggshell. Although it was small, a balcony onto the courtyard let in a pool of light, creating an impression of spaciousness which the high beamed ceilings expanded. Of the furniture, Elaine said, "Spanish Provincial. A little overdone, but at least it's comfortable." Then she pointed out the red tile floors, which would be easy to clean, the fireplace where they could grill meat on a hibachi, the kitchen which would be perfect once they painted the cabinets, and the bathroom which lacked only a shower curtain and rug.

Carter's mouth soured and he grew angrier as she spoke. The pain in his head seemed attached by stinging wires to the one in his knee, so that every movement meant an agony of mounting rage. Decorating an apartment was such a paltry diversion from the real reason they had come to California. "No," he snapped. "We can't afford it."

"Of course we can."

Her eagerness confounded him. "Elaine, we're not here to play house."

"I know damn well why we're here. And if I forget, you'll remind me."

"That's not fair."

"Is it any fairer for you to talk about why we're here? For two weeks I've been groping through these problems, and at last I have them worked out. How do you think I feel when you . . ."

"Maybe the same as I felt when I got off the bus and you acted like someone had delivered a slab of beef."

"Oh, Carter, I'm sorry. I explained why I was that way."

He emptied his lungs in a slow sigh. "I'm sorry too. But like you, I've been thinking this through. We're going to have huge medical expenses. Before I left I talked to a fellow who once lived in L.A., and he said the best place to work is a supermarket. They pay union wages, and I figure if . . ."

"Carter, let's not discuss it now. We have weeks. Months!" Leaning her head on his chest, she clasped him tightly in her arms. "You haven't even unpacked, and we're both too excited and upset to think straight."

As her tears dampened his shirt, he didn't know why he was angry, why he was arguing . . . unless in an attempt to convince her and himself that he would have preferred to stay at his old job and in his old room. An absurd notion. Resting his chin on the top of her head, he rocked her until his smarting eyes shut. "I'm putting myself to sleep."

"Why don't you unpack and lie down? I'll be right back. I have to wash my face."

The bedroom, too, had a beamed ceiling and three tall windows which provided a view of a lemon tree, and beyond its branches of shriveled fruit, North Harper Street. Furnished in the same style as the living room, it contained a chest of drawers, a night table and lamp, and two single beds which Elaine had pushed together so that their carved headboards formed one broad relief. On the wall was a childish chalk drawing of stiff roses in a lopsided vase.

In the closet, smelling of mothballs, Elaine's winter coats and suits hung in plastic bags beside a row of summer dresses, skirts, and slacks. On the shelves were hatboxes, stacks of neatly folded sweaters, and spare linen. Carter counted nine pairs of shoes which toed the rear wall. But he didn't need much room. He wedged in his raincoat, three suits, and slacks at the end of the railing and stuffed the remainder of his clothing into the bottom drawer of the bureau. After shoving his suitcase under the bed, he stretched out on the blue spread.

Though his fatigue had taken on new dimensions of giddiness, he didn't want to sleep until he was secure in this new place. The bed seemed to sway with a lunging motion like the bus. Or maybe this sensation issued from the strong beat of his heart. He had made a terrible start. Having ridden three thousand miles to help her, he had already come close to saying and doing what he recognized was best left unsaid and undone.

Still he didn't want to skate along the surface like Elaine. If they intended to stay off thin ice, they had to test every crack and explore the caverns of darkness underneath. But as usual she believed things would be easy, and this worried him. He had to convince her she was wrong before she sent them both crashing through.

"Can't you sleep?" Elaine climbed into bed, her hairline wet from the scrubbing she'd given her face.

"No. My body's on the bus and my mind's back in Kansas. I've been lobotomized by all that boredom. But it's better now that you're here." Unfastening the ribbon, he loosened her hair and combed it with his fingers. It was long and dark enough to be a nun's cowl. "Why don't you wear it down?"

"Too much trouble. It gets in my mouth and tickles my nose."

"Why have long hair if you're going to hide it?"

"It's easier to take care of."

"Long hair's very sexy. That's a scientific fact. It reminds men of other places where it grows in profusion."

"My God, I'll always wear a scarf."

Laughing, he lifted her on top of him, kissed her, and scooped his hand inside the jersey, up the smooth column of her spine, until he discovered a brassiere. As he unhooked it, there was a yielding of flesh against his chest. Then he rolled Elaine over to expose her breasts, which were whiter and larger than he remembered. She shivered, and the nipples tensed into tight buds.

"They're bigger," she whispered. "I had to start wearing a bra."

"Do you suppose it's milk?" He traced one of the blue veins that marbled her bosom. Even the scar was enlarged.

As Elaine shivered again, his finger lost contact and hung limp in midair before he leaned down to kiss her eyes closed. Along the incline of her belly, he tested for other changes. It was harder, fuller. Inside her slacks, he touched the soft tangle of hair, then withdrew his hand to tug at her zipper.

"Let me." Sitting up to undress, she sought the correct expression for her face and chose her brittle grin. But Carter could see the commotion in her eyes, and having removed his own clothes, hesitated above her, his desire in momentary flight. Suddenly he realized what she had meant on the ride from the bus station. He didn't know her either—this woman whose body, cleft into globes and swollen curves, contained mysteries she wouldn't explain and he doubted he could learn.

Arms straight by her sides, thighs pressed together, she lay rigid on the bedspread, her smile faint and falsely serene, her figure geometrically perfect like a piece of Egyptian mortuary art, so that the scar, in spite of its graceful arc, seemed the work of a malicious vandal. Then, miraculously, the statue quickened to life. She lifted her hands. "I'm cold. Come keep me warm."

He found no part of her cold, and the innermost point of her thighs was warm and moist. The moment she guided him in, he started to come. The sensation was of a silk scarf drawn out slowly and steadily. He tried to hold back, but it was impossible. As he pitched forward, Elaine locked her thighs around his waist, whispering distinctly in his ear, "Oh God," whether in passion or disappointment, he couldn't tell.

Alone, cold, and naked, too tired to cover himself, Carter tumbled headlong into sleep with the sound of running water washing his inner ear. He was at sea, rudderless and adrift on a high rolling tide, amid the smell, even the salt taste, of brine, which had settled into a rhythm, a deliberate yawing in the pulse of his brain. In submarine distortion Elaine's face loomed before him, her head swaying fitfully, again whether in endless negation or in the narcotic reflex of desire, he couldn't say.

He woke mumbling, "How long have I been asleep?"

"A few minutes. You must be dead tired."

"How are you?" he asked, realizing he hadn't satisfied her.

"I'm all right." She had dressed and stood before the bureau mirror, braiding her hair. Her eyes in the glass seemed to avoid his.

Getting up, he pulled on his trousers and went to her as she was about to coil the braid at the back of her head. He started to put his arms around her, but struck by some futility or redundancy in the gesture, did not.

"Why don't we go out?" she said. "I've seen enough of the apartment for one day."

Silently they cruised the gaudy boulevards of West Hollywood. Perhaps Elaine knew where they were headed, but Carter did not, nor did he care. He set the

Thunderbird free like a boat on a slow river current, and the traffic swept it along. He had pushed beyond the final barrier of fatigue to a crystalline state in which every sound and sight had the hot precision of the pain in his knee, the same fierce flicker as the neon which burst on and off all around them. On a billboard advertising an antidote for indigestion, a plastic heart burst, came back together, and broke again.

The road ended at a palm-lined palisade overlooking an empty beach. Heavy air, blown about by sea breezes, seemed to threaten a storm, but there were no clouds and the last light of day could be seen far out on the Pacific where the sun was funneling its fire into the water. Carter parked, fed the meter a dime, and walked Elaine down a rocky stairwell. At the bottom the wind died and the roar of traffic merged with that of the sea, a monotonously repeated rush and retreat. As they stepped out of their shoes and trudged over the sand, Carter took Elaine's hand, yet his mind, uncomfortable after so many missed connections, pursued its protecting ironies. He imagined that to anyone on the cliff they must have looked as cloyingly romantic as an album cover or a cigarette ad.

Dropping their shoes on a dune, they walked nearer the water, and with cool sand clinging to their feet, continued along the shoreline, on the edge of the continent, intent on savoring a last hour along before turning to face what was to come. At a jetty they sat on the damp stones and watched darkness coast in with the changing tide. Far out where the water gleamed a deeper green a crest of foam gathered, combed higher, and broke for the beach. As it pitched against the sand, then quietly glided back to the channel, Carter said, "I'm sorry about today."

"Don't be."

"I didn't want to start like this. We got off on the wrong foot and . . ."

"It was bound to be hard in the beginning," she said. "I don't think we should worry about it."

Carter couldn't conceal his exasperation. "From what I've seen, you're not worried about anything. I don't want to upset you, but . . ."

"For two weeks I did plenty of worrying." She spoke tranquilly, and though the air had become cooler, she didn't turn to Carter for warmth. "It cost me a lot of time and effort to get myself together, but I'm here now, and the big problem as far as I can see is how we live, how we look at, the next six months. We can make them hell on each other, or use them to grow and enjoy ourselves. I'd rather do it that way, wouldn't you?"

"Of course." But he wasn't sure exactly what she meant.

"Would you really? To be honest, from what you've said, I assumed this was a great trial for you. You acted like you wanted to grit your teeth and cross six months off the calendar.

"I know you're worried," she went on. "There are bound to be bad moments. It would be stupid to deny that. But they'll work out if we let them. This is a chance for you to try new things, try yourself. Don't settle for a job in a supermarket. You're too good for that. You could land a more challenging position and have something to show for it when this . . . this whole situation is over."

Though often mercurial, subject to moods he didn't understand, she had never spoken like this, and the change jarred him. Her indifference, her disdain for ambition and saving grace of self-mockery had disappeared and been replaced by a humorless determination. She talked as if she had come to Los Angeles to help him. Here in a new place, she said without a flinch of embarrassment, he could be a new man. His only limitation would be the breadth of his vision. Was she joking?

But when she said, "You could even go back to school," he realized how serious she was. "UCLA had night courses. Have you ever thought of becoming a lawyer? You'd make a fine one."

Soon she was a captive of her own enthusiasm, and the projects she outlined offered her an escape from the present, from the reality of her predicament. For this reason, and because the plans she proposed for his future seemed a guarantee of their future, Carter didn't interrupt. But then suddenly, like a break in a life-line, Elaine released his hand. "My God, our shoes! The tide will wash them away." Vaulting from the rocks, she raced over the sand.

Forgetting his bad leg, he jumped and ran after her. His knee ached, and the ocean air singed his lungs as he surged past her, opening yards of darkness between them. She laughed, cried out, "Wait!" and quit chasing him, but he wouldn't stop. Sprinting through ankle-deep foam, he refused to turn and confront Elaine, or whatever else pursued him.

Chapter IV

1

That night they squeezed into one single bed, made love, talked, listened to the noise from Sunset Strip, and didn't doze off till two A.M. Then at dawn, thrust out of sleep by a disturbing dream, Carter woke to watch the windows fill with tawny light like three tall glasses taking on wine. Naked beneath the covers, Elaine had curled onto her side, and he embraced her from behind, one hand on her breasts, the other on her belly. Her breathing was deep and steady. He could hear it clearly and feel it in the rise and fall of her chest in his arms. For once he didn't wonder who she was or why she had chosen to confide in him, but rather whom she had loved enough to let him lie next to her like this. Certainly not the older man he had seen at La Grenouille. The young fellow, the big redhead, was more likely, yet she hadn't seemed to care for him, and in his drunkenness that particular night he couldn't have done much damage.

Caressing the fullness of her belly, he decided it wasn't love that had brought this about. Just another mistake, blind and impersonal, which the answerable parties could explain no better than he could. Otherwise—Carter's mind leaped ahead—she would have married months ago and he wouldn't be here now. So how could he object? And what good would it do to ask questions?

At seven o'clock, careful not to wake Elaine, he went into the bathroom to shave. Although he'd slept little in the last few days, he felt remarkably fresh and vigorous. Even in the unflattering fluorescent light, he looked robust, alert. The muscles of his chest and shoulders, too broad to be contained by the medicine-cabinet mirror, flexed neatly under his tanned flesh. Maybe she was right, he reflected, scraping lather from his lean cheeks.

In a new town he could do whatever he wanted. Of course, he still didn't care about a career, and in daylight her advice seemed no less ludicrous and out of character, but he agreed that a good job would make it easier to pay for an apartment where he could continue sleeping with Elaine. At this hour, early in so many ways, the notion had a sufficiency, a coherence all its own. It didn't really matter what he did as long as he had Elaine and a place to be alone with her.

After donning his new blue suit, he darted a glance into the bedroom, saw Elaine was asleep, and quietly closed the front door behind him. A fountain in the courtyard freshened the air, which smelled as starched as his shirt collar, much more like spring than autumn. On North Harper Street a team of Japanese gardeners marched from yard to yard, mowing lawns, clipping hedges, pruning shrubbery, and raking leaves. The high slant of their lip-song never rose above the hiss of sprinklers which spat out long ropes of water. Sunlight on the spray created a small rainbow, a sheltering dome that hovered over the men. They broke beyond it only to toss onto a truck the exotic refuse they had gathered—gleaming magnolia leaves, unripe coconuts, a basket of hibiscus blooms, and a heap of sweet, slowly drying dichondra. Like fragile toys they hurried up the block, working with no wasted effort, and apparently no strain.

Carter wished he had a job like theirs, up in the heady air of dawn, dizzied by the scent of last night's jasmine, domed by a rainbow, and back home by noon. But he had set his sights higher, as Elaine said he should. Lengthening his strides, he outdistanced the gardeners.

Traffic on Sunset Strip was stalled from Crescent Heights to La Cienega, and hippies padded barefoot among the stranded autos, hawking the L.A. *Free Press* and hassling motorists for fouling the atmosphere with exhaust fumes. Carter walked west, past the Body Shop, a burlesque house whose marquee asked "Had Your Oil Changed Lately?" Over the sign someone had pasted an orange poster: *Male Chauvinist Pig—Support the Liberation of Women and All Oppressed Peoples*. On the other side of the street the Hollywood Hills hunched their brown backs into a hazy patch of smog, which obscured what appeared to be a number of large castles. Below them, on narrow shelves of rock, nested pastel villas, Oriental pagodas, Swiss chalets, and cantilevered cottages. The cars, the houses, the hills themselves gave the impression of hasty construction and utter impermanence. The slightest disruption might destroy everything.

Carter bought the *Los Angeles Times* at a coffee shop, and sitting at the counter, opened a newspaper for the first time in three months. It seemed that the source of Elaine's advice might have been the classified section, for promises of Money, Position, Prestige, and Opportunity leaped from the page like startled fish from a pond. Relieved to see so many jobs available, he skimmed from aerodynamic engineer to zoologist, circling the best prospects, then paid for his coffee and hastened back to the apartment.

Elaine was in the bathroom, running the water full force. Carter put on a pot of coffee, but before it had begun to perk, she shut off the faucet and returned to the bedroom. From the door, he asked, "Don't you feel well?"

"I have an upset stomach."

"Can I bring you anything? Coffee?"

"No. I'll sleep until I feel better." Blowing him a kiss, she rolled over.

Carter sat next to the telephone, and since it was too early to call anyone, fretted with his shoelaces, knotted and reknotted his tie, and after fighting the temptation, picked up the newspaper. He skipped from the front page to the sport sheet, and ignoring the articles about Vince Lombardi, spent a quick hour reading about this season's heroes. He even studied the box scores and the racing results. The Reds and the Orioles were bound for the World Series, the Rams had won three straight, and there was a snapshot of an immense young man in gym shorts standing on the scales in a slaughterhouse. "Schoolboy Grid Star Hailed as Game's Biggest Player" read the caption. He weighed three hundred and eighty-six pounds.

At nine he dialed his first number, and was mildly surprised that the position had been filled. Had he waited too long? Before he had a chance to ask, the secretary broke the connection. Quickly he made four more calls —to a research and development plant, an accountant's office, an insurance company, and a real estate agency

—but in each case was told he was too late or unqualified. How did they know unless they interviewed him? Again there was no time to ask.

Shaken, he poured another cup of coffee before reconsidering the classified section. Already his meaty list of prospects looked skeletal, and in the next few minutes the bones themselves dissolved. He had no success until he sifted the dregs at the bottom of the page where the ads tended to be brief, impassioned, and ambiguous. Addressing bored secretaries who didn't bother to inquire about his age, experience, or background, he arranged two appointments. But in both instances when he requested additional information, the voice at the other end became edgy and evasive and would reveal nothing except a salary—$140 a week for one job, $125 for the other.

He felt he was off to a poor start. The extravagant ads, as well as Elaine's encouragement, had led him to expect more—maybe, ridiculous as it sounded now, a firm offer over the phone. Even when Elaine emerged from the bedroom, recovered from her morning sickness, and assured him two interviews were a heartening start, Carter couldn't forget the seamless indifference of the voices he had talked to.

"When are your appointments?" Elaine asked.

"The first is in Van Nuys at two. The other's in Burbank at three-thirty."

"Good. You'll have plenty of time. If you run into trouble on the freeways, there's a map in the glove compartment. Why don't . . ."

"I won't have any trouble."

"I'm sure you won't. Do you plan to wear that suit?"

"Is anything wrong with it?"

"No. But why don't you take it off so it won't be wrinkled?" Loosening the tie, she unbuttoned his shirt. "Let me to it." She stripped him to the skin, as a mother might a child, led him to the couch, and shrugging the nightgown from her shoulders, made a swaying motion with her hips so that the material piled up at her feet. Stepping free of it, she lifted her right foot higher than she had to, as if she might start to dance. Her legs were lean and sleek, tanned even on the inner thigh. She looked so tall, so graceful, at ease within her supple skin, he rose up to meet her.

At noon Carter put on his uncertainty along with his clothes. He ignored her final encouragement, grinned at a joke she cracked, and left. Of course, he'd had job interviews before, yet this seemed different, like everything out here. Three blocks from the apartment he pulled the Thunderbird to the curb and studied a map of the city, on which the convoluted freeway system squirmed off in all directions, reminding him of schematic charts of the human digestive tract. Entering, he might be swallowed and spat out at any one of a dozen dead ends. He remembered yarns about hapless motorists who had missed the correct exit and been lost for hours. Already nervous, he didn't wish to risk this, and decided to follow secondary roads and side streets out to the valley. But after taking this meandering route, he arrived twenty minutes late for his first appointment.

The flat cinder-block building sat at the edge of an abandoned drive-in movie, where a sign commanded *Support Our Boys in Vietnam*. Passing in front of the blank screen, he walked through heat mirages on the macadam and a field of aluminum speakers that glinted like enormous trumpet flowers. Inside, a girl at a Samsonite table stopped her macramé work and directed him to a room where three dozen applicants squatted on the floor around a man in shirt sleeves. Most of them appeared to be high school students.

"Your name?" the man called out.

"White. Carter White."

"Okay, White, Have a seat. Be on time tomorrow. To begin again for the latecomers, lemme repeat that the hundred-and-forty-dollar salary is just an approximation. I mean, it's what the average, strictly mediocre guy can make with our outfit. Frankly, we don't want that type, because"—he beat his fist into his palm—"if you're aggressive, if you're a hustler, you'll make a hell of a lot more. What we're talking about is straight commission sales. Me, I started two years ago, and now I pull down four hundred a week."

When the man displayed an imitation-leather-bound book and said, "This set of encyclopedias will sell itself. All we need is somebody to collect commissions. It's like taking candy from a baby," Carter backed out of the room.

"Is it over?" asked the girl.

"No, just beginning."

Angrily he strode across the parking lot. Not even the air-conditioned comfort of the Thunderbird could cool his temper. Surely selling encyclopedias wasn't what Elaine meant by a challenging position. But driving to Burbank, he was beset by doubts, which the site of his second appointment did little to allay.

He circled the block twice to be positive he had the right address. Behind spindly pillars rested a narrow neo-Colonial monstrosity with a neon sign, *Dave Furber's Film-land College*. Unable to imagine what it might be, Carter entered more out of curiosity than in the hope of landing a job.

"The college," Dave Furber, the president and dean, explained, "is dedicated to preparing young people for careers in the film industry. Basically it's an eight-week course, divided into two semesters, with seminars in everything from movie editing to repairing the popcorn machine. We're willing to offer you our thirty years of experience in return for your untapped talent and energy. Do you think there's a match between your amibitions and our operation, Mr. White?"

Uncertain what he'd been asked or offered, Carter said, "It sounds like an interesting position. The salary is a hundred and twenty-five dollars a week?"

Perturbed, Mr. Furber folded his liver-spotted hands. "It seems avarice is the curse of our age. If money is what matters to you, show business may not be your best bet. But I can almost guarantee one twenty-five or better upon graduation."

"Graduation?"

"Yes. Eight weeks from tomorrow." Furber spoke faster. "The tuition and fees are four hundred dollars, but if you're a veteran, you may qualify for the GI Bill. And if you haven't been in the service, we've had excellent luck obtaining deferments for our students."

"You mean this isn't a job? There's no pay? You said on the phone . . ."

"Calm down, Mr. White. You mustn't be impatient. I assure you it'll lead to a lucrative position. You'll be the envy of . . ."

"To hell with your lucrative positon."

That evening when he told Elaine, she acted neither surprised nor disappointed and seemed more interested in the roast she was preparing. "Well, at least after these appointments you'll have a better basis for comparison."

"Comparison! Aren't you listening? They weren't interviews. In one case there wasn't even a job. The whole experience was like leaning against a wall that suddenly gave way."

"Carter, there's no reason to be angry. It's only the first day."

Next morning Carter spent an hour on the telephone trying to cull from two columns of slippery promises a few solid prospects. He made an appointment for the afternoon, but didn't hold high hopes for it, and as he waited, time passed in agonizing slowness. Elaine slept late again, then stayed clear of him, for which he was thankful. He was in no mood for more of her assurances.

Today he had gone beyond the classified section and sport sheet, and opening the first page was like opening a vein. Charles Manson and the dark-eyed members of his family stared out with swastikas scratched into their foreheads. On page three Jimi Hendrix thrust a guitar, like a massive plastic phallus, between his thighs. He was dead, drugged by sleeping pills and drowned in his own vomit. An ecologist on page seven said that was how everyone would die, unless something was done. He didn't reveal what. "By 1980 the world will have suffocated in its own stench and detritus."

Gradually the articles merged into a murky stain on Carter's mind like the smudge of printer's ink on his fingers. He didn't want to leave the apartment. He wasn't afraid. There simply seemed no use. Whether what he had read was actually the news, or someone's terrifying fantasies, he thought it indicated insanity was afoot everywhere. Yet no one seemed to have noticed except him.

That afternoon he broke out of the eggshell apartment and drove to a motel in Pasadena. The Kon-Tiki-Tel, built to look like a Polynesian village, consisted of fifteen hoochlike units, roofed with fireproof rods that had been painted the color of bamboo. The waspish owner, a sunburnt little man in Bermuda shorts, met him at the front desk and asked at once, "Where the hell have you been?"

"I got lost," said Carter, who had avoided the freeways. "I don't know the city too well."

"Yeah, how well do you know the motel business?"

"Not very, but . . ."

"Ever had any experience?"

"Not really, but . . ."

"Did you take any economics or accounting courses in college?"

"Not exactly, but . . ."

"What the hell did you take?"

"I was a history major."

"Why didn't you tell me on the telephone?"

"You didn't ask, and I didn't know it was important."

The man groaned. "This I don't believe. What makes you think you can be a night clerk?"

"Look," said Carter, fighting to control his temper. He foresaw the threat of another futile trip and tried to save the situation. "The newspaper mentioned nothing about qualifications, and neither did you. I'm willing to learn. I need this job."

"People in hell need ice water, but like you, they're wasting their time. Go back to school and become a teacher. History, for chrissake!"

Carter was tempted to dive across the desk and throttle the man, but suspected he was the type to keep a revolver under the counter. Boiling, he slammed out of the office and through the Polynesian village.

As he headed west to Hollywood, his anger simmered beneath a sky which spurted flames where the sun had burned a hole in it. Speeding toward this charred opening, he saw it erupt and spread orange lava the length of the horizon. Soon ashes the size of feathers scudded along the streets, whipped by a parched wind. The radio announcer said a brush fire was burning out of control in the Santa Monica Mountains. A flashing thermometer on the Bank of America building registered ninety-eight.

The apartment, although bright, was strangely cool, and Elaine sat on the bed in a crisp white robe, drinking a gin and tonic. A ladder of sunlight, slanting through the blinds, climbed over her shoulder and up the wall. "I just took a shower. Why don't you fix yourself a drink? You must be roasting in that suit."

"Have you seen the sky? It looks like there's been a volcanic eruption."

"My God"—she laughed—"you do have ashes on your shoulders. I saw a volcano once in Hawaii. Very interesting. Here, let me brush you off."

"There's a fire in the Santa Monica Mountains."

"Where's that?" She gestured for him to lean over.

"West of here. They say it's out of control. This is the craziest damned city."

Bending down, he pressed his lips to her damp hair as she swept the dust off his suit, wafting from the folds of her robe the fragrance of cologne. He was beginning to feel better until she asked, "Any luck today?"

"None."

"Don't look that way. There's nothing to worry about." Smiling, she cooled her hands on the highball glass, touched her cheek, then his. "Something will turn up. I was thinking you might call a couple of the large corporations in town. They won't hold a little initiative against you."

What they did hold against Carter was his un-completed degree and lack of experience. The job market was tight, the personnel manager at Bell Telephone told him, and he would be wise to return to college. So after wasting a morning, he resumed digging in the debris of the classified section, angry at the flatulent claims and promises.

In the ensuing days he talked to men in flashy suits about selling tupperware, used cars, high-risk insurance, and low-grade aluminum utensils. On rare occasions they rejected him before they had raced through their absurd spiels, but more often there was no relief until they had run down like wound-up toys. They implored Carter to believe in them, in their product, in the cause. The job was secondary. Even they were expendable. The larger scheme alone mattered, and before one could work, he had to pledge allegiance to it.

Finally, with infinite restraint, Carter would inquire whether there was, in fact, a job, and a moment later would find himself out on the street, as if he'd asked the most impertinent question. There were no jobs anywhere. Yet though the well was dry, the empty barrels rumbled on, unable to admit it was more than a temporary decline. Then at the apartment, listening to Elaine, he had to fight an inclincation to strike out at her. By the end of the week he felt the fires that had ravaged Southern California were smoldering in his stomach.

Friday morning he made an appointment with Moylan Fingerhut at Fist, Inc. An ad in the *Los Angeles Times* had said simply, "I want forceful and aggressive men." The women who answered told him to repeat his name, then gave an address in Culver City, but nothing else. Although he feared another disappointment, he had no choice. He set out at once and arrived at a squat, fortress-like building which barricaded a strategic corner and maintained its vigil through slotted windows. Its metal edges looked menacing as razor blades, reflecting splinters of light on the concrete fist which burst from the front lawn. Bigger than an automobile, it bore the letters F-I-S-T across its knuckles and, below, in smaller print, First International Security and Trust. Inside the building a long counter had been sectioned off into semi-private stalls by sheets of soundproofing.

Carter stepped into one and spoke to a woman who had a pencil stuck in the waves of her lacquered hair. Plucking it out, she flashed a smile that blinked off and on like a traffic light. "Is that W-H-I-T-E?"

He nodded. "I came . . ."

She spun her swivel chair to a file cabinet, flipped through a drawer of cards, then smiling, said, "Your first visit to Family Finance? Here, have a souvenir calendar." She passed a square of plastic through the barred window. "The Future Depends on Trust" was inscribed at the top. "What amount, up to five hundred dollars, would you like, Mr. White?"

"There must be a mistake. I'm looking for Fist, Inc."

"We're a subsidiary of First International Security and Trust. Confidential treatment and complete security are guaranteed."

"I have an appointment with Mr. Fingerhut," he said, still confused.

She jabbed the pencil, eraser first, back into her hair. "Why didn't you say so? Can I have the calendar? They're for our customers."

Carter's confidence slipped as low as his aching leg and he limped off in the direction she pointed.

Fingerhut, clad in chino pants and a blue polo sweater, occupied the doorway of his office, pressing his palms against the lintel, performing isometric contractions. "Be right with you," he grunted, his face red, the veins in his neck thick as cigars. A hulking man, middle-aged and well over six feet, he had fists like chunks of driftwood, knobby forearms, both bearing the Marine Corps insignia, and close-cropped sandy hair. In a shoulder holster under his left armpit, he carried a revolver. His face looked raw and shaved from the top of his ears to the stiff collar of his shirt. But two inches below his lipless mouth the razor had skipped a spot where a deep cleft crudely halved his chin.

"Whew! That does it for now." He sucked in three sharp breaths, smacked his flat belly, and gave Carter's hand a vigorous shake. "I like to keep fit, but with all the desk work I do, it isn't easy. Come on in. What's that name again?"

"White. Carter White."

The dingy room contained a metal desk, three straight-back chairs, and a filing cabinet. Overhead hummed two circular fluorescent lights. Carter blinked, reminded of an army barracks or a police station. The cubicle appeared sturdy enough to be the cornerstone on which the entire building stood.

Fingerhut lit a cigar butt he had filched from an ashtray on the desk. "Before you sit down, let me have a look at you. What do you go, anyway?"

"Pardon?"

"How big are you? Weight? Height?"

"Six-two. One ninety-five." For some reason, Carter added an inch and ten pounds to his size.

"Not bad. You have a good frame and could carry more weight. A good appearance, too. Step over to that file cabinet."

Like a drunk at the scene of an accident, Carter tried to walk the line. He'd encountered bigger men and never been intimidated, but Fingerhut had a habit of shifting his weight knowingly, so that a great pack of chest muscle stretched his sweater thin. Next to him, Carter felt very small.

"Hmm. That's what I thought. You limp, don't you?"

"A little." His cheeks burned, embarrassed by the ease with which Fingerhut had spotted the injury.

"How'd it happen?"

"Vietnam," he said, eager for any leverage.

"Too bad. A mortar? I caught one myself on Okinawa.

But it didn't hobble me. Does it slow you down much?"

"No. It doesn't bother me."

"I reckon you could build it up if you went on a weight program. Take a seat, White, and let's talk. I don't believe in wasting time. What we have here is a job for a collection agent to help me out. I've got more work than I can handle." As he spoke, Fingerhut prowled in heavy, stiff-legged strides around the desk. Since he had almost no neck, he carried his head oddly on his broad shoulders, like an earthenware mug whose contents he was afraid of spilling. "It's a simple matter. People borrow money and they don't pay it back. Naturally, we go after them. It's a tough job and it calls for a special kind of man. A take-charge guy. A scrapper. Now I could give you a lot of silly damn tests, but they wouldn't tell me what I want to know. What you have here!" He thumped his chest. "I'm gifted with a sixth sense, and size up a man just by looking at him. White, I think you've got what it takes. Some people would fork our dough over the minute they saw you, because you look respectable, you look like authority. But other people"—he clenched his fist —"you'd have to squeeze."

Though Carter believed he was expected to say something, he didn't know what. Fingerhut had started to stalk him again.

"That bum leg bothers me, but I won't hold it against you. God forbid I should hold military service against anyone in this day when every flappy-wristed fairy is dodging the draft. No, I respect a man who's been in action. It prepares you for life. What do you think, White?"

"I think I'd like to know more about the job," he said, mustering a short burst of enthusiasm. "Would I be working for Fist, Inc.?"

"It's all Fist, Inc., but there are half a dozen departments. You'd start with the collection unit of Family Finance. After that, it depends on you. We have room for expansion. This is a big industry, and it can only become bigger, because the country is crying out for security and trust—and that's what I intend to give them. How much do you know about our operation?"

"Not much. Not as much as I'd like to," he lied.

Moving like a poorly made automaton, bracing his back and cradling his head, Fingerhut tramped behind the desk and sat down. "Let me tell you this, we're big. The fourth largest dealer in safety, security, and public protection in the state. And we're growing every day, because performance counts and news travels fast. That's my motto. We're lucky to have hundreds of fine men on our team—special police, industrial investigators, private investigators, collection agents, and undercover agents. Just last spring we entered the technical hardware field and began to merchandise tear gas, anti-personnel sprays, and nerve gases. Our next project is to make the operation total electric, using computers and systems equipment. If you want to beat the criminal element today, you have to keep up, keep ahead, keep a foot on their necks." He hunched forward, anxious not to be overhead. "Our ultimate aim is a program not only to capture and punish felons, but to crush out potential criminals before they have a chance to break the law." Abruptly he pitched to his feet. "That's the story here at Fist. It's a first-class outfit. Good, tough boys right on down the line. We accept nothing but the best, White. Do you have any objections to taking a polygraph test?"

"I . . . I don't think so."

"You don't think so?" Fingerhut shot him a sidelong glance.

"I've never taken one."

"If you have nothing to hide, there'll be no problem." Fingerhut jabbed his cigar, little more than a lump of ash, back into the tray. "But that comes later, before we hire a man."

"Look, Mr. Fingerhut, I . . ." Carter attempted to interrupt, realizing what a polygraph test could reveal. Any one of a hundred questions, any mention at all of Elaine, might ruin him.

But Fingerhut bore on. "You've been in the service, right?"

"Yes."

"You own a car, right?"

"Yes."

"What make? What year?"

"A new Thunderbird."

Fingerhut stopped in his tracks. "A what? Where did you get it?"

"I . . . uh, my wife's parents gave it to us as a wedding present."

"You're not hiding something from me, are you?"

"No. What would I have to hide?"

"A gift from your in-laws, huh? No shit. They must

68

have big bread." Testing the bristles of his hair with the palm of his hand, he looked as if he were passing new judgment on Carter. "I don't know, White. I just don't know. What rank were you in the army?"

"Second lieutenant."

"Hmm, that's what I was afraid of. You're a college boy, aren't you?"

"I only had three years." For the first time he emphasized he didn't have a degree.

Going to the file cabinet, Fingerhut unlocked the top drawer, took out a new cigar, and passed it beneath his spread nostrils. "My sixth sense is acting up on me. The more you talk, White, the less I think you're my man. A T-bird. Rich in-laws. Three years of college. An officer." He ticked off each offense by rapping his knuckles on the cabinet. "What the hell are you doing here? I'm looking for a man who's anxious to make a career."

"I need a job." Now that Fingerhut was losing interest, Carter feared he would never find one. Although he didn't care to work for Fist, Inc., his prospects were meager, and regardless of Elaine's advice, didn't seem likely to improve. "My in-laws don't support me. I'm on my own and I'm willing to work. I have a wife and she's expecting a baby."

"No, White, you're not my man. You'd stay six months, maybe a year, and whine for a promotion. Christ, you'd try to take over the whole damn place." He leveled the cigar on Carter like the barrel of a pistol. "I know you college boys. You think you're too good for the rest of us. But for all your education you haven't got the guts to go out and knock down doors to get our money."

Carter wanted to deny it. Fingerhut's raw smirk dared him to deny it. But remembering what the polygraph test might reveal, he stared back at the cleft of Fingerhut's chin, which might have been hewn with an ax, and said, "You're right. I'm too good for you." Then he quickly departed.

To postpone returning to the apartment and Elaine in a foul mood, he stopped at a park on Melrose Avenue, which was lightly powdered by ashes that had blown down from the hills. The lawn, the palm trees, the tropical plants, everything appeared hoary with age, and the sun burned out of control, its flames fed by tinder-dry clouds. The air itself seemed on the point of spontaneous combustion.

69

Yet Carter was far from alone. A legion of men lay sprawled on the ground, or sat propped against one another on the benches, breathing poisonous fumes that the people Fingerhut would have had him pursue— singed their throats and smarted their eyes. These were debtors, the defeated. Walking among them, Carter remembered stories about the Great Depression, and thought that money was the least of many things these men lacked. Like him, they no longer believed. They looked at the opulence beyond the park, and feared if they went to grasp it, they would plunge through to the darkness on the other side.

But whereas they were resigned to this knowledge, he was angry. Despite deep misgivings, he had wanted to believe Elaine's assurances but now suspected he'd been tricked, betrayed. Her words were a mockery of his ability, an absolute ignorance of reality. Regardless of her intentions, Elaine's naïve encouragement had put added pressure on him. Not just any job would do. He had to find one that satisfied her, that corresponded to the capabilities she said he possessed, and since he had found none at all, he felt doubly inadequate. If only he could bring her here, he thought, and show her these men.

It was late. The sun had started to sink; the bodies on the grass began to stir, eager to escape before dark. From end to end the horizon was furrowed with mad scarlet streaks that spiraled to earth like bandages torn from an open wound. Carter hurried along with the crowd, then broke away sheepishly, unlocked the Thunderbird, switched on the air conditioner, and sped past the men whose eyes showed no envy, no interest, no life.

At dinner there were candles and a bottle of wine on the table. Again Elaine wore white, and in the flickering light, looked as cool and nonflammable as the whitewashed walls. They seemed to be sitting in an asbestos box, safe from the fire storms outside, yet Carter, still on edge, ate and said little. Noticing this, Elaine asked a few questions, then lapsed into silence, her appetite, also, lost. At last she mumbled, "Stifling," snapped out the candles with her fingers and stretched out on the sofa.

Feeling no desire, driven by some force of defiance or resentment, which he had never associated with sex, much less love, Carter knelt next to the couch and kissed her hard on the mouth. As he awkwardly labored to un-

70

dress her, Elaine didn't object, but didn't help either, and though her eyes watched him closely, she said nothing. In his hands her breasts felt heavy and inert, and it was doubtful that he could, or ever had, aroused her. Yet this doubt, too, drove him on, and he continued to work his grim techniques until she drew back, saying, "Don't wait for me, Carter. You go ahead."

He straightened angrily, cracking his knees, and slammed out of the apartment. The sound of his footsteps, the rush of blood in his ears, beat in tune to the methodical bump and grind from the Body Shop. He waited at the corner of North Harper and Sunset, wondering where he was going, what he had done. Above him a sign announced *Amateur Night. C-Cups or Better to Qualify,* and at the base of the hills, a bottle of J&B Scotch slanted like a space ship across a billboard, shedding gruesome green light on the passing cars.

Despite the noise and the glitter of neon, he struggled to make sense of his predicament, which went beyond sex, money, and the job that kept eluding him. It seemed to him Elaine lived in a different world, a real one perhaps but one which didn't include him, and couldn't account for what he had experienced. It was as simple as that. While she thought life was easy, he knew it was not and wanted to warn her before it was too late. If he accomplished nothing else in California, he had to convince her that life was more than a matter of choosing among attractive alternatives. Mistakes happened, resisted control, and roved about freely as germs. Already in her womb she bore one small doom and would have to face this fact before she delivered.

He returned to the apartment, determined to make his attitude clear. But as he joined her in the kitchen, where she was ironing his shirts, the clarity of his convictions jumped out of focus.

"Do you feel better?" she asked. Although her eyes were swollen, Elaine appeared serene and self-contained. She had let down her hair and changed her dress for a nightgown.

"I'm fine. There's nothing wrong with me." He tried to smooth the edge from his voice. He couldn't blame her for what she didn't know. He would have to teach her. "But I've decided if I don't find a job next week, I'll check out a few of the supermarkets in the neighborhood."

The iron slowed, halted, and she balanced it on its

heel. Filigrees of blue and gray shimmered on its face. "I don't think you've given yourself a chance. You've only had a few appointments, and there's no rush."

"No rush! Don't you read the papers or listen to the news? We're practically in a depression. Men everywhere are out of work. I saw them in the park today."

"Please, don't worry about money." She draped his shirt on a hanger. Carter was surprised at the sureness of her gestures. He had never pictured her at domestic chores, but she seemed to do them well. "I can always cash one of my bonds."

"No, don't do that. Money isn't really the point I'm trying to make."

"What is, Carter?"

"It's that . . ." He clenched his hands into fists, seeking the best words to express his ideas, then opened them, having grasped nothing. He couldn't say it without upsetting or insulting her. "I'm concerned about you. The world is a lot different than you think, and I don't want you to be hurt."

"That's funny. I feel the same about you, Carter. You act so sad and angry sometimes, and I want you to be happy. Maybe I'm selfish. You see, when you're unhappy, I am too. There's no reason for us to have problems, unless we make them for ourselves."

He sighed and sat at the breakfast bar, watching her iron the wrinkles from another shirt. What she said sounded reasonable—at least here in the apartment, late at night, it did. Weary of wrangling, he let the subject die. "Who taught you to be such a little homebody?"

"No one. We had servants. But I used to sneak into the kitchen at night to practice. I've gotten pretty good, haven't I?"

"Terrific. Maybe we'll hire you out as a maid."

Saturday they stayed in out of the heat and corrosive stench of smoke. A desert wind whipped flurries of ashes past their windows, but the turbulence didn't trouble Carter again until Sunday, when, as he read the newspaper, all his doubts crept back like the tendrils of a stubborn, gloom-seeking vine.

As always, to balance the bad news on the front page, there were in the classified section numerous toothsome guarantees of happiness, success, and security. He had dutifully circled half a dozen of the most lavish promises when someone knocked at the door. He looked immediately to Elaine, who shook her head. It couldn't be for her, and she wouldn't answer it. She ducked into the bedroom as he opened the door on a hefty man dressed in blue cord pants and a Ban-Lon sweater. With a toss of his head, which didn't disturb his pomaded gray hair, he beckoned Carter into the courtyard, but when Carter wouldn't come out, he seemed unsure of himself. He thrust his hands into his pockets and a shrill little voice asked, "Is that girl your wife?"

The man's lips hadn't moved, but the voice repeated, "Well, is she?" and a tiny woman stepped from behind him. She was thin as a spike, with long arms that hung at her sides like wet twisted ropes. Her face was an unfortunate combination of acute angles—a chin pointed as a tack hammer and a hooked nose sharp enough to pry out nails.

"Yes, she is." Carter shut the door behind him.

"Then you're Mr. Yost," said the man.

"No. My wife . . ." He shifted his weight onto his good leg. "That's her maiden name. My name is White."

"The lease says Yost." The woman rocked back and forth on the balls of her feet, ready to defend herself against deceit.

"We were separated for a while." Carter watched the man pull out unsteady hands to light a cigarette. The smoke he exhaled was laced with the scent of bourbon. "Who are you?"

"Chuck Regan, the manager. We live over there." He nodded across the courtyard. "Your wife gave us false information," he mumbled almost apologetically. "She didn't say she was married and . . ."

"She certainly didn't mention she was pregnant," Mrs. Regan snapped.

Carter felt a curious commotion in his belly. "Who said she's pregnant?"

"I got eyes. She's five months along if she's a day."

"We have rules against kids," said Mr. Regan in a gentle voice. "I mean I don't hold anything against them personally. I had three of my own, but . . ."

"You had! That'll be the day. I had them and they damned near split me in half." Then to Carter. "I feel sorry for the girl, but the other tenants are bound to notice and they won't like it one bit."

"We didn't know about the rule."

73

"Read the lease. It's right there."

"Couldn't we stay until the baby's born? asked Carter, unreasonably displeased at the prospect of switching apartments now that he had settled into this one. "Maybe we could sublet."

"That's all right by me," Regan said to his wife.

"Okay. If anyone asks, tell them you're leaving the minute the kid is born. Tell them it'll never set foot in this apartment. Understand?"

"I understand."

Blushing, Regan was reluctant to end the conversation on a sour note. "We're from Cleveland. How about you? From back East, I bet."

"Washington, D.C."

"I've never been there, but it would have to go some to beat L.A., especially in winter when everyone at home is freezing his butt off. Well, glad to meet you."

As he shut and locked the door, Carter thought the man, Chuck Regan, could have been anyone. Even the baby's father. Someday, any day, he might open the door or answer the phone and it would all be over.

"Who was it?" Elaine called from the bedroom.

"The landlord," he said, hurrying to her. She sat against the headboard, reading a magazine. "He knows you're pregnant."

"Oh?" She didn't bother looking up.

"It's nothing to worry about," he said, as though she had acted distraught. "You are pregnant and people are going to notice. But why the hell did you use your real name? You should have told him you were married and used mine."

"I didn't think of it. It didn't seem important."

"From now on we've got to think of everything." As he said this, the skin at the back of his neck crawled from the false melodrama. It was nothing. Just a nosy landlord.

Yet late at night as they lay in the same single bed, he thought how strange it was that although they were isolated and alone, he should feel someone was always watching, that something was bound to happen. This was the fear which drove him—that he would lose Elaine—and it turned his love into an agony which she saw only as sullen anxiety. Lifting her head onto his shoulder, he thought that no matter how he acted, this was how he felt—he loved her and desperately didn't want anyone to find them.

Chapter V

Monday the *Times* ran an ad for "Talented and Ambitious Young Men to Fill High Paying Junior Executive Positions." By reflex Carter circled it, and at the same time harbored a malignant contempt for the rhetoric and whoever was responsible for it, and perhaps also for himself, since he had to regard it seriously. For a rebellious moment he swore he wouldn't call, yet knew he had no choice. At nine he dialed the number, and a woman answered, full of mindless cheer, "The David Felix Employment Agency. Hold the line and Mr. Brown will assist you."

Carter started to hang up—it was stupid to pay for a job—but caught himself and decided to see what the agency had to offer.

"Eddie Brown here. Rap away, babes."

"I read your ad about junior executive positions."

"Yeah, we got a boatload of them. Why don't you zip down here and try one on for size?"

"I'm serious. I need a job," said Carter to moderate the man's enthusiasm.

"I'm serious too. Isn't everybody? Come see us."

"If you don't have any jobs, please tell me now, so I won't waste my time and yours."

"Look, man, I'm not putting you on. There's a basket full of jobs right in front of me. But we have to talk first before I know where we're at."

"What's the fee?"

"Don't sweat that. We'll discuss it later. Where are you?"

"West Hollywood."

"Good. Get on the Santa Monica Freeway. We're at 126 Hoover Street."

Carter hung up, furious, intending to forget the David Felix Employment Agency, but when his other calls proved fruitless, he again had no choice except to try Eddie Brown.

An hour later, having crept through miles of congestion on Wilshire Boulevard, he entered that trough of urban blight he had plumbed his first day in Los Angeles. Parking the Thunderbird, he marched up Hoover Street, reminded of the decaying heart of every city he had seen. Only here the billboards were bigger, gaudier, and there were palm trees, desiccated by grime and exhaust fumes, waving their shredded fronds like unimaginably tall dandelions gone to seed. The air, stale as a vast gymnasium that had been sealed for a year, stung his eyes till they watered.

When he came to 126, a narrow red-brick structure which bore on its sides a room-by-room blueprint of the adjoining buildings that had been razed for parking space, he hoped it would be air-conditioned. It was not, and the agency was on the sixth floor, a slow ascent in an airless elevator which left the smell of dirty pennies on his fingers. The more Carter saw, the less he cared to go on. No good would come of it, he was certain. But the same despairing realization that he had no alternative drove him down the hall to 831, a brilliant buttercup-colored room, lacking drapes or blinds. There were perhaps a dozen desks, each attended by a man in shirt sleeves. Most of the applicants appeared to be Negroes or Mexicans, and Carter was the lone one wearing a suit and tie.

A secretary asked his name, dialed three digits, and spoke to a man whose voice would have been audible withut the phone. "Mr. Brown will see you now." She directed Carter to the left.

"You must be the jumpy one I talked to. I thought I'd scared you off. Eddie Brown here. Sit down, man, and loosen up." Seated in a swivel chair, Eddie shoved back from the desk but didn't rise or put out his hand. He had on an open-collar purple shirt with billowing sleeves, a black leather vest, and blue love beads. His blue-and-white-striped pants tapered at the thighs, than flared below the knees, folding over the tassels of his pointed-toe boots. Small and wiry, he might have looked like a doll styled vaguely along the lines of a movie star if it hadn't been for his beaked nose. "What's your thing? What are you into? Your background?"

After so many disappointing interviews and having already lost hope that Eddie Brown could help him, Carter refused to summon up his usual pretense of eagerness.

Sinking onto a chair, he said wearily, "I don't have a background. I attended college for three years but didn't finish a degree. I was in the army nine months, then received a medical discharge. The only real working experience I've had was as a waiter in a night club. Now I'm married and need a job."

"Hey, babes, cool it." Eddie bent forward, elbows against the desk, shoulders hunched high as his earlobes. Though his long hair hung in thick shaggy curls, it couldn't conceal the dandruff which peeled in flakes from his inflamed scalp. "Jesus Christ, somebody's liable to hear you!" Glancing in both directions, as if about to cross a dangerous street, he whispered, "look, kid, it's okay to tell me that, but I hope to hell you don't come on this way at the job interview. Death, certain death. Admit to anyone that you're desperate and he'll dump on you and rub it in. Stay cool, act like you couldn't give a rat's ass, and you're in. They'll love you. Listen to me and I'll have your head straight in no time. First thing to remember"—he stiffened his index finger—"find an image and don't blow it. It's all in how you come on. Take what you told me. I could make it sound terrific. It's something you learn in this business. So relax. We're going to do all right by you. What did you study at school? Any business, economics, or accounting?"

"No, I majored in history."

'History! Where was this?"

"A small college in Pennsylvania."

Frowning, Eddie asked, "How long you been in L.A.?"

"A week."

"Man, you're nowhere. You're batting zero. How old are you?"

"Twenty-two."

"Lemme lay it on you straight, kid." As Eddie talked from the side of his mouth, his face reddened like his scalp. Only the bony tip of his nose remained white. "To any employer in L.A. you don't rate. You're lower than whale shit, and that's beneath sea level. You're too young, you don't have a degree, you got no experience, and you're new to the area. How long you been married?"

"Six months," said Carter after an instant of flustered hesitation.

"Don't bullshit me. I see you're lying, and you can bet your sweet ass an employer would too. What you say

77

sounds like one of two things to me, both of them bad. Number one, maybe you're a college kid who decided to cut out for a semester and come to the Coast for some action. In January you'll be hauling ass back East. In which case you're no damn good to anyone. Or, number two . . ."

"That's not true."

"Lemme finish. Or, number two, you knocked up a girl, married her, and have a good reason to be uptight about a job. In which case you still aren't exactly golden, because people can tell you're jumpy and nobody wants to hire a man who's liable to split after a few months."

"Look, you've got me all . . ."

"I got you all nothing," said Eddie. "I don't care which is true. You walk out that door, I'll never see you again. If we do business, I get my commission and I'll still never see you again. Your bag don't interest me in the slightest except as far as it helps me find you a job. So wise up. The way I figure it, we have to do a special number on you. With most clients I rap away until I think I know them, then I try to get them a job that fits. But you, I know everything already and it adds up to nothing. Before I help you, I have to decide who you are and what you can do. I think we'll work on a whole new image, a new dossier, an imaginative background."

"I don't have to lie to get a job," said Carter, who had been pushed far enough. "I came here for information, not a lot of foolish advice. If what I am isn't good enough, I'll . . ."

"You'll what? Sleep in doorways? Eat at the Mission? Don't hand me that shit. These are hard times. And who said anything about lying? Once you're working, an employer could care less what you told him. The important thing is to learn how to tell it. And, kid," he whispered, "lemme remind you, your trouble isn't that you're not good enough. It's that you're nothing. Now gimme a minute to think."

Before Carter could answer, Eddie slipped a clean sheet of paper from the desk and started to scribble. He wasn't actually writing. He was doodling, sketching large scrolls and figure eights. Although anger had replaced Carter's despair, he believed it amounted to the same thing. He had wasted a morning and wouldn't find a job.

"You said you were in the army?" Eddie interrupted his artwork.

"Yes. For nine months. Look, if you don't mind, I'll . . ."

"What happened?"

"I told you. I received a medical discharge. Now why don't we wind this up?"

"Not a mental, I hope."

"No, I busted my knee."

"Vietnam?" Eddie asked eagerly.

Carter nodded yes, and a rubbery smile seized the man's face. "Hot damn, now you're talking. Did you get a medal?"

"No, I fell off a truck."

Eddie shut his eyes, slumped back in the chair, and shook his head, looking immensely pleased. "It doesn't matter. Don't tell me any more. I'm beginning to get the picture. This opens all kinds of possibilities."

While he eased into a blissful, reflective doze, Carter darted an anxious glance about the room. Fortunately no one was paying attention to them. He would have left if he had known anywhere to go other than the apartment or the park.

"Yeah, babes, I think I have it." Smiling, Eddie emerged from his trance. "Your problems are solved."

Struck by the man's verve and his crude, uncanny insight, Carter longed to believe this, but murmured, "Really?"

"Does a wild bear shit in the woods? It's a cinch. What type of job are you looking for?"

"Something . . . you know"—he took heart—"creative and challenging." Elaine's words sounded ridiculous when he said them.

"Oh Christ, every schmuck who comes in here wants a challenging and creative job. What do they mean? Half of them are about as creative as a fucking fireplug. But leave it to me. I got just the spot for you. And why not? You're a nice-looking kid. You're tall. You have a little education. You almost had your ass shot off by a Chink. I tell you, we're going to do all right. Now let's go eat lunch and see what we can work out."

"Wait a minute." Carter caught his arm. "Are you serious?"

"Kid, I'm always serious. It's in the bag."

Breathlessly Carter pursued Eddie Brown down the hall, into the sweltering elevator, and out onto the sun-parched pavement, and as he attempted to keep pace with the little man, who at five feet six had the loping stride of a long-distance runner, his legs buckled and his toes thudded against curbstones. He wanted to demand why Eddie was so sure, but couldn't squeeze out more than a syllable, for the monologue had intensified and Eddie's rasping voice worked like a shuttle ceaselessly weaving a web. Logic, syntax, and grammar eluded him from time to time, but a tireless energy, a compelling power out of all proportion to his size, stayed at his command and allowed him to talk without pausing for thought or air. At once he saw through Carter's feeble lies and tossed aside the few filaments of truth as being of slight importance. Ruthlessly Eddie forced him to confront the emptiness of his life, then laughed and argued that it afforded them an unusual advantage. They would start with a clean slate.

In a small chromium diner, which looked like a pullman car stranded on a street corner, they sat at the counter and ordered hamburgers and coffee. Eddie continued talking, and during the meal, lit a cigar, which he used for emphasis, punctuating his remarks with pointed thrusts, calibrating the changes in his voice and mood with the flick of an ash, as if he exercised as much control over the tobacco as he did over Carter. Both burned at a speed to his liking, and the effect was not simply to batter Carter into acceptance, but to kindle in him a desire to share Eddie's vibrancy.

At last he halted an instant, then asked, 'What's your name, anyway?"

"Carter White."

"Ugh! I don't like it. Carte Blanche. We'll have to fix that too."

"What do you suggest?"

"We'll decide later. First I have an admission to make." He slung an arm around Carter's shoulder. "Kid, you remind me of myself. No shit, you do. Seven years ago when I came to L.A., I was broke, scared, married, and thoroughly screwed up. Plus I had two kids. You are married aren't you? You weren't lying about that?"

"Yes, I have a wife." Carter lowered his eyes to the counter.

"And she's pregnant?"

"Yes."

"You kids! You're all too much. You just don't know how to keep it in your pants. But I dig you, because like I said, you're the old me. You see, when I was in the navy, I married a California girl and brought her back to New York. Jesus." He shook his head ruefully at the memory. "I wonder what was on my mind. A massive mistake from the start. When she hit that city, she came unglued. Hated the weather. Said people were cold and rude. Was scared of spics and niggers. She claimed one would slip a dong to her in the elevator. Day after day she handed me the same line of shit until my head was completely bent out of shape. What could I do?"

With a magnificent shrug, he threw up his hands and in the same motion reached for the mustard. "When a chick starts to moan, you got no choice. You'll learn that. So we compromised. We came to L.A. and, kid, for the first three months I hated it. For my money they could have taken the whole city and stuffed it up their ass. The heat dried out my scalp, the smog made my eyes water, and I had two accidents. Every time I set foot on a freeway, I spaced out. Man, I was dying to go back to New York. But then suddenly—this is the important part, so pay attention—suddenly everything changed. *I* changed. Me, who hadn't changed since he was nine. It wasn't any one thing, just being out here in the great weather, going to the beach, grooving on good people. All at once I was a new man, and my wife couldn't stand me, which was okay by me, because by then I couldn't stand her either. So we split. She took the kids and moved out to the Valley, and now I have this town on the half shell. I mean girls, grins, bread. I wouldn't go back to New York if they made me mayor. Why the hell should I? Leave that dump to the dregs and misfits and fuck-ups. It's what they deserve. I say every tight-butted babe on Sutton Place deserves to be raped by a nigger, and every nigger deserves to be greased by a cop, and every cop sliced up by a spic, and every spic should die with a dirty needle in his arm. It's what they're asking for if they stay in that roach nest. But me, I got out and I'm staying out." He took an emphatic bite of the sandwich, but seemed to have forgotten his point— if he had one.

"You're doing all right, then," prompted Carter, who'd barely touched his sandwich.

"Oh Christ, yes! This is a town of extra-ordinary opportunity. It's five, no, maybe more like ten years ahead of the rest of the world. And lemme tell you . . ." He slapped Carter playfully in the ribs. "You'll make it, kid, just like I did. And I'm going to help you, because I dig

81

you. You're young. You're in a jam. You knocked up your girl. You need . . ."

"You said that. Not me."

"Don't try to fox Eddie Brown." He laughed leeringly. "Here, have a cigar."

"I don't smoke."

"Good. Don't start." Biting the end off, he lit a match, inhaled, and slouched against the counter. "Kid, you're my kind of guy, and to show you where my heart's at, I plan to do you a big favor. How would you like the complete and personal Eddie Brown treatment at half price?"

"What's that?" asked Carter suspiciously.

"Lemme put it this way. I know a big restaurant company that's begging for someone like you. They want a bright fellow to learn the business. It pays one-fifty a week to start, and after that it's up, up, and away." He made a missile of his cigar and blew a stream of smoke in its wake.

"I'd be very interested to . . ."

"Sure you'd be interested. Who wouldn't? But if you go there now, they'll toss you out on your ass. You're jumpy and you got a lot of rough edges. You need the complete and personal Eddie Brown treatment. If we do it through the agency, it'll cost you five hundred bucks. Now, I was thinking we could handle this little deal just between the two of us. I have the rest of the week off. Tomorrow at my place we could begin the treatment at a special reduced rate. For two hundred and fifty dollars I'll train you and guarantee a job. Understand? Just a personal transaction. This way nobody gets hurt."

"Nobody but the people upstairs," said Carter, on guard and bitterly disappointed that the little man appeared to be a fraud. He had wanted to believe.

"The people upstairs!" Eddie winced. "For crying out loud, forget them. They have a hundred deals cooking. Why be a jerk? I'm trying to give you a break. But of course if you . . . " Eddie sprung to his feet.

"No! Wait. What's the Eddie Brown treatment?"

"It's what you need," he reemphasized. "I'll work with you personally over my vacation."

"What is it exactly? I want to know before I pay two hundred and fifty dollars."

"Look, kid, I can't *exactly* tell you. It's everything. I'll teach you to put balls in your spiel. Since you really got nothing to offer, you have to come on double strong. We'll hit all the little details and work up to the big picture. Just looking at you, I notice twenty or thirty things that need improvement. Shine your shoes. Never wear a white shirt. Wear one with a bit of color, and buy some new ties. You're not applying for a job at the morgue. Don't use that bear grease on your hair, and let it grow. You'll look older. See what I mean? Plus the matter of filling in all the holes in your background and providing the right answers for the questions you'll be asked."

"How do I know it'll work? How do I know you'll come through with a job?"

"You really are in bad shape. Trust me, kid. The two of us will go over to that phone booth and call the personnel manager of the company. You can talk to him yourself, if you want."

"What's the name of this restaurant chain?" asked Carter, still wary.

"Hey, you think I'm crazy? If I told you that, you'd go there and blow the whole damn deal. First fork over the dough and undergo a few days of treatment. Then I'll put you in touch with the guy."

"I don't have two hundred and fifty dollars on me."

"How about a check?"

"I haven't opened a bank account yet."

"Look," said Eddie, as a flake of dandruff floated from his head to the counter, "I'll meet you halfway. Gimme a hundred bucks now and the rest later."

"Twenty-five dollars," said Carter, certain he could afford the risk for that amount.

"Okay, it's a deal. I want to prove something to you." He rose and headed for the phone.

"How do you know I'll pay off once I have the job?" asked Carter, following him.

Eddie finished dialing, then patted him on the cheek. "You're a cute kid, but don't try to shaft me. This guy would drop you like a bad habit if I gave him the word." Sticking a finger in his ear, he turned his back to Carter. "Yeah, honey, I'm fine. Lemme speak to Don Reichlederfer. Hello, Don? Eddie Brown here. Not bad. I found the man for you. Would I lie? He has more brains than he knows what to do with. He took the Wunderlich Test and his score was out of sight. You'd need an IBM machine to add it up. He's a good-looking kid. Twenty-five. About six-two. A big fella. Nice head of hair. Okay, you're

83

not looking for a beauty queen, but I tell you he's what you want. Yes, he's married. No, not tomorrow. I'll send him later this week. Maybe Friday. I'll call the day before."

"We're in business," said Eddie, hanging up. "Reichlederfer is creaming his jeans over you. He knows I wouldn't recommend a bummer. We better whip you into shape so I won't look like a sucker. Call me tomorrow at eight-thirty. I'll be in bed. Let the phone ring. My number's in the book. Now lemme have that twenty-five bucks. I have to get back to the office before they start to bitch."

Not until he had driven halfway to West Hollywood did Carter feel strangely let down and edgy. As the electric rush of excitement, now tepid as dishwater, ebbed from his pores and congealed into clammy perspiration on his back, he was afraid he had made the wrong decision, and couldn't comprehend what, other than utter desperation, had persuaded him to take Eddie seriously, to suffer his insults, and to place twenty-five dollars' worth of confidence in him. However he looked at it, he thought he had paid too high a price. Even if Eddie didn't cheat him, even if he did land the job, he believed it would have cost him too much, maybe not in money, but in something less tangible—an erosion of his character, of the already threadbare fabric of his identity. Since his first lies weren't sufficient, he would have to submit to the little man's baroque imagination, setting himself at two removes from the reality of his nothingness, and knowing full well that the added distance wouldn't change anything. It would have been bad enough to have gone through an agency—to buy a job—but to sneak in through the back alley—to steal it as an accomplice of Eddie Brown's—deprived him of all the satisfaction he might have felt.

At the apartment, as he glumly explained the situation to Elaine, she broke into a smile and said, "That's wonderful. When do you start?"

"I don't have the job yet, I go for an interview Friday. It's a sure thing," he said, feeling it was anything but certain, and seeking the means of impressing upon her how much it had cost him—again not necessarily in money—to get a job which would satisfy her. "Meanwhile the employment agent will train me not to make a fool of myself."

"What kind of job is it, and how much does it pay?"

She held onto his arm, apparently as excited as he had been an hour ago.

"It's with a restaurant chain and pays a hundred and fifty a week."

"Great! Which chain? What will you be doing?"

"I don't know. They didn't tell me."

His tone brought her up short. She let go of him and her shoulders sagged. It seemed to require all the slender strength of her neck to prevent her voice from quavering. "Aren't you happy?"

"At least we'll have a roof over our heads." Then he went into the bedroom to change clothes.

"You seem upset. Or angry," she said, dogging his heels. "Don't you want the job? Was the agency fee too high?"

"It should have cost five hundred bucks, but I worked out a deal with one of the agents—a little chiseler named Eddie Brown—and I'll pay him two-fifty."

Her smile widened, showing her straight white teeth. "Why, Carter, you're a better businessman than I thought."

He hadn't anticipated this enthusiasm, and didn't know what to say. Turning from her to the bureau, he drew out a clean shirt, and when he was dressed, went back to the living room. Elaine kept her distance now, perhaps expecting him to burst into laughter and say it was a joke. There was no job. Maybe his sullenness itself was the joke and he was pretending to be upset just to tease her. You got two letters today," she said. "They're on the coffee table."

Careful not to show his surprise, he opened the envelopes.

"Carter, what is it? What's . . .?"

"One's from Mrs. Vaughan," he said, thinking she meant the letters. "She wants my share of August's phone bill. The other's from my brother-in-law, Ray, with the address of an old friend in Pasadena."

"What else does he say?"

"Nothing."

"That's odd."

"Not really. We don't have much to say to each other any more." But instead of throwing both letters away, he slipped them into the pocket of his Levis.

That night for the first time he slept in his own bed, which although it was next to Elaine's and she occasionally reached over to touch him, provided the privacy he desired. For more than an hour he stared into the darkness, attempting to imagine what he looked like lying there, and when that proved impossible, he tried to determine the exact contours of his body, so that he might gain a sense of release in thinking, This is Carter White. His perimeters. His form. Again he failed, and felt himself a shadow, like the others in the room.

"Is anything wrong?" asked Elaine.

"No. I'm tired. I have to think." He seemed to imply the two were synonymous.

As he set his mind in motion once more, he picked up the beat of the Body Shop, the sound of a television somewhere in the building, footsteps on the sidewalk below the window, the scent of jasmine. A car rounding the corner of Delongpre and North Harper shot its high beams through the Venetian blinds and stretched a lopsided section of railroad tracks across the ceiling. Elaine's breathing became deep and regular.

And yet, acutely aware of this, Carter was deaf to his own heartbeat, blind to the outlines of his body. He could think only of the two letters in his Levis, holding them in his mind like priceless coupons, like guarantees of his existence. This dark room didn't encompass the whole of his life. He had been elsewhere, had done other things—had made phone calls, if nothing else—and for the moment this sufficed.

Chapter VI

1

After a long, sound sleep, the best he'd had since coming to Los Angeles, Carter woke well rested, certain for the first time of where he was and what he had to do. He'd land a job with Eddie's help or without it. What he did scarcely mattered, for in six months he and Elaine would leave this place, and his real life would begin. Meanwhile he could tolerate anything that kept them together and paid the bills.

At eight-thirty Eddie's number rang eleven times before a ragged voice answered, "Yeah?"

"Eddie Brown?"

"Yeah." A loud yawn stretched the word twice its normal length.

"This is Carter White."

"Who?"

"Carter White. I spoke to you yesterday."

"Oh, yeah, Carte Blanche." Eddie coughed up a laugh. "Gimme a minute to wake up. I put in a long night."

"You told me to call."

"Yeah, yeah. Lemme think. Jesus, we're off to a flying start. Where are you?"

"West Hollywood."

"I'm on Franklin Avenue, just past La Brea, at the Mediterranean Cascade, apartment fourteen. Come on over."

The Mediterranean Cascade, with its whitewashed walls and narrow windows, looked like a fortress of the French Foreign Legion constructed out of papier-mâché for a high school play. Guided by signs, Carter coasted into an underground garage, which was silent save for the buzzing of fluorescent bulbs. He parked the Thunderbird and ascended in an elevator to the courtyard, where the sun was burning rags of mist from a swimming pool. A waterfall gurgled through a garden of palmetto plants and rubber trees and splashed into a stone basin. Carter couldn't tell which was louder—the purling water or the electric pump that pushed it along.

At apartment 14, one flight up, overlooking the pool, Eddie Brown opened the door in a white terry-cloth robe and red rubber sandals. His eyes were swollen from sleep and his hair was bent out of shape like a Brillo pad. "Come in, kid, but watch the dog shit."

Sheets of newspaper scattered over the living-room rug were soiled by the droppings of a black toy poodle, which now teethed on the arm of a chair. "Tiger, stop that," shouted Eddie, smacking the dog's ears. "The fucking mutt is going to get me evicted. Had breakfast yet, kid?" He stepped over to the stereo and shuffled through a stack of albums.

"I had coffee."

"Have another cup. There's a pot on the stove. Fix me one too."

Dirty dishes were piled high in the kitchen sink, and oyster shells littered the drainboard. A few of the smells had been used as ashtrays, compounding the fishy smell with cigar and cigarette smoke. A dozen empty beer bottles arranged like bowling pins stood on the table, and one pan on the stove had grown enough mold to resemble a petri dish. As Carter rinsed two cups, Eddie came in, pursued by Janis Joplin in stereo and the poodle, its paws rapping on the linoleum.

"Jesus, that bitch can sing. Make mine strong, kid, and leave the rest of this shit as it is. The cleaning girl will wash it, if her lazy black ass ever shows up again."

"She's dead, you know," said Carter, cutting off the water.

"Who, the nigger?" Eddie appeared mildly interested.

"No, Janis Joplin. I heard it on the radio this morning. She died of a drug overdose."

"You don't say? People are dying this year who never died before." He was rummaging in the refrigerator. "Want some yogurt?"

"I've never tasted it."

"Here, try a pint of strawberry. It'll put hair on your chest and lead in your pencil." As he handed Carter the cardboard cup, he said with uncharacteristic solemnity,

"First lesson of the complete Eddie Brown treatment, don't die. At least don't die stupid. You gotta survive if you want to win. We'll sit out on the balcony where there's room to think."

The full force of the morning sun fell on the balcony, and as Carter drank his coffee, ate the yogurt, and listened to Eddie and to Janis Joplin's "Summertime," he believed he was experiencing the initial effects of the complete treatment. Relaxing for the first time in a week, he let it all soak in—the heat, the advice, and the new taste—as Eddie said he should.

"The most important thing to remember is style and quality." Eddie warmed to his subject. "How you come on, what you wear, the kind of car you drive, they're what count out here. So go first class. Shoot for the big payoff every time. It all evens out in the end, and you might as well be playing for top stakes when the cards start to turn your way. The main point is to play the game. Don't hold back. That's what losers never learn. They get gummed up in the chicken shit, while the winners clean up on the chicken salad. Okay!" As Eddie clapped his hands loudly to catch himself before he rambled too far, Carter restrained an incredulous, jittery laugh. He had heard all this before in locker rooms, yet although Eddie evoked the image of a Jewish and patently bogus Knute Rockne urging on the Irish, Carter didn't interrupt. "Lemme repeat, you have to be in the game to win, and you might as well fly first class if you want to make it worth your while."

Eddie tilted back, squinted, and spread the lapels of his robe away from the matted hair on his chest. "Christ, feel the sun. That's California for you. You could almost reach out and grab it like a big luscious tit." He shot out a hand, which flopped on his belly. "Do you have a middle name, kid?"

"Raymond."

"Raymond! Your family must have been high on gin and glue when they doled out that handle. Carter Raymond White. Horrible! The first time I heard it, I thought, Carte Blanche. Just popped into my head. You should drop it altogether, or change it to Clint Williams or Curt Walters so you won't have to throw out your monogram shirts."

Carter roused himself from his drowsiness. "I told you yesterday, I don't intend to lie to get a job."

Wearily, Eddie sighed. "Okay, keep the name if it makes you feel better. It'll hurt, but maybe we can compensate. But we have to root this lying business out of your brain. We're choosing, selecting, not lying. And like, who cares? Nobody will know, and I need leeway if I'm going to make anything out of you."

"Change whatever you want, except for my name."

"Fine. We'll just change everything around it." He sighed again. "I better have another cup of coffee. I see you mean to make me earn my money."

Over a second, then a third cup, Eddie continued his lecture—when, that is, he wasn't yelling at the dog, hailing people on their way to work, or telling Carter about them in garrulous digressions.

"Now there's a sweet piece." He pointed to a girl crossing the courtyard. "I've had my eye on her for a month. Note the legs. Tight and long enough to squeeze the life out of you. It comes from keeping her balance in bad weather. She's an airline stewardess. You know, they have to meet high standards, and don't I wish I was the cat checking them out."

Later, after shouting "Morning, John" to a man in a gray silk suit, he whispered, "That guy runs the numbers racket in L.A. He's worth a mint. But wait, one day they'll find him belly up in the pool." Pulling a grave expression over his face, he said in an avuncular tone, as if he were unconcerned about his fee, "You know, kid, bread isn't the only thing. The biggest kick I get from my job is watching a guy develop. No shit, sometimes I feel like an artist, and I plan for you to be my masterpiece."

"I hope I don't disappoint you," said Carter, unsure whether the man was serious. He drained his cup, and when Eddie's expression didn't change, asked, "Where's the bathroom?"

"Straight through the living room. Watch out for the dog shit."

Light-headed, he ambled unsteadily through the living room, saw two doors, opened the one on the left and entered a bedroom, where a naked blonde was combing her hair before a full-length mirror. Her mouth parted to form a puzzled letter O, but emitted no sound. Her hands still strained at a tangle in her hair, lifting her breasts up and out to pink, pointed nipples. He could see she didn't use peroxide.

Smiling, she shrugged, said in a guttural accent, "I thought you ver Eddie," and resumed brushing.

"Excuse me." He shut the door, forgot the bathroom, and stumbling back to the balcony, walked through a fresh dog dropping.

"Step in it, kid? I warned you." As Carter cleaned his shoe with a napkin, Eddie scooped Tiger onto his lap and playfully yanked the poodle's ears. "Goddamn mutt, I ought to grind you into hamburger."

Almost at once the girl, dressed in a yellow miniskirt, joined them, nibbling a straw-colored strand of hair. "I have to go, Eddie."

"Don't you want coffee?"

"I can't. I'm late." Keeping one dubious eye on Carter, she leaned down to kiss Eddie's forehead. "Thanks for dinner."

"Don't mention it, doll." Eddie tightened his arm around her waist. "Before you split, I'd like you to meet another client. This is Carte Blanche. Carte, Ebba Sjostrom."

"The name is Carter White," he said, standing.

"Hallo."

"He signed up for the complete Eddie Brown treatment, too, but not the one you're getting. Try to remember what I taught you." Patting her rump, he winked at Carter. "You got big things ahead of you, doll."

"I von't forget."

"Watch it on your way out. Someone made a mess on the living-room floor."

"Vy, Eddie, I thought you ver housebroken." After pecking his forehead again, she departed, and as she struck out over the courtyard, her hair swung in one direction, her behind swayed another, and her purse yet a third—each gesture as studied and affected as the amateur theatrics of any young girl who knew men were watching her.

"Christ, look at that action," said Eddie. "In a few months she'll be the most valuable property in L.A. She has the greatest tits in Southern California, and they're not stuffed with styrofoam and silicone either, which puts her one up on most chicks out here. *Playboy* already offered two thousand to do a spread on Ebba, but we're holding out for three. Can you believe her?"

"Not at all," muttered Carter.

"It's the biggest break of my life! She ran right into my arms at a discotheque. She'd only been here a few weeks.

Came over from Sweden to be an *au pair* girl in Beverly Hills. What a waste that would have been." Chasing the dog from his lap, he rose, stretched, and asked, "What time is it?"

"Eleven-fifteen."

"Shit, kid, the morning's shot and we haven't done a damn thing. Tell you what. You stay out here. Take off your shirt and sunbathe. Once I've shaved, I'll phone the Plush Pup for a few burgers, and after lunch we'll bear down and work. Meanwhile review what you've learned.

Carter couldn't recall everything he had been told, but remembered the words "quality" and "thinking big," which in his drowsiness he vaguely associated with Ebba Sjostrom's breasts. Sizable, yet not too large, their chief merit was shape—the full curves which ended at sharp points—and color—pink and white. As the sun warmed his bare shoulders, he shut his eyes, and cushioned by a gauzy daydream, thought of Elaine. He wished she were here. It would be like last summer when . . .

Promptly this straightened his spine and threatened to eat through his sense of well-being. In his place, what would Elaine be doing? Was this the way to get the right kind of job? She would extract everything possible from these hours and coolly appraise Eddie's advice, rather than accept it without question.

But somehow—perhaps the sun had drugged him—he believed he was progressing at his own rate. For once he wasn't tense or worried. Surely that constituted progress, and although Carter might appear lethargic and indifferent, the little man's unflagging zeal had struck a spark inside him.

During lunch Eddie continued the lecture and interrupted himself only once, as Carter salted his cheeseburger. Snatching the shaker from his hand, he demanded, "Have you tasted that?"

"Not yet."

"Then why are you sprinkling salt on it?"

"I like salt."

"Christ, kid, think! Don't you have a brain? How do you know there's not salt already on that burger?"

"I don't. But I . . ."

"Exactly. And what you're doing employment-wise is committing suicide. Suppose I was interviewing you and I saw you burying your burger in salt before you'd tasted it. I'd figure you were an unstable nut who doesn't think things out first. Believe me, these people have a scoreboard and they keep track of little fuck-ups like this. You gotta be on your toes."

Afterward Carter ate slowly and warily, and when he had finished, Eddie smacked his belly, yawned, and furiously scratched his scalp. "Jesus Christ, kid, I'm wasted. Watching you eat nearly put me to sleep. Wanna go for a swim? It'll wake us up."

"I don't have a suit."

"I've got hundreds. We'll swim a few laps to bust the cobwebs out of our brains, then buckle down and work."

Eddie tossed a pair of surfing trunks from the bedroom, and Carter changed in the bathroom. Noticing in the mirror he had renewed his tan, he reflected that so far the complete treatment was much like summer camp. Yet he wouldn't object to anything which spared him the anxiety and dislocation he had suffered for the last week.

When he came out, Eddie was waiting in a red knit jersey and matching trunks. "Lemme see your leg. I've had experience with these things."

Carter gingerly lifted it to display the curved scar.

"Christ, are you kidding?" He knelt for a closer look, and testing the raw nerves with his finger, caused Carter to shiver. "You limp for this? A big ox like you? I wouldn't feel it if I had it on the tip of my tongue. Lemme show you something, kid." Standing up, he pulled back the sweater to reveal on his belly a jagged patch of skin the size, shape, and vermilion shade of a maple leaf. It appeared a fist had punched through Eddie and the hole had been packed with red clay.

"God, how did you do it? Were you in the war?" The sight of it made him slightly sick at his stomach.

Eddie snorted. "Yeah, that's it. I was in the war. I was in everything. Take a little advice from me, kid. Once you have a job, quit limping. It gets on people's nerves. Nobody likes a cripple for long."

Warm color came to Carter's cheeks. "Maybe you'd like to try walking on it awhile."

"Okay." He nodded. "Suit yourself." Whirling, he led the way from the apartment to the pool.

While Carter swam, Eddie sat in a deck chair, a loose-leaf binder on his lap, his eyes masked by convex green sunglasses which gave him the sinister, polyhedral gaze of an insect. Fondly he kneaded the loose flesh and livid scar on his belly, as if they were a handsome acquisition which, as much as anything, staked his claim to excellence. It was impossible to tell if he was angry.

"Aren't you coming in?" asked Carter to break the silence.

"No, kid, I don't swim. I have punctured eardrums."

"Oh, I'm sorry. I . . ."

Don't be. They have their advantages. Like when I'm eating a chick, I breathe through them. Where did you say you come from?"

"Maryland," he answered after a lull.

"City or country?"

"The suburbs. It was . . ."

"I get the picture." He scribbled in the binder.

Carter swam the length of the pool, stood in the shallow end until the sun dried his shoulders, then paddled back to Eddie. Swirling water on his leg summoned up memories of the whirl-pool treatments at Walter Reed—the best hour of each day. It had taken him from the depressing ward to a bright, airy room where a blond therapist encouraged him. Unfortunately she was married, and her sharp diamond always cut into his arm as she helped him out of the tub.

She had said it would be six months before he walked without a limp. Now more than a year had flashed by, and with some embarrassment he realized Eddie was right. It was time to stand alone, free of crutches or excuses. Stirring his bad knee back and forth, he promised to concentrate on each step from now on.

Carter clung to the edge of the pool waiting expectantly as Eddie jabbed a period to the final sentence. "Here's how it stacks up. You're twenty-five years old. Nobody's going to ask for proof, but believe me, the extra age will help. It means you've been married over three years and aren't the type of nitwit who marries a girl and knocks her up in the same night. I got you down for those three years of school, and if you're careful, they won't hurt you. Listen close. You paid your way through three years of college by working in the cafeteria. So you already know the restaurant business. But just before your senior year, you were bugged about Vietnam. The war was eating at you all the time. You didn't know whether you were for it or against it. The news only confused you, so you decided to enlist and see for yourself. Watch it on this one, kid. You could get clobbered. There's no saying how people stand. Just tell them what you think they'd like to hear."

"They can check my record," said Carter, displeased.

"I'm not a rookie at this game. There's no record that says *why* you went into the service. Just tell them you joined the army, volunteered for Vietnam, and were wounded. Nothing else. Act like it's too painful to discuss. They'll think you're a hero, if you let them." Removing his sunglasses, Eddie chewed at the earpiece, and like a film director, consulted the script. "Incidentally, you were married right after basic training, before you left for Vietnam. One of those crazy romantic weddings people love. I hope to hell you're not putting me on. You better have a wife."

"Of course I do."

"Okay, you were sent home and stuck in a hospital. Nobody will dare press too hard for details. Keep it simple and quiet, and they're bound to feel for you. That's the important thing. Let them imagine what that bum leg is like. If you really want to limp, this is your chance."

"Hey, wait a damn minute. I've had enough of that."

"What did I say?" Eddie asked innocently. "Practice your new style of walking when you have the job. Can we go on? After you rested a few months, regaining your strength, you started to work for your father-in-law."

The water became glacial. "That's pushing things a . . ."

"Lemme finish. I won't make you stick your neck out. Now then"—he referred to the script—"your wife's old man owned a nursery."

"A what? This is silly."

"A nursery. A place where he grew bushes and flowers, out in the sticks of Maryland. But when the old bugger died, the business collapsed. This way there's no sweat about references. You been in the army and you worked for your father-in-law. Don't mention anything else. It'll only screw you up."

"That's nonsense. I could furnish good references."

"Forget it. You have all you need right here." He rattled the pages. "After the old man died your mother-in-law cut out from the East Coast for La Jolla, and you and the wife settled in L.A., where you could start a career and still be near the old gal in her declining years." Eddie cracked the binder shut. "How does it sound?"

Confused, Carter couldn't say whether Eddie's audacity amounted to a twisted brilliance or simple-minded absurdity. "Do you think it'll work? Wouldn't it be easier to . . ."

"Does a fat dog fuck? Of course it'll work, if you do what I tell you. Now climb out of that pool and lie in the sun. I want you looking tanned and healthy. I'll be inside typing up these notes." Glancing at the binder, he grinned. "I swear to Christ, kid, sometimes I amaze myself. This stuff is terrific."

At first, as he lay beside the pool with the tips of his fingers in the water, the sun soothed Carter and he tried to convince himself that Eddie and his scenario were "terrific." But then he wondered again how any of this could lead to a job. It was one thing to be amused by Eddie, to listen to his advice and laugh along with him, but quite another to act upon it. If the treatment didn't succeed, Carter would be angry and disappointed. Yet if it did succeed . . . Somehow it seemed worse to think that people were so pathetic they would embrace an abyss if it were cleverly disguised and attractively packaged.

Carter shivered as evening shadows lengthened across the courtyard. Once the little man was out of sight, his script sounded ominous, not so much a callous effort at deception as a haunting admission that words alone screened one from nothingness. No amount of laughter could cover this, and Carter was reluctant to go upstairs and accept the menacing vitae sheet. Yet he couldn't remain here much longer. In the wet bathing suit he shivered uncontrollably. It was at least six o'clock, the sun had climbed the far wall, and Elaine would be worried.

Dressed in his terry-cloth robe, Eddie sat on the sofa, a portable typewriter in his lap, tapping out the notes with two stiff fingers. Tiger darted about his feet, snapping at his bare ankles and at the loose threads dangling from the robe. Eddie appeared not to notice the dog or Carter, who had emerged from the bathroom after changing clothes. Carter hesitated, raked a hand through his damp hair, then blurted, "This is stupid."

"Huh!" Eddie grunted, hunting the correct key.

"It's insane. All I want is a job."

"What?"

"I said this is insane. I'm looking for a job, not a starring role in your fantasies."

"Kid, have you seen Sunset Strip lately?"

"I live a half a block from it. What does . . ."

"So what's insane about this?" His fingernail flicked the paper. "When everybody is running around the streets dressed like a freak, you're the one who looks crazy. You're the one who doesn't have a job. Of course it's insane. The whole world's a fucking nut house. But I didn't make it that way. I just live here and get by the best I can. So what are you going to do? Keep beating your meat about how crazy things are, or find yourself a job?"

"I want a job, but . . ."

"No buts. This is how it's done. And you should be glad. Since everybody else is flipped out, it'll be easier for you. While they're thrashing around, you can coast on the waves they make."

Carter set out from the Mediterranean Cascade with his notes and sped recklessly down Franklin Avenue, carried along on the precarious crest of a wave which broke against the bulkhead of cars at the intersection of Hollywood Boulevard. The entire day, and especially the details of Eddie's scenario, had begun to lose shape, to disperse like a newspaper photograph held too close to the eye. Only a mass of confusing dots danced before him.

When an angry horn sounded, he accelerated again, lurching like a puppet cut loose from its strings. Ahead the traffic moved toward the sun with the quick silver flicker of a snake slithering into its hole. The gleaming serpent of cars threatened to drag Carter along with it, until he broke to the left, followed Sunset a few blocks, and took a second left onto North Harper. Parking in front of the apartment, he paused a minute to regain the lunatic clarity of Eddie's vision. Although it seemed an insult to accept the little man's instructions, Carter didn't feel safe in ignoring them. If the world was half as mad as he suspected, Eddie Brown might be the best mentor to have.

Elaine came out of the kitchen in an orange dress. Over it she wore a small apron of crisp white lace. "Where have you been? I was worried." She sounded perturbed, and a wan smile masked her annoyance as transparently as the apron covered her dress. "I've prepared a special dinner. Beef Stroganoff. I hope it isn't ruined."

Then as the smile faded, "Is anything wrong? Your fore-head is red."

He wiped his brow, which was warm, almost feverish. "Sunburn, I guess. We spent this afternoon outside talk-ing. And working, of course."

"To think I felt sorry for you." She reached behind to untie the apron. The stiff bow snapped as it unknotted. "It was so hot here, I was sure you'd be miserable in your suit coat. How did it go today?"

"Fine." Lingering in the hall, as if he didn't know whether to stay, Carter jangled the car keys.

"Is this man worth the money?"

"Yes. I think so. Sorry I'm late. I'll wash up." He kissed her lightly as he pushed by on his way to the bed-room.

For the balance of the evening he evaded her questions, avoided her eyes, eluded her silences, and finally as he lay in bed, ignored the slow and deliberate manner in which she stripped off the orange dress, then her slip and underwear. She was near enough that he could have ca-ressed her hips, her buttocks, her hard belly, but though he was tempted to, he did not. The gentlest touch would have brought on more questions, and he didn't wish to talk. How could he explain about Eddie when he himself didn't entirely understand? Yet he believed . . . What? He had changed, was changing. She must have seen that.

Lifting her nightgown up to the light, she examined its diaphanous weave for flaws, or perhaps for reflections of her own mistakes. The gown gave her body a blue, luminescent tint, which deepened as she put it on. Switch-ing off the light, she crawled beneath the covers of her bed.

"Good night, Carter. I hope you feel better by morn-ing."

In fact, he felt better at once, for in the dark the tidal wave of Eddie's words washed over him and he reviewed the script for his new life. He had been married three years. His mother-in-law lived in La Jolla. He had worked in a nursery. He was twenty-five . . . At last he was asleep.

2

Carter's eyes rolled open at seven, half an hour before the alarm, and he was so eager to continue the treatment, it required a stern exercise of the will not to leave at once. He remained in bed until the urgency subsided, then hearing the Japanese gardeners at their weekly rounds, got up and went to the window.

The reedy music of voices, the feline purr of their mower merged with Elaine's murmurous breathing. Sleeping on her side as always, she had one leg outriggered to support the swollen discomfort of her belly. He regretted his silence of the previous night, and promised to explain things soon—as soon as he understood. Meanwhile the best he could do was reassure her by his presence, that regardless of his confusion, he wouldn't fail her. When one of the gardeners started to prune the lemon tree, releasing a tart scent like after-shave lotion, he headed for the shower.

Eddie was eating breakfast with the airline stewardess they had seen in the courtyard yesterday. A tall girl, she had muscular legs and a friendly, vacant expression. A leatherette overnight bag, blue like her flight uniform, was on the couch.

"Betty, this is Carte Blanche, one of my clients. Take a good look. When I'm through, you won't recognize him."

"I think he looks okay like he is. Hullo, Card." Her nasal twang had an echo of the heartland. "Want an egg?"

"It's Carter," he corrected her. "I've eaten. I'll sit on the balcony."

"Yeah, why not study your notes? I want you singing that tune like a canary by Friday." To Betty he said, "The kid has talent, but doesn't know how to use it yet. Mark my words, though, he's bound to make a ton of bread. Maybe when he's in fat city he'll fly us up to Vegas."

"How fun! The girls all tell me . . ."

He removed his coat and shirt, and lounging in the sun, memorized the notes, then played with the poodle and watched the tenants set off for work. Lazily content, he considered himself not so much truant as above the mindless hustle, as though this freedom were part of the treatment. By ten o'clock the only sound to disturb his reveries was the tuneless humming of an old Negro who sauntered around the pool wielding a long-handled net to scoop out eucalyptus leaves that had sailed down on soft air currents from the Hollywood Hills.

"Tiger seems to like you," said Eddie, stepping onto the balcony, slapping a black plastic leash against his thigh. "How about taking her for a walk?"

"Why?"

"I'm trying to housebreak her. Sick of having dog shit all over the apartment. Just drag her around the block a couple of times. Say forty-five minutes. You're a prince, kid."

Carter noticed Betty's overnight bag agape; the toe of a stocking protruded like an impudent tongue. The bedroom door was shut, and he thought of his money. He didn't intend to pay two hundred and fifty dollars for the privilege of walking Eddie's dog.

But as he hiked up Franklin Avenue to La Brea, steering Tiger from one palm-shaded patch of grass to the next, his anger eased. It was a brisk morning, which would warm by noon, then cool that night. Each day in Los Angeles seemed a miniature of three quarters of a year in the East—spring in the morning, summer in the afternoon, and autumn at evening. Winter alone was absent, and Carter wouldn't miss it.

On Hollywood Boulevard he stopped at Grauman's Chinese Theatre, read the list of Academy Award Winners, inspected the hand- and footprints on the sidewalk, and strolled toward Vine Street, past cut-rate liquor stores, souvenir shops, and cheap boutiques, specializing in crotchless panties and nipple-less bras. After an hour—time enough, he thought, for even a sexual athlete—he backtracked to the Mediterranean Cascade.

Eddie opened the door, his face bearded by shaving cream. "Christ, kid, where you been?"

"You said you wanted to be alone."

"Not all day. I didn't have the time or inclination to waste the complete Eddie Brown treatment on that chick. Her idea of sex was to keel over in the sack and act like a wooden Indian."

After he'd shaved, Eddie ordered lunch from the Plush Pup and continued yesterday's lecture as if nothing had intervened. "There's one matter I haven't mentioned, kid, and that's timing. You ought to learn to pace yourself. The worst mistake a guy can make is getting impatient. I've seen a lot of good men ruined because they didn't think they were progressing fast enough. Trust me, kid, and I'll bring you along just like you should be. You'll learn and you'll grow, but so slow and gradual you won't know it."

"I must admit, I've been . . ."

"Of course you have. It's natural. But relax." Eddie waved a French fry. "There are two important items on the agenda today. First, you have an appointment at a hair stylist's."

"I just had my hair cut."

"Yeah, a butcher must of done it. It's a wonder you didn't need plastic surgery afterward. A little styling will cost fifteen bucks, but it's worth every penny. What the hell, you're a good-looking fella. Why hide it? You have to play all the angles. Then tonight at seven-thirty you're scheduled for a lie-detector test in Brentwood. The guy is doing it in his home as a favor to me."

"What? Why a lie-detector test?"

"Jesus, kid, don't jump out of your skin. It's routine. Some companies won't hire you unless you're bondable."

"I don't have the money. I'm already paying two hundred and fifty dollars and I . . ."

"The polygraph won't cost a dime. Like I said, the guy's doing me a favor."

"You mean a restaurant will demand a lie-detector test? I don't believe it."

"I don't know what they'll want. Maybe everything. Maybe nothing. But since it's free, why not do it? There's nothing to worry about unless . . . unless you're not telling me the truth. Hey, do you have a record?"

"Of course not."

"Don't bullshit me."

"I'm not. It's just that . . ."

"Okay then, quit bitching. Your appointment at the hair stylist's is in fifteen minutes."

Carter proceeded to Mel Tuttle's Tonsorial Shop with the same disquiet he felt about the polygraph test that night. Again he told himself he balked because of the money, but he knew better. While he feared the lie detector for the truth it might reveal, he hesitated outside the hair stylist's, reluctant to risk more changes and revolutions. After scrutinizing the snapshots in the window—they showed Mel Tuttle sculpting the hair of Hollywood's leading men—he had trouble opening the door.

The scent of bay rum battled the cigar and cigarette smoke which coiled in burly clouds around the light fixtures. Few customers talked, and everyone acted ill at ease, as a covey of homosexuals attended half a dozen beefy men who presented aggressive evidence of their masculinity by reading *Playboy* and *Sports Illustrated*. Large, elegant, and carpeted in a deep rust-colored pile, the room was strung with insipid threads of sound, too attenuated to be called music. They added a bothersome distraction which clung to Carter like spiderwebs.

Mel Tuttle met him, a decal smile pasted to his face, which, if the tired eyes were any indication, wanted desperately to relax. "Do you have an appointment, sir?"

"Yes, Eddie Brown sent me."

"Of course, you're Mr. White. Come to my chair. I assume this is your first visit?" he said after a glimpse at Carter's hair.

Blushing, Carter nodded.

"Excellent." With a dexterous flourish he slipped the coat from Carter's shoulders, checking the label as he passed it to an assistant. Then he clapped his hands soundlessly, struggling to gather enthusiasm or simply to strengthen his wrists. "Mr. White, I hope you'll trust me and my taste. The first visit is most important. It's the foundation for everything that follows." He spun the plush barber chair away from the mirror. "It would be a shame if you lost heart halfway through. Andrew, his smock. Please be seated," he said after the assistant, a mincing mulatto, had tied a rubberized sheet around his neck.

Folding his arms, Tuttle circled Carter, his head tilted pensively to the left, like a sculptor inspecting a block of virgin marble. "Marvelous cheekbones and the forehead's an inspiration. But the part in your hair absolutely must go."

"Why?" Unnerved, Carter didn't care to yield anything.

"Your hair is too thick." Roughly Tuttle ran a hand through it. "It looks like someone carved the part with a wood-burning set. The natural sweep of your hair is to the right. You should let it pursue its own course. Unfortunately there's not much to be done about the sideburns. They're too short. Let them grow. They might give your face body, which it badly needs."

As Tuttle knuckled shampoo onto his scalp, Carter thought once more of the money. A stupid waste of fifteen dollars. To endure another little man's insults. For a haircut he probably wouldn't like. And what he hated most was knowing he was entirely in someone else's hands.

His scalp cooled as Tuttle rinsed the suds, then used a comb and straight razor to shape Carter's hair in soundless strokes that dropped wet locks into his lap. After applying a dense lacquer, he drew a net over his head.

"Andrew, bring the dryer." Shielding Carter's eyes, Tuttle rotated the chair toward the mirror. "No peeking. Just ten more minutes."

Suddenly hot air shot into his ears, and when Tuttle stepped back, Carter saw a startled man on a throne, swathed in a rubberized sheet, crowned by a dryer that looked like a bishop's miter.

"God, it's hot!" he hollered.

"It's supposed to be. You have . . ." The rest of the sentence couldn't penetrate the humming silver helmet.

Reminded of madmen and mysterious rays, of forces out of control, Carter thought his bewildered face could have been an advertisement for a horror movie in which insidious machines ran amok, destroying the cellular structure of their victims. He closed his eyes, and that was better. Though the torrid air still needled him like an electric current, it was now a pleasant shock that stimulated new nerves and senses. He remembered that in those stories he'd read victims of amnesia were often subjected to dramatic cures which jolted them into recognition or burned their minds completely clean. They were ready in the end to start life anew.

"Andrew, pull the plug." Tuttle peeled off the hairnet. "Let's see what we've accomplished. Oh, yes, much better. Don't you agree, Mr. White?"

The mirror presented a strange, glassy-eyed captive. In that first instant it appeared that everything had changed. The part was gone, his hair canted rakishly off to the right, and his features had fleshed out and matured. He looked reserved, strong, rather than rawboned and haunted.

"Jesus Christ," he whispered.

"Do you like it?"

"I don't know." He swiveled his neck.

"Careful! The setting solution hasn't cooled."

"Jesus Christ," he repeated, but recognizable traits were beginning to crawl over his face like objects into a developing photograph. The conversion seemed less drastic. He flashed a tentative smile, as would someone who'd had plastic surgery and wanted to see if his well-modeled features were as immobile and impermanent as they looked. They weren't.

"You do like it, then?" asked Tuttle.

"Will it stay like this?"

"That remains to be seen. Don't wash your hair until it has discovered its natural contours, then apply a dependable setting solution. I recommend my own brand."

Outside on Las Palmas Avenue, carrying two spray cans of Tuttle's Stay-Tru Magic, which he hadn't known how to refuse, Carter studied the people he passed, hoping to judge by their eyes what he hadn't succeeded in doing with his own. Finally he thought he would let Elaine decide whether the haircut was an improvement.

Yet this annoyed Carter, who suddenly didn't care to subject himself to her appraisal. He could draw his own conclusions and knew it would all seem ludicrous to her —the Eddie Brown treatment, as well as the haircut— unless or until he found a job, and since he wasn't sure, himself, of the connection between what he had done in the last three days and what she expected, he was unwilling to allow Elaine, who had experienced none of it— neither Eddie's compelling voice nor the artistry of Mel Tuttle—to evaluate his progress. Buying a paperback at Pickwick's, he parked on Sweetzer Avenue, read until dinnertime, and headed for the apartment, planning to eat quickly and leave for Brentwood.

Elaine was in the kitchen, and he waited a moment at the doorway until she glanced up and did an exaggerated double take. "My God, what have you done?"

"Nothing." He feigned surprise.

Her eyes narrowed as she neared him. "You look . . . You've had your hair cut!"

"Styled," he said, his voice poised between acute embarrassment and arch defiance.

"You're kidding. Turn around. You don't look like the same person. You seem . . . older, more sophisticated."

"Eddie Brown thought it would be an improvement." He disclaimed both credit and blame.

"It is. But I'll need some time to get used to it."

"A minute is all I can spare. I have an appointment to take a test for the job."

"What kind of test?"

"General aptitude," he said, fearing she, too, would realize how easily a lie-detector test might shatter the spindly under-pinnings of their life. "Is dinner ready? I don't want to be late."

Elaine bowed her head and bit at her lower lip, the habitual gesture which led him to suspect she had suppressed her true thoughts.

3

Carter sped west on the Strip, which at dusk had fallen into a period of temporary peace. Not all the neon had blossomed and few cars were on the street. As he passed UCLA, the sun burst its rind like rotten fruit, staining the sky with mango brilliance, but the extravaganza was wasted. No one was out, and high fences screened most of the houses.

He found the address on a street walled by cypress and pine trees. A dry rasping noise grated his nerves as the Santa Ana wind, laden with lava-like heat, boiled over the asphalt through the leaves and shattered against the tireless buzz-saw of window air conditioners. From an arched entrance in the shrubbery, he peered beyond a chest-high chain-link fence to a stonehouse, square as a fortress. *Beware of Dog, Ring Bell before Entering* warned a plaque on the gate. When he pressed the button, an electric lock uncoupled and the gate swung wide.

"Come ahead. The dog's in his pen," called a man from the porch, and even at this distance, through the dimness, Carter recognized the cleft in his chin. It was Moylan Fingerhut from Fist, Inc. Wearing gym shorts and a tight T-shirt, he strode down the walk, a slab of raw meat in his right fist. As he stopped in awkward slow motion, his muscles flexed. "Hey, don't I know you?"

"Yes. I'm Carter White." He fought to keep his voice under control. "You interviewed me last week. Eddie Brown sent me for a polygraph test."

"I thought so. I never forget a face. It's my business. Come around back while I feed the dog." Fingerhut, barefoot, marched over the Augustine grass, his shaggy brown legs sturdy as tree trunks. "Still haven't found a job, huh?"

"I'll have one by the end of the week," said Carter, regaining his composure. No longer tempted to turn and run, he nevertheless wondered if he could refuse to take

105

the test, claiming he was sick. But that would rouse Eddie's suspicions. And Fingerhut's. He was trapped.

In the back yard a wire pen imprisoned an enormous German shepherd, which growled and sprang against the fence. Rising on its hind legs, it was as high as a tall man.

"Down, Patton! Step back, White. He doesn't like strangers." Tearing off a sliver of meat, he tossed it over the wire, and Patton torpedoed into the air to catch it before it touched the ground. "Look at that bastard. Smartest damn dog I ever owned. And mean as hell. He'll attack anything that moves." Fingerhut threw him another chunk. "After I've trained him, I plan to mate him and produce a team of superdogs. Maybe a cross between a German shepherd and a Doberman. There are hundreds of people who'd pay top dollar for a good attack dog."

"How do you know Eddie Brown?"

"In my business I meet all kinds. Some a lot worse than Eddie."

"He seems like a nice guy." Even to Carter this sounded like a question.

"Isn't that what you'd expect from a Jew? They're all nice when they smell money." Heaving in the last hunk of meat, he expelled a rumbling laugh. "That must be how they lured them into the ovens. Wave a few bucks in front of a kike and he thinks he can walk on fire. But Eddie Brown, he's a typical small-time chiseler." Fingerhut harshly cleared his throat, hocked, and spat into the pen. Patton leaped up to snare the oyster. "He's the type who'd have talked his way out of the ovens, if you know what I mean. He's got a tongue like cotton candy and a mind like a steel trap."

"I don't think talk about Jews and ovens is very funny."

"Don't you?" Wiping his bloody hands on his shorts, he struck out toward the house. "You've been brainwashed. It's all a lot of propaganda. I'm in a position to know that not nearly as many Jews were killed as people think."

"You mean like five million instead of six."

"Nobody kept count, and now West Germany, East Germany, Israel, and the Jewish cartels all have reasons for hiding the exact number. A lot of them just pretended to be dead, collected their insurance, emigrated to Israel or the United States, and made a mint." Removing a ring of keys from his belt, he unlocked the basement door.

"But it doesn't do them any good." He locked the door behind them and switched on the lights. "In the end most of them die of cancer. It's in their blood."

Paneled in knotty pine, the basement looked like a hunting lodge or the game room at a men's club. The polygraph machine had been set on a pool table, a moose head mounted over the fireplace, and a brace of rifles secured in a rack next to six chalky cues. On the walls hung a rotogravure of plaques, certificates, and framed snapshots of Fingerhut beside a sailfish, Fingerhut with his boot on the head of a dead grizzly, Fingerhut in the Marines, Fingerhut with movie stars, Fingerhut with J. Edgar Hoover. The relentless air conditioner had chilled and filtered the air so that it yielded the antiseptic smell of ice cubes hardened out of chlorinated water.

Carter shivered, and wondered if anyone, even a grotesque like Fingerhut, could be exactly what he seemed. It sounded as though he believed what he said, but it was impossible to tell since he had turned such a stern, unblinking surface to the world. One could test him anywhere and never touch a seam or soft spot. Yet what cavernous crevasses underneath caused these brutal reverberations?

"Have a seat." He motioned Carter to the green felt table. "Ever taken a polygraph test?"

"Never."

"Everyone should from time to time." Picking up a clipboard, Fingerhut sat opposite him and thrust a thumb into the cleft of his chin. "Before I hook the wires to you, I have a few questions. What's your full name?"

"Carter Raymond White."

"Age??"

"Twenty-t . . . twenty-five."

"Father's occupation?"

"He's dead."

"Wife's maiden name?"

"Why all these questions?"

"For comparison. The machine can't say when you're lying unless it knows when you're telling the truth. Wife's maiden name?"

"Yost," he answered, seeing no harm in it. "Elaine Yost."

"Father's occupation?"

"I told you. He's dead."

"Not yours. hers."

107

"This is ridiculous."

"Look, White, I'm doing you a favor. I could be working with Patton or watching TV. Show a little cooperation or the deal's off. Father's occupation?"

On quick reflection and despite his reluctance, Carter again saw no harm in the truth. "Foreign Service."

"Yeah? Where?"

"Costa Rica."

"That's where you get your money."

"I don't have any money."

"There's no time to discuss that. Place of previous residence?"

"Washington, D.C."

"Did you like it?"

"Is this question for comparison too?"

"No. I worked in Washington for a while. I might have stayed, but I couldn't bear living around niggers. They're the worst criminal element in our society."

"Worse than Jews?"

"It's not even close. Do you know the High's Ice Cream stores?"

"Yes," he said, unable to imagine where this would lead.

"Do you have any idea how often they're robbed? More than four hundred times a year! Some ghetto stores are stuck up two and three times a night. A group of, well, let's say, concerned private citizens asked me to investigate."

"I guess you put an end to the robberies," Carter needled him.

"That wasn't my job. I was hired to find out how a chain of retail stores could be robbed four hundred times a year and remain in business."

"Maybe they have crafty Jewish managers."

He shook his head so vigorously Carter thought it might tumble from his shoulders. "Better than that. They have about one half of the United States Senate behind them."

"You can't be serious."

"I couldn't prove it. Nobody could. It's so secret even the CIA isn't aware of the whole story. But I have reason to believe that the High's Ice Cream stores, along with a number of other nationally known firms, are subsidized by Congress. What I mean is, the liberals have discovered how to dole out your money and mine to the coons.

They secretly distribute it to stores like High's, then pass the word for those black bastards to take what they want. Can you imagine?"

"No, I can't," said Carter. "Are there any more questions?"

"What? No. Let me plug you in."

Using adhesive tape, Fingerhut attached wires to Carter's temples, wrists, the palms of his hands, and after ordering him to unbutton his shirt, coiled one, cold as an earthworm, over his heart. Carter thought he felt some vital essence—his courage, wits, or endurance—bleed into the brown box, which emitted a hum as several scratching needles registered his reactions on graph paper. Just as he had that afternoon, he believed he was at the mercy of a sinister machine, a portable electric chair perhaps.

"Breathe normally, don't twitch, and answer yes or no."

Tense, short of breath, and fidgety, Carter tried to joke. "My palms are sweating. Will that cause a short circuit?"

"Never happen. This baby doesn't react to water. It has a taste for blood and keeps a count on your pulse." He stroked the box. "Is your name Carter Raymond White?"

"Yes."

"Are you twenty-five?"

"Yes."

"Are you married?"

"Yes."

"Have you ever lived in Washington?"

"Yes."

"Are you under contract to Eddie Brown?"

"More or less. I assume you . . ."

"Yes or no?"

"I told you, I . . ."

Fingerhut switched off the machine, and for a moment the needles scraped dryly like fingernails on slate. "Look, I don't want a debate. You're wasting my paper."

"I never signed a contract, but"—he attempted to catch a hint from Fingerhut's tiny gray eyes—"we have an agreement."

"Okay, why the big deal?" He switched on the polygraph. "Are you under contract to Eddie Brown?"

"Yes."

"Have you ever been arrested for a felony?"

"No."

"Do you have any mental, spiritual, or physical handicap which would prevent you from being a good employee?"

"No." To divert himself and stay calm for the difficult questions, Carter stared at the stuffed moose head.

"Is your father dead?"

"Yes." The wire over his heart nipped his flesh at this truth.

"Are you married?" Fingerhut double-checked.

"I . . . I'm married."

"Yes or no?"

"Yes."

"Is your father-in-law in the Foreign Service?"

"He is."

"Yes or no, dammit."

"Yes."

"Hold it." Fingerhut cut the power. "Something's screwed up. Are you juggling your feet?" As he consulted the scrawl on the graph paper, he explored the cleft in his chin as if expecting to detect an answer there. "The machine says you're telling the truth on the important questions, but lying on the others."

"I'm nervous."

"Maybe," said Fingerhut doubtfully. "We'll do it over."

This time the electric current seemed to stream in the opposite direction, channeling strength and confidence into Carter, and with repetition his lies slid out easily, unnoticed, he was certain, by Fingerhut. The man was like his machine, cunning and exact, but limited. If Carter ducked beyond his range, he would be safe.

When his answers became increasingly assertive, Fingerhut broke in. "That's enough."

"Well," Carter said, detaching the wires, "did I pass?"

"Yeah, sure." He was folding a long strip of graph paper into an envelope. "Were you afraid you wouldn't?"

"I knew I would. Now what? Shall I give Eddie the results?"

"No. I'll do that."

Carter's hand lingered a moment in midair before falling to his side. "Thanks for the help."

At the apartment the lights were out and Elaine had gone to bed. Although not in the least tired, he undressed and crawled under the covers, pleased with his performance at Fingerhut's, pleased, in fact with the entire day. But when Elaine murmured, "Carter?" he hesitated before answering, "Yes?"

"I was lonely and decided to sleep until you came back. Somehow I feel better in the dark. How was the test?"

"Easy."

"I knew you'd do well." She touched his face.

"I'm sorry I woke you. Go to sleep. You need the rest."

"I'm wide awake. Tell me about the test and Eddie Brown. Do you like him? Are you learning . . ."

"Elaine, it's late. I have to be up early. We'll talk tomorrow." Kissing her hand, he folded it onto the sheet, moved to the edge of his bed, and lay awake long past midnight. He thought of Washington, and although he didn't miss it, remembered it fondly, falling asleep to an image of the river. It gleamed deep blue, rather than septic yellow, and Carter was on the bottom of a boat, looking up at a white triangle of canvas which sliced the sky into a widening furrow. As the wind rose, the sail bellied and tilted to the starboard. The keel cut through the water, giving off a glimmering spray and an illusion of great speed.

The final day of the complete Eddie Brown treatment dawned chilly and overcast, and the courtyard of the Mediterranean Cascade was dim as a cellar. A gray sheet of mist paved the pool, muffling the sound of the waterfall. Upstairs, the newspaper was under the welcome mat, and Carter checked his watch. Ten after nine. Yet he had to knock for five minutes before Eddie answered the door in red silk pajama bottoms and a hairnet.

"Oh Christ, kid, it's you." He snatched off the hairnet, exposing a greasy solvent on his scalp. "You scared the hell out of me. I thought it was my ex-wife. What time is it?"

"After nine."

"Shit, I just went to bed." He scratched the bushy hollow of his chest, powdering his paunch with dandruff. "This goddamn vacation will be the death of me. I'll have to go to the office to recover."

111

"Do you want me to come back later?" He gestured toward the bedroom.

"What? No. Nobody's here. Ebba cut out a few hours ago."

"Ebba?"

"Yeah. After you left for Mel Tuttle's, Ebba breezed in on me. She can't get enough. We did it every way except swinging from the chandelier. She could be a one-man sex circus. A nympho-acrobat. How did you make out?"

"I had my hair styled."

"It's out of sight." Eddie fished a cigar from a dish on the coffee table and staggered toward the bedroom.

"I passed the polygraph test, too."

"Great. I need some sleep if I'm going to get it together tonight. See you in a few hours."

Carter fixed coffee, ate a cup of yogurt, fed Tiger, and filled the dog's water dish, which looked as if it had been empty for days. Then after leafing through the *Los Angeles Times*, he stretched out on the couch, and with Tiger dozing beside him, fell into a deep slumber.

At noon the phone woke him, and he answered in a voice husky from sleep.

"Eddie, I have only a minute. The family's out and I vanted to talk. I vish you ver here." It was Ebba Sjostrom.

"Wait a minute, I'll . . ."

"Don't hang up. I don't know ven they'll be back. How do you feel? I'm like jelly inside. Of all the times and vays I've been kissed, I've never been kissed there."

"I think I'd . . ."

She giggled. "How did I taste? Can't you talk? Is someone wit you?"

"No, it's not that." At this point it seemed impossible to say he wasn't Eddie.

"Come then. Vat did I taste like?"

"Pickled herring."

"Eddie, I hope not. I keep very clean."

"No. I was kidding. It was like a piece of fruit."

"I'm so glad. I'd rather do that than anything. Or I'd rather start that vay and end wit what we did in the bathtub. Oh, I hear the car in the driveway. I'll call again. Remember, I love you."

Carter gently cradled the receiver, and as he stretched

out again, sleep eluded him, but part of Eddie's advice returned. California was like a big luscious tit you could reach for and grab. It wouldn't move, wouldn't hide, and wasn't afraid to give you what you desired—or give it to you whether you wanted it or not.

At two o'clock Eddie burst from the bedroom. "That's what the doctor ordered. A few hours in bed—alone! Christ's sake, kid, let's have some light in here." As he shot back the balcony curtains, an oblong of sunlight fell across the carpet. "Beautiful day. Why aren't you outside?"

"It was chilly and gray the last time I looked."

"Gray and chilly? Never. Not on my vacation. You say the lie detector test went okay?"

"That's what Fingerhut said."

"Do you have the results?"

"No. He said he'd pass them on to you later."

"Hmm. Strange." Eddie scratched his right sideburn, examined his fingernails, and said, "The guy's got a screw loose. You never know what the hatchet-faced moron is thinking."

"He spoke highly of you, too."

"I'll bet. The fucking pig would like to make a lampshade out of my ass."

"How did you two become friends?"

"Friends! Being friends with Fingerhut would be like having a meat grinder for a buddy. I met him a few years ago when I was late paying back a loan to Family Finance. He hounded me all over the goddamn city until I squared my account. After that I tried to throw him a little business once in a while, the way you'd throw raw meat to a wolf. I didn't want to have the bastard breathing down my neck. Now we have a nice give-and-get relationship. Sometimes he gives and I get, but more often it's the reverse. It keeps him from busting my ass. He's the kind of guy who lurks around waiting for you to fuck up. Then he won't quit until he runs you down."

"Why the hell did you send me to him? Or am I another hunk of raw meat?"

"Relax, kid. I told you why I did it."

"Does the test matter?"

Raking his left sideburn, Eddie seemed distracted. "Not really. Anyhow, you said you passed." He kicked Tiger away from the hem of his robe. "Mel Tuttle did a good job on your hair. I can't think of anything I forgot.

113

Unless you have more questions, why not take the rest of the day off. Your interview is tomorrow at eleven."

"You haven't told me the name of the company."

"All in due time, babes. First there's a matter of some bread. Two hundred and fifty bucks, to be exact."

"I paid you twenty-five."

"Okay, we won't fall out over loose change. Lemme have the difference."

"You'll get it when I have a job."

"After what I taught you, it's in the bag. These people are bound to love you. Don't you believe me?"

"Yes, but . . ."

"But you won't gimme the dough. All right, have it your way. What's your phone number and address? I'll call tomorrow."

"I want the name and address of the company first."

"Something tells me you learned too much, kid. Don't let it go to your head. The office is at 1750 Beverly Boulevard. Danny Boy's Restaurants. Now what's your number?"

When for the fourth night in a row Carter remained in his own bed, Elaine said nothing, but her teeth had worn a groove in her lower lip, and she couldn't sleep. It seemed to Carter she must have sensed that he had changed. She might even have been experiencing a small part of what he had felt several nights ago—a recognition of loss and uncertainty, a groping for familiar limits only to discover that they had disappeared and nothing had replaced them. Moving closer, she reached for him, but her hand fell short.

Carter heard Elaine's restlessness, the light fall of her hand, her uneven breathing, but didn't dare disturb the fragments of his new character that had yet to coalesce. Silently he ran through the script for his interview till he was satisfied he knew it by heart, then he thought of Eddie and Fingerhut and all the other people and places he'd seen since arriving in L.A. It seemed he lived in a land of billboards. No one was real except him. And, of course, Elaine. Yet something propped up those walls of cardboard, and unless he learned what, he was liable to trip in the darkness over quivering wires and unyielding braces.

Chapter VII

1

Friday morning Carter woke early and waited in the living room, pleased to be alone. Skimming the *Times,* he drank three cups of coffee, which sent his pulse racing untiil it seemed his harried mind might take leave of his body. Random thoughts dive-bombed from a distance, unerring as arrows, and although the precise words of Eddie's advice escaped him, the essence of the complete treatment, of the breathless vitality of his voice, wound Carter into a tight knot. He knew he would get the job, but was anxious to put the interview and his long week of temporizing behind him.

On an end table his fingers tapped a nervous rhythm which his feet rapped out on the tile. This fidgeting made him jumpier. Forcing himself to sit still, he stared at a Picasso print which Elaine had tacked to the white-washed wall. The colors red and black streaked the card-board, suggesting a bloody clot of sun and a bull with bold, outsized horns. In the fireplace was a new hibachi. A few gray feathers had drifted onto it from a bird that nested in the chimney, and the curlers of dust—the only evidence, other than the hibachi and the print, that they had lived in the apartment—nuzzled in the corners, for Elaine, sensing something tentative in this week, wasn't yet interested in cleaning.

At ten-fifteen he couldn't hold off any longer. Going out to the car, he hurried to Sunset Strip, where traffic was at a standstill. Heat shimmered from baked enamel and wisps of smoke waved from each exhaust pipe. A crowd of hippies, shouting and pinwheeling their arms, had surrounded a cream-colored Bentley in which an imperturbable silver-haired lady sat with both hands on the wheel, her serene eyes straight ahead, as if she were cruising through rather tedious terrain. From a dent on the right front fender red lines fanned out like a hasty sketch of the Japanese flag, and as the crowd parted to let a cop through, Carter saw a brawny chimpanzee in an Uncle Sam suit, face up on the pavement, blowing bubbles of blood from its nose.

Executing a U-turn, he coasted to Beverly Boulevard and drove east into residential areas, breathing the medicinal scent of eucalyptus and the rich mask of ivy and boxwood hedges. Then, farther into town, there was only the smell, almost the feel, of the smog which this hot morning had gathered in patches like grazing sheep on the hills. Though traffic was heavy, he ran four amber lights and arrived early at 1750.

Broad and low, the building squatted beneath a neon sign several stories high, on which a sprightly green leprechaun supported a gigantic platter saying *Danny Boy's*. The green-tile façade was set off from the street by a retaining wall and a square of white gravel. Two palmetto plants shaped like Oriental fans were reflected once in the plate-glass window, then in a mirror behind the receptionist's desk. As he opened the door, electric chimes played a few bars of "Danny Boy" and a red-head gazed up from the magazine she was reading.

"My name's Carter White. I have an appointment with Mr. Reichlederfer."

Removing a pendulous earring, she lifted the receiver and dialed three numbers. "Mr. White to see you." Then smiling, she nodded to a door nearby.

When Reichlederfer greeted him in the hall and applied a firm handshake, his blue eyes darted quickly over Carter before dropping back into the sparkle of an unflinching smile. Though the hair had gone gray at his temples and in an uneven patch above his forehead, he was lean and tanned, a trim athlete in his early forties. He spoke crisply, as if ready to bark out a command or break into laughter. Throwing an arm around Carter's shoulder, he pulled him into another room. "Danny Boy" started and abruptly stopped.

Paneled in stained wood, the starkly finished office gave an impression of cheapness and total impermanence rather than the intended modernity, and emanating from the formica-topped tables, Naugahide chairs, rayon curtains, and plastic ornaments, was the faint odor

116

of a chemistry lab. Reichlederfer motioned Carter to sit in front of his desk. Over his head hung an enlarged photograph of a double-decker cheeseburger oozing ketchup and mustard at its edges.

"What did the agency tell you about our operation, Mr. White?"

"Only that it's first rate." To his own ears this rang ridiculously false, but Reichlederfer didn't appear to notice.

"Good. We think we do the best job of presenting ourselves. So if you'll pardon me, we'll talk about Danny Boy's for a minute before we talk about you. Danny Boy's is young, ambitious, and growing. In a few years we'll break ground for branches throughout the state, and we'll have to have men trained in food service management to staff them. Since we don't want other companies' rejects, we've inaugurated a program to teach the food service management business from the ground up. It's hard work, but the pay is good and the job is full of creative opportunities."

"I see. That's . . ." Carter was let down already by the description of the job and by Reichlederfer's tone, which sounded dramatically inappropriate. After Eddie's advice, he'd expected . . . He didn't know what he'd expected. ". . . very interesting."

"We believe the best training is on-the-job. Our men begin in the kitchen. Or, too be exact, beneath the kitchen, where we prepare our meats and breaded items. From there they proceed to the deep-fat fryer, the grill, the steam table, the sandwich and salad block, the Talk-a-Tray unit, the dessert board, and to the dining room itself, where they learn table-waiting techniques. By that time they have a pretty firm grasp of the food service management business."

"Very interesting," he repeated, and groped through the script. "I helped put myself through college waiting tables. It'll be good to return to the . . .uh, restaurant food management service."

"Glad to hear you've had experience, but part of our job will be to correct the unprofessional habits you picked up."

"Of course." Carter smiled, certain Reichlederfer was joking.

"This isn't a simple business," he said, deadly earnest. "It'll be months, maybe a year, before you're capable

117

of commanding your own operation. For a few hours each day you'll do nothing except study our menus and recipes. I might mention these recipes are patented. Only staff members, managers, and trainees have access to them. They're unsophisticated, but very effective. Generally our approach to food service is dual-pronged and falls under the headings of Preparation and Presentation. I'm convinced that one is as important as the other. Here, I'll show you. Pull your chair around." From the top drawer of the desk Reichlederfer took a brochure which, under clear shelds of plastic, pictured cheeseburger platters, trays of onion rings, ice cream sundaes, milk shakes, and baskets of fried shrimp.

"You can see the crucial importance of an eye-catching presentation. After years our research office has realized that customers don't go to restaurants because they're hungry. They go when they're bored. If they want nutrition, they stay home and eat some dreary mush. The instant they enter Danny Boy's, we make every effort to amuse them, to convince them they're in a different world. We do this by the unique combination of a memorable taste and an attractive preparation. State law limits us a little, but our policy is never to sacrifice our distinctive flavor for an unproven value."

After Carter had murmured, "That's interesting," a third time, Reichlederfer snapped the brochure shut. "Enough about us. Now let's talk about you, Mr. White. But first I'll call in Ned Cervik, the manager of our Santa Monica outlet."

When he pressed a button, a section of the wall paneling slid back and out stepped a short, powerful man whose face was cruelly pitted with acne scars. On his balding head a dozen small scabs might have prefigured more pockmarks, but the perforations seemed too perfectly round and symmetrical to be a natural skin affliction. They were the early stages of a hair transplant.

After he had pumped Carter's hand, they sat down and Reichlederfer said, "Mr. White was about to tell us about himself."

"I heard on the intercom." Cervik pulled a ballpoint pen and a notebook from his pocket. "How old are you, Mr. White?"

"Twenty-five."

"Married?"

"Yes."

"And what does your wife do?"

He couldn't remember whether Eddie had covered this. "She's going to have a baby in February."

"Wonderful," said Reichlederfer. "Your first? You must be excited."

"Kids are great," said Cervik, "if you like noisy vegetables.'"

"Ned, I didn't know you had children."

'Christ, yes. One of each kind. Three."

Their laughter echoed eerily off the plastic ornaments.

"Did you attend college?" Reichlederfer asked.

"For three years."

"You didn't graduate?"

There had been no change in Reichlederfer's expression or voice, but the cords of Carter's throat drew taut. "No, I joined the army. I'd planned to finish afterward, but things didn't work out."

"How long were you in the service?"

"Nine months." Now both their expressions did change, and Carter readied the oft-repeated scenario. "I received a medical discharge. It wasn't a serious wound. I was lucky."

"Were you in Vietnam?" asked Reichlederfer.

Carter felt a touch of guilt and embarrassment. Nothing, it seemed, could justify this cynical use of the experience, and as if on cue, his leg began to throb. "Yes, I was there . . . for a short time."

"That's too bad," said Cervik.

"What have you been doing since your discharge?" asked Reichlederer.

"I was in the hospital . . ."

"Yes, of course." As Eddie had anticipated, they didn't dwell on this.

"Afterward I worked for my father-in-law as a sales representative. He owned a nursery and landscaping company."

"Where was this, Mr. White?"

"In"—was it Washington or Maryland?—"in Washington, D.C., and the suburbs." He split the difference, and launched out on his own. 'We had contracts with a number of housing and apartment developments, and with some state and federal agencies. I don't have to tell you how much the government spends just to keep the White House lawn in shape," said Carter, who had no idea.

"Did you have the White House contract?" asked

Reichlederfer. "I thought the Department of the Interior cared for national monuments."

"Of course," he said hastily. "I only mentioned the White House as an example. Although once we did sell them a hundred and fifty azalea plants for a special reception." Half-moons of sweat spread under his arms.

"You don't say?" Cervik lit a cigarette, and in the glow of the match his face looked like burnished pigskin. "What's the name of this company, and why did you leave?"

"My father-in-law died suddenly and the business folded. I didn't have the experience to manage it myself, so my mother-in-law liquidated her holdings."

"And you came out to Southern California," said Reichlederfer. "Well, I don't blame you. It's a wonderful area, especially for young people."

"Yes. When my mother-in-law moved to La Jolla, we settled here to be near her. I could have gone to San Diego, of course, but I thought Los Angeles would be more challenging."

Cervik clicked back the point of his pen and stuck it into his breast pocket. "I don't have to hear any more."

"We want people with your attitude," said Reichlederfer. "I'll have to admit I'd prefer a man who had a degree and a background in food service management, but I . . ."

"To hell with that," said Cervik. "I'll teach him all he needs to know. He's got the desire. That's what matters."

"Well, do you have any questions, Mr. White?" Reichlederfer acted rushed. Evidently he had more questions himself and a few doubts he would have liked to clear up, but Carter allowed him no time to reconsider.

"Yes. When do I start?"

"Monday," said Cervik.

Reichlederfer stood up. "There are a few forms to fill out. I'll send a secretary in. Then we'll go out to lunch and celebrate. Ever been to the Phone Booth? It's fun. But don't tell anyone we're dining with the competition."

Two hours and four martinis later, when Carter returned to the apartment, his tongue tasted like a pine cone and he was clammy from the effort of answering questions, eating roast beef, and ogling nude waitresses, all at the same time. He was drunk, but felt good, delighted by the ease with which he had deceived Cervik and Reichlederfer. In the courtyard the fountain splashed metallically and he waved to Mrs. Regan, who was staked out on the other side next to a mop. After fumbling at the front-door lock, he stumbled through the hall to the bedroom.

Elaine slept on the spread, wearing a yellow slip that, in the sunlight let in by the windows, clung like a wet second skin, and as she fretted from side to side, in flight from one dream, in search of a better, the nylon wrinkled above her hips to reveal that she wasn't wearing panties. At last she lay still, facing him, her left leg straight, smooth, and brown, her right leg crooked at the knee and raised to balance her belly. He took off his suit coat, shirt, and tie, sank onto the bed, and rubbed her buttocks in a widening circle.

"Is that you, Carter?" she murmured.

"No, the milkman." He chuckled, tasting pine cones again, and slowly explored her body. Its softness shaped itself to his fingers—the cool curves, the silk of her inner thigh, the glossy hair. "This is a fine welcome for the conquering hero."

"Sorry. I couldn't keep my eyes open. Just call me Sleeping Ugly. Did you get the job?"

"Sure." He moved his hand between her thighs. "Don't you wear panties any more?"

"They're not panties! Only old perverts call them that. They're pants, and I never go to bed before I've taken them off." She rolled onto her stomach, her legs slightly parted.

"Sounds like a dangerous habit that could . . ." A frozen stream coursed through his veins, and he feared she could feel it in his fingertips. "Is this a lesson you learned at your mother's knee?"

"How did you guess? Every night at bedtime she reminded me to take off my underpants. When I asked why, she said to give myself a chance to breathe."

"So that's what it's for."

"Among other things."

Carter lifted the slip up her back, over a column of vertebrae smooth as carved ivory. "No bra either?"

"It's there."

As he unhooked it, Elaine rose on hands and knees and shook the slip and bra over her head and down her arms. Then she stretched out on her stomach again, while Carter undressed and lay beside her, caressing her back and the warmth of her inner body. When he tried to turn her over, she whispered, "No. I want to stay like this," and easing onto her, he was suddenly inside her, hard against a pressure equal to his own. She rose up on her knees once more and swayed her hips, as Carter, in a kneeling position, seemingly suspended her above the bed on the strength of his cock, which she impaled herself upon, searching for some hidden source within her. Holding her hips, he leaned his chest across her back, resting his face at the nape of her neck, eyes closed against the play of her long hair. He felt in control until she found what she was searching for. Carter himself thought he'd found it as she sighed and spread her legs to the limit of the bed, then closed them, bringing him to a climax, too.

They lay together a long time in the lemony light, and he saw expanding rings on a pond, then the sea at morning, surging toward shore with slow, dawn rollers which threw a fine spray of foam and sand.

The phone ended it, drilling them both through the base of the spine. Elaine tensed like a dreamer tripped by a mysterious wicket that tumbled her out of sleep. Still inside her, beached on her brown back, Carter kissed the salty tast of her shoulders. Then he went to answer the phone.

"Hello, kid. How did it go?"

"What?" Carter mumbled.

"Don't give me that 'what' bullshit. It's Eddie Brown. Did you get the job?"

"I got it. And you're calling about your money."

Eddie's laugh was like gravel raining on tin. "You're learning fast. Before the complete treatment it would've taken you a month to figure that out. Fork over two hundred and fifty bucks and we'll part bosom buddies."

"Two twenty-five."

"Small mistake. I gotta have the rest. My ex-wife is bitching about late support payments."

"I'll send it to you."

"I want it in my hand. Tomorrow is my day to play Mother Goose and I'm taking my kids to Universal Studios to some kind of Mexican fiesta. While they're watching the greasers, I'll meet you at the front gate at one-thirty."

"I'll be there."

"You better be. I'd hate to have to call Reichlederfer."

"I said I'd be there and I will."

122

"Don't act Frank Lloyd righteous, kid. Just bring the bread."

To escape this intrusion, Carter hurried back to the bedroom, but Elaine was gone. The rumpled covers carried an angular imprint of her body and a hint of perfume. Or perhaps the scent was from the lemon tree. It stole in through the window on an evening breeze that brought gooseflesh to his shoulders. He shivered once before he heard running water, and relieved, went to join her in the shower.

2

Next morning they kicked off the covers and stayed in bed, talking and watching the oblongs of sunlight at the windows expand to fill the room. From somewhere in the building the smell of pastry and brewing coffee made their stomachs rumble. A phone rang and rang but no one answered. In the distance a radio broadcast a football game from the East Coast, where it was already afternoon, and closer, in the courtyard, the fountain ceaselessly splashed.

'One night we'll sneak out," said Elaine in a conspiratorial tone, "and skinny-dip in the fountain."

"It's too small. There wouldn't be room for both of us."

"Then we'll go one at a time. The important thing is the dare."

"Mrs. Regan has probably thrown in thumbtacks."

"You're a damn spoilsport." Laughing, she gestured to the drawing of stiff roses. "Why don't we throw that in with the thumbtacks? It's awful."

"Of course it's awful, but it's what we have instead of television."

"Do you want to buy a TV?"

"I wouldn't mind seeing a few games this fall."

"Oh God," she groaned. "I detest football."

"I'll teach you to like it."

"I doubt that."

"What'll we do, then, for entertainment?"

"Stay in bed together. You know, the idea of sleeping with you has always excited me as much as sex."

"Aren't they the same?"

"No. They don't have to be. But I have an embarrassing confession. When I was a little girl and heard people talk about making love and sleeping together, I thought sex lasted all night. Isn't that silly?"

"You must have been very disappointed when you discovered how wrong you were." He was afraid he had insulted her, but jokingly insisted, "Were you?"

"No, I like it."

"You sound serious."

"I am. Maybe sex can be what we have instead of television."

"Or along with it, at half-time during the games."

Jumping on his chest, she pinned his shoulders with her knees. "You're impossible."

"I try to be."

As she bent over to kiss him, she was smiling and kept her eyes open. Minutes later, coming inside her, he was open-eyed too, sensing, as she must have, a welcome otherness, a distance which made him acutely aware of the dark-haired girl he felt so close to. He saw her face, her brown arms, her breasts, yet despite the separation—maybe because of it—thought of them as being parts of him as surely as his own hands.

Only afterward did the distance matter. Falling away from each other, their bodies reasserted their boundaries. Side by side, they touched lightly at the shoulders, hips, and thighs, but seemed worlds apart. A voluptuous fatigue floated them over shallow ripples of sadness and into sleep.

Carter woke first and thought of his parents. His mother, the small woman who wore a timorous stripe of lipstick on her mouth. His father who had always acted tired. They'd slept late on weekends, then nappd on Sunday afternoons. For the first time it didn't seem unlikely that they had lain together like this, and at the moment Carter could not resent—could only pity—their timidity, their sadness. And his own. Perhaps, he thought, it was the same repeated effort and repeated failure, filled with other pleasures though it might have been, which had chastened them into silence, smaller gestures, and less dramatic leaps to bridge the gap between them.

Stroking her smooth flank, he roused Elaine for company and whispered, "We should get up. It's a shame to waste the day."

"We're not wasting it." She was awake at once, and stretching her arms straight up, flickered sunlight from her fingertips. "We're savoring it, and I hope you're not the type who usually bounds out of bed and does exercises. Sometimes when I was little, I didn't get up all day. In Japan there were no children my age, so I'd stay in bed, make a house under the covers, and play with my dolls."

"You had dolls?"

"Of course. For a long time they were my best friends."

"That must have been lonely."

"It wasn't too bad." She sat up. "I hate sad, dreary childhood stories, don't you? Everybody has them and they're all the same—self-pitying and dreadful."

"I wouldn't mind hearing yours."

"You just have. I had a very happy childhood, especially when I was old enough to attend receptions and dinners. By the time I was sixteen I'd had my first proposal. A Peruvian attaché kissed me and begged me to live with him forever in Lima. It was all very romantic. We were on a steamer in the South China Sea."

"And what broke up this romance? Or are you secretly married to him?"

"Like a fool I told Mother, and Daddy had him sent home. I never saw him again, but I received a card—a holy picture of Jesus with seven swords stuck in his heart. On the back it said, 'Why Hast Thou Forsaken Me?'"

"The man had a flair for the melodramatic." Displeased with Elaine and with himself for being jealous, Carter, too, sat up. "I'd better get dressed. I have to meet Eddie Brown this afternoon."

"No, don't go yet. You haven't told me about your job."

"Sure I have. I'll be working for a restaurant chain called Danny Boy's."

"Yes, but what will you be doing?"

"I'll be a management trainee, learning the business from the ground up. God only knows what that entails."

"It should be a good future reference, if nothing else."

Carter couldn't suppress a laugh. "That doesn't sound like you, and I don't want to look at it that way."

"What do you mean?"

"Opportunity, future references, experience, prestige—I'm sick of the words. I kept seeing them on the classified page, arranged as a ladder. But where's the ladder leading? And why start up unless you know?"

"You have to start sometime."

"Do you? You don't understand. It's not a simple matter of climbing the ladder, doing your job, then calling it quits. There's always a higher rung, and if you take one step, you have to take the next. Everything is linked. You land one job, because it sets you up for another. If you don't stop and think, you find yourself climbing a very tall ladder until at the last moment they switch it around and you're headed down instead of up."

"Don't you want this job?"

"Of course. I don't mind work, especially when I have a reason." He touched her belly. "Maybe I'll decide to make a career of the restaurant business."

"You're teasing me now. But I think you should get your money's worth. I'm serious, Carter. Why waste this opportunity?"

"You must have talked with Eddie Brown."

"Oh?" She pulled the sheet up over her nakedness. "Great minds move in the same direction."

"You might not want to move in his direction, if you met him."

"What's he like?" she asked in a lighter voice.

"A little guy with bushy hair and a hook nose."

"Jewish?"

"Probably. He's a high-powered, jive-talking hustler from New York who thinks of his life as an experiment in education and self-improvement. Yet for all his emphasis on quality, his apartment, his belongings, and his personal life are a mess."

"You should accept his advice and ignore his example." Smiling, she patted his bare knee. "Meanwhile I'll make sure things are in order here. My mother always said the person who's messy in his drawers is likely to be messy in his mind."

"Your mother sounds like the last of the Great Western Philosophers." He wrestled her close for a kiss. "I'll bet you were never messy in your drawers, were you?"

After they had showered and dressed, Elaine prepared bacon, lettuce, and tomato sandwiches, and as they ate at the breakfast bar, Carter said, "What color shall we paint the cabinets?"

"What cabinets?"

"The ones over the sink."

"Oh, those. They can stay like they are. Carter, how much do you owe Eddie Brown?"

"We owe two hundred and twenty-five dollars. Is there enough in the account?"

"Yes, but it is an awful lot."

"It would have been more if I'd gone through the agency."

"Too bad you didn't find a . . . Oh well, I guess it couldn't be helped. Carter, I was wondering, what could Eddie do if you didn't pay him?"

He put down his sandwich. "I don't know. We made a deal. I gave him my word."

"Yes, but"—she grasped his hand—"legally what could he do?"

"Legally, not much. But he threatened to call Reichlederfer and have me fired. Anyway, I don't want to cheat him."

"Cheat him? Oh, come on, Carter. It wouldn't be hard to say who the real cheat was. That's why he threatened you. He's afraid. He knows he couldn't call Reichle-whatever-his-name-is, because then he'd have to admit he'd cheated the agency. You could just as easily threaten to tell his boss and have him fired. Do you see what I mean?"

"That's no reason not to pay him."

"Don't you hate to let that crook have your money, when we need it so badly? After all, how much good did he really do you? You said he was a messy little chiseler. How could he help you? Don't be modest. You got the job yourself."

"It's hard to say. I know I owe him something," he protested feebly. It wasn't mere avarice or self-serving evasion which left him reluctant to concede how much Eddie had helped. Now that the treatment had ended, it was impossible to take it seriously—or to imagine he had ever required help. Maybe that was the final measure of Eddie's effectiveness.

"Why don't you pay him fifty dollars? He'll be happy to get it."

"How about seventy-five? That'll make it an even hundred I've paid him."

He couldn't tell if he was bargaining with her or with his own conscience, and Elaine didn't allow him time

127

to decide. "Fine. That's more than enough. I think I'll come along. Just for the ride."

They folded back the top on the Thunderbird and carved a cool path through the warm air. On the Hollywood Freeway a smell of wood smoke suggested early autumn. The radio announcer said another brush fire had broken out in Verdugo Hills.

At the front gate of Universal Studios, Eddie Brown had a little curly-haired girl in his arms, and looked more ridiculous than Carter remembered, wearing tassle loafers, a pair of blue bell-bottom Levis, and a sleeveless tie-dyed T-shirt that exposed tufts of hair on his shoulders. Obviously this man's advice couldn't have meant much.

"Is that him?" asked Elaine. "This is terrible. He looks like a troll."

Carter crossed the street, repeating that Eddie had done no more than sell him a name and an address, for which a hundred dollars was adequate payment. But it didn't work. He felt awful, yet couldn't turn back.

"Hi, kid. I was beginning to worry. Who's the babe in the T-Bird?"

"My wife. Here's your money."

"Who's the man?" asked the little girl.

"A client, doll."

"What's a cleint?"

"Cool it a sec. So the chick's your wife. Not bad, even if she is knocked up. Is the T-Bird yours? I let you off cheap. I should have charged . . . Hey, what's this shit? There's only seventy-five bucks."

'That's all I can afford." He struggled to muscle some conviction into his voice. "And face it, Eddie, that's all you deserve."

"Daddy, what's wrong?"

Setting down his daughter, Eddie hiked up his Levis. Small as he was, he acted as if he might start punching. Bracing his bad leg, Carter readied himself, but felt foolish. "Look, kid I warned you not to jerk me around. I could cause you awful grief. If I call Reichlederfer Monday morning, you're out on your ass, back on the streets whining for help."

"I don't think you'd do that, Eddie, because if you call Reichlederfer, I'll call the agency and then you'll lose *your* job. So what good would it do you? You earned a hundred dollars."

"A hundred dollars! A hundred measly bucks. You think that's all I care about? It's the principle. I went to bat for you, kid. I wasted my whole vacation trying to create something out of your sad-ass, no-talent life. Jesus Christ"—he scratched his scalp—"I produced a work of art from a wagonload of horse shit, and this is my thanks. A hundred fucking bucks." He flourished the money in Carter's face, but thrust it into his own pocket. "At least gimme another fifty so it's worth my while."

"I . . . I don't have it."

Eddie glanced at the Thunderbird, then at Elaine, and nodded. "Yeah, sure. You're learning fast, kid. Keep it up and you'll win an early grave." He picked up his daughter.

"What's a client, Daddy?"

"I didn't say a client. I said a chiseling prick. But don't mention that to your mother."

"Any trouble?" asked Elaine as Carter returned to the car.

"No. Not really." He watched Eddie pass through the gate and out of sight.

Chapter VIII

1

In the ensuing weeks—at night after work, or as they drove home from a movie, or lay awake in bed, struggling to keep sleep at arm's length like an incalculable bore and waste of time—Elaine often asked, "What are you thinking? I can never tell from your eyes."

"I'm thinking I love you," Carter would answer.

"No. I want the truth."

"It's true. This is the happiest time of my life."

"Is it really?" She would touch him as she asked, and he sensed in her fingertips the same thrill he heard in her voice. If he touched his own fingertips to her throat or belly, he felt life. It beat delicately, like a caged hummingbird, against his hand.

Although he readily repeated what she wanted to hear, he realized it might have been more truthful to say that this was the single time in his life, for Carter seldom reflected about the past or deliberated out loud about the future. Living in the present, with Elaine as his fixed point, he labored long nights inside her, and constantly sought new positions, places, and opportunities to make love.

One weekend they traveled south of Tijuana and registered at a deserted hotel for no reason save the desire to make love in a different location. It was as if they believed they could create a past for themselves by filling the moment full of experiences that might have happened to them separately long ago. Gazing out from the terrace, Elaine said it resembled the Costa Brava. Where the mountains crumbled into the sea, the littoral was little more than a jagged wall with minute, curving beaches, like desperate white fingernails, clinging to its rim.

That night they drank margaritas at the bar until the

lights blinked out, then swam naked in the pool and made love on their knees at the shallow end. Moonlight transformed the water to a chunk of cobalt and washed the whiteness of Elaine's breasts with phosphorescence. As cool air climbed his back, Carter toiled twenty minutes to come, and when he did, it seemed to last almost that long. Twisting against him, Elaine threw back her head, baring the softness of her throat and dampening the ends of her hair.

Afterward she swam two sleek laps and said, "I feel like a fish laying its eggs. Do you suppose there's any truth to those tales about girls getting innocently pregnant in swimming pools?"

"Not a chance. Chlorine would kill the sperm."

"You don't have a romantic bone in your body."

Laughing, he lunged, but she eluded him, her wet flesh swelling in the satisfaction of its curves, too slippery to be contained. As she wriggled away, he pursued her.

If from time to time Carter recognized he was sloughing off the familiar contours of his character, the change didn't cause any loss of sleep—unless from the dizzying pleasure he gained by realizing that as he lost his old self, he won a new one in its place. It seemed a chink of warm light had widened in a wall of darkness, and for this light, in all its forms, he had cultivated a tropism. At last he was liberated from those fearful images which had hidden like stingers in his head. Now he saw nothing lethal in the lead-streaked sky, nothing catastrophic about the evening sun. Although it descended in a shroud of smog, it would soar full-blown in the morning to burn off the haze.

Meanwhile, during the night, there was the laughable crescendo of neon on Sunset Strip, strong enough to undress him, to steam away his fears. This was the city's greatest gift, a grotesqueness which could be funny rather than frightening. If, as Eddie Brown alleged, everyone in Los Aneles was insane, at least no one considered the situation serious, for the town, bountifully tolerant of distortion, parodied all its worst paranoias and, thus, achieved partial triumph over them. Once Eddie had said, as if it were an article of faith, "No one can die in Los Angeles before dawn. It's a city ordinance, and by daybreak the sun would nurse you back to life."

In their apartment, particularly the bedroom, the afternoon light lingered longest, just as it had on the sundeck in Arlington, re-creating the bright bell jar that sheltered them from the disorder outside. Shored up by pillows against the headboard, they talked for hours, and while evading the most hazardous issues, sought something essential in the ordinary. Did you date much in high school? Where were you when Kennedy was killed? As a kid did you look in the mirror and recognize the face, but wonder who was behind it, who was doing the wondering? Their answers, however commonplace, inspired an unquestioned intimacy.

Other evenings, since Carter rarely received mail, Elaine read her letters aloud—the ones she got and the ones she sent—perhaps as much to prove she had no secrets as to amuse him. She carried on an effusive correspondence with a few cousins in New York, a tepid one with an old girl friend in Boston, and a brisk, formal one with her grandmother. Also, a number of men wrote her, and she answered, signing herself, "Love, Elaine," depending, she explained, upon how long she had known them. It sounded so mechanical, he asked why she bothered, and she said she didn't care to disappoint old friends. "Besides, if I don't write, they'll know something's wrong, and I don't want to rouse curiosity."

"Does anyone else know?"

"Know what?"

"About the baby"

"Do you think I'd tell"

"Not even the father?"

"I guess he knows." She couldn't conceal her irritation. "He either knows or he doesn't."

"Yes, he knows."

"Has he written you?"

"I'd tell you if he had. Honest, Carter, I would."

"I believe you."

Most of her letters, certainly the longest, came from her parents in Costa Rica, emblazoned with stamps of exotic birds and flowers and jowly generals who peered through tinted glasses. Using an Osmiroid pen, Mrs. Yost wrote in a stilted script matched by her own tone. She thought it "vulgar and inconsiderate of you, Elaine, to flee Washington so suddenly. None of our friends can comprehend why. And, frankly, neither do I. I understand acting on impulse, but why did your impulse lead

132

you to such an improbable place? Have you met anyone with whom you have the least bit in comon? I hope your travels have prepared you for the low-life of that city. Although I'll admit nothing could have prepared me for San Jose. The weather and food are abominable, the servants inept, at best, sullen and rude at . . ."

Her father, Donald Christian Yost, dictated his letters to a secretary who typed them on official embassy stationery. Though gentler and more congenial, he, too, disapproved of Elaine's hasty departure and expressed his dismay by misquoting and slackly paraphrasing writers whom he must have read, if at all, years ago. "Youth has always been an age of rebellion, but in this era true rebellion and non-conformity would be to accept responsibility and undertake a mature path of self-fulfillment. Although your mother and I have kept a light rein on you and wouldn't wish to curtail your freedom, we have faith you'll use your talents wisely. I appreciate your desire for the unusual, but unless you wish to live what one poet has called a life of silent frustration, I urge you to . . ."

At first Elaine made no effort to defend her parents. She read their letters, then fell quiet almost defiantly, challenging Carter to object or pass judgment on them. He never did. Realizing she was linked to her family by a sentiment he couldn't understand or share—it seemed more like grudging loyalty than love—he waited for her to break the silence, and she always did it obliquely with a pointless remark to which he would add another. The sound of their voices in that echo chamber of a room reminded Carter of water filling an empty basin a drop at a time. He didn't feel safe until it attained the correct depth and the talk flowed in a steady stream.

When the Yosts kept urging Elaine to return to Washington, she said, "I resent their attempts to control my life. And I resent their innuendos."

"Calm down. You can understand their feelings," said Carter, who hadn't revealed his own.

"No, I can't. They've always acted like this."

The next night she handed him a letter she had written them. Thoughtfully worded, it showed she was well aware of their wishes, but reasonably committed to asserting her individuality. Clearly, though she had often lived alone, she had never been on her own. Now she seemed determined to make a break.

Because he believed the Yosts wouldn't care for him, Carter was pleased she'd done it with no encouragement and no mention of him in the letter, yet an indirect reference to his influence. "I'm disappointed," she wrote, "if you have the impression I'm off on an irresponsible skylark. I haven't touched a penny of my graduation money or Grandmother's trust fund. I'm self-supporting for once. I have a management trainee's job with a large restaurant chain and I've enrolled in two night courses at UCLA—one in International Law, the other in the Cultural and Intellectual History of America. My plans remain indefinite, yet I'm confident . . ."

Since it was he who had registered for courses at UCLA, Carter thought the letter indicated how proud she was of him, and it let him take pride in himself. By any standard he had done well, and he felt this doubly when her parents wrote back, considerably chastened. "The job will be a good reference, if nothing else," they echoed her opinion with uncanny accuracy. "The history class should be entertaining and stimulating," said her father, "but don't short-change the law course." Suggesting she have a Dun & Bradstreet rating run on the restaurant chain and that she sit for the Law Board examination, they closed with apologies, declarations of affection, and a hope that they would hear from her soon—which they did.

Not in the least disappointed that the break hadn't been final, Carter now looked forward to their letters and accepted the praise and encouragement as his.

Oddly, given the potential of the situation for bitter discord, their one real argument concerned religion. On a Sunday morning after breakfast Elaine asked, apropos of nothing, if he still considered himself a Catholic, and he answered without hesitation that he did.

"You can't be serious."

He should have ignored her tone—it was as though he'd claimed he believed in unicorns—but said in a thorny voice, "Can't I?"

For a few minutes they nibbled at the edges of the subject, like a couple of cautious sparrows pecking a stale crust of bread. Then after they had admitted a general ignorance of systematic philosophy and owned up to a host of prejudices and misconceptions, he attempted to put a polite end to the discussion. "I guess it's a matter of personal preference."

"But you never go to church," she persisted.

"Would you like me to start?"

"Don't act so damn defensive. I'm just trying to understand why you think of yourself as a Catholic. Or why you'd want to."

'Because I am one. A bad one. Wanting to has nothing to do with it."

"Do you think what we're doing is a sin?"

"Elaine, why ask that?"

Her back drew perceptibly straighter. "Do you or don't you?"

"I haven't thought about it."

"But you do believe in sin, don't you?"

"Yes. Don't you?" By her expression he knew each question and answer was weighted by tons of jagged, subsurface ice.

"Of course not. In fact, I think it's so silly and irrational, I . . ."

"Maybe what you call silly and irrational is what I'd call sin."

"Then you're committing a sin right now by acting nonsensical."

"I'm not acting any way." He got off his stool. "I simply happen to believe in God."

"Incredible. I suppose you'd insist on raising your children as Catholics."

In his anger he was about to blurt, Yes. Hell yes. But he said something worse. "I don't have any children."

Elaine tilted her head as if to balance an object on the point of her nose, and the brittle smile he believed she'd left behind in the East flattened her mouth and nipped it up at the ends. "I see." She banged her hand very hard on the breakfast bar, stood trembling while the smile quaked to pieces, then rushed into the bedroom.

An hour later when he was about to apologize, she came out, red-eyed, and murmured she was sorry. Carter promised to watch what he said from then on, and afterward each shied away from the other's sore spots. He didn't mention the past or her family, and Elaine no longer inquired about the future or his job.

But for Carter, Monday nights continued to be difficult. Although he wouldn't confess it to Elaine, he found the law course and his classmates a deadly bore. Herded into a vast, reverberating amphitheater with a hundred students, he thought of the army, of briefings and field

135

problems, of the unfathomable jargon, pointless and pro-lix. As a bell above Royce Hall tolled out the hours, only the itch of chalk dust in his nostrils kept him awake.

Wednesday the history class was better. In a seminar room he and a dozen others, directed by a Professor Durand, discussed Cotton Mather, Jonathan Edwards, Thomas Jefferson, and F. O. Mattheissen. Although he cautioned them against facile comparisons, Dr. Durand did an excellent job of detailing the origins of the country's current strengths and weaknesses. No matter how tired he was, Carter came home charged with new ideas, eager to do outside reading.

But early in November, on Elaine's advice by way of her parents, he applied for the Law Board examination that January, and she bought him a booklet entitled *Preparing for Law School.* As they reviewed the chapters concerning the exam, it soon evolved into a contest, for while Carter was better at the briefs, Elaine could answer all the questions on art, literature, and music.

"I can't believe it," she said repeatedly, goading him on with laughter. "You must know who Jascha Heifetz [Wittgenstein, Le Corbusier, Brancusi, Rilke, etc.] is."

Yet once Carter learned a name or fact, he didn't forget, and to acquire background information, he carted home reference books from the UCLA library.

"No fair!" cried Elaine. "You're turning into a grind. I haven't studied in months."

"If you can't stand the competition, drop out of the race," he proclaimed in a Slavic accent. "I will bury you. You, your children, and your children's children will live under my rule. All knowledge is now my province."

From his job at Danny Boy's, which proved to be a lot less fascinating than promised, but also less difficult than he had feared, he gleaned one irrefutable conclusion—he didn't wish to remain in the "restaurant food management service business" any longer than he absolutely had to. Otherwise his training program under Ned Cervik produced no more than sore feet and inexpressible boredom. He tried to regard the drudgery as a test of his maturity, a measure of his personal growth. Then, when this failed, he attempted to view it as evidence of his devotion to Elaine. In the end he was reduced to looking upon it as merely a means for making the hands on the clock move faster, for lopping off all the odd hours when he wasn't with Elaine or in class—and, of course, as a way of paying for maternity clothes, tuition, books, rent, food, medical expenses, and the used TV they bought.

As Reichlederfer had assured him he would—it seemed more like a threat once he started—Carter commenced his training in a dank basement, supervised by a blue-black cook whom everyone, even the Negroes, called Luke the Spook. Wielding a meat cleaver, Luke chopped chickens into identical chunks, which Carter dipped in egg batter and rolled in bread crumbs. When he'd mastered the technique, he progressed to filet of fish, butterfly shrimp, and, trickiest of all, onion rings.

"Shit, you give away too much of the man's bread crumbs," the Spook continually admonished him, thrusting trays of onion rings back under his nose. "Them things look fat and lumpy as snow tires. Do 'em again."

After two weeks he cracked the crust from his fingers, washed egg yolk off his hands, and graduated to the second plateau—the kitchen—delighted by the warmth, the light, and other people. But he displayed such ineptitude at the simplest tasks, he was asked to step aside during the lunch and dinner rushes to "observe restaurant food management procedure" or to butter hamburger buns. At the periphery of constant frenzy, he became a chronic clock watcher and fastened his eyes upon the gloating Longine's whose red hand raced, while the black ones barely crawled. It was like the army again, hurry up and wait. There were only two speeds—double time and none.

One day during lunch he saw a large roach tightrope the electrical cord and invade the clock through the winding stem, only to have the second hand swing down upon it like a bloody scimitar. Terrified, the insect tucked its antennae and scurried in a hectic circle to avoid decapitation, but the tireless blue ultimately knocked it kicking on number six.

When he knew enough to assist in the kitchen, Carter imagined himself as that roach, racing in mad circles with a sharp blade at the back of his neck. But his cunning and stamina surpassed the insect's. He learned to stand clear of the deep-fat fryer's spitting grease, he no longer burned his thumbs on the bun warmer, and scrambled eggs seldom escaped his spatula and slithered onto the floor. He could slice an onion without slitting his wrists, prepare a cheese omelet according to the customer's order, and survive six hours at the steam table ladling out over-cooked vegetables. Eventually he gained the grudging respect of the colored kitchen crew, who called him T-Bird and ribbed him about being a newlywed and an expectant father. (Cervik must have told them this.)

Although he assumed the boss kept him under close scrutiny and reported his progress to Reichlederfer, he couldn't guess what Cervik thought of him. Yet he wasn't worried, for Cervik treated his employees as equals, and they, in turn, treated him as a great deal less. Obviously they had something on him. Or he feared they did and quietly suffered their insolence. He said nothing even when they referred to his superior as Rippledorker. Toby, the oldest woman in the kitchen, planned the menus, ordered provisions from the commissary, supervised the cooking, did everything in fact, except count the till.

Occasionally Cervik asked, "How's it going, Sport?" but wandered off before Carter answered. Their first conversation came the afternoon Carter advanced to the Talk-a-Tray unit, the machine which controlled curb service. At appalling length Cervik demonstrated the intricacies of the operation, then gesturing to a window which overlooked the parking lot, said, "That's the other problem. All day you have your nose rubbed in it."

A group of teen-agers had gathered after hours of surfing. Some still wore wet suits, glistening black from the ocean, and paraded around their cars, stiff-legged as Martians, rough-housing and shouting to friends. When they peeled away the rubber to reveal firm pink flesh, the girls looked as though they were blushing from knee to neck. Their boyfriends briskly rubbed down the tender goose bumps.

"Jesus, do you see them?" Cervik said, brushing a hand over the scabs of his hair transplant. A few follicles had taken root and sent up stubble. "Already they're getting more ass than you and I have had in a lifetime. Look how they dress. Look how they act. When I was a boy in Chicago, we had to pay money to see something like that. Now it's everywhere you go—stag movies, naked women, beat-off books. I tell you, pussy is driving people nuts." He sighed wistfully. "I was born twenty years too early for every revolution you can name—financial, social, or sexual." Then grinning, he gave Carter a playful punch in the shoulder. "But why am I telling you? You're not too old to get the juices going. Don't be a selfish bastard. Spread the sperm. That's my motto."

"I'm married," Carter reminded him.

Cervik poked him again. "That's your problem, Sport. I have my own. A man my age has to pick his spots."

One spot Cervik had picked lay close at hand. He and the cashier, Rita, a stocky blonde with teased hair which she arranged in tiers like a beehive, arrived at Danny Boy's together each morning, ate an invariable lunch of BLT's in his office, and departed arm in arm after reckoning the day's receipts. Their affair was common knowledge to everyone except his wife, her husband, and Reichlederfer.

In the afternoon when Carter descended to Cervik's office to review menus and recipes, the air smelled of cigarette smoke, perfume, and bacon grease, and the ashtrays bristled with butts which bore the carmine print of Rita's fleshy lips. Strands of her hair, singed by peroxide, had curled on the carpet like dozens of wedding rings. But for Carter this was the best time of day. Although small enough to cause claustrophobia, the office was soundproof and could be locked from the inside. Extracting a dozen cards from the file cabinet, he would spread them on the glass-topped desk, sit down and study.

SHRIMP COCKTAIL: In a #6 fruit cup on a #9 plate with a slice of lemon, a garnish of parsley, and tartar or cocktail sauce.

HOT FUDGE SUNDAY: In a #8 dessert dish with two scoops of vanilla ice cream, two tablespoons of chocolate, a topping of Commercial Grease, and a wooden parasol which the customer can keep.

DANNY BOY BURGER: A single beef patty served with bun and pickle (onion optional) on a #3 plate.

The cabinet contained hundreds of these entries, and he promptly committed to memory a sufficient number to satisfy anyone who might quiz him. In addition, he memorized a few menus, classifying them under headings which amused Elaine.

1. Polyglot imbecility: "chili con carne en casserole," "succulent juicy roast beef au jus."

2. Blatant anachronisms: a ham sandwich called "the Twister," and a mint gelatin ring named "the Hula-Julep Hoop."

3. Flatulent alliteration: "taste-tempting tenderloin of beef en brochette turned to perfection."

4. Flaccid rhetoric: "a fabulous, fun dessert for the discerning palate."

After the first month, although he remained in the office the allotted two hours, he didn't bother studying. He read, prepared for his night courses, or tried to think, which was most difficult, since the room was cluttered with distracting knickknacks and souvenirs. There were three *Playboy* calendars—1965, 1967, 1970—a ceramic ashtray shaped like a dog turd, and a plastic figurine of a little boy peeing a stream of bubbles. Beneath the glass top of the desk, pieced together in a madman's jigsaw puzzle, were snapshots of Cervik's wife and children, of Rita and him, of four Irish setters, a two-dollar bill, three Indian-head pennies, ticket stubs from football games, and half a dozen lewd limericks. Across one wall arched a stuffed sailfish, glinting gray and blue, lethal as an artillery shell, its sail stiff as angry hackles. But in its flat black eye lay a look of purest bewilderment, as if the fish could see how far it was from water and knew it would never return.

Carter avoided this dazed eye and seldom looked at the glass-topped desk, which transformed his face into a confusing collage of trivia. After his study period he mounted the stairs to the kitchen and plodded through the hours until six o'clock. Then he hurried home, feeling not so much a sense of relief as an emotion closer to satisfaction. He had completed another day in which nothing had gone wrong. It was a stupid job, he admitted, but it paid for the things he valued, and no matter how insane his duties, he had Elaine and the apartment awaiting him. As he passed through the city, the scene appeared always the same—a sky as luminous as fish scales, tall palms against it, an endless chain of headlights in one direction, red taillights in the other, and at the center of it all, Carter at the wheel of the new Thunderbird, advancing for once without caution toward an undefined goal.

2

What Elaine did during the day, Carter never knew. When he asked, she said, "Nothing but wait for

140

you," and though there might have been an undertone of irony to encase her words in italics, she seemed determined to convince him and herself that she delighted in this cloyingly domestic role. She cooked, cleaned, washed and ironed their clothes, and rarely ventured out of the apartment except to shop at the supermarket on Santa Monica. Of course she didn't care to make friends, and at times behaved as if she suspected someone were trailing her. Even the ubiquitous Regans set her nerves on edge, especially Mrs. Regan, who noticed they received mail under two names and wanted to know why. Whenever they were in the courtyard—the tiny woman straight as a stake to which her tottering husband had been tied like a fifty-cent balloon—Elaine drew the Venetian blinds and refused to go out.

Although Carter quit the apartment each day for Danny Boy's, he tired soon of their isolation and doubted it was good for them. They seldom read the newspaper or watched TV—never the news—and in two months had three phone calls, every one a wrong number. If asked, he would have declared he was satisfied with Elaine's company, and said the apartment seemed very nearly a perfect place, but his contentment needed to be nourished and he felt an itch for other people, other places, if only to reassure himself of the value of what he had. Despite twinges of guilt, he often thought of Eddie Brown, regretted he had swindled him, and wished they could spend another afternoon talking.

But their solitude continued, and it was embarrassing—maybe worse, frightening—not to know of De Gaulle's death until after his funeral, not to learn of the typhoon that had wiped out three hundred thousand in East Pakistan until a week later. Carter felt queasily vulnerable, and believed while they weren't watching, when they couldn't protect themselves, something, anything, might happen. So after working overtime during the Thanksgiving weekend, he asked for the next Thursday and Friday off and decided to drive to Palm Springs, as though this would put them in touch with what was going on around them.

Elaine said nothing until they had gone beyond San Bernardino into the desert, where the land dried and crumbled. Since the sand here was packed solid and there were no trees, they saw few signs of the wind, but heard it seethe at the Thunderbird and fight to wrench the

141

wheel out of Carter's hands. Leaning across the console, she rested her head on his shoulder so that he couldn't see her eyes and she couldn't see the countryside, which resembled a copper platter with sharp scalloped edges.

"I think I have agoraphobia, but it affects me in a funny way. When I traveled with my parents I used to imagine what would happen if they abandoned me in an empty space, so big, its size alone could kill you. What frightened me were the thousands of tiny things that must have been hiding there. If you fell overboard in mid-ocean, it wouldn't be the sea's depth that got you, but a shark or a teacup of water in the lungs. And if you were lost out here"—she sat up to stare at the desert—"a scorpion or snake would put an end to you before the wind, and heat, and hugeness could."

Carter refused to fill the silence with facile assurances. Adjusting his image of her childhood, he waited for her to go on. But she pointed to an oasis of date palms and spoke in a lighter voice. "This might be North Africa."

"Even with the mountains in the background?"

"There are mountains in Algeria and Morocco. From Marrakech you see snowcaps all year round. But the sand there is reddish, and the mud houses rose-tinted."

'There must be other differences." They sped by a motel whose main office was a concrete tepee, then passed a colony of mobile homes, a reptile farm, and a stand selling dates, date-nut cookies, date shakes, and a pamphlet entitled "The Sex Life of a Date."

"Maybe you and I will travel someday. There are a lot of places I'd like to show you."

"Hey." He squeezed her thigh. "We are traveling."

"Of course, but you do want to see Europe, don't you? I wouldn't like to be stuck in one spot for the rest of my life."

'Neither would I. And we won't be."

She withdrew into herself a moment before saying, "It won't be easy for them."

"Who?"

"My parents. They're not going to understand about us. They think . . . No, they don't think at all. They don't know what to think. Everything's changed too much. Their image of an ideal life was a long party where everyone drank a lot but no one got drunk and ugly, and where everyone acted witty and flirted but no one did anything wrong. Or at least no one got caught. Now all their friends are very witty alcoholics and failures whose marriages are breaking up."

"You can't blame them," said Carter to ease her dismay. "You don't know what they've been through and . . ."

"Oh, I don't blame them. It's just that my parents have crazy ideas about what I should do. They see me as sort of a second Clare Boothe Luce. When actually all I want is . . ."

"What?"

"I guess what I want is . . . to find out. I never had the chance around them. Then, in college, it seemed the wrong time. There were too many parties, too many boys, too many books. I can't honestly say I spent twenty minutes thinking about the future until the spring of my senior year, and by then it was too late. At times I'm tempted to tell my parents the truth about me and all I've done, just to show them how far off base they've been."

"You can't blame them," Carter repeated, suddenly the impassioned defender of people whom, on principle, he disliked. "That wouldn't make sense."

"You're right. It would ruin them. They'd never get over it and . . ."

"I don't know about that, but it wouldn't serve any purpose. And think what it might do to us."

She nodded, gazing out where the wind had unearthed a few wavering tongues of sand and shot them across the scorched asphalt.

Oddly, after coming to the desert for the heat, the first side trip they took in Palm Springs was a ride on the aerial tramway to the top of Mt. San Jacinto, where clouds combed through the ponderosa pines, tearing loose tattered flurries of snow. The sealed car, drawn along greased cables, penetrated the haze like a diving bell. They might have been under oily water or in smoke, and couldn't tell whether they were soaring or plummeting until at the summit the sun pierced the clouds. Half a foot of snow had bent the youngest fir trees into frozen tunnels, arches, and arcades.

Most of the passengers, dressed in summer clothes, remained in the restaurant at the end of the line waiting to be lowered to the warmth of Coachella Valley. But Carter and Elaine, who wore sweaters and welcomed a hike, marched through the stone-and-timber room, out into the snow, trailing fluted cones of frost. To the east, far below, was Palm Springs, an iridescent green against the bleached sand, with its hundreds of blue back-yard swimming pools. Falling steeply from beneath their feet, a meadow of drifts appeared on the point of avalanching into the desert, and it blinded them when the sun slipped through the mist once more.

"God, wouldn't you love to ski down?" said Elaine.

"It looks like you could coast right into a swimming pool."

"*Can* you ski?" She glanced at his leg.

"I don't know. I used to water ski. I'd like to try."

"That's something else we could do in Europe. Rent a chalet in Kitzbühel and spend a winter learning to ski."

"Yes," he said, smiling, and used both hands to measure the prominence of her belly. "Just as soon as we've recovered."

The sun had stayed out, but a cloud crossed her face. Elaine pulled back sharply, and must have been standing on a slick spot, for she lost balance, skidded a few feet, and toppled into a drift.

"See what I mean?" Carter laughed as he helped her up. "You're not ready for the big slopes."

She twisted free again and very slowly and deliberately brushed the snow from her slacks, slapping hard at her thighs and calves. Carter saw tears in her eyes. "Did you hurt yourself?"

"I'm fine. I'm not just as grateful as I used to be. Let's start back."

"You look cold." He took her arm as they scaled an icy path toward the restaurant, feeling a frigid wind at their bare necks.

While they awaited the tram Elaine quietly sipped a cup of hot chocolate and Carter had two beers. Then when the gleaming car emerged from the depths, shedding clouds like seaweed, they stepped aboard, she twined her fingers with his, and shut her eyes during the descent.

They stopped at a lavish motel that cost far too much, and Carter hoped it would help recapture their expansive mood. Elaine did act buoyed, but only because of its preposterous stab at elegance. "A marvelous example of twenty-third-century Colonial," she proclaimed in the voice of a tour guide. "Look at this bathroom. It's as big as a gymnasium."

Peering beyond her shoulder, he saw a pink space like the inside of a yawning cat's mouth, and gold fixtures wrought into a birdlike grace. It recalled the Yost apartment in Arlington, and he wished they had gone elsewhere.

"At least the tub is nice." She approached the huge sunken square in the far corner. "Would you like a bath?"

"No, I'd probably fall asleep and drown. I'll lie down until dinner."

"You'll be sorry," she said, unzipping her slacks. Although smiling, she seemed petulant. "I'm going to take a bubble bath. I'll bet you haven't had one in years."

"Wrong. I bet I haven't had one ever."

He was aware he had done more than decline the bath, and didn't know why, unless it was that fleeting memory of the apartment in Arlington, or the brittle smile she had brought out again like an old snapshot in a plastic envelope. When she looked that way, compressed and self-contained, and her words were crisp as foil, he couldn't reach her and, frankly, didn't care to try.

Sprawled on the bed, he listened as rumbling water filled the tub and slpashed higher in his mind. The noise deepened while he dozed off to troubling dreams which snared him just beneath the surface of sleep. He was out on a river, water-skiing in the wake of a speed boat, weaving a pattern of white spray, when suddenly he cut back over the curl and remembered his bad leg. Before he could protect it, he smacked down parallel to the boat, suffered a cold shock of pain in his knee, and collapsed. The green blur of shoreline darkened as he went under, clawing at the slender lifeline of his own air bubbles. He rose, groaning, struggled clear of sleep, and stayed motionless until his heart stopped pounding.

In the bathroom he found Elaine still in the tub, apparently asleep. With eyes shut, hair tucked neatly under the turban of an orange towel, she looked contented, and he hesitated to wake her for fear her face, now placid, would pinch tight into that plastic grin. But it was seven o'clock and he was hungry.

"Elaine," he called.

"Hmm."

"Time for dinner."

"Ummmhmm."

'You'd better bail out, or you'll shrivel."

"I hate to move." She lifted her eyes, blinked once, and left them open.

He extended a hand, which she gripped with wet fingers, and as she broke from the shell of bubbles, he didn't recognize her body. It couldn't have altered overnight—he tried to recall the silhouette in bed beside him —much less in the last two hours, yet he hadn't noticed the extent of the changes until now. Retreating to the sink, he took another look, as if expecting distance or a new perspective to transform her. But when she had rinsed away the soapy foam which girdled her waist, she appeared swollen, ungainly, and for the first time, undeniably pregnant.

Unsteady on the damp tile, she slewed her feet out to the sides to support her belly and the baby, which during the seventh month she carried high. Her protruding navel had burst inside out, and two crooked red stretch marks widened on her left breast, intersecting the white scar she'd had since childhood. On her hips and behind were others, deeper and darker.

As he had done earlier, Carter placed his palms on her warm belly, and her reaction was the same. She drew back, saying, "I know. You don't have to tell me. I'm ugly."

"No." He held on to her.

"Yes, I am. I'm fat, I walk like a duck, and have marks all over my skin."

"You look fine to me." He kissed her cheek where a tear shimmered. "But when we get back, you ought to see a doctor."

"Oh, Carter, it's happening, isn't it? I'll grow bigger and uglier and there's no way to stop it." She began to sob.

"Don't cry."

"I'm afraid."

"No, you're not. You'll be all right."

"I am afraid, and I can't pretend I'm not."

"No." He rocked her in his arms. "I'll take care of you."

Chapter IX

Neither mentioned the matter again until Sunday night, when as they traveled back to L.A., Carter reminded her to make a doctor's appointment Monday. Then he brought up a subject one of them had to broach sooner or later. 'You'd also better ask how to put the baby up for adoption. Maybe the doctor could tell you. Or you could call the Florence Crittenden Foundation."

In answer he heard the hum of late-evening traffic. The air, especially after the desert, was cool and at last full of the foreboding melancholy of an East Coast autumn. On side streets the tires crushed fallen sycamore leaves. "Elaine, are you listening?"

"Yes." Her voice was dry and disembodied as the leaves.

"It has to be done."

Once more she was silent, and Carter didn't press her. But in the morning, before leaving for work, he taped a note to the bathroom mirror: "Make doctor's appointment."

At Danny Boy's, prior to disappearing into his office, Cervik sent Carter on to the next plateau, the salad and sandwich block, with accurate, yet useless advice. "Careful in there, Sport. Don't cut your knuckles off."

By noon Carter had half a dozen nicks, and the wounds stung wickedly from spicy sauces and dressings. Toby, who was busily dicing vegetables, wasted no sympathy on him, for her own fingers were notched by pink scars. Even after years of practice, she cut herself, but bled very little, and when she sliced off a black scrap of skin, she meticulously moved it to the edge of the cutting board, where it dried into a hard raisin. But Carter bled profusely, ruining two bacon, lettuce, and tomato sandwiches and one chef's salad.

At quitting time Toby assured him, "You doin' real good if you ain't lost a finger this day. Tomorrow you'll be carefuller, and by next week your hand'll be tougher than a hickory switch."

Hurrying home, he couldn't outdistance the absurdity of his job any more than he could shake the stinging from his fingers. He doubted he could endure it much longer —not just the ennui and weariness, but the stupidity. Yet how, and where, would he find anything better?

He was tempted to skip his law class that night, since he probably wouldn't be able to hold a pen and the boredom would only remind him of Danny Boy's. But then it occurred to Carter—and with such simplicity he marveled he hadn't thought of it sooner—that he could complete a degree at UCLA with two years of night school, or a year of extension courses and one semester full time. The idea promised an eventual escape from this senseless job. Of course, it also entailed staying in Los Angeles long after the baby was born, but he didn't think Elaine would mind.

He called her name as he entered the apartment and was irritated when she answered from the kitchen instead of the bedroom. Fat, he thought, going to her. Both of them were getting fat, and at the moment this meant more than gaining weight. Was it poverty of imagination that had permitted them to subside into the predictable, the most pedestrian roles? While she played the cheerful housewife, he played the industrious hubby, neither of them aware until now of how effortlessly they had yielded to what they would have sworn they didn't want.

"What did you do today?" she asked from the stove.

"Fix about four hundred finger sandwiches." He showed his lacerated hands. "I'm working the salad and sandwich block, and may bleed to death before I'm through. This job is beginning to . . ."

"Poor baby." She stooped to check the oven. "I'm baking you a birthday cake."

"My birthday's in April. Look, I . . ."

"I know. This is to make up for the twenty-two you had before I met you. Besides, I'm in the mood for a celebration and couldn't think of a better excuse to satisfy my craving for sweets."

"Very sneaky." Then postponing the news about his plans, he asked, "Did you call a doctor?"

Rearranging a strand of hair, she stood up. "No."

"Didn't you see my note?"

"Yes, but I was restless this morning. I took a walk

148

down to La Cienega and came home full of energy. Once I started the cake, I forgot about the doctor."

"What time is it? Maybe you could . . ."

"No, it's too late," she said sharply. "I'll do it tomorrow." They ate dinner silently, and Carter went to UCLA in a bad mood and returned in one that was worse. Next morning he noticed his message on the bathroom mirror, and leaving it there, set out to confront another idiotic test of courage at the cutting block. If he could tolerate this, the least she could do was call a doctor.

By noon he bled steadily, and during his two-hour study period, bathed his smarting hands in a salt-water solution. He considered phoning Elaine to jog her memory, but didn't. Annoyed by the pain, he didn't want to take it out on her.

That evening as he unlocked the door a stale compound of odors—mostly cigarette smoke and coffee grounds—smacked him in the face. Elaine lay on the living-room couch, asleep under her bathrobe. Every ashtray bristled with cigarette butts. In the kitchen the coffee pot was still plugged in, and Carter unhooked it and transferred three dirty cups from the drainboard to the sink. Returning to Elaine, he shook her by the shoulder until she mumbled, "Oh, it's you. Good. I was lonely."

"It looks like you had company." He roosted next to her.

"God, don't mention it."

"Who was it?"

"The Regans. The drain was clogged and I asked him to fix it. But she did the work. He offered encouragement and handed her wrenches. He's just had a prostate operation. Last year she had a hysterectomy, but has never felt better. Ask me anything about their medical history. I know it all. You see, she's an expert on plumbing and pregnancy. Although she likes pipes, she's strictly against babies. She asked me everything from how often I go to the bathroom to the size and capacity of my pelvis. That one took my breath away. I should have told her to ask you."

Carter laid a hand on her hip, as if expecting her to bolt. "Did you call a doctor?"

Her smile vanished in stages—fading from her eyes, her cheeks, then her mouth—and she heaved a great sigh.

149

"There we go again. Didn't I tell you the Regans were here?"

"All day?"

"I don't know when they arrived, but they didn't leave until four-thirty."

"You could have called this morning. Honestly, Elaine, you . . ."

"Carter, is there a reason for this, or are you simply trying to upset me?"

The question gave him a moment's pause, and when he answered, he couldn't conceal his anger. "You're more than seven months pregnant and should see a doctor. It worries me."

"You're positive that's all?"

"What else would there be?"

"It's sweet of you to worry, but . . . but . . ."

"But what? Look, you realize a doctor is just the beginning."

"You seem to enjoy reminding me."

"You're not being fair."

"I know, I know." Tears sparkled on her eyelashes. "I've been dreading this. We've kept it a secret so long, I'm not sure I could discuss it with a stranger."

Carter could say nothing except the obvious "Honey, you've got to," and although he whispered it gently, her head bowed beneath the weight.

"Would you rather I did it?" he asked. "Call a doctor and an adoption agency?"

"Would you, please?"

"All right. But once I've contacted an agency, it's up to you."

The following day Carter locked Cervik's office and sat gazing at the sailfish's desolate eye, then at his own eyes jaggedly reflected in the glass-topped desk. Suddenly, like Elaine, he dreaded telling their secret, for he knew it would bring about changes which it was impossible to prepare for. But he dialed the Florence Crittenden Foundation, and when a woman answered, experienced a last moment of indecision before saying, "I'd like some information about adoptions."

"Are you interested in adopting a child, or do you have one to relinquish?" She spoke like a saleswoman, certain of her customer, inquiring about an inconsequential preference in size, style, or color.

"I'm calling for a friend. She wants . . . has to give up her baby, and also has to see a doctor. Could you recommend one?"

"We have physicians, as well as registered nurses. Florence Crittenden is a non-profit organization which accepts girls without distinction as to race, creed, or national origin. No one is turned away, and payment is based upon the client's need. Most girls come in their fourth or fifth month and stay at the home until after the baby's birth, or until . . ."

"Do the girls *have* to live at the home?" Carter cut in.

"Well, I . . . That's what we're here for," she said, departing from her prepared script.

"That's not what we . . . what she's looking for. Couldn't she stay with her family?"

"There are agencies which handle that type of case. We don't."

"Would you know the name of one that does? A reputable organization with doctors."

"Most of them have doctors. It depends on what you want. Does she have a religious preference?"

"No. She'd simply like the baby to be delivered by a competent doctor and placed in a good home."

"Why don't you contact the Harold Wendell Agency? If they won't handle the case, they'll tell you who will."

At the Harold Wendell Agency he spoke to Miss Donna Dugan, who listened patiently, then proposed an appointment that Saturday. Carter hesitated.

"How far along is she?" Miss Dugan coaxed him out of his silence.

"Seven months."

"Oh, that's very late. Certain options are already closed. Has she seen a doctor?"

"No. Not since she found out. About these options, what . . ."

"I'd advise you to bring her at once. First, so she'll receive medical attention and, secondly, because the agency requires a series of consultations—ten in all—before a baby is relinquished."

Carter wondered whether he should check with Elaine. But this irresolution exasperated him. He was behaving worse than she had. "We'll come Saturday."

"Is eleven convenient? I'll schedule her for the doctor afterward. Could I have her name, please?"

"Elaine. Elaine White."

Carter hung up, nervous and perspiring, relieved he'd agreed to handle the arrangements. He doubted Elaine could have managed in her present frame of mind. No matter how fumbling and tongue-tied he'd been, he had gotten the information, and once he calmed down, he felt a sense of satisfaction that they had crossed the first hurdle.

That evening when he told Elaine, she acted pre-occupied and said nothing. "Are you listening?" he asked.

"Yes." In bed against the headboard, she bore over her shoulder and breasts a bright stripe of sunlight. "Thank you, Carter."

He moved to block out the sun. "You're set up for a doctor's appointment, too."

She thanked him again, then excused herself, saying she had to start dinner.

He felt an unreasonable disappointment, far keener than his satisfaction, but tried to be patient. He knew Elaine was upset and he didn't blame her, even if her behavior did seem out of character.

Twice that week he saw her staring out the window at the shriveled fruit of the lemon tree. She said nothing to him—wouldn't explain or share her fear and grief—and it hurt him that she didn't. For the first time he was left out, and it amazed him Friday night when as they un-dressed for bed she broke long hours of silence to ask, "Will you go with me tomorrow?"

From the corner of his eye he watched her in silhouette as she shrugged a maternity dress from her shoulders. A clinging white slip accentuated the size of her belly.

"I'd like you to be there," she said. "I need you."

It was what he'd waited to hear, yet he held back. "I should study. I have tests next week and the Law Boards in January."

"I'll be lost without you."

"There's a map in the glove compartment," he said, not unkindly. "Take the freeways and you won't get lost."

"Won't you please come? You could bring your books and study while you wait."

"All right, I'll come."

Late into the night they lay on their backs beneath the light covers and listened to the racket from Sunset Strip. In muffled tones they talked as though they didn't want to disturb what went on outside, and they spoke with sad voices, in startling contrast to what they said. But then, exhausted by their meandering conversation, they matched their words with their melancholy tone, and discussed childhood, family misfortune, and early sorrow. At last Elaine opened herself to him, uncovered by any cloak of irony, vulnerable before Carter and the bad memories she had never admitted.

She told him of her father's assignment in Haiti when she was thirteen. Of the Negro nuns who taught her at Port au Prince's only decent school. Ash-black in the white habits they wore like a penance in that fierce heat, their tongues at Communion time were pink as a dove's. A Protestant, she had had few friends. She was tall and skinny, and the other children called her Birdlegs. The lonely nights were like this one, long and sleepless, full of strange noises, dry waving palms, and feathery moths which flapped out of the darkness and circled with the fan above her bed. She had begun to touch herself, she said, at first to feel the new changes in her body—the sore nipples, the mist of hair between her thighs—and then to cool the fire her hands had kindled.

When she was quiet, he felt the even newer changes, passing his palms over her heavy breasts, her belly where the baby kicked against his fingers, and deeply between her thighs.

"No, not tonight," she whispered. "Don't go inside me. The doctor will know."

"It doesn't matter."

She didn't answer. Working her way down his stomach, she set her cool lips to his cock. Carter's muscles strained as he groped blindly in the darkness, touched her hair, and stroked the soft strands.

2

Saturday dawned bright, hot, and muggy, more like July than the first week of December. Yet Christmas shoppers in short-sleeved shirts crowded the streets and sidewalks as Carter and Elaine cruised up Crenshaw Boulevard. Los Angeles, especially Hollywood, seemed far away when they came to a neighborhood of identical cinder-block homes, over which loomed a few larger wooden houses, paint-peeled, gaunt, and gray as skeletons, divided by flimsy partitions into cheap rented rooms and apartments. Palm trees and hibiscus blooms suggested subtropical decadence and lent this district of trash-littered streets, storefront churches, and rusty abandoned cars the look of a southern town in midsummer. But the impression was called into question when they saw so many Mexicans and Orientals among the Negroes.

"Are we almost there?" asked Elaine.

"It shouldn't be far."

She took a drag on a cigarette, examined the filter, and tossed it out the window. "My stomach and I ought to strike an agreement. I think I want to smoke, but it disagrees." From her purse she picked a shiny bullet of lipstick and brightened her mouth. "Carter, what should I tell these people?"

"There's really not much to say. Just tell them the truth."

"I mean about you." Her hands shredded the Kleenex which she'd used to blot her lips. "The woman—Miss Dugan—must wonder who you are. Shall I tell her?"

"Why not?"

"It's bad enough being pregnant, but if she learns we're living together, she'll . . ."

"You're being silly. She deals every day with stranger predicaments than ours."

"She doesn't deal with me every day. Couldn't we say you're my brother?"

"Are you serious? She won't believe that."

"I really don't care. At least we won't have to discuss it."

"You're inventing a problem where none exists."

"Please, Carter. It'll be easier this way."

"Do what you want. It doesn't matter to me." Yet deep down it did, and he believed the lie would be more than a harmless equivocation. "That must be it."

Surrounded by a wrought-iron fence, a white frame house, by far the biggest and best kept one on the block, commanded the crest of a sloping lawn. Along its front was a broad porch whose steamboat Gothic fretwork gave the building the frothy appearance of a wedding cake. There was nothing to denote the nature of the place, except a bronze plaque on the gate pillar: *The Harold Wendell Agency*.

"I'm afraid," said Elaine.

"Don't be. I'm here."

After parking the Thunderbird, he crunched over the gravel, conducted her through the front door to a foyer done in walnut paneling, and said to the switchboard operator that they had an appointment with Miss Dugan.

"I'll tell her you're here. Won't you have a seat?" She took them across the hall.

Small and smelling of must, the room had a narrow window which let in light but no air, and looked as if it had been shut tight long ago and forgotten. Odds and ends of old furniture created the shabby, dispirited atmosphere of an attic. Although Carter wished he were outside, he said to Elaine, "It's not too bad."

She settled awkwardly into an overstuffed chair, poked through her purse, searching for something, then snapped it shut, having gotten nothing. She appeared to be holding her breath, counting to herself.

"Relax." He sat opposite her on a couch.

A soft rap at the door saved her the effort of answering.

"Hello, I'm Donna Dugan."

The woman was dark, trim, and short, and at first looked their age, maybe younger. But she possessed a gravity and assurance that belied her size, and there seemed nothing spontaneous about her gestures. As she approached to shake hands, a web of lines was visible at the edges of her mouth and eyes. Although over forty, she wore a suede miniskirt that showed her fine legs, sheathed in patterned stockings, to their best advantage. On the crown of her head a pair of silver-rimmed sunglasses was pushed back like an outlandish barrette to fasten her shock of brown hair.

"Now, you're Elaine White. I remember that. But did I ever get your name?"

"Carter White."

Smiling, she nodded, and seemed momentarily unsure of herself, perhaps worried that the smile revealed her wrinkles. "Please sit down." She shut the door. "I suppose since you've waited this long, you've talked over your decision thoroughly." She sat beside Carter on the sofa. "Of course, it's too late for a therapeutic abortion, but . . ."

Carter couldn't say whether she saw some fleeting sign of surprise on their faces, or had halted purposely to trigger a response. But he reacted and so did Elaine. "Maybe you weren't aware that California permits abortions, under certain conditions, up until the twentieth week of pregnancy. Well, I guess there's no reason to go into it. Even with this option closed, you must have questions."

"What has to be done before the baby's born?" Carter asked.

"A great deal. Elaine has to have medical care. She'll be examined by one of our doctors after the conference." As she crossed her legs, a grating sound escaped her inner thighs. "What's most important, you have to be absolutely sure you've made the right decision. That's why we require these consultations. I hope I'll be able to help. I'm a trained psychologist and do my best to become friends with the girls and, when possible, their husbands."

Although in saying this Miss Dugan had not looked at Carter, Elaine asked, "Maybe you've told my brother, but could you explain how you select parents for the babies?"

Now Miss Dugan did glance at him before shifting to Elaine with no change of expression. "We're extremely cautious, I'll assure you. Prospective parents fill out questionnaires, submit recommendations, take a battery of tests, then undergo a period of consultations, just like the girls. The most common problem . . ."

As the woman answered the question at length, Elaine looked down into her lap and offered no indication she was listening. Because of this, Carter himself had difficulty concentrating on what Miss Dugan said.

"It's not easy to match people with babies from a similar racial, religious, and economic background. That's another reason these consultations are important. They'll determine the type of parents your baby is placed with. If we're to find a suitable couple, you'll have to tell me about yourself, your family, and the baby's father."

Her monologue, which bordered on the formulaic, finally made the woman falter. Elaine continued to peer over her belly at the hands knotted in her lap, and Carter, at the mention of the baby's father, kept his gaze on Miss Dugan. He wished Elaine were beside him so the two of them could stare down this small, dark woman whom he immediately considered their enemy. It might have been the dim corner in which she sat, but Miss Dugan looked dusted with ashes in the hollows of her cheeks, on her upper lip, inside the triangle parted and closed by her thighs.

"I might add"—she roused herself with an uncomfortable grin—"for most girls this is a time of great emotional strain. We give them support and professional help when they need it, and encourage them to confront their problems and learn something from the experience."

As she paused again, Carter realized it was part of her routine to dispense information piecemeal, then wait while it sank in. He wouldn't have minded, except this called attention to Elaine's silence. Trying to draw her into the conversation, he said, "That makes sense. If a girl wants to understand herself, she has to be honest. Unless she knows why she got pregnant, I don't imagine you could help her."

Miss Dugan flashed a smile, and Carter felt he'd scored a point in an unstated contest between them and Elaine, who refused to play. "Oh, there's a reason for whatever we do, although it's not always easy to face it."

He looked at Elaine, at the top of her bowed head, where her hair was parted in a straight white line. "Miss Dugan, could I speak to Elaine alone for a few minutes?"

"Certainly." She came to her feet at once, well practiced in accepting the unusual.

As the door shut, Carter studied its stained, cracked surface, which resembled alligator hide. The air in the room rested upon them like a great stone. He could hear Elaine's breathing. Through the window burst a bar of sunlight, murrhined by shiny motes of dust, and among them shone her eyes, which she had raised to meet his.

"What's wrong?" she asked.

"I think you should tell the truth. You should level with Miss Dugan and with yourself. Why waste time fooling her? If you wantted to, you could get something out of this."

"Like what?"

"You might learn why you've been upset this week."

"I don't need her help to know that."

"Okay, then you might learn how to cope with it, and understand what has happened."

Her eyes narrowed. 'Are you sure it isn't you who wants to understand?"

"We both have a lot to understand, and none of it's easy. If there were something you could explain, I'd ask. You've got to pull yourself together. It's not like you to act this way."

The stark white part reappeared.

157

"Look at me," he said. "You have to go through these sessions with Miss Dugan. Didn't you always tell me to take advantage of opportunities, to . . ."

"You're right, Carter, but . . ."

"Of course I am. You don't have to hide from the truth. Let's tell Miss Dugan."

She held his shirt sleeve. "Will you do the talking?"

"Yes, at first. After that, it's up to you." He touched her cheek, then called in Miss Dugan.

While she reclaimed her seat on the couch, he remained standing and said, "I'm not Elaine's brother, and we're not married."

He stopped to read her reaction, and when there was none save for bland professional indulgence, he experienced an instant of doubt. Maybe they should have kept lying; the truth might destroy them. But he knew if their lives were ever to come unkinked from the lies they'd told, it was time to start unraveling them. Although this realization didn't make the telling much easier, he went on. "I'm not the baby's father. I thought if Elaine wanted to benefit by these consultations, you should know the truth."

Elaine noisily struck a match. The sound set Carter's teeth on edge and the smell of sulphur burned in his nostrils.

"Well," said Miss Dugan brightly, "it takes a man to establish the facts, but now it's time for girl talk." The uncertain smile came to her face, gathering its well-powdered wrinkles. "May I have a few minutes alone with Elaine? It's standard procedure."

Carter looked at once to Elaine, positive she would protest, but she was rearranging the ashtray on the arm of the chair.

Stunned, he stood in the hallway, staring at the alligator-hide door, unable to fathom what had happened. Though he'd warned Elaine it was up to her, he hadn't expected to be shut out, but at his abrupt dismissal by Miss Dugan, it was as if the lid of a mysterious trunk had closed him off from her. Now she was alone, and so was he, and it was difficult to believe he'd done the right thing.

To avoid the appearance of eavesdropping, he roamed deeper into the agency, stopped at a water fountain, and stepping on the pedal, shot a cold stream of liquid, tasteless as cellophane, into his mouth. He saw no one—perhaps it was lunch time—and the worn wooden floor sank silently beneath his feet. At the end of the hall he entered a room where folding chairs surrounded a desk whose scarred surface was papered by purple mimeograph sheets, sickly sweet as every test Carter had taken in college.

Sitting down, he read on the sheets an explanation of California's new abortion law and how this might affect the Harold Wendell Agency.

Under no circumstances should a counselor's prejudices or religious principles interfere with a client's decision. Since a mischosen word and even a gesture can put additional pressure on the most stable woman, I strongly recommend these guidelines:

1. Explain objectively and in detail every option—relinquishment, retention, and abortion.

2. Never prejudge a case. We're an adoption agency, not a religious or moral institution.

3. Let the *client* make her own decision. Don't try to influence her. And *remember*, every word counts. Do *not* mention the word "baby" until the client has committed herself to having it. During the first few weeks when there's still the possibility of a D and C, the unborn baby should be referred to as "cells." After that it can be called "the embryo," or "the fetus," as the case may be.

"Oh, here you are," Miss Dugan interrupted him. "I'm sorry the room's a mess. We had a staff meeting this morning." Swiftly she collected the mimeographed sheets, plucked the one from Carter's hand, ripped them in half, and scattered the shreds in a wastebasket. "They're not for the public."

Carter got up, angry—whether at Miss Dugan or what he had read, he couldn't say. "Where's Elaine?"

"In the doctor's office." She folded her arms, hugging them to her breasts. "I want to thank you for bringing her. We had a wonderful chat. She's a charming person. Because of the pill and the ease of abortions, I don't see many educated and well-bred girls any longer." She swayed in a balanced motion that made the sunglasses saddled on her head wink bright and dark. "If there's anything you'd like to discuss, please feel free. I'm at your service too."

"I'll keep that in mind."

"You must have questions." She gave a dubious arch to one eyebrow.

"None at the moment."

"It's a shame Elaine didn't come sooner. We're really rather limited in what we . . ."

"I think I hear her in the hall." Lifting his bad leg to relieve a jab of pain, he started around her.

"One last thing, Carter." She caught his arm. "Elaine is a sensitive, intelligent girl. Be patient with her. She thinks she's awful and ugly. You and I know better, and she needs our encouragement."

"I'll take care of her."

"I know you will." Her fingers tightened in a friendly squeeze. "See you next week."

3

Carter guided Elaine down the front steps, offered his arm as they crossed the gravel parking lot, and opened the car door for her as if this were their first date. Twice she murmured, "Thank you," but said nothing more until they had passed through the gate, and he asked, "How was it?"

"Not as bad as I'd feared." Taking the pack of cigarettes from her purse, she tossed it out the window. "Dr. Sachs ordered me to quit smoking. Remind me if I forget."

"What else did he say? Are you all right?"

"Yes. I'm in perfect health." The corners of her mouth curled into a faint smile. "He's a very sweet man, and has three adopted children. He told me some women are born breeders, and pregnancy makes them bloom. Do you think I've bloomed?"

"Yes, that's the word for it." He ran a hand over her belly.

"Don't tease, Carter." Though in a better mood, she was still skittish, and Carter wisely withdrew his hand. "He also wrote a prescription for my stretch marks."

"Shall we stop and buy it?"

"Not now. Later."

"Let's not forget."

Unbuckling her seatbelt, she leaned over to kiss his cheek. "I'm sorry I've been such a bitch. I don't know what I'd have done if you hadn't come."

"I don't know what I'd have done either. It should be better now. The first meeting was bound to be the worst. That's one more hurdle behind us."

"I suppose."

"Did you like Miss Dugan?" He labored to keep the conversation alive.

She shrugged and fidgeted, apparently already wishing for a cigarette. "At least she's young. Or acts like she is. I was afraid I'd be stuck with a dowdy old lesbian in a shirtwaist dress and sensible shoes."

They laughed together. "You've read too many bad novels. Were you upset when she ushered me out?"

"No. I expected it."

"What did you talk about?"

"Nothing, really."

"She must have said something. You were in there half an hour."

"Oh, she reemphasized the importance of the consultations and told me to feel free to call on her any time." After the slightest catch, her voice quickened to attach these words to the ones she had just spoken. "She also asked if I'd considered an abortion."

"What did you say?"

"That I'd thought about it, but after discussing it with you, decided not to."

"Are you sorry you did?"

"No. I don't believe I could have gone through with it. Not alone. And even if you'd agreed to help me, that would have finished us."

"Why?"

"I know it's not logical, but I couldn't imagine us going on afterward as if it hadn't happened. It would have been horrible to have nothing in the end. This way we're trying to make something good come out of my mistake. You understand."

"Yes, I do. Did Miss Dugan?"

"She didn't say."

"I'm amazed she mentioned it at all. Did she ask about me?"

"No."

"She didn't say anything?"

"No."

"I told you she wouldn't." But he was surprised. "Are you interested in eating dinner out? You shouldn't have to cook. You've done enough today."

"You know what I'd really like?" She turned to him, suddenly revived. "To dress up and go to the best restaurant in town. Tomorrow I'll start keeping sensible hours and watch my weight, but tonight I'd like to enjoy myself one last time."

"Fine. We'll do it, and it won't be the last time."

After his days at Danny Boy's, Carter had no desire to eat out, yet he didn't want to disappoint Elaine now that she had begun to rally. So at the apartment, while she dressed, he phoned Scandia's, Perino's, and Chasen's, but in each case was told it was too late to reserve a table. When the list of better restaurants had dwindled by more than a dozen, he had to settle for Trader Vic's.

Elaine must have overheard this, for as he came into the bedroom she acted astonished that her plans had been dashed, and though she said nothing, her eyes accused him. With a few quick strokes she completed her make-up and stalked into the living room.

Carter, too, was astonished—mostly at the utter precariousness of her mood—and was tempted to shout, What the hell is wrong with Trader Vic's? Why did it matter where they ate? But then he remembered Miss Dugan's advice. He had to be patient.

He mixed them both a strong bourbon and water, which they drank at the far ends of the couch, peering over the polished tile to the fireplace. Since they rarely left the bedroom, this room disturbed them. They didn't know where to focus their eyes, and the heat heightened their discomfort.

Outside, clouds had overtaken the sun, wrapping it in a raglike winding cloth which sifted a pale yellow light through the Venetian blinds. Carter felt moisture on his back and saw it cluster in tiny beads on the bridge of Elaine's nose. Even a second round of drinks failed to refresh them or loosen their tongues.

Not until they were in the car, on their way, could they talk—about the jaundiced sky which promised rain, about how hungry they were, although they weren't, about the traffic on Santa Monica Boulevard stalled by a locomotive lumbering along tracks they'd never noticed

before. Elaine laughed and said Los Angeles was preposterous. Then Carter laughed. They arrived at Trader Vic's
in paroxysms of laughter and ordered Mai Tai's, which
sweetly thickened their tongues. Near their table a waterfall trickled over plastic rocks, each drop followed by
reedy notes of music. Carter was reminded of a loudly
ticking clock, and as his body took wing with the drinks,
his mind remained grounded, for despite their facade
of high spirits, something whispered that he should be
on guard.

A moment later he saw why. Leaving the flowers in
the glass, Elaine raised the Mai Tai to her lips, and her
faultless skin reflected the funereal pallor of gardenia
blossoms. Believing that the petals hid her, she stared
directly at Carter, and her eyes, gleaming out of that hothouse jungle, had the same frantic expression she had
worn for days. He hoped the drink would catch her before she faded altogether, but it didn't. She laughed
once more, then grew silent and stopped pretending she
was happy. It seemed to Carter they had struggled to a
summit and were now tumbling down the far side.

When dinner came she listlessly pushed the sweet-
and-sour pork around her plate. "We could be anywhere
in America. One Trader Vic's is like another. A poor man's
Honolulu. Once in Hong Kong . . ."

"Elaine, do me a favor." He clasped her hand. "Don't
tell me what this reminds you of." Angrily she tried to
retrieve the hand, but he wouldn't let her. "You always
told me not to worry about the future. You said it would
take care of itself. Well, why don't you stop chewing over
the past?"

After this neither of them spoke, and they ate with
great speed and precision. Carter bent over his plate,
careful not to spill a morsel. He blotted his mouth after
each bite and laboriously worked the utensils. He felt
just as he had at sixteen when he'd first asked a girl out
to dinner—that the act of eating was unimaginably coarse
and no amount of attention to good manners could disguise his awkwardness. At last he despaired of the patience Miss Dugan had recommended, paid the bill, and
they departed.

They drove up Sunset, screened off from the crowd
and the noise by the Thunderbird's tinted windows. The
street fizzled for miles in either direction, shooting sparks
like a long, slow-burning fuse. At every bar, night club,

and discotheque, Carter was tempted to stop and wrench some satisfaction from this night whose lights promised so much, yet delivered nothing. But it was useless. Elaine wasn't in the mood, and now neither was he.

Dressed for dinner, they sat in the apartment watching TV—something they seldom did—as if counting on that gloating purple maw to swallow their problems. Elaine produced a pack of cigarettes and performed an elaborate ritual in lighting one. She tamped it on the arm of the chair, struck a match, waited for the sulphur to burn off, inhaled deeply so her face glowed for an instant like a jack-o'-lantern, then exhaled, extinguishing the flame. Carter didn't remind her of Dr. Sachs' orders. He knew she hadn't forgotten.

When she'd smoked the cigarette down to its filter, Elaine crushed it in an ashtray and went into the bathroom to shower—something they usually did together. Carter couldn't remember the last time they had made love. That night in Palm Springs? No, just last night. But he recalled more clearly a sunlit morning months ago when he had wakened to see her standing nude beside the bed, a dollop of toothpaste on her finger. After feeding him its sweetness, she slid beneath the covers, her arms lean and cool, their tongues tasting like candy.

Now she was ashamed of the body that had been her triumph. Any other time Carter would have assured her she was desirable, but tonight, when she had made her irritation apparent, he was weary of hiding his. After she had come out of the bathroom and gone to bed, he sat through the late news and part of a movie, took a shower himself and joined her at two o'clock.

Elaine was still awake. Several times he started to speak, but a lingering aftertaste of the long day's discontent left him mute. Though this wasn't what Miss Dugan meant by patience, it was the best he could do.

Outlined by the light at the windows, Elaine's body began to shake. Tears coursed over her cheeks. Choking back a sob, she let them flow. Her fingers clutched the sheet and stretched it taut. Then she sat up and buried her face in her hands.

Throwing off the covers, Carter came around to her side. "What's wrong?"

As she twisted away, his arm slipped from her shoulder. "The baby."

"Don't you want to give it up?"

"No. Of course not."

'Would you like to keep it?"

"You know we can't. There's nothing to do."

"Yes, we could get married and keep the baby ourselves."

"Carter, don't say that." Then in a calmer voice, "Please let me alone for a few minutes."

Leaving the lights out, he stumbled into the living room and fell heavily onto the sofa, wondering as he had all day what had gone wrong. Although Elaine had good reason to be upset, it was difficult, especially in the dark, for him to piece things together. He'd anticipated some trouble, but hadn't thought she would fall apart. Now where did he fit in? She said she didn't want to relinquish the baby, yet didn't want to keep it either. Or was she simply reluctant to marry him?

It was impossible to know, and as the darkness gradually dissipated, he was distracted by all that entered their apartment at this hour. Far from a safe bell jar, it seemed insecure, the walls crumbly and spider-cracked, the shadows menacing. Through the windows pounded the crude beat of the Body Shop, while jasmine blooms bled their cheap perfume. He heard a startling noise behind him and whirled to see Elaine on her way to the bathroom. As her pink gown passed down the hall, fleeting and insubstantial as a shadow, he had an eerie premonition that if he shot out a hand, it might crash through her.

He shut his eyes as Elaine returned and said, "Carter, you can come back to bed."

He didn't answer.

"Please, Carter, before you catch cold."

Rising, he realized some definite, dramatic gesture was needed, and thought of making love to her, yet this struck him as empty. Maybe worse—unwise, desperate— for if it failed, they would only face deeper turmoil.

As he got into bed, she crawled to his side, wrapped him in her arms, and said, "I've been a bitch. I *am* a bitch."

"Elaine, it's too late to talk. We'll . . ."

She clapped a hand to his mouth. "Let me finish. You were right. I should stop living in the past. It was never any good. People were always telling me what to do. If it wasn't my parents, it was someone else. That's why

I'm pregnant. He wanted to get me pregnant. I think he planned it."

"You don't have to tell me. It doesn't matter."

"It does!" She gave him an impatient shake. "You have to know how it happened. He asked me to marry him, and told me to start taking the pill. I didn't want to. I didn't want either one. I'd just stopped taking it, and knew if I started again, he'd have a claim on me and I'd wind up marrying him. Do you understand? Do you?"

Carter wasn't sure what she meant and was tired of being pushed back and forth. "No. I don't understand."

"But you have to."

Her voice was a high-pitched whine, and he supposed she was still drunk, yet he asked wearily, "Why did you keep sleeping with him?"

The room became very quiet. "It's hard to say. I liked him. Or did at first. Afterward . . ."

"Forget I asked."

"No. You have a right to know. It's just not easy to explain. It doesn't even seem real anymore. He was only the second man I'd slept with. I wanted to believe I was very mature and liberated, but like most girls, I was always told it was wrong, and although that didn't keep me from doing it, I thought there had to be a reason. So I decided I loved him, and by the time I learned I'd deceived myself, it was too late."

They lay motionless a few moments, then Carter touched her arm to reassure her. She misunderstood and kissed him. He wanted to stop her, to tell her no, but she would have misunderstood once more. So he rolled her onto her back and raised the nightgown up to her neck. Entering her, he buried his face in the cool silk.

Afterward she whispered, "I'm sorry. I love you."

Chapter X

Sunday it rained, and as the storm lasted the rest of the week, Los Angeles blurred at the edges and bled streams of grease and paint. Shallow gutters overflowed, washing the sidewaks ankle-deep in water. Then the water ominously clouded with silt, and mud slides buried back-yard barbeque pits, automobiles, and people. By Tuesday a few hillside houses could no longer hold on to their foundations. Trailing pipes and electrical wires, they plunged into the canyons, smashing themselves to kindling. Swimming pools pursued them, spilling chlorinated water and scattering blue shards like giant robins' eggs.

For Carter and Elaine, the catastrophe provided a diversion from their personal problems, from the questions they might have had to ask themselves. Or from silence. Gratefully Carter thought winter had arrived—at least what little winter Southern California could expect—and with the season at bedrock, he believed their relationship might settle onto a securer footing.

Yet although the weeks soon merged into a familiar pattern, the apartment never again seemed a refuge and Elaine didn't recover. It occurred to Carter that while she encouraged him to widen his experiences, she had reduced her own to protect herself at the point where she was weakest—at her core where the baby stirred. And now that the doctor and the adoption agency were forcing her beyond these diminished boundaries, she had no defense except a sad amazement that the pregnancy had caused troubles she could neither foresee nor subdue.

Carter did his best to help. He often called from work to break the monotonous isolation of her days. He bought her extravagant gifts, rarely reminded her of Dr. Sach's advice about dieting and cigarettes, and never complained when she spent hours worrying about her clothes and applying make-up. Then—most difficult—he patiently endured the tantrums which beset her after these lengthy preparations when she looked into the mirror. Repeatedly he assured her she was not, and never would be, ugly.

Purchasing the ointment Dr. Sachs had prescribed he gave her slow massages each evening. In bed on her stomach, she scarcely looked pregnant, and the tan on her back gleamed like dark shellac as it tapered toward her waist. But her hips had broadened, and on her behind, inch-long lines crawled across skin that had been drawn too tight. As Carter tenderly tried to heal these wounds, they seemed to lengthen and multiply like voracious crimson leeches gnawing her flesh.

When she rolled over, he saw the marks had burned deeper brands on her breasts. The one white scar was a delicate thread on which the others had been strung. As Carter smoothed the salve onto them, her nipples tensed, and invariably she winced from embarrassment, not pain, whispering, "I'm ugly."

"No." But to avoid the scars, he raised his eyes to hers, which she closed. He moved his hand, then, between her legs, where on her inner thigh a sheath of muscle, flawless as a silk pennant, narrowed to her knee. There were parts of her untouched. He wanted to touch them, and going inside her, believed he had. The final, the best, stroke of the treatment was his love.

Fortunately his job at Danny Boy's made fewer demands. Or perhaps he had become shrewder at dodging them. His "study period" gradually expanded from two to three hours, and although he often arrived late and left early, Cervik didn't object. In fact, he'd started to treat Carter as a protégè, clapping him on the back, calling him Sport, and praising his progress. During the second week of the rains, complaining of severe headaches and sinus problems, Cervik asked him to do the yearly inventory, and Carter welcomed the chance to break the routine and lose himself in what proved to be a time-consuming but effortless task for anyone who could count higher than a hundred.

Assisting him, Luke the Spook was wary at first of the new white man who had substituted for the old easy-going one. Sullenly he stamped around the walk-in freezer, shuffling frozen pork chops, steaks, and hamburger patties like a man, all knuckles, dealing his first hand of poker. He dropped slabs of meat on the floor, kicked them into the corner, and using a snow shovel, scooped them into plastic bags, grumbling the crudest estimate of their number. But when he realized Carter wasn't a threat, his arithmetic improved, and he passed the days discussing the boss.

"You take Cervik. He says his nose is stopped up. There ain't no way that could be true. He'd just have to try another sniff of Rita's quiff and he'd be running straight pipes down to his toes. Shit, man, what else could they do in that office? There ain't no room to stretch out in. If you're asking me what's wrong with him, I'd say it's them new hairs on his head. Anybody knows hairs are like trees. They got just as much underground as they do on top. They've probably drilled down and clogged his nose holes. What do you think?"

"You might be right."

"You like Cervik?"

"He's been good to me."

"He's afraid you'll steal his job. Somebody better do something soon, or we'll all be in the breadline."

"Actually, I was hired to take your job, Luke."

"It's yours, man."

Monday the sun returned, the mud hardened, and the rain was resurrected as wavering lines of heat into a smoggy sky. Along the boulevards Christmas lights winked off and on, holly wreaths wilted, and while the Boy Scouts preserved their spruce trees by hosing them with water, Santas, sweating behind cotton beards, offered their padded laps and hired ears to suspicious children. Anyone who had a house with a view stopped searching for Catalina and looked east to see if there was snow on Mt. Baldy.

That afternoon a waitress interrupted the inventory to tell Carter he had a phone call at the cashier's desk. Since he had just spoken to Elaine, he doubted it was she, yet couldn't imagine who else it might be. Squeezing behind the counter next to Rita, whose broad hips left little room, he covered the receiver with his palm and waited for her to allow him some privacy. But Rita remained where she was, rump against the cash register, and filed from her fingernails a pink powder which drifted onto the cigars, after-dinner mints, and candy bars.

"Hello," Carter said at last.

"Hi, kid, Eddie Brown here."

Quickly he cupped a hand to the receiver again and jerked his head.

"I can't leave the money," said Rita. "And like, who's listening anyway?"

Moving the length of the cord, he got a better grip on the phone and touched it gingerly to his ear. "Hello?"

"Back on your feet, kid? I thought you had fallen out for good. We have business to discuss."

"I don't believe we do," he said evenly.

"You don't? Well, you'd better give it another thought. I've got you by the ass."

Carter stuck a finger into his opposite ear, as though afraid Rita might hear Eddie through it. "If you'll check your records, you'll . . ."

"Fuck you and your records, kid. If I don't get my money, you're in big trouble. I have information somebody should be willing to pay for."

"We've already talked about this and decided to drop it. Maybe I should refresh your memory."

"Hold it. I'll refresh yours. Ever hear of Donald Christian Yost? He works at the American embassy in Costa Rica and has a daughter named Elaine, who's not married. Starting to flash yet, kid? Or do you want me to call this guy and let him know his daughter is knocked up?"

"Who told you that?" As Carter shouted, Rita stopped filing her nails. "What do you want?"

"My money."

"Where are you?"

'Never mind. We'll get together when the time's right. Like—lemme see—tonight at seven. Don't be late, kid. I'm expecting your old friend, Moylan Fingerhut, too. See you at my place."

The dead phone dangled from Carter's hand until Rita poked the nail file at his shoulder. "Hey, you finished? Better hang up. We're supposed to keep the line clear for carry-out orders."

From a pay phone booth, Carter told Elaine he had to work late that night and mumbled a hasty excuse which obviously puzzled her. But he recognized it was best if they didn't talk again before he had resolved matters with Eddie Brown. Then, after she broke the connection, he kept the receiver to his ear, as if listening to something other than the dial tone, and attempted to grasp what had gone awry. He'd known it was unwise, as well as wrong, to cheat Eddie, but he thought he had covered himself.

170

Now Fingerhut was in on it, too, and Carter couldn't guess why, unless . . . He cradled the receiver in its aluminum cup. It had to be the lie-detector test. Drawing upon the spotty information he'd furnished, Fingerhut had discovered everything else. Or if not everything, then enough to put Elaine and him at Eddie's mercy.

Despite the overhead fan that chattered like a trapped pigeon against the aluminum panel, Carter was warm and a swift pain seized his knee. They had over eight hundred dollars in the bank, and he was willing to pay every cent to keep Eddie and Fingerhut quiet. He didn't want anyone, not even Elaine, to know what they had found out, for this might be the jolt which would send her into hysteria.

Biting his lower lip as he'd often seen her do, he wondered how he could prevent her from noticing when he withdrew their savings. And how would they pay their medical bills? He slumped against the pebbly metal. The truth had burst out, painful as surgical pins, and seemed to jeopardize everything he had done. If Cervik learned, he would lose his job. If the Yosts were told, he would lose Elaine. If . . .

At this thought, he jerked upright, and the pain moved from his knee to his belly. He was angry—mostly at himself. No matter what her parents learned, there was no reason to lose Elaine, and as for a job, he could always get another.

Putting weight on his bad leg, he pushed against the pain, as if to hold it off by an act of the will or fight through to the other side. When the knee stopped throbbing, he rejoined Luke the Spook in the basement, and worked quickly and methodically, counting stock, stacking it on shelves, and filling the ledger with inflexible numbers and notes.

Though the rush-hour traffic had slackened, Carter took his time driving to Eddie's and arrived twenty minutes late, not wanting to appear eager or intimidated. As he coasted into the garage at the Mediterranean Cascade, he caught a glimpse of Ebba Sjostrom leading Tiger on a leash along Franklin Avenue, but she didn't see him. In the courtyard the waterfall gurgled biliously, a pump behind the foliage filtered chemicals into the pool, and from an unattended charcoal grill smoke rose in random semaphore. There was no one in sight.

Eddie answered the door at the third knock, and for his own unfathomable reasons, clasped and pumped Carter's hand. "Come in, kid. Jesus Christ, come in. You're looking great. The hair could use a trim—better give Mel Tuttle a call—but otherwise okay. I was afraid you'd self-destruct once the treatment was over. Have a seat. Fingerhut will be here in a minute. How about a drink?"

Declining, Carter sat in a chair which, like all the others, bore the print of Tiger's teeth. The upholstery had been shredded to tangles and flapped in a sloppy fringe about the bottom. But the newspapers and dog droppings had been replaced by a tidy red sandbox in the corner.

Eddie was fidgeting with the stereo, then as a record dropped onto the turntable, he danced a few steps. "Like it? That's Sly and the Family Stone. A heavy group, if ever I heard one."

Though he wore a gray flannel suit, white shirt, and blue tie, it was unlikely anyone would mistake him for a stockbroker. His trousers were flared and the coat, cut in snugly at the waist, was sleeveless, exposing the puffed, transparent material of his shirt. The tie was actually a kerchief, jauntily knotted and tossed back over his shoulder.

"Look," said Carter, "why not tell me what you want?"

"You know what I want."

"All right, how much?"

"Wait for Fingerhut." A drink in hand, Eddie stood at the front door—a paltry barrier to flight.

"You might as well know, I didn't bring much money. Tell me your price and if it's reasonable, I'll . . ."

"Hey, kid, you aren't in any position to say what's reasonable."

"Ever heard of blackmail? It's against the law."

Eddie rattled the ice in his glass. "I don't know what's got into you, but you'd better set your mind right if you don't want me to make that call to Costa Rica. And don't moan about the law. You're the one who screwed me."

"Just like you were screwing the agency."

"Now we're name-calling. You're a schmuck, kid, but I dig you. So don't gimme a hard time." Eddie left the door to mix another drink. "Sure you won't have one? Okay, suit yourself. Really, kid, I said it before, but you're the image of the old me. You're your own worst enemy. That's what I've been thinking since I talked to Fingerhut." He chuckled. "How the hell did you get into

172

this fix? Sounds like something I'd do. Only I'd find a way to pull out. I don't understand why you didn't have your girl scraped. Or if you planned to stay with her, why you didn't marry her."

"You were right the first time. You don't understand," said Carter, hoping Eddie didn't know the entire story.

"Maybe I do, better than you think. I'd hate to see you fuck yourself up."

"Then why gouge money out of me? We're going to need it for doctor bills."

"Oh, that. That's business. You shouldn't have tried to put one over on me. Besides, I saw the T-Bird, and from what Fingerhut says, her family has dough. This won't break you. But lemme warn you, kid"—his face grew serious—"I'd look this one over real careful. There aren't too many ways to come out of it a winner. Since the baby's not yours, that makes a bad situation much worse. Keep your . . ."

"What! Who told you that?"

"Fingerhut."

"How did he know?"

"That son-of-a-bitch knows everything. He has eyes in the back of his head, and agents everywhere. Don't cross him or he'll . . ."

At a heavy knock on the door the stereo needle skipped a groove. "Speaking of the devil, that must be Hatchet Head." Eddie went to let him in.

Growling on a choker leash, Patton sprang into the room, dragging Fingerhut, who had on a blue suit and wrap-around sunlasses, and carried a black briefcase under one arm. He bore a remarkable resemblance to a blind beggar, and as always, walked in an unsteady gait—more so now that the dog jerked him off balance.

"Jesus Christ, hold on to that bastard," said Eddie, giving ground as Patton lifted his snout above cruelly pointed teeth.

"Heel, Patton! Heel, dammit!" Wrenching the leash, Fingerhut raised the dog onto his hind legs, squeezing from his throat a tortured whine of submission. When he fell back onto his front paws, Patton skulked behind his master's thigh and followed him obediently across the room. Fingerhut knotted the leash to the leg of a wrought-iron table and commanded him to lie down before he seated himself, unzipped the briefcase, and removed a sheaf of papers. "Have you told White why we're here?"

"He knows."

"I don't know anything. What is this?"

Fingerhut pivoted awkwardly from the waist up, leading with his massive chin in which the cleft gaped like an empty eye socket. "I won't mince words. You're a liar, White. You violated your verbal contract with Eddie Brown."

"What contract?" Carter saw no advantage in conceding anything, and intended to fight on every point.

"Listen to the little . . ."

Fingerhut raised a hand to restrain Eddie. "During the polygraph test, you answered yes when asked whether you were under contract to Eddie Brown."

"Maybe I was lying."

"That's not what the machine said. As a matter of fact . . ."

"Okay, Fingerhut, this isn't Perry Mason. Quit beating around the bush. I want my money."

Lunging straight ahead, Patton nearly buried his fangs in Eddie's buttocks.

"Down, Patton! Stand clear, Eddie. You're riling the dog."

"Goddamn! He could have chomped off both ass cheeks in one bite."

"I don't have all night." Carter started to get up, but at Patton's malevolent growl, reconsidered. "What do you claim to know?"

"White, we know everything. We know you're not married. We know Elaine Yost is pregnant and we know that her father *doesn't* know—about you or the baby. The two of you are living illegally in a state of lewd cohabitation. It's a crime punishable by . . ."

"Oh wow, Fingerhut, let's not overdo this." Eddie turned to Carter. "The point is, unless you cough up the cash, we'll call this guy Yost and tell him about his daughter."

Fingerhut wheeled sharply on Eddie. "Remember what I said. No blackmail! You don't have the right to demand punitive fees. You can collect the money he owes, plus expenses, but nothing more."

Now Carter did rise, cautiously keeping the chair between the dog and him. "This is nonsense. What proof do you have? Who told you these lies? And how do I know you won't use them even if I pay you?"

"I hope you're not questioning my professional integrity. The polygraph test provided proof, but friends of mine in Washington did a little additional digging, and there's no way you can worm out of this, White. As for what will be done with the evidence, you have my word as a licensed private detective that the matter will end once you've paid off."

"Suppose I don't agree"

"Then Eddie will use the information to recover his damages."

"Which means calling her father and blackmailing him."

"Not at all. He'll simply ask Yost to make good the debts you and his daughter have incurred."

"She had nothing to do with it."

"That's a question for the courts to decide—if you care to carry it that far."

"All right, how much do I owe you?" he asked of Eddie.

"Five hundred bucks."

"You're crazy."

"I'm quoting the standard fee."

"You said two hundred and fifty, and I've already paid a hundred."

"That was a special discount—before you rooked me. I've got expenses. Fingerhut and . . ."

"I won't pay it," Carter said adamantly to drive down the price.

"I'm telling you, five hundred's the standard rate."

Carter looked to see if Fingerhut approved.

"Leave me out of this." Pulling a cigar from his breast pocket, he lit it and leaned back, impassive behind the wrap-around sunglasses. He had set the case in motion— had unearthed the facts, "the truth," as he called it—and nothing else mattered to him.

"It's not worth a penny more than two hundred," said Carter.

"Where in hell's your head at, kid? I have to have four hundred to break even."

"All right. I'll give you four hundred," Carter suddenly agreed.

Caught off guard, Eddie nodded. "You're jerking me around like a yo-yo, but I'll take it just to get you out of my hair."

"Since I paid a hundred in October, I owe three hundred more."

175

"I don't believe you. You'd steal the nickels off a dead nigger's eyes. Four hundred!"

"When do you want it?" asked Carter, weakening.

"When do I want it!" Eddie smacked his forehead in exasperation, scattering dandruff from his parched scalp. "I want it now. This minute!"

"I told you I don't have any money on me."

"Write a check."

"I don't have my book, and there's not enough in the account," he lied.

"What do you suggest? Monthly installments?" Allowing Patton wide berth, Eddie stepped over to the stereo and switched it off. "I only have so much patience."

"I could give you two hundred next week and the balance after the first of the year."

"What can you do?" Eddie sighed wearily, addressing no one in particular. "You deal with losers and they drain you. Okay, kid, call me when you have the bread. But I'm warning you, if you gimme another hand job, I'll send Hatchet Head after you." He nodded vaguely toward Fingerhut and Patton.

"Who the hell are you referring to?" Fingerhut dropped the briefcase, spilling papers, and lurched to his feet along with Patton. "I ought to . . ."

"You ought to pick up your bookbag and go home. You'll get your money when I get mine. A lot of help you've been!"

"You better watch your mouth, little man, or . . ."

Patton was barking and the wrought-iron table had begun to totter, when the front door opened—it was as if a vacuum had been cracked—and Ebba came in, carrying Tiger. "Oh, aren't you finished?" The poodle squirmed out of her arms, yapping playfully, and dashed at Patton, who lowered his head savagely, toppling the table behind him. Tiger ran right into his jaws, as deep into the crunching teeth as she could go, and Ebba and she let out the same high keening wail. Carter's ears popped.

"Call him off," screamed Eddie. "Call off your goddamn dog."

"Heel, Patton, heel!"

Unheeding, he tossed his head, snapping Tiger like a flimsy rag.

"I'll give the bastard a heel." Eddie dealt him a vicious kick in the ribs. But althouh Patton shot back one dark implacable eye, marking his next victim, he didn't drop Tiger.

Fingerhut hurled Eddie aside, grabbed Patton by the raised fur at his neck, and drove the cigar deep into the dog's ear. Patton's mouth split to the limit, flashing full of white teeth and a curled pink tongue, and emitted a harsh cry. Tiger tumbled limply to the floor, moaning much like Ebba, who had collapsed into Eddie's arms.

"Heel, Patton!" When Fingerhut smacked the dog on the snout, the jaws snapped shut like a sprung trap. Patton tucked tail and retreated, and Fingerhut picked up what was left of Tiger, whose backbone had burst through the fur. Though she had ceased whimpering, her tiny paws still scrabbled the air.

"Give her to me," said Eddie.

Carter, too, extended a hand in instinctive supplication. But Fingerhut muttered, "This dog's dead," and to make sure, twisted her neck. As Tiger's bowels burst, a long black string popped onto his shoe.

"You simple shit, you've killed her." Seizing a brass lamp, Eddie rushed Fingerhut.

"Wait a minute. Calm down." Fingerhut flinched, surrendering the poodle.

"Get out of here before I crack your head open."

"I . . . I didn't mean . . ."

"I don't give a damn. Get out." Eddie hugged Tiger to his chest.

Recovering, Fingerhut drew himself up to his full height, gathered his papers and briefcase, and hauled Patton out the door.

More than a minute passed as Carter stood by helplessly, silently, having almost forgotten why he was there. Then Eddie said, "You, too. Get the hell out of here. And don't forget my money." Stroking Tiger's matted fur, he murmured, "This is your fault."

Carter descended to the dim garage, where Fingerhut, his foot on the bumper of a station wagon, was using a Kleenex to buff his shoe. In the front seat Patton had his wet snout against the windshield, fogging the glass with his quick, heavy breath. As Carter walked by, the dog barked and Fingerhut said, "I want to talk to you."

"I don't have anything to say to you."

"Then maybe you'd better listen." Discarding the Kleenex, he straightened to his full height, just as he had done upstairs. He depended on his size and could make

177

himself appear bigger by sucking in his breath like a blowfish. But Carter noticed for the first time that their eyes were level. Fingerhut might even have had to lift that cudgel of a chin one grudging centimeter, and his weight alone wouldn't intimidate Carter. Perhaps realizing this, Fingerhut played a new card. "How would you like to learn the name of the baby's father?"

Carter hadn't intended to stop, but did.

"You ought to know." Fingerhut sounded sincere. His mind, which must have operated much like the polished revolver he packed under his armpit, couldn't conceive of anyone who didn't share his voracity for facts, his intolerance of the unknown.

"I'm not interested," Carter managed to say.

"Think it over. I'll give you the information cheap, as a favor. You must want the truth."

As he had done earlier that day, Carter pressed on his bad leg, fighting back the temptation. "What would you know about the truth?"

"I know the name of the father and a few other things, too. I'll let you have . . ."

"Go to hell."

"Hey, wait a minute." He clutched at his elbow, but Carter wrenched free and went to the car. Driving up the ramp, he saw Fingerhut in the rear-view mirror, his foot on the bumper, briskly shining his shoe.

Carter's anger subdued his confusion, then his better judgment overcame both. If he didn't calm down, Elaine would see something was wrong, and though he was certain he'd handled Eddie and Fingerhut correctly, he feared telling her where he had been. She might have a breakdown, or a miscarriage.

Yet it would be hard to fool her—much more difficult than duping Fingerhut and Eddie—and, moreover, he didn't want to deceive her. He valued their closeness, realizing it was his complete honesty with her which allowed him to live a lie with everyone else. Now he'd have to live a deception at home too, and of all the misfortunes this might cause, he regretted most the threat of being excluded from her.

Wearing a white flannel nightgown, Elaine sat on the couch, shivering in the dark. She had pulled up her feet and hugged her knees to her breasts. When he flicked on a lamp, she averted her eyes, but he could see she'd

178

been crying and for an instant thought she knew, that somehow someone had told her. "What's wrong?"

"Where have you been?" she asked angrily.

"I told you I had to work."

"No, you didn't. I called the restaurant and you weren't . . ." Choking and coughing, she began to cry.

He tried to take her in his arms, but she wouldn't let him. "I was lonely and wanted to talk to you, but you weren't there."

"I was . . . Christmas shopping. I'd planned to surprise you. I didn't mean to scare you."

"I wasn't scared." She sniffed. "Just hurt that you lied to me."

"I didn't lie. It was supposed to be a surprise. I couldn't find anything. You'll have to come with me next time."

She blotted her cheeks on the sleeve of her nightgown. "I guess I was a little scared."

"About what?"

"Everything. Maybe that you'd leave me. And that made me so damn mad I . . ."

"You know I wouldn't."

"That's not what I meant. I was mad at myself. I've become such a clinging vine. I didn't use to be like this."

"And you won't be once it's over."

"No, I won't. I swear I won't." She smacked her knee. "But now there are so many horrible things that could happen. I can't stop thinking about them, and there seem to be more every day. What if something's wrong with the baby?"

"There won't be."

"What if there is? What if it's deformed or retarded or . . ."

"Elaine, don't do that. No matter what happens, we'll take care of it."

A look of annoyance came to her face. "That's easy for you to say. But if it is deformed, no one will adopt it, and I'll have to live with that thought."

"No, it's not easy for me to say, and I'll have to live with it too. That and a lot else. I know this is hard on you. Don't make it impossible by worrying about things that are out of your control."

Sobbing, she whispered, "Yes. You're right," and lowered her head to his lap. She wanted to say more, but when nothing would come, he carried her into the bedroom. As he tugged the covers up to her shoulders, she

179

managed to murmur, "I'm not mad any more. Really, I'm not. I just can't stop crying. Please, lie down beside me."

Still dressed for work, he stretched out on the spread and stroked her wet cheek. The caress comforted them both. Elaine was quiet, and Carter closed his eyes. He hadn't realized how tired he was. He tried to stay awake by thinking over the day, but the darkness weighed heavily upon him. It took energy even to stroke her cheek and, at first, sleep itself seemed an exertion. Yet finally he dozed off with his hand touching her damp face.

Chapter XI

1

When Carter woke, something slipped from his shoulders. Elaine's robe. Her bed was empty, and he heard her in the kitchen. In spite of his clothes and the rumpled covers, he had slept soundly and felt refreshed. As he saw by the clock radio, he was an hour late for work, yet he didn't hurry and wasn't worried. Last night all the adrenalin had been wrung out of him, and he was glad to have gotten past that.

In the bathroom he had lathered his cheeks and begun to shave when Elaine brought him coffee. She, too, seemed better—serene and unconcerned, as if crying had become such an integral part of her life she no longer had to account for it. Draped in the white gown, with her hair down and her face free of make-up, she looked like a young girl at her First Communion. "Do you mind if I watch?"

"It won't be interesting. I never cut myself. My skin's too tough."

"My father is fair-skinned and each morning has tiny pieces of tissue paper stuck to his face."

"A brave man."

"Would you like more coffee?"

"I've barely touched this cup." Carter scraped his upper lip. "I have to draw some money from the account."

"Do you have the checkbook?" She was in the doorway, her shoulder against the jamb.

"Quite a bit of money," he emphasized.

"Is there enough?"

"Yes. I'll need about two hundred. You see, I have to join a union at work, and there's a Christmas collection for the kitchen crew, and the car has . . ."

"If you have to buy any other gifts, I'll look in the

shops around here. How about your sister and her husband?"

"We'll send a card."

"Do you mind if I buy a few things for relatives and friends?"

"Of course not. As long as you're careful." He smacked aftershave lotion on his face. "The money may get tight when we pay our medical bills."

"I could always cash . . ."

"No, we'll make it on our own. Excuse me. I have to dress." He kissed her as he passed, pleased she had asked no questions, and positive she wouldn't find out about Eddie and Fingerhut."

When Carter arrived at Danny Boy's, Ned Cervik called him to the office, but instead of a reprimand, offered a bloodless smile and said, "Sit down, Sport. Good job you did on the inventory. I'd forgotten half the supplies we have in stock. We won't fold this month after all."

Carter sat in front of Cervik, so close their knees touched, and once again wondered what Rita and he did in here. Only a contortionist could have warded off cramps.

"It's not easy to get good men these days. Not young ones." The smile drained into his pockmarks like water through a sieve. He was nervous, and if there had been more room, might have paced. Gingerly he raked his fingers over his scalp where new hair had rooted. Its curving strips resembled rows of eyebrows, an amazed expression multiplied a dozen times. "A word of advice, don't count on your children. My oldest boy is in North Beach shacked up with a nigger."

"I'm very . . ."

"No, no." Cervik waved his hands. "Don't worry about my troubles. Although I have plenty. It's hard for a man my age to change. Hell, it's hard at any age!" He glared, as if Carter had suggested he was old. "This is a bad time for Rita, too, and I'm helping her out. She's a wonderful girl. You'd agree if you knew her like I do. She's had a rough life. She's divorcing her second husband, and I . . . I imagine I'll marry her."

"Congratulations." Carter feebly sought to relieve the

silence, which he didn't understand any better than the conversation.

"Of course, I'm already married and . . . Look, Sport, all I really want to do is congratulate you on your progress. Before long you'll have a Danny Boy's of your own. I've spoken to Reichlederfer, and he agrees you have talent, but lack experience. So I'm going to let you have a crack at the yearly report. It should be a hell of a challenge." He opened a desk drawer that contained a colorful rat's nest of receipts, bills, and canceled checks. "Everything's right here. All you have to do is put it in order and fill out the ledger."

That afternoon Carter cleared the desk top, but because of the pastiche of trivia under the glass, it still looked cluttered, and when he dug out the tangle of papers, the confusion increased. He made two piles, one for requisitions and invoices, the other for receipts and canceled checks, then had to start a third stack for Cervik's personal effects. There were unpaid bills, unanswered memos, dunning letters from lawyers, a summons, and an odd miscellany of mementos—motel matchbooks, a red rayon scarf, an ankle bracelet, and three miniature bottles of Scotch from an airplane flight.

He couldn't comprehend why Cervik had allowed him —had ordered him—to sift through this debris, unless, in utter bewilderment himself, he hoped Carter would find some meaning in his life. But Carter could only conclude the obvious—that Cervik was aging and in agony because of it, that he had a wife and children, yet was in love, or otherwise involved, with Rita Phipps. The restaurant appeared to be in worse shape than his personal affairs. The records didn't indicate how deeply it had fallen into debt, but Cervik was on shaky grounds and again had placed his faith—perhaps this was the ultimate measure of his despair—in Carter's ability to rescue him.

Carter didn't welcome the assignment, for the mess this man had made of his life reminded him of the chaos he had struggled to govern in his own. Though he thought the tide had turned, he knew his battles were far from won and was unwilling to be swept into Cervik's. Yet he worked the rest of the week, elbow-deep in confetti, and through sheer artifice and arbitrary selection, finishd on Monday. He had no idea whether they were correct, but sturdy columns of figures paraded across the pages, and now just one layer of disorder remained, preserved beneath the pane of glass.

Tuesday afternoon, buoyed by this success, he asked for a few hours off and drove downtown to pay Eddie Brown. They met in the nickel-plated diner on Hoover Street, where Eddie greeted him with the same amicable exuberance he had shown in his apartment. He couldn't have forgotten how that evening of angry accusations had ended. Yet he seemed to assume that a bond still existed between them, for if Eddie was a chiseler, he was, also, a sculptor of sorts, driven by creative passion, and he felt a special fondness for Carter, his masterpiece. Slinging an arm around his shoulder, he dragged him onto a stool. "Take a load off, kid. You're looking good. I watched you walk up the street and you acted like you owned it. What's more, you didn't limp. Did you know that?"

"No." People in the diner were staring.

"I'm glad you stopped. On an older guy a limp sometimes looks good. But you're young. Why screw things up with a limp? Here, lemme buy you a cup of coffee."

"I can't stay. The boss thinks I'm taking my wife to the doctor's."

Chuckling, Eddie ordered the coffee anyway. "Your wife! Christ, kid, you got that guy by the balls."

A mirror behind the counter presented a warped image of them and of the scene beyond the front window. Pedestrians and automobiles passed by, but to Carter they seemed stationary and the diner appeared to be moving, chugging along over rusty rails. He and Eddie looked like men who had traveled—in opposite directions. While Eddie wore a maroon Edwardian coat, Carter had on a conservative business suit, and although they might have come from different centuries, he looked older. Perhaps it was his size.

"Here's your money." To jostle his vision into perspective, he extracted an envelope from his breast pocket. Of course, this little man had the goods on him, yet seen in the mirror, Carter might have been a rich uncle surprising his nephew with a gift. "I'll have the rest after New Year's."

"Sure, kid. How's Elaine? You must be cut off by now. Maybe I could set up a trick for you."

"She's fine."

184

Eddie folded the envelope, kissed it, and stuffed it into his wallet. "This bread is going to a good cause. Ebba and I are flying up to Vegas for the holidays. Think of us Christmas Eve. We'll be doing a stand-up quickie at the kino tables."

"That'll put my mind at ease." Smiling, Carter said, "Can I ask a personal question?"

"They're the only kind I like."

"Are you ever sad?"

Eddie laughed. "All the time."

"I'm serious."

"So am I. Even when I'm joking."

"Do you ever feel down?"

Swiveling on the stool, Eddie scratched his scalp. "Yeah, sure. I don't let it bother me, though. I got no time for it. Worrying about what might happen, or what has happened, is shit for the birds."

"If you don't worry, worse things might happen."

"What are you, a preacher? Look, kid, I'm no fool. I take care of myself and I'm on my toes all the time. But I could get up from this counter, go outside, and have some dumb fucker drop a brick on my head. Am I supposed to worry about that? Christ Almighty, there wouldn't be time for anything else."

"What do you do when you're depressed?"

"Nothing. Just live and let it pass. It's like anything else. It comes and goes, if you give it a chance. But when you pick at it, it bleeds. That's why I say thank God for work. If it weren't for jobs, there'd be a lot more loonies loose on the streets. Speaking of which"—he stood up— "I'd better go back upstairs." He cuffed Carter on the arm. "Buck up, kid. Don't sweat the small stuff. You shouldn't worry about all the crazy shit that drops out of the sky. It'll hit you sooner or later. You just have to be ready to shake it off."

"Thanks. That makes me feel much better." Carter couldn't help smiling sourly. Then he brushed a large flake of dandruff from Eddie's velvet lapel.

"Any time, kid."

2

As Christmas approached, Elaine responded to the holiday season with a zeal he couldn't comprehend or share. She took a childish delight in decorating the apartment and in sending and receiving gifts. Each day the mailbox disgorged dozens of cards from her relatives and friends, and she taped them above the fireplace in a tall triangle like a fir tree. As its limbs expanded, she glowed at the sight, and her face reflected brilliant colors. Carter presumed she was flattered that people had remembered her, but as she told him one night, the matter was deeper and more complex.

"A week ago I couldn't believe I'd live to see Christmas. Oh, it wasn't that I thought I'd die. I was just so miserable, I couldn't imagine a time when I wouldn't be. Then as the cards started coming, I realized there are people, places, everything, out there, and someday this will be over. It may sound stupid, but I'd lost sight of that." Embracing him, she said, "I can't wait. Can you?"

"For what?"

"For Christmas, silly."

She bought a strand of lights for the front window, a yule log for the coffee table, a wreath for the door, and a small fir tree. She loved the scent, the colors red and green, the sense of her own renewal. From daily shopping trips down Santa Monica and Sunset boulevards, a red flame, like a poinsettia leaf, had blossomed on her cheeks.

But that Saturday, when Carter mentioned her appointment at the Harold Wendell Agency, the flames flickered out. She begged him to come along and insisted he drive. Chain-smoking and biting her lower lip as they cruised downtown beneath a canopy of lights, she said nothing, yet he didn't have to ask what was wrong. Again it was as if she had forgotten she was pregnant and in Los Angeles to relinquish her baby.

While she went off with Miss Dugan, Carter waited in the lobby. He had brought along his law books, but after a perfunctory glance at one text, he leafed through a stack of magazines, reading the ads, the counter-news. Opposite an article about breast cancer was an ad for brassieres. A picture of a handsome Negro who had just bought life insurance faced an editorial on race riots. Laid out cheek by jowl were a report on an airplane crash and a snapshot of a Caribbean island which was two hours by air from New York City.

He hoped Elaine wasn't too shaken. From the beginning he'd feared her seasonal euphoria wouldn't last and that she would take the fall hard. At least he could help her more now that her blind confidence no longer matched the airbrushed faces which peered up at him from the magazines. At these cosmetically smiling cretins he could only stare back in disbelief, reluctant to press too hard, tear through the slick surface, and find on succeeding pages the familiar fear, hopelessness, and failure.

"I'm sorry to disturb you. Elaine told me you'd be studying," said Miss Dugan, who could see he wasn't.

He left *Look* open to a feminine hygiene ad.

"How have you been?" she asked.

"Busy."

"Have I told you what a remarkable girl Elaine is? So mature and articulate. We never have trouble with even the most difficult subjects."

"I'm glad it's going well."

"Are you?" Her eyebrows arched. "You're an amazing person yourself. You seem to lack any resentment. I'd like to talk to you sometime."

"About my lack of resentment?"

"I'm sure we'd have other things to discuss." She folded her arms and crossed her legs at the ankle so that the slightest movement set off the grating from her stockings. As always a pair of sunglasses was saddled on her head. "Unfortunately Elaine was distracted today. Is anything wrong?"

"She forgot her appointment and was upset when I reminded her. I think it's easy to understand why."

"You do? Maybe we could discuss that during our talk."

Since Carter didn't reply, Miss Dugan mumbled a few more remarks, then left as Elaine emerged from the doctor's office, carrying a manila folder. She looked cheerful and buoyant again. Kissing his cheek, she apologized for making him wait, and when they went outside, suggested he fold back the Thunderbird's top.

Though clear, the day was cool, especially in the shade, and he asked, "Do you think it's warm enough?"

"We'll turn on the heater."

But the heater, even at its highest speed, was little help once they reached the freeway. Carter shivered, and Elaine slouched low on the seat, looking up at the sky. A rash of goose bumps spilled down her throat and onto her hands, which clasped the folder.

"This is exhilarating," she said as the Christmas euphoria reappeared. "Would you stop at Century City?"

"Do you have to buy medicine?" He thought the folder contained prescriptions.

"No. A surprise. A Christmas present. I've gotten a gift for everyone except you."

"You don't have to. I . . ."

"No, I want to." Her cold hand gripped his wrist.

At Century City they entered an elevated garage, where the squeal of tires unraveled his nerves as they circled the ramp, searching for a parking place. He tried one narrow slot, sawing the car back and forth a few minutes, but grew impatient and drove on to the next level. His goose flesh felt permanent; he couldn't stop shivering. Elaine's face was raw from the wind and she hugged her arms across her breasts. Yet she was still smiling, and once he'd found a place, she hurried him to the escalator.

Along the concrete mall shoppers marched, slightly out of cadence, to the tune of Christmas carols broadcast by loudspeakers in the shrubbery, and they bore their gaudily wrapped packages with seasonal abandon, as though they had discovered in compulsive buying a source of joy and release. About the eyes they resembled Elaine, intoxicated by the glitter. Also like her, they hastened through the shadows, sensing there an intimation of real winter, of icy mortality deep in the stone buildings.

A plastic ten-foot-tall Santa occupied a huge alcove at one department store, smacking his red belly with rubber hands and asking at electrically timed intervals, "Ho, ho, ho, and what do you want?" Crowds of children gathered about, giving careful consideration to their answers. Nearby a lady in a Salvation Army uniform tucked her buttocks together, waddled around a pot, and rang her bell.

Elaine led Carter to the men's department at I. Magnin's, where she'd had a beige suede coat put away for him. As he tried it on, another bell, making a much different sound—a persistent *bong, bong, bong*—seemed to toll the minutes rather than the hours.

"Do you like it?"

"It's very nice." He couldn't work any spirit into his voice. "How much does it cost?"

"That doesn't matter. Turn around. Do you think it

188

fits?" she asked the clerk, a Christmas substitute, a few years younger than they.

"It's perfect through the shoulders," he responded with poorly counterfeited expertise.

"I'd have to buy a whole new wardrobe," said Carter, staring into a three-way mirror. It was a handsome coat, but something held him back. Her enthusiasm, even her generosity, puzzled him. "I don't have any pants to match."

"This coat can be worn with anything," said the clerk.

"How much is it?" he insisted.

"Two hundred and ten dollars," said the boy before Elaine could interrupt.

"No fair. You're not supposed to know." She produced a book of traveler's checks. "If you like it, I want you to have it."

Carter slipped the coat from his shoulders into the clerk's hands. "No."

"Don't be silly."

"Shall I have it wrapped?" asked the clerk.

"Yes."

"No." In the background the bell *bonged* half a dozen times. "Where did you get that money?"

"Never mind." She had signed one check and started a second.

Carter urged her off to one side where the boy couldn't hear. "Is it from the account? We're going to need it. Don't you remember I withdrew . . ."

"It's my money. I brought it for emergencies. There's plenty more."

"No, don't use it," he said, bewildered and a bit angry. "This is no emergency."

After this first purchase, they tramped silently and grimly from one department to another. She bought him three shirts and an electric razor. He got her a cashmere sweater and a beautiful nightgown of imported lace. Rubbing its softness to her cheek, she said she would wear it in the hospital—at which he bought her a red silk robe. When the orgy of commerce had finally ended, they walked to the car, hearts heavy, arms laden with gifts. Carter wished he knew what was wrong. The plastic Santa still slapped his hollow paunch and asked what everyone wanted.

While Elaine prepared dinner, he sat in bed, swaddled in a woolly blanket, warming himself. On the bureau their gifts, wrapped in glinting foil, looked like gold ingots decorated with superfluous bows and ribbons, and on the top box rested the manila folder. For half an hour he wondered not so much what was in it as why he cared, why it caused his heart to pound. He knew he shouldn't open it. It was an insult to Elaine that he wanted to. Then, to end the matter for good, he asked himself how he would like it if she looked through his personal possessions, and that ruined everything. He had no secrets, and wouldn't have minded. And so by a curious reverse logic he concluded he should look, if only to prove how foolish he had been.

Shrugging the blanket from his shoulders, he threw his feet over the edge of the bed. His chattering teeth might have been audible to Elaine in the kitchen. One step brought him to the bureau, and he flipped back the thin sheet of cardboard.

There, under the heading of Mother's Confidential Statement, was the information he had paid Eddie Brown to hide, including a name, William Garrett, which answered the question "Father, if known?" Farther down, after a query about religious preferences, Elaine had scribbled "I'm Episcopal, but wouldn't object if the baby were placed with any family of a standard Protestant background—Methodist, Lutheran, or Presbyterian."

He stared at the page a full minute, his emotions in turmoil. He couldn't tell whether he was angry, afraid, profoundly shocked, or all three. Shutting the folder, he climbed back into bed and pulled up the covers. Though he'd stopped shivering, he felt very cold.

His first impulse was to confront Elaine with this evidence . . . Of what? The baby had a father, whether Carter knew his name or not, and her religious beliefs—he was surprised she had any—were her own business. But why had she left the folder where he would see it?

Thinking back over the day, he pondered the part Miss Dugan might have played in this. Was there, in her praise of Elaine, an implicit judgment of him . . . that he wasn't good enough for her? Carter bristled at the suggestion, and his angry blood beat faster, just as it had when she'd stood before him in the waiting room, her arms folded and legs crossed. He couldn't have said whether her attitude was one of instinctive self-protection or coiled malignancy. She appeared to fear and dislike him at the same time. Perhaps she had passed on to Elaine this tangled reaction. There was something insinuating in the way she probed. What did she want to know? What had she said to Elaine? Or Elaine to her?

For the remainder of the week questions came in clusters he couldn't answer. It might have helped to talk to Elaine, yet that would have upset her, and his strategy had been to keep her calm, to postpone all doubts until after the baby was born. On Wednesday, when she received a card from her parents with a cashier's check for five hundred dollars enclosed, it took all his powers of self-control to curb his irritation. The imperturbability with which she accepted the money, and without a word to him, put it into her purse, made his delicate handling of Eddie Brown seem pointless and melodramatic. She could have paid him out of her petty cash.

3

By Christmas Eve Carter imagined himself the legendary Dutch boy, determined to hold back the cold shrouding seas. In the living room this particular dike of molded concrete seemed to have surrounded him. The apartment offered no shelter now. Even had he possessed the agility, he didn't have enough fingers to plug up all the leaks, and here was one barrier too high to hurdle. He could only wait and watch as other chinks widened in the protective walls. He knew he and Elaine would drown unless he kept his head clear, above the riptide.

They ate early that evening, showered separately—although Elaine insisted on this, she didn't say why—and curled up in their robes next to the tree. She had shampooed her hair and left it down to dry, and in shifting needles of brightness, it glittered like the strand of lights in the window. She was checking her Christmas card list to make certain she hadn't forgotten anyone.

Though Carter had a book—*Preparing for the Law Boards*—in his lap, he couldn't study. The examination still seemed a long way off, and the subject bored him. As the autumn quarter ended, he had resigned himself to a C in law. But his history professor, Dr. Durand, had written on his term paper: "This is a well-reasoned essay, full of insights I wish you had developed further. Your ideas seem to be your own, fairly gained and personally expressed—which is one way of learning what others have said before you. Next time try to do more research. Have you ever thought of graduate school? I'd be happy to recommend you. A—."

The grade pleased him. He'd done well in the course and had enjoyed it. But the professor's question, presenting other possibilities, bothered Carter. When he mused about the future, he never got much beyond late January, when the baby was due.

"How do you usually spend Christmas?" Elaine interrupted his woolgathering.

"A lot like this. When my parents were alive, I went home. Marion and Ray were there, too."

"Was it a happy occasion?"

"Not particularly. I don't mean it was sad. You'd have to know my family to understand. They never got excited. They were quiet. Maybe 'shy' is a better word."

"That's too bad."

"No, it wasn't bad. It just wasn't anything special."

"I wonder why your sister didn't send you a card?"

"We don't have much in common any more."

"That's a shame. Christmas was a wonderful time in my family. No matter where we traveled, we dragged along our ornaments and decorations. We even hung our stockings. In some countries the people must have thought we were crazy. Of course, on Christmas day we went to church and to the embassy for turkey dinner. You went to church, too, didn't you?"

"Yes. To midnight Mass."

"Are you going tonight?"

He paused a second to be sure she was serious. "No."

"I thought I might go with you."

"To a Catholic church?"

"At Christmas, what's the difference? I've been to midnight Mass before and . . ."

"The same difference as every other day of the year."

"You know what I mean. Everyone attends church at Christmas. It doesn't matter where."

"You don't believe in God," he said, trying to keep his voice neutral, "yet you'd go to church?"

As her cheeks reddened, she fretted with the ends of her damp hair. "It's like your believing, yet not going."

"I certainly wouldn't go tonight. Not after skipping all year."

"At least you're consistent. Why don't we drop this. It's silly." Before he could speak, she slipped her arms around his neck. "Every time we talk about religion, you remind me of a Jesuit. Maybe you missed your calling." Propping her head against his chest, she whispered, "I'm lonely. I'll be your family this year, if you'll be mine."

He felt he had to convince her of something about himself, not his religious beliefs. After all, what did it really mean to be a Catholic? But a hard knock at the door cut him short. "With both families present and accounted for, who could that be?" He gave her a reassuring pat. "I'll get it."

Carter was dumbfounded to see the Regans, and couldn't respond when Mr. Regan wished him Merry Christmas.

The man was wearing one of his golf outfits, a powder-blue sweater and yellow trousers. Mrs. Regan, her mouth pinched between her sharp nose and chin, looked as though she wanted no part of him.

"Thought you might like company tonight. And maybe a drink." Regan held out a bottle of bourbon.

"Glad to have you. Won't you come in?"

"We'll only stay a minute," Mrs. Regan said as she entered.

Mr. Regan, preceding Carter into the apartment, said over his shoulder, "Guess what the weather is back East. Twenty-six and snowing in Cleveland. Forty-three and raining in Washington. The poor suckers." In the living room he collapsed onto the couch, and although he'd already had too many, asked for a bourbon and water.

His wife refused to drink. Instead she applied a bony hand to Elaine's belly, and the palm must have been cold and clinical as a stethoscope, yet because of its brittleness, sensitive to vibrations. "It just keeps coming, doesn't it? I bet you're miserable."

"I feel fine." Elaine smiled, moving the woman's hand.

"Yeah, now you do, but wait. Do you know what it's like?" She lifted her upper lip to expose yellowing teeth. "It's like pulling your lip up over your head."

"Honey, please."

"Don't honey me. I know what I'm talking about. If people have to have babies, there must be a better way." She sat on the sofa, a calculated distance frrom her husband.

Once they'd settled, they had nothing to say. The Regans were as uncomfortable as Elaine and he, and

193

appeared to recognize that their one common ground was loneliness. Carter regretted they couldn't start by acknowledging the fact, for this might have led to a less limited communication—if nothing else they would have said one thing that was true—whereas ignoring it could only deepen their isolation.

"Well, we had a tenant run out last night," said Mrs. Regan. "The apartment was a mess. Trash in the sink, Tampax in the toilet, and three . . ."

To her relief, she was interrupted by another knock at the door. Carter was far from relieved, and as Elaine looked to him, he couldn't conceal his distress. He knew no one else in Los Angeles whom he cared—or dared—to see. Walking reluctantly through the darkened hall, he answered the door for Ned Cervik and Rita, who darted in swiftly, as though they were being followed.

"Merry Christmas, Sport. Just in the neighborhood and decided to drop by. Didn't roust you out of bed, did we?" He tugged the lapel of Carter's robe.

"No. It's good to see you. How did you find us?"

Rita handed him a rabbit-skin stole. "Your number and address are in the . . ."

"At Danny Boy's we keep close tabs on all our employees. I could use a drink."

When Carter introduced them, the Regans appeared nervous, but Cervik's bluff good humor soon put them at ease. Then he turned to Elaine with boisterous flattery, while Rita, restraining the hem of her red velour miniskirt, sat next to her and asked, "When are you due?"

"Late January."

"Isn't that exciting? I have two of my own. One by each husband. They're a lot of trouble, but they're worth it, if you know what I mean. They're good company and all." Her hair, recently rinsed pink, glowed above the red dress like the revolving globe on a barber pole.

Carter and Cervik went into the kitchen to mix drinks. "Hope you don't mind us barging in on you, Sport."

"Not at all."

"Good. Rita said you wouldn't't." Loosening his tie, he leaned over the breakfast bar. His porous face and perforated scalp had the consistency of pumice stone. He looked very old and very tired. "Well, I did it." He toasted Carter with a shot of bourbon. "I told my wife I'm leaving."

Carter didn't know whether to congratulate him.

"She took it harder than I expected." Cervik's eyes watered when he drank. "Thirty years is a long time. But you can't hold back what has to happen. Here's to the new year." He emptied a second jigger.

Back in the living room, as Carter sat down, an uncomfortable silence settled along with him. Although the congregation of loneliness had increased by two, nothing had changed, and again he wondered whether they shouldn't discuss this.

Instead they talked about Christmas. Or, that is, the others did, corroborating what Elaine had said. Christmas had been a special occasion when they were young, and they looked on it fondly, though they admitted it didn't have much meaning unless you were a child or had children. After saying this, Cervik, Rita, and the Regans stared into their laps, at the core of themselves from which children had come, then glanced at Elaine as if expecting—and hoping—she would give birth at any moment.

Carter regretted he had said he wouldn't attend midnight Mass and was tempted to suggest that they all go. Anything to escape the apartment. If they stayed much longer, they might . . .

The phone rang, and six heads snapped straight. Elaine turned to Carter, and he looked away, racking his mind to remember who else had their number. In a murmurous, threatening intrusion a few names oozed to the surface. Eddie. Fingerhut . . . It rang again. "Aren't we popular tonight?" He reached for the phone.

"Long distance calling person to person for Elaine Yost."

His throat tightened. "Elaine, it's for you. Probably an old boy friend." This got a laugh, but when he released the receiver, it bore a moist palm print.

"Mother! What a surprise!" Her expression was one of alarm rather than surprise, and her cheeks paled like warm wax in the lamplight.

"It's her mother calling from Costa Rica," Carter explained. "We'd better hold it down."

No one had said a word. They were looking at Elaine. When he realized what he had revealed, he closed his eyes and wanted never to open them. At six points on his body—temples, wrists, chest, and knee—there was a steady beating pulse. Though he looked up at last, he couldn't read Cervik's reaction.

"Fine," said Elaine as the color came back to her face. "I hear you perfectly. I'd love to say hello to Daddy. Yes, I got your card. Thanks for the gift. Sorry, it was impossible. Of course I miss you. No, I'm not lonely. I have friends here. A small, impromptu party. You know Southern California."

As she let them speak, Carter tried to catch her eye, but couldn't.

"Sounds like they don't trust you with their little girl," said Cervik.

"When you have a daughter, you . . ." Regan finished on a failing breath and a loud hiccup.

As they all laughed, Carter was relieved. Maybe Cervik hadn't heard her say Daddy. Hadn't heard him say Costa Rica. "How can you please in-laws?"

"With lots of grandchildren," answered Rita.

"My plans are indefinite." Elaine attempted through vagueness to satisfy her parents without divulging anything to the others. "What a shame you couldn't make connections. I'm glad you called. Merry Christmas. Love to you both."

Hanging up, she let out a harsh, erratic laugh. "Did I sound properly repentant? It's been weeks since I've written them."

Carter winced as she said "them," but there was still no indication Cervik understood.

"A letter isn't too much to ask," said Mrs. Regan.

"I do feel bad about not writing."

"How do your parents like living out at Costa Mesa?" asked Regan. "I played golf there years ago."

"Costa . . ."

"Golf's big everywhere these days," Carter rescued Elaine.

"I think it's a bore," said Rita. "My first husband always had a club in his hand, and when he wasn't hitting a golf ball, he was beating me and the kids."

"That's enough to make anyone swear off the game," said Cervik, rattling the ice in his glass.

"But Costa . . ."

"How about a refill?" Carter cut in again, and this time Elaine realized something was wrong—something more drastic than the phone call.

He served Cervik a triple shot in a thumbleful of water, and hoped for the best. Fortunately he could count on Rita's being oblivious. For a moment they had difficulty discovering a topic of conversation until Carter mentioned Danny Boy's, and the Regans took up the slack, asking Ned Cervik about an order of bad onion rings they had once eaten. Mrs. Regan flourished at this recollection of food poisoning and painful bouts in the bathroom, for while scatology was her penchant, plumbing was an absolute fixation.

"Well," she concluded, "I'll have to admit, it cleaned out our systems."

At this, she dragged her husband to his feet, asked for the bottle—no more than an inch of bourbon lay at the bottom—and said good night.

When the liquor disappeared, Cervik and Rita's spirits flagged, and they, too, decided to leave. "Sport, it's been a treat. Take care of the wife. And as for what I told you about Rita and me," Cervik whispered in boozy intimacy as Carter accompanied them to the front door, "mum's the word. You know how rumors get around. One happy family, right?"

Tottering, Rita rose on tiptoes to plant a wet kiss on his cheek. "I think Helen is marvelous."

Then they strolled off unsteadily, propped against one another.

Carter sat for a few minutes, gazing through Elaine, who had folded her legs up under her robe and pulled her hands in at the sleeves, so that her face and black hair seemed strangely suspended above a cloud of pink cotton.

"Do you think they know?" he asked.

"My parents?"

"No, Cervik and Rita," he said, irked at her slow grasp of the situation. "If he was listening, he must realize I lied to him. What else he suspects . . ."

"What have you told him?"

"Briefly, that after your father died we moved out here to be near your mother, who lived in La Jolla."

"Why didn't you let me know?"

"Look, if I started to tell you every lie I've had to concoct since I got to Los Angeles, we'd still be here tomorrow afternoon. Half the time I can't remember which story I've told to whom." He tilted a highball glass to his lips.

"What shall we do?"

"Nothing." The sip of whiskey left an aftertaste of ashes, for one of Rita's soggy cigarette butts had sunk to the bottom of the glass. "If Cervik doesn't mention it, I won't. If he does, I'll tell a few new lies to smooth over the old ones. The worst he could do is fire me. I think we have enough money, don't you?"

"I'd hate to have him know."

"Why? Once the baby's born, we'll never see him again."

"That's not the point."

"What is?"

"I don't want *anyone* to know."

"Sometimes I think you're sorry I know."

She jerked her chin up. Why do you say that?"

"Forget it." He set the glass on an end table. "how about your parents, did they sound suspicious?"

"No. Just surprised that a man answered the phone. It was odd talking to them. For some reason I wanted to tell them about the baby. Isn't that peculiar? It seemed natural to share the news with them. The one bad thing they said was that Mother was in Mexico City last month and had planned to fly here for a visit. Somehow she missed connections." Elaine expelled an uneven sigh. "God, what would we have done?"

At this moment the danger of her mother learning the truth struck Carter as distinctly less menacing than the unnamed, undefinable gloom that had engulfed him. "There would have been nothing to do."

"Well," Elaine mused, "she might have called first from the airport."

"So what? You couldn't run away. You'd have had to face her."

"Yes, of course. But you'd have had time to move out. There wouldn't be any sense complicating matters. It's bad enough to . . ."

"What?" A flash of heat singed his throat. Yet when he touched his tongue to his lips, they tasted cool and sterile as dental instruments. The fire inside him quickly died, and he didn't have the endurance to ask why she would hide him. The question could only lead to a lean, attenuated answer, another question, a slimmer answer, and finally pin them against a stony barrier of silence. "I'm tired," he mumbled. "It's too late. Let's go to bed."

Chapter XII

1

Perhaps it was this question he hadn't asked, or the answer he doubted she could give, or his fear that Cervik knew more than was safe which made Carter miserable during the last week of December. At Danny Boy's he couldn't think, and at the apartment he tried not to. They made love every night in an unspoken admission that contact desperately demanded to be reestablished, but though they touched, they couldn't talk, though they had always assumed their bodies were bearers of truth, they learned the act of love could be a lie, or at least an evasion.

New Year's Eve, sitting by the tree, they ignored one another and looked outward, hoping something would happen. Another phone call. An unforeseen visit. Anything to alleviate the tension which now affected Elaine as much as it did Carter.

Yet nothing happened, and to soften the silence, they switched on TV and watched the inexorable passage of the New Year across the country. In New York City it began as a glowing ball plunged toward the crowd in Times Square. An hour later at a hotel in Chicago people in paper hats danced the box step to sounds of the forties and kissed for the cameras. By the time 1971 crept into Salt Lake City, the town was asleep.

As midnight moved nearer, Elaine begged him to build a fire. It would have been their first.

"It's too late," he said.

"It might cheer us up."

"There's no wood."

"We could use old newspapers."

He didn't answer, but believed that building a fire tonight, after not having had one all fall, would be naggingly

199

false—as false as going to church on Christmas when he hadn't been during the year. He didn't care to be cheered up that way.

At twelve the television throng at the Beverly Hilton beat itself into a frenzy that lasted two minutes as measured by the announcer's watch. An aging cowboy with confetti on his toupee wished for victory in Vietnam, while a voluptuous starlet hoped for peace. Afterward in an old movie the governor of the state scored touchdowns against an imaginary foe.

Later Carter lay spread-eagled in bed, dreaming he was a diver who had plunged from the high board. Serenely he sliced through the air, weightless and invulnerable, until at the last moment he realized he was about to land wrong. Groaning, he pitched out of sleep, yet still felt he was falling. Something was coming and he didn't know what. Crawling to Elaine, he embraced her from behind, but her belly was almost too big to be contained.

Happy to have the holidays end, he helped Elaine take down the lights and throw out the tree, which had shed a circle of brown needles. Monday he started the last unit of the training program—waiting tables, serving up club sandwiches, French fries, and onion rings, and pocketing wet coins left in puddles of Coke. Cervik mentioned nothing about his visit, the phone call, or his own marital problems, but he continually and somewhat apologetically assured Carter he would soon have a restaurant to manage—a promise which would have worried Carter had he not been certain he would be gone by then.

During his study period he read novels, daydreamed, or, less often, reviewed for the Law Board examination. Although law school was one subject which could rouse Elaine from her silent distraction, Carter didn't share her enthusiasm and didn't understand how serious she was, until the night before the exam she treated him like an athlete in training. When he tried to make love to her, she said she didn't think they should.

"Are you afraid it'll drain my memory?"

"Don't make fun of me. You ought to go to bed early and . . ."

"This won't take long."

"You could use the time to review your notes. Would you like me to press your blue suit?"

"What for?"

"To wear tomorrow."

"Christ Almighty, I'm not going to wear a suit. Do you think the Attorney General plans to be there to check us out?"

Refusing to show her irritation, she coaxed him by the arm, "Come on. You're acting like a little boy. This is important. Have a warm drink and go to bed."

Carter skipped the warm drink, but went to bed, bewildered.

In the morning she was cheerful and solicitous, fixed him breakfast, and hid her dismay when once more he wouldn't hear of wearing a suit. She even asked a few review questions.

Too puzzled to pay attention, Carter couldn't understand her behavior, and found these high spirits as baffling as her bad moods. Maybe more so since he remembered the gloom beneath her smiles and dreaded its return. Again, as at Christmas, she seemed to have placed absolute faith in something outside herself, while ignoring what was obvious and most important. Bustling about the apartment, she might have been oblivious, for all he could tell, to the swollen womb which preceded her.

When Elaine dropped him near Royce Hall and headed for her appointment at the Harold Wendell Agency, Carter had a fleeting impression that he didn't know where he was. After a semester of night courses, he didn't recognize the campus in daylight. But this accounted for only one level of his dislocation. It was as if he had awakened from a long, restless sleep. Of course he was here because Elaine wanted him to sit for the Law Boards. But why? He had no intention of becoming a lawyer.

Yet he started up the fieldstone steps, in stride with several dozen other men, figuring he'd paid and studied for it, he might as well take the test. Elaine had been right. Everyone except him wore a suit and tie, and this angered Carter. He paused to let them pass, focusing his resentment upon his classmates, only to have it lash back upon him. He was more incensed at his own indecisiveness. There was no reason other than money—the amount too small to remember. Ten dollars? Fifteen?—to waste his time.

He couldn't blame Elaine. It was his fault, his refusal to confront the truth, which left him at the brink of a wounding admission. While she had employed any device to forget the baby—he recalled her enthusiasm for cooking and cleaning, her eagerness to be entertained, her reluctance to contact a doctor and an adoption agency, and, of course, her elaborate plans for him—Carter had used the baby and Elaine to forget himself. He had postponed his future, always with the excuse that he could do nothing until the baby was born. Now he recognized this for the self-serving deception it was and wondered what he would do if it weren't for Elaine, or if she weren't pregnant.

The answer was surprisingly simple. He'd continue his night courses. Perhaps go to school full time. That seemed sufficient for the moment. Turning his back on Royce Hall, he went to the student union bookstore to check the syllabus for Dr. Durand's course next quarter.

It wasn't until early evening, as he waited for Elaine at the main campus gate, that he admitted it was one thing to tell her he had no desire to study law, but quite another to say he hadn't bothered to take the exam after all their planning and reviewing. She'd see it as an insult, and though this hadn't been his intention, it would be difficult to convince her otherwise.

As the sun faded, the air grew cool, and he wished he had worn a sweater. Soon the street lights blinked on, then a line of cars streamed past for the basketball game at Pauley Pavilion. A few fans whistled and catcalled, and one hurled a ball of crepe paper in Carter's face.

Elaine was late. He didn't have to look at his watch. He could sense it by his agitation, by the dull ache in his leg. But he worked to curb his impatience. He didn't want to be angry when he told her his decision.

At last she pulled up in front of him, motioning to several packages in the back seat. "Sorry. I lost track of the time. I was blue and thought it might perk me up if I bought a few things to wear when I'm skinny again." Her smile was already thin. "How was the exam?"

"Not bad."

Awkwardly she climbed over the console, while he came around to the driver's side. He turned east on Sunset, but had no intention of going to the apartment, for the place was tied too closely to their old plans. Cutting to the left, he passed between high white pillars into Bel Air.

"Let's go sightseeing," he said with false geniality.

"It's awfully late."

"Maybe we'll spot a star."

"Okay. But not too long. I'm tired."

In the gathering dusk the houses—those not screened by tall hedges or electrically charged fences laced with ivy—were large, but looked weightless and hollow behind their ornate façades. Only the lush vegetation—and it might have been plastic—seemed to anchor them in place. Yet it wouldn't have mattered if a stiff breeze had blown them away. The neighborhood made no more impression on Carter than the stylized props for a bad high school play. "How was Miss Dugan?" he asked.

"Same as always." Elaine appeared genuinely interested in what she saw.

"And how's that?"

"Very kind and helpful."

"Does she ever ask about me?"

"Sometimes."

"What?"

"How are you and what you're doing."

"How am I? What am I doing?"

He laughed, but she didn't. "Aren't you going to tell me about the exam. Do you think you did well?"

"I didn't take it."

"Oh?" She said nothing else, yet this one word was barbed as a fish hook. Her quick resignation—obviously she'd anticipated this—rankled Carter, for he hadn't been sure until that morning what he would do.

"I don't want to be a lawyer," he said. "I thought I might as well take the exam, but when I got there, it seemed a waste of time. No matter how high I scored, I wouldn't have changed my mind."

"Oh?" she said again. "What do you plan to do instead?" She was watching the road as if she expected it to squirm out from under them.

Circling in a cul-de-sac, Carter coasted back toward the gate. "Instead of what?"

"Instead of becoming a lawyer."

"I'd never decided to become one. I took the course to see if I liked it. I didn't. It would have been two years before I entered law school. So this doesn't upset my immediate . . ."

"Yes, but what do you plan to do?"

"Take things a step at a time. I'll complete my degree in history."

"What will you do with a degree in history? Have you ever thought of that?"

"Yes. I haven't decided. I have a few years to make up my mind. In these last few months I've learned a lot, and . . ."

"But you did decide not to take the exam."

Carter couldn't talk and drive at the same time. Pulling to the curb, he switched off the engine. There were no other cars on the street, and none passed. "I know what I don't want, Elaine. I'll have to work out the rest. Is there anything wrong with that?"

The silence was suffocating, and Carter nudged a button to lower his window. He couldn't see if she was chewing her lip, but would have bet she was. At a house nearby, a light went on, then the entire lawn was illuminated as a man emerged carrying a hose.

In a startling reversal Elaine asked, "What are you thinking?"

"Nothing," he said bluntly so she'd know he was lying.

She looked out the window at the man tending his dichondra. "I was thinking how much I miss winter. Real winter with snow and ice. I like warm weather, but . . ." Her voice didn't so much die as disappear, like a stone thrown down a deep well. When she spoke again, she sounded far away. "Dr. Sachs told me we shouldn't make love any more. I mean you can't go inside me. The baby's dropping and we have to be careful."

It was foolish to ask hadn't he always been careful and since this was the least of his questions, he said nothing.

"You can still hold me. I won't break." Brushing her lips past his cheek, she whispered, "Let's go home. I'm cold."

Carter tried to be reasonable, tried to accept what she'd said and prove it by an increased tenderness toward her, but two facts were linked too closely in his mind. When he told her he wouldn't go to law school, she said they could no longer make love. He knew they weren't—couldn't be—connected, yet . . .

That night as the lights clicked out, he kissed Elaine, and she locked her hands at his neck as though she was afraid he might flee. Kneeling in the center of the bed, they undressed one another, then Carter kissed her throat, her breasts, her stomach, and both her thighs. When he moved his mouth between her legs, she held his head by the hair, but he felt far away from her, reminded of times last summer, before they had made love at all. Looking up, he saw the smooth white slope of her belly, striated by red stretch marks. Her face was out of sight. Groaning, she lifted her legs over his shoulders and squeezed in spasms.

Elaine was soon asleep, but he remained awake. The fear they had lived with for months—that they might be discovered and forced to part, that at any minute they might be ruined by a mistimed decision or a mischosen word—seemed small now when set against his far greater fear that nothing would ever happen, that things would go on this way forever, with Carter sliding down her sleek body, away from it, out of her life.

2

In mid-January, two weeks before the baby was due, clouds of smog tumbled out of the hills, unspooling dirty gauze. Thunderheads appeared to be building, though no rain fell, and each day the smog dissipated just enough to expose a pallid sun, like the last weak ember flickering in a heap of dead ashes. This dull glow where the sun should have been and the acrid stench in the air made it seem something was burning, a fire no one could put out. Pedestrians bled bitter tears and tucked their heads to their chests to get nearer their lungs and relieve their parched breathing. Some held handkerchiefs, like surgical masks, over their faces, yet nothing could screen out the ozone and the gritty particles of filth which drifted everywhere in a strangling suspension.

The leaves browned and curled at the edges, schoolyards were abandoned, and the *Times* reported that two cats and five dogs had died of air pollution. But these were quickly forgotten when a number of respiratory patients passed away in fits of choking. The newspaper started to print on its front page a macabre box score of smog victims.

Though Carter drove the air-conditioned Thunderbird to and from work, his eyes were rheumy, and he used up wads of Kleenex sneezing black powder. Elaine, who spent her days in the apartment—dust roved through the rooms insidious as germs, speckling the whitewashed walls, the linen, and furniture—came down with a cough, but she didn't complain, didn't say anything, in fact. Carter didn't speak either and never touched her except when they made the only love allowed them now. Each time he kissed between her thighs he had to acknowledge how few, how feeble, their points of contact were.

One afternoon, as Carter prolonged his study period twenty extra minutes, he got a call from Eddie Brown. "Christ, kid, we're up to our asses in a recession. I've gotta have my money."

They arranged a rendezvous at the diner on Hoover Street, and with Cervik's permission, Carter left Danny Boy's, eager to see Eddie. Though he hoped this would be their final meeting, he looked forward to spending an hour with the one person who knew the truth and didn't care, who could laugh and joke as the city flaked off in minute pieces.

Eddie was late, and the narrow, nearly empty Pullman car rattled to the noise of traffic outside. Once more Carter had an impression he was moving, that rusty iron wheels ran loudly beneath him. Leading where? He waited a moment in the doorway before the waitress shouted he was letting in smog. Coming to the counter, he ordered a Coke.

He decided what he liked most about Eddie, who, after all, was a shyster and blackmailer—Carter attempted to weigh this in the balance, but couldn't—was his sense of humor, his vitality, even his cunning. Regardless of the situation, he would be a survivor. Carter couldn't conceive of Eddie in his predicament. As he'd said, he might have fallen into it, but would have found a way out.

"Like a refill, dearie?" The waitress, a young girl, had the sexless dignity of somebody's aunt. Across her belly lay a brown line from leaning against the counter.

He accepted a second Coke, nursed it a few minutes, then stepped into the phone booth and dialed the David Felix Employment Agency. The secretary was flustered when he asked for Eddie. "One minute and Mr. Prinella will assist you."

As the line broke, a brusque voice asked, "Who's this?"

"I asked for Mr. Brown."

"He doesn't work here."

"I spoke to him yesterday. We have an appointment."

"Oh." The voice softened. "If you're a client, we'll be glad to . . ."

"I'm not a client. I have to talk to him."

"Are you a friend?"

The man made this sound like an accusation, yet Carter refused to be intimidated. "Yes, I am."

"If I were you, I'd advise him to hire a very good lawyer."

"Why? What's wrong?"

"Ask him. I'm sure he'll be glad to tell you." He slammed down the receiver.

Carter started for the counter, but couldn't bear a third Coke. He left and crossed the street, where he could see the agency and the diner. If Eddie had lost his job, it wasn't likely he would fail to collect his money. What kind of trouble could he have had. Had he been caught with his hand in the till?

The smog bothered Carter and his eyes brimmed with tears, giving the seedy, run-down block an even grimmer quality of distortion. Everything looked old and coated by decades of grime. Underfoot were chunks of brick, scraps of trash, and crumbling concrete. The building in front of him had the appearance of ancient stacked newspapers, ragged and dog-eared, the lines of paint obscured by age.

A flatulent bus came around the corner, and in its tinted windows Carter caught a glimpse of himself—tall, tanned, dressed in a summer suit. The reflection, he thought, bore no resemblance to him. Yet there he was, there he went, big, broad-shouldered, and self-contained. He had changed more than he'd realized, and against this drab background, stood out in bold relief. He didn't look the type to worry about anything. So why was he waiting? At once he went to the car. If Eddie wanted his money, he could come get it.

3

As he pushed through the door at Danny Boy's, Rita handed him a slip of paper. "Someone phoned and asked you to call back."

"A man?"

"No, a woman." Broad bottom swaying, she resumed her post at the cash register.

"My wife?"

"Hey, like how would I know?"

In the pay booth he unfolded the slip of paper, but didn't recognize the number. Maybe Elaine had gone into labor. After he'd dialed, he pressed a hand to the green panel, its bumpy surface like enormous goose flesh.

A woman, Miss Dugan, answered.

"Is anything wrong?" he asked.

"Not really. Are you free to talk?"

"I'm in a booth."

"When can I see you?"

"I'll be with Elaine this Saturday."

"That won't do. I don't want her to know."

"Know what?"

"That we've seen each other. Like most pregnant women, she's a trifle paranoid and might think we're talking about her behind her back."

"What do we have to talk about?"

"It's a question of completing the adoption. Could you come to the agency today?"

"I guess, if it's really . . ."

"It's quite important."

"I'll be there in half an hour."

Returning to the cash register, he had Rita tell Cervik he was going out again, then stepped back into the smog. He had no idea what Miss Dugan wanted, and for once didn't attempt to guess. After so many mistakes, he knew well the desolate dead ends of his imagination.

But after battling the rush-hour traffic on Santa Monica Freeway and restraining his wild surmises, he remembered Eddie Brown the moment he entered the Harold Wendell Agency. There had to be a connection between him and Miss Dugan's phone call. Suddenly Carter had a thudding headache.

"Do you have any aspirin?" he asked Miss Dugan, who met him at the front desk.

"Yes. Upstairs. We'll talk there."

Her cramped office, ill-lit by a naked light bulb that dangled from a black cord, had been gerrymandered from the end of a hall. To the lone window clung a fire escape freshly covered with chromium paint, and as evening sunlight slanted through it, the slender struts, steps, and guide wires spun a weblike shadow on the wall behind Carter. On the window ledge were six dolls dressed in national costumes, and off to the left hung a degree from Stanford and an abstract design fashioned from fallen leaves.

Taking a chair in front of the desk, Carter washed down the aspirin with a cup of water.

"How have you been?"

"I'm all right," he said.

"And Elaine?"

"She's all right, too."

"She usually is, isn't she?" Miss Dugan sat at the desk, and the cushion sighed. "She never complains, never refuses to co-operate. I'm sorry the relationship has to end." She picked up a pencil and tapped it on the blotter. "But I guess you'll be happy when this is over."

Carter didn't answer.

"Elaine seemed upset again last Saturday." She switched subjects without changing expressions. "I had a feeling she was holding back. Is anything wrong"

"Did you ask her?" Crushing the paper cup, he tossed it into a wastebasket.

"As a matter of fact, I did. She said I should ask you. If something's bothering you, please don't take it out on her. The two of us could talk it over."

"I don't take things out on anybody, and I'll tell you when I need help."

"Do that, Carter. And remember, there are times when we need help, yet don't know it until it's too late. I'm sorry we haven't had a chance to talk. If nothing else, it might have helped me with Elaine. You do understand the importance of these consultations, don't you?"

He nodded.

"A girl has to be sure of her decision. Once the papers have been signed, it's too late. Some of them want their babies back. We've even had cases where married women relinquish babies without their husbands' consent."

Since he didn't believe she'd asked him here for this, Carter said nothing. She would make her point when it pleased her. But as he waited, his curiosity soured into depression. He was sick of this woman and tired of talk about unwed mothers and the problems of adoption.

"There are a few questions I have to ask. I hate to pry, but the information is crucial and will be kept confidential." She ceased tapping the blotter, and on her strong jaw he noticed a whorl of light brown hair. "Elaine says you're not the baby's father?"

"I told you that the first time we met."

"And the two of you aren't married?"

"What are you getting at? You know we're not."

"I had to be sure." From the top drawer of the desk she removed a manila folder. "I'd like you to sign this release stating that you aren't married to Elaine, are not the baby's father, and therefore have no claim to it. This will complete our records. No one else will see it. I'll be the only witness."

"If no one will see it, why do you want it?"

A look of exasperation passed over her powdered face, pinching the forehead into a crooked ladder of wrinkles. "It's to protect Elaine and the adopted parents from legal action."

"Since I'm not her husband and I'm not the baby's father, why should my name be involved?" He shoved the papers back across the desk, thinking this would force her to the point. Yet the act also reemphasized his exclusion.

"Carter, be reasonable. In living with Elaine, you've become very much involved."

He said nothing.

Miss Dugan ran the pencil along the edge of the papers. "Carter, why did you stay with Elaine?"

"Because I love her."

"Why don't you describe your feelings a little more fully?"

"Because it's none of your business."

The pencil halted a second, then pushed on, straight as the electrocardiogram of a dead man. "Don't you think it's important to understand why you came?"

"I understand why I came. I love Elaine. Isn't that the best reason?" As he spoke, he realized she didn't care about the reason.

"And what do you look for in return? After the baby's born, what will you demand of Elaine?"

"Who's asking, you or Elaine?"

"Carter, let's stop answering each other with questions."

"I don't have to answer at all. Save your questions for her. She's the patient."

"I have asked her."

"What did she say?"

"That's of no importance until I hear your point of view." More gently she said, "Elaine is anxious about what you'll expect once the baby's been adopted. She thinks you'll want a permanent arrangement. Under normal circumstances, this might be welcome, but Elaine has many unresolved conflicts. Also, she understands what a serious matter marriage would be for you and . . ."

"Isn't it serious for everyone?"

"Of course. But you're Catholic, aren't you?"

If there was a logic to her question, it eluded Carter. His first impulse was to say no, he wasn't a Catholic, or that he was a bad one. But unable to understand her motives, he hesitated, afraid one renunciation would lead to another, then another, until he had nothing left. "Yes, I'm a Catholic."

"Well, there you are." She smiled, satisfied.

"I don't follow."

"She's aware of what marriage means to a Catholic."

"What the hell are you saying. We haven't talked very often about marriage, much less religion."

"Well, she has spoken to me, and your religious convictions concern her."

"Nonsense. I don't even go to Mass."

"That's not the issue."

"What is? Is she prejudiced against Catholics? That's something out of another century."

"Let's just say Catholics look at life differently. You don't have to be a bigot to think their attitudes toward birth control, the Pope, church dogma . . ."

"Wait a minute. What have they got to do with Elaine and me? We've lived together five months and Catholicism has never caused problems."

"That's not Elaine's story."

Of all the things she might have said, this seemed the least likely, the most absurd. "I don't believe you."

"Be honest, Carter. First you refused to let her have an abortion. Second . . ."

"That's a damn lie! I simply said she didn't need my help if she wanted an abortion. What did she tell you?"

"Carter, calm down."

"I want to know."

"Essentially she said you had different values, different life styles. Of course, you . . ."

"Does all this mean she doesn't want to marry me?"

"Well . . ." As she temporized, he heard the dry hiss of her stockings, and she need have said no more. Yet she lamely added, "I couldn't say. She's preoccupied at the moment. It's a very . . ."

"I know. A very difficult time. Well, she shouldn't worry," he said bitterly. "I won't twist her arm."

"Of course you won't. You're mature enough to know . . ."

"Don't get me wrong." He resisted the wedge she tried to drive between them, but too weary for anything except the truth, repeated, as if it were a formula, "I love Elaine." As Miss Dugan shifted her weight, he saw the window behind her fast filling with darkness. Though he thought he understood everything, he had to hear her say it. "Doesn't she love me?"

"Carter, I can't answer that. After all, Elaine spoke in confidence. I know she has a great deal of respect and . . ."

"Oh Christ, stop it." Carter stood up. "There's no sense talking if you won't tell the truth. You called me here to say something, but if you won't do it, I'm leaving. I'm sick of your innuendos."

"You're wrong. I simply hoped you wouldn't upset Elaine in these last weeks. Now I'm afraid I've upset you. I'm sorry, Carter."

"Why did you say she didn't want to marry me?"

"Please. That's not what I said. I told you I didn't know. I thought we could chat and . . ."

"What about my being a Catholic?"

"That's a potential problem you and Elaine will have to discuss after the baby's born." She spoke in a soothing whisper. "I thought if I pointed this out, it might make things easier on both of you. As for why I called, I need your signature on these papers."

"And I told you . . ." In the confusion, Carter's angry defiance died. For all his probing, he had touched nothing solid. Miss Dugan had eased off each question and refused to offer a straight answer. "Give me the damn things," he muttered, signed the documents, and turned to go.

"Just a minute." She brought him up short of the door. "I want you to promise not to mention any of this to Elaine. Particularly in your present mood. I won't be responsible for what she might do. Would you like to wait here until you've cooled off?"

Carter slammed the door behind him.

Yet he did wait in the car on the parking lot. Smog made the night profoundly dark. The lights in the Harold Wendell Agency winked off a window at a time, and a few people came out, but no one said anything to him. Soon he had the graveled lot and the silent grounds to himself. As Miss Dugan's ambiguous comments crackled hotly in his brain, he stared at the dashboard clock and was startled by the swiftness of the fluorescent hands. They left him slightly breathless. After all the days he'd wasted marking time, the minutes now measured him, taking their toll of his energy and concentration. He supposed he should be thinking, should be angry or in turmoil, but he felt and thought nothing. He was in shock, sunk in the dead hollow center of his emotions.

After two hours he started for home and revived a bit on the freeway, taking refuge for a few minutes in Miss Dugan's reluctance to be precise. She had never stated outright that Elaine didn't love him or didn't want to marry him. She admitted she didn't know and wouldn't have told him if she did. Maybe there had been a mistake. Worse than a mistake, an intrigue on Miss Dugan's part. She'd never liked him.

But these vain delusions had collapsed of their own accord by the time he reached North Harper Street. He parked beneath the bedroom window and looked up through the crooked limbs of the lemon tree. Although it was only ten o'clock, all the lights were out.

Had Elaine left him? Or simply gone to bed early? It didn't matter. Nothing did. He asked himself if he should bother going in. He had the checkbook and the Thunderbird. Tomorrow he could be . . . Where. Alone. For the first time he felt more than married.

He labored up the front steps. His headache had returned, and he remembered Miss Dugan's warning. He was to do nothing, divulge nothing, demand nothing. He had never in his life experienced such an utter sense of his own nothingness.

In the hallway he waited until his eyes adjusted to the darkness, then crept to the closet and hung up his suit coat. Through the bedroom door he could see Elaine's reclining silhouette. Her face was turned to him, but she said nothing and he assumed she was asleep. Quietly he closed the door. He couldn't bear to look at her, couldn't bring himself to lie down beside her.

Although he had no appetite, he went to the kitchen and took out bread, bologna, and a tomato to make himself a sandwich. He examined each object as if it had its own peculiar secrets, then feeling dizzy, shut his eyes.

Unfortunately his ears had no lids, and they picked up every sound. Leaning against the sink, he cupped his palms over them.

The morning his parents were buried he had stood before the bathroom sink brushing his teeth, thinking what an appallingly imbecilic act it was. Five miles away his mother and father were locked in metal boxes, their clean teeth icy and useless, while here the mirror showed a man with flecks of foam on his lips, a pink stick in his mouth, and a sick ache in his belly. But he knew if he stopped, he would never start again. Absurd repetition was all important. Shaving, showering, combing his hair —they had carried him through the funeral as surely as Librium had lifted Marion out of her hysteria. The trick was to keep busy, not to think.

Raising his head, he picked up the butcher knife and began to slice the tomato, but somehow cut his ring finger instead. The blue gash didn't bleed till Carter squeezed his knuckle and a livid hinge of flesh flapped loose. The blood plopped onto the white porcelain drainboard in a neat pattern of circles which merged into one large spot. Watching it, he smiled, for the wound gave focus to the pain he had been hiding for hours.

He let it drain a moment longer, then went into the bathroom for a Band-Aid. After he had wrapped the finger in adhesive, he decided to forget about eating and go to bed, for once the pain faded, there would be nothing to do except think, and that could lead nowhere.

Elaine was on her back now and he suspected she was awake. Yet he left the lights out, undressed silently, and slid beneath the sheets on his side. The single beds seemed far apart. Elaine's soft breathing bridged the distance like a melancholy whisper from another time or place. He hoped she wouldn't cry, for that would ruin his resolution to pay her no attention.

"Have you eaten?" she asked.

"Yes."

"Are you tired?" She turned toward him.

"Yes. And you?"

"I can't sleep." She giggled nervously, and he didn't recognize her voice. "I feel like I was punished and sent to bed early. I've been waiting for you."

"I had to work late. Cervik said . . ."

She crawled closer to touch him. "Carter?"

"Yes?"

"Do you love me?"

No question could have shocked him more. It sliced through him as keenly as the butcher knife, and there was no defense against it. After an instant he conceded that he did.

"Please say it."

"I love you."

"You don't act like you do. You never talk any more. Is it because I've gotten fat and ugly?"

"Of course not, I . . ." He was tempted to tell the truth—that he didn't trust her, that Miss Dugan, in refusing to say anything concrete, had by her evasions implied . . . What? "I've been tired."

"You seem angry. And even if you are tired, you could speak to me and give me a kiss before you go to sleep. I'm lonely."

Again he wondered whether Miss Dugan had lied. Or was Elaine lying now? "I've been thinking."

"About what?"

"About you. Me. Everything. Sometimes I ask myself what will become of us when this is over—after the baby's born and adopted—but I don't have any answers."

"Neither do I." She rolled onto her back. "I try not to, but I think about it all the time."

Before he could ask what she had thought or concluded, she said, "Carter, I want to make love with you. Not like we've been doing. The real way."

"We can't."

"Yes, we can, if we're careful."

"I don't think we should. Why don't you tell me what . . ."

"I want you inside me."

"What about the baby?"

"It'll be all right." She sat up to remove her nightgown.

"What about us?"

"What?"

"What about us? You said we never talk any more."

"We'll talk tomorrow night."

"All right. There are some things I have to tell you." He put his hand on her belly. "You'd better stay on top."

"No, you." She drew him onto her.

"Wait a minute, Elaine."

"No. Go ahead. Don't wait for me."

Placing his palms flat against the sheet on either side of her shoulders, Carter straightened his arms, and raised

215

his weight above her. The whiteness of her belly glowed like a hill of snow, and as he toiled inside her, she took his face between her hands and whispered something he couldn't understand.

It was over quickly for Carter, and he moved down between her thighs. But Elaine stopped him. "No. Stay here beside me." As she rested her head on his shoulder, he felt warm tears.

"What's wrong? Why are you crying?"

"I'm not. Not really. I'm happy."

Chapter XIII

1

Carter woke to the rich aroma of bacon. Elaine was humming in the kitchen. When he had shaved and dressed, she called out that his eggs were ready. Though still in her nightgown and robe, she had combed her hair and put on make-up, which meant she'd been awake at least an hour. She set a place for him at the breakfast bar, and served a lavish meal with no worry about how many dishes and pans she was using. She ate nothing herself, but appeared to take pleasure in every bite he swallowed. Sipping coffee, she smiled as Carter self-consciously praised the cereal, bacon and eggs, toast and grapefruit. Then after she'd cleared the plates, she kissed his cheek and whispered, "I love you." Walking him to the door, she kissed him a second time and said, "I'll be waiting for you."

The day at Danny Boy's was a senseless interruption, but he skipped the study period, resisted his natural inclination to analyze what had happened, and worked till he was exhausted, worked till cooking grease seeped through the bandage and stung his cut. He swore he was through making problems for himself, and since there seemed no way that Miss Dugan could have been right, he thrust her from his mind altogether. His plan was to get through the next few weeks, quit his job, and go off alone with Elaine. They needed rest, and time to talk and reassess their future.

As he left the restaurant that evening, a fine mist fell from the smog, beading in mercury pellets on the windshield and hood of the car. Sunset Strip wriggled with snakelike reflections of neon, and driving was dangerous. He had to park around the corner on Delongpre, then hurry through the drizzle to the apartment. When he opened the door, cold air rushed out at him, and as he closed it, there was an echo through the rooms. Thinking Elaine was asleep, he turned up the thermostat, called her name, and stepped into the bedroom.

Both beds were empty and unmade. "Elaine." Her name echoed eerily as the heat grumbled on behind the baseboards.

In the living room he switched on a lamp, and despite the foul weather, assumed she was out shopping. But when he bent over to pick up the newspaper, panicked, racing blood brought on doubts. She might have gone into labor. Or had a miscarriage. Although in that case wouldn't she, Miss Dugan, someone, have contacted him at Danny Boy's? It was foolish to worry.

He stretched mightily to relieve the tightness in his chest, then turned on all the lights, removed his coat and tie, and went into the kitchen, where the breakfast dishes were stacked in the sink, stained by soapy bubbles. Nothing had been taken from the freezer for dinner. Obviously she'd decided to wait for him to get home.

Or had something, in fact, gone wrong? Someone might have shown up suddenly. Her parents? A friend? The baby's father? He considered and quickly dismissed the idea of asking the Regans.

It was almost seven. Too late. She should have known he would worry. He thought of the police, but that seemed far-fetched, melodramatic. He dialed Danny Boy's instead to ask if anyone had called. Rita said no and hung up to keep the line clear for carry-out orders.

Carter prowled the apartment searching for a note and even got down on his hands and knees to check under the sofa. When he glanced into the bedroom again, he noticed what he hadn't seen before. Most of Elaine's cosmetics had disappeared from the bureau. In the closet her clothing was in disarray, and her raincoat, several dresses, and a suitcase were missing.

He dialed the Harold Wendell Agency, and getting no answer, grabbed up the telephone directory to look for the name Dugan. There were six Donnas listed, and he dialed five before he got the right one and blurted, "Is Elaine in the hospital?"

"No."

218

Her voice indicated she knew he'd be calling, but he was in no mood to spar. "Where is she? Is anything wrong?"

"Elaine told me what you've done. I'm very disappointed, Carter, and sorry I spoke to you the other day. I thought you were mature . . ."

"What are you talking about?"

"Don't play games. You told Mr. Brown Elaine's business."

"Who?"

"Mr. Brown."

"Oh God," he groaned.

"So it is true. Why did you do it?"

"Where's Elaine? I have to speak to her."

"That's impossible. She's very upset."

"Is she at your place? There's been a mistake."

"She's not here. But of course you're right. There's been an awful mistake. I only wish I knew what drove you to do it. You should have talked to me instead of to Mr. Brown. I'm afraid you need help very badly."

"Look, goddammit, I've had . . ."

"Get a hold of yourself, Carter. I don't intend to argue."

"Okay, we won't argue. But for Christ's sake tell me what happened and when I can talk to Elaine."

"That's up to her. As for what happened, I suggest you ask Mr. Brown."

"I haven't seen him in weeks. What did he do?"

"He barged into the apartment, told Elaine he had damaging information about her, and threatened to call her parents unless she paid him."

"Did he hurt her?"

"Not physically, but she's dangerously distraught."

"She should have contacted me. Why did she run off before I had a chance to . . ."

"Because you broke the trust she had placed in you, leaving her at the mercy of this malicious blackmailer."

"He's not malicious. He just wants the money I . . . we owe him. And I didn't tell him about Elaine. He found out on his own. Ask her if she remembers the day we drove to Universal City to . . . Oh, hell, just have her call me."

"I'll try, but don't count on anything."

His life became a nightmare which dissolved only when he fell asleep. But waking next morning brought it all back. She had left him, and it was painful to lie close to the sheets on Elaine's side, which tempted him to bury his face in her cool perfumed pillow. Throwing off the covers, shivering barefoot on the tiles, Carter crossed his arms as if to cradle a broken vessel in his chest. Outside, the drizzle had ceased, yet a black foreboding sky threatened more of everything—rain, smog, and filth.

He dialed Eddie Brown's number, just as he'd done dozens of times in the last twelve hours, and as he listened to it ring, he could easily imagine what had gone wrong. Having missed Carter at the diner, Eddie had come to the apartment and attempted to extort money from Elaine, who had reacted predictably, first in fear, then flight. Now Carter had to keep Eddie from calling the Yosts in Costa Rica, and convince Elaine he hadn't betrayed her. But at the Mediterranean Cascade no one answered.

He phoned the Harold Wendell Agency, where Miss Dugan was as distant and indifferent as she had been the night before.

"This is absurd," he protested. "I have to speak to Elaine."

"She's free to call any time."

"Did you tell her what I told you?"

"Yes, I saw her this morning."

"What did she say?"

"Very little. She's still upset."

"I could straighten this out in a few minutes."

"Have you contacted Mr. Brown?"

"I can't reach him." Eddie and Elaine weren't the only ones he couldn't reach. Speaking to Miss Dugan was like struggling to reason with a stubborn child. "If I explain how this came about, will you pass the word on to Elaine?"

"Yes, if I think it'll help."

Drawing a deep breath, Carter began by repeating himself. "I didn't tell Eddie Brown anything. He got his information from a private detective. You see, we owed him money, and he threatened to call her parents unless I paid him. I didn't let Elaine know because I thought it would upset her. At least I was right about that. But Eddie didn't show up for the last payoff. Instead he came to the apartment and talked to Elaine by mistake. He probably assumed she was aware of the arrangement." When Miss Dugan said nothing, he asked, "Don't you believe me?"

"It doesn't matter what I believe."

"Will you tell Elaine?"

"Yes. She'll have to make up her own mind."

He hung up, furious, unsure whom to blame. He didn't know why Elaine hadn't called, unless Miss Dugan wasn't relaying his messages. There had to be a way to reach her, yet none of the desperate measures he courted seemed likely to work. To his regret, he had no choice except to wait.

For the remainder of the morning he paced the floor to distract himself from the slow unwinding of the hours, from the slender hands on his watch which crawled from one numeral to the next. Twice more he phoned Eddie Brown in vain, then remembered Fingerhut. Surely he could help—if he wanted to, if he could be convinced to. After all, he too was at fault, for like a mad dog needling marrow from a bone, he had exposed them, and despite his warning, Eddie had tried to blackmail them. Carter set out at once for Culver City.

Fist, Inc., had been trashed. The windows were boarded up and obscenities, revolutionary slogans, and the word PIG had been painted on the wooden planks. Several armed guards kept the pedestrians moving and eyed every car that passed. One protected the pole from which a shredded American flag fluttered. The company symbol—a massive concrete fist—had been reduced to rubble, and scorched chunks of it lay everywhere on the lawn. A work crew busily bulldozed the shards onto dump trucks. But in bold letters a sign over the door announced *We're Still Open*.

Inside, other guards buttressed the walls, as if the blast had left them too weak to stand on their own. Carter went to the same woman at the counter, but she didn't flash her traffic-light smile. When he asked for Moylan Fingerhut, she pulled a pencil from her hair, scribbled his name, and pressed an intercom button. A harsh

221

voice broke the monotonous buzzing of the plastic box. "What does he want?"

"I have to see you," Carter shouted.

"Why?"

"Business. It's about Eddie Brown."

"Send him in."

As Carter's footsteps echoed before him in the corridor, he had the impression he was headed for the center of a crypt. Next to the water fountain he saw one last guard, a burly man with a thick neck and sloping shoulders, who slumped against the cinder blocks like a side of beef. His eyes followed Carter as he rapped the metal door at Fingerhut's office.

"Who is it?"

"Me. Who do you think?"

"Who?"

"Carter White."

Locks untumbled, a bolt slid back, and Fingerhut swung open the door, his left arm in a sling, his head swaddled in bandages. Because of the sling, he had strapped the shoulder holster over his right forearm. "Come in, White, and be quick about it."

"What happened?"

"Anarchy, pure and simple. Violent, cowardly anarchy." Slamming the door, he locked and bolted it, and struggled toward the desk. Once seated, he placed the pistol on his knees and propped up his cumbersome jaw by thrusting a thumb into the cleft. "The night before last they swarmed over us like locusts."

"Who?" Carter sat in front of the desk.

"All of them. The weirdos, queers, dope addicts, niggers, and Jews. They smashed the windows, blew up the fist, and tore down the flag."

"It looks like they got you, too."

"Not before I made my mark on a few of them." He lifted his chin proudly, then had to lower it to lighten the pain. "We're ready for them this time. So I say if there has to be a bloodbath, let's get it over with." Banging his hand on the desk, he set the metal ringing. "Now what do you want?"

"Eddie Brown is blackmailing me, even though you guaranteed he wouldn't. I paid him half his money. I have the rest, which he never showed up to collect. But yesterday while I was out, he came to the apartment, told Elaine what he knew, and threatened to call her parents unless she sweetened the pot. She panicked and . . . uh, ran off. Jesus, Fingerhut, she's nine months pregnant. You have to find her."

"What's the point, White? You want me to put a tracer on her?"

"Yes. Locate her and Eddie. He has to tell her the truth. You see, she blames me. She thinks I told Eddie."

"What?" He squinted quizzically. "How do you know?"

"From a woman at the adoption agency."

"And how did she know?"

"She's in touch with Elaine."

"Why don't you ask the woman where she is?"

"I have. She won't tell me. I've tried to send messages through her, but I'm not sure she's delivering them."

"Look, White, I can't be bothered about your girl running off. Work it out yourself."

"There's no time. I don't want her to think I let her down."

Trussed up in the sling and bandages, Fingerhut shifted uncomfortably. "Sounds to me like she let you down. Why not save your money and my time, and . . ."

"I don't want your advice, Fingerhut. It's partly your fault that she's gone. Find her!"

Fingerhut put the holstered pistol onto the desk. "This case doesn't interest me."

"I don't give a damn whether it does or not. You're responsible. You're an accessory to blackmail."

"You're full of bullshit. I'm not responsible for Eddie Brown. And don't get pushy or . . ."

"I'll let the police decide who's responsible." Carter stood up.

"Sit down."

"No."

"I think you'd better."

"I'm sick of you, Fingerhut. I'd like to see you behind bars."

In a stagelike gesture, Fingerhut clasped his hand to the revolver.

"Is that supposed to frighten me?" asked Carter, too angry to back down. "Are you threatening to shoot?"

"Of course not." Though he kept his hand on the gun, Fingerhut blushed. "Why don't we talk this over?"

"There's nothing more to say."

"Why don't you sit down?"

"I'd rather stand." But he did move next to the chair.

223

"What is it you want again?"

"Find Eddie Brown before he calls her parents, and make him tell Elaine the truth."

"Is that all?"

"No. I have to know where she is and when the baby's due."

"Okay, write down your phone number and the name of the adoption agency. I'll see what I can do." He relaxed his grip on the gun. "Do you think this will bring her back?"

"Do you care what I think?"

"Not much."

"Then why ask?"

"Would you like a little advice, White? Don't waste your time on this girl. If she wants to leave, there's no way to stop her."

"Save your advice, Fingerhut. I'll be waiting."

At the apartment he resumed his post by the telephone and stayed there for three days while the words of Fingerhut's unwanted advice ate at his will power with the slow corrosion of acid. After hours of effort he could understand why Elaine had left—in panic she believed he'd betrayed her, and considering her precarious mood, she might have done much worse—but it was inconceivable that she wouldn't give him a chance to explain.

Angrily he slammed from room to room, determined to pound an answer from the concrete walls that he smacked with his open palms, the furniture he kicked, the bed he thumped futilely with his fist. Yet there was no response, and his body stiffened and took on greater density. He became aware of its every process. Particularly the most annoying burden, the troubling beat of his heart. It, along with eating and breathing and all the brute mechanics of moving from morning to night and the precious blind moments of sleep, exacted an agonizing toll. He was tired, yet rarely got any rest, for even as he lay on the couch, cold and lonely, he burned inside with memories and regrets.

He skipped classes that week and stopped working altogether. As he told Cervik by telephone, he didn't think he and the food service management business were compatible.

"You must be joking," said Cervik. "You're the best trainee I've ever had."

"No, I'm afraid it's not for me."

"Sport, don't do this to me. Reichlederfer will raise hell. It may mean my job. He's very high on you."

"I'll tell him it has nothing to do with you."

"He won't believe it."

"I'm sorry. I'll do what I can."

"Come back," Cervik begged. "You'll have your own restaurant in a few months. Quit then, not now."

"I couldn't do that."

Seconds after he hung up, the phone rang.

"You ungrateful shit."

"Who is this?"

"Don't play dumb. It's Rita and you know it."

"I'm sorry, but I . . ."

"You're going to be more than sorry. Do you realize you're breaking up my marriage?"

"I thought you were already getting a divorce."

"Not that marriage, you asshole. You're breaking up my next one—to Ned—before it starts. Don't we have a right to a little happiness?"

"Of course, but there's nothing I can do."

"Oh yes, there is. You . . ."

He broke the connection and left the phone off the hook. Sorry as he was for Cervik, Carter couldn't endure the distraction of work or study, and was unable to accept responsibility for anyone else's suffering. He wanted Elaine back, nothing more or less, and although the waiting was torture, he had no intention of diverting himself through meaningless drudgery. He ate little, couldn't read or watch TV, and didn't leave the apartment. Since he wished their love to last, he thought he should be willing to brave a torment that would continue as long as Elaine was gone. Only this sense of perpetuation, even if of his own agony, satisfied his need for meaning and completion.

That afternoon he cradled the receiver, but it didn't ring again until early morning, when Carter rose, straining for it before he was fully awake. The tile floor stung his bare soles as he ran to the living room.

"Carter, how are you?" Hearing Reichlederfer, he sagged onto the sofa. "Cervik says you're not happy. I trust you've straightened out this misunderstanding."

"No, I haven't."

"Is he getting on your nerves? You could switch to another restaurant. Hell, you'll have your own in a few months."

"It's not Cervik. He's been good to me. I just . . ."

"Another firm? Howard Johnson's and Hot Shoppe may be bigger . . ."

"No, it's not that."

"Why not take a few days off and think things through? You have a very special opportunity at Danny Boy's."

"Thanks, but that wouldn't change my mind."

There was a long pause, and on Reichlederfer's end, a grinding sound, as if he were gnashing his teeth. "Listen," White, we've invested a hell of a lot of time and money training you."

"Mr. Reichlederfer, I'm expecting an important call. I've quit and that's it."

Like yesterday, he had no sooner hung up when the phone rang. Thinking it was Reichlederfer, he considered not answering, but didn't want to risk missing word from Elaine.

"Christ, White, where were you? I don't have all day." It was Fingerhut.

"Any news?"

"Yeah. Eddie has disappeared, and you're not the only one looking for him. If he contacts you, let me know at once."

"How about Elaine?"

"That was easy. She's at the Harold Wendell Agency and the baby's due any time."

"Did you see her? What did she say?"

"I didn't see her myself."

"Then why are you so sure she's there? Did you speak to her?"

"No, but I have ways of knowing. That's what I'm paid for."

"Can you get a message to her?"

"I suppose. If it's short and simple."

"Tell her to call me. Tell her I'll explain. Ask her to . . ."

"Calm down, White. One thing at a time."

"Just have her call me," he said, regaining his composure. "And one more thing, phone me the minute she goes into the hospital. I want to be there when the baby's born. I don't care what time it is."

"I do. I don't work twenty-four hours a day."

"If it's late, have one of your agents call."

"You really are wound up, aren't you? Did it ever occur to you why she left? If you'd listen to me, . . ."

"I have no interest in listening to you."

Carter was relieved for a few hours simply knowing where she was. Though tempted to try to see her, he was certain Miss Dugan wouldn't let him into the agency, and so stayed rooted by the telephone, awaiting Elaine's call. But when Fingerhut had had more than enough time to contact her and there was still no word, his high spirits soured into a sullen anger. He couldn't understand.

That night he dreamed of phones that rang and couldn't be answered, of receivers transformed to quicksilver at his touch, of distant conversations crackling with static. Then he saw Elaine in the bedroom door, taunting him until he reached for her and she raced down the hall. He caught her by the nightgown, but it tore loose as she laughed and disappeared into the wall.

He woke, clutching the twisted sheet, and almost at once drifted back to sleep to see her again. This time as he shot out a hand it crashed through her stomach, a fine trickle of sand fell out, and she sank moaning into the floor.

Actually it was Carter moaning as he fumbled for the bed lamp. When he pulled the chain, light exploded onto the pink spread, and he sat up to fight against sleep which had become a kind of sickness, a dizzying descent into darkness. But being awake wasn't much better, for he had to resist a suspicion that love was a lie, as cruel and unreal as his nightmare. Since last summer it had allowed him to accept the idea of death, and had been one reason among many that he'd come to California with Elaine. Despite all its special agonies, the time had promised a direction, a purpose, a stay against his dread that nothing meant anything, and everything would amount to nothing in the end. But with Elaine gone, the bottom had dropped out, and he wondered if love, too, was a deceit so subtly crafted it could conceal that it was only a little death, pregnant with others, leading to the big one.

He got up and went to the window. It was raining. Water beaded on the glass in perfect silver pellets, inside of which swam hundreds of black dots. They looked like cells his father might have studied under the microscope, simple organisms that pulsed with life or disease. He couldn't say which, and wouldn't have known how to separate the filth from the silver, the fever from the vital matter. That task would require not a scientist, but an alchemist, a man such as Eddie Brown, who flourished on both silver and filth, like an unconquerable strain of insects that ate poison for strength. How silly it had been to think they could fool him. Or fool themselves.

Carter left the window for the living room, and on a whim, although it was one A.M., dialed Eddie's number. He wished he could ask what Eddie believed—what did his ilk do when the world caved in around them—but there was no answer.

Switching on the light, he lowered himself onto the sofa, determined to stay awake until exhaustion overtook him, or he had heard news. He could only be a slave of that squat black indifferent toad so long before it released him, or ceased to matter.

At two-thirty it rang, and he answered before it could ring again.

"She's been in labor two hours," said Fingerhut, his voice raw from sleep. "But she has a long way to go."

"Where is she?"

"Downtown at California Lutheran Hospital. It's off the Harbor Freeway at 1414 South Hope Street."

"I'm . . ."

"Hang on, White. If anyone asks how you got this information, don't mention my name. Eddie Brown's in big trouble. If you hear from him, phone me."

"I'll talk to you later."

He returned to the bedroom to dress, his heart pounding in bold strokes. All he asked was a few minutes to tell her . . . ask . . . Perhaps he wouldn't have to say a thing. By now she must have known. Still the words and phrases shuttled through his brain as he groped for the ones which would convince her.

Turning east, he traveled Sunset Boulevard, where even at three A.M. heavy traffic tore at the sleek wet satin of asphalt. Through the drizzle, headlights squinted like weary eyes, blood-shot and half blind from the glare. Progress was slow. At Gower Street, as a dozen drunks dressed as cowgirls and cowboys crossed against the light, one dropped a bottle of liquor, which shattered on the pavement in jagged pinpoints of fire.

On Hollywood Freeway cars sped bumper to bumper,

side to side at sixty miles an hour, like a length of glinting chain mail. Then after a metallic rattle and the sharp scream of brakes, they stopped dead, engines idly revving, tailpipes tossing out rings of exhaust fumes. Above the pavement curved a row of aluminum arc lights whose fluorescent tips sprayed purple onto the roadside ivy. The vines had withered to reveal a writhing nest of black strings, with only here and there among them a healthy leaf, spade-shaped as the head of a serpent.

Drumming his fingers on the steering wheel, Carter tried to think. But what was there to think? He would take her in his arms. When he asked her to come back—both of them burdened with memories—how could she refuse? If they hoped to get in out of this chaos, they had to be together.

The traffic stuttered around an accident in the passing lane. Seven cars had locked at the bumper, telescoping into one smoking tube. At the center of the pile-up, the doors of a Chevy had flapped wide like wings, and the driver must have been a Fuller Brush man, for mops, combs, plastic dishracks, bottles of shampoo, and tubes of facial cream popped beneath Carter's tires. This sound was surpassed by the racket of a police helicopter carrying off the injured.

At last Carter gained the Harbor Freeway and left it for South Hope Street, where California Lutheran Hospital loomed over a desolate terrain of parking lots and seedy shops. The lobby looked new, however, and a Negro, mopping the marble floor, directed him to the maternity ward. In an elevator, he was lifted through several distinct zones of odor—orange juice, oatmeal, cod liver oil, and disinfectant—then deposited in front of the Expectant Father's Waiting Room.

At the nurse's station a stocky girl with a cap on her knot of reddish-blond hair supported her sleeping head in cupped palms. Carter cleared his throat twice to rouse her.

"My wife's here I just got into town and would like to know how she is."

"Name, please."

He guessed blindly. "White. Elaine White."

Spinning a circular file, she picked out a card. "Yes, she arrived a few hours ago and is in labor."

"May I see her?"

"I'm afraid not. Not until afterward." She offered a

pale smile of reassurance. "Your wife's card hasn't been completed. The duty nurse must have thought you'd give us the information. Is this your first baby?" she asked, rotating her chair to an electric typewriter.

"Yes."

"How exciting. What do you want?"

"It doesn't matter. Could you tell me how she's doing?"

"I'm sure she's doing wonderfully, Mr. White." After winding the card onto the platen, she examined the nail on her index finger, tested it with a nibble, and asked, "What's your wife's maiden name?"

"Yost."

"Isn't that on the card?"

"No."

After this she rapped out a dozen questions—age? address? family illnesses?—as her pudgy fingers, each dusted with red hairs at the knuckle, raced to keep up with his answers. He was reminded of that night months ago at Fingerhut's. Now it was too late to hide the truth. Or to hide from it. The most dangerous questions were his own, and Elaine alone had the answers.

"Your occupation, Mr. White"

"I . . . uh . . . I'm unemployed at the moment."

Her milky eyes lifted in a sidelong glance. "Do you carry Blue Cross, Blue Shield, or any other health insurance?"

"No."

"Do you plan to pay cash or by check?"

"We've made other arrangements."

The typewriter wheezed as she switched it off, and impatience brought color to her cheeks. "Are you a charity case?"

"Of course not."

"Pardon me, but who will be paying the bill?"

"I will."

"Mr. White, you just told me you'd made other arrangements."

"Miss Dugan at the Harold Wendell Agency was supposed to tend to this. I was to pay her later."

Her eyes closed, as if she were bored beyond reckoning. "Is this an agency case?"

"Is that what you call it?"

Ripping the card from the typewriter, she flung it in a wastebasket. "Why didn't you tell me the baby was up for adoption. We have a special record for agency cases. You may go to the waiting room."

Carter seethed as he stalked through the hall. It wasn't the nurse's fault, of course, but it wasn't his either. Why hadn't Miss Dugan seen to this? And after he'd signed the release, after Elaine had left and never called, why was she registered in his name? Unless . . . His mind reversed itself. Unless she intended to return, in which case she could do whatever she wanted.

In the waiting room there was no one save a black boy about fourteen with an Afro haircut, big and bristling as a coonskin cap. His insolent eyes sounded Carter, then glanced away. Chastened by the boy's cool, Carter calmed himself and sat in a green vinyl chair. On the wall was a framed crewelwork copy of the Expectant Father's Prayer.

> He waits in the wings
> While an angel sings
> And brings a bundle of glory down from the skies.
> It's the flesh of his flesh, which in his eyes
> Bears the mark of a mother's love
> And a radiant smile from up above.
> He prays his child will win happiness, fortune, and fame,
> But most of all that he will remember from whence he came.

There would be scant glory in this little bundle's birth. With some shame, he realized he had never even thought of the baby as a person. If anything, he'd considered it a force—the fate that had brought Elaine and him together, driven them West, and now apart. Afterward they might be reconciled or, with nothing to bind them, drift farther apart. For the first time he wondered about this baby who would soon be not only the source of problems, but, like everyone else, their object. Dragged into the dark stream of life, he would be born and no one would care. Could this account for Elaine's behavior? Her depression, withdrawal, and final panic?

Abruptly he got to his feet. Again he was using the baby, this time as a rationalization for Elaine's actions. Rather than do this, he walked a well-worn path in the carpet, oblivious to the boy and to anyone who passed the open door. He must have looked like an archtypical expectant father, harried, fretful, and nervous. Wiping his forehead, he found it moist. He couldn't dispel the baby from his thoughts. It needled its way in and swam elusively like the specks of dust in the silver beads on the windowpane. What would become of it? Was he responsible since he'd refused to help Elaine have an abortion? He had believed there was a value in allowing the baby to be born. What was it? Simply that more life, even if it meant more death, was better than no life at all?

"Hey, man, you awright?"

"Yes," he mumbled to the black boy. "Just nervous."

Carter sat and picked up a magazine. Though he couldn't bear to read, he flipped the pages, studying the photographs and the advertisements with absurd concentration, trying to replace his gnawing fears with these vapid images. But sight of one toothy, lunatic grin after another did little to relieve his anxiety. He began to whisper silently, Don't let her die. Don't let the baby die. He couldn't remember asking more fervently for anything.

An hour later a vivacious nurse, determined to smile, burst into the room. "Mr. Johnston, you've had a . . ." then seeing Carter and the boy, trailed off. She glanced over her shoulder, thinking Mr. Johnston might be there, and her calves, encased in stockings, looked pink and thick as sausages.

"What did you say about Johnston?" asked the boy.

"Surely, you're not Mr. Johnston."

"I'm Raymond Johnston. Where's my mother at?"

"She had a baby boy. What do you think of that?" The nurse readied her smile.

"Where is she?"

"In the recovery room. How would you like to see your baby brother?"

"Okay, lemme have a look at him."

Before the nurse left she asked Carter his name, and said, "I'm sorry. I didn't know you were here. They took Mrs. White to the delivery room half an hour ago. It shouldn't be long now."

Putting aside the magazine, Carter went to the window. It was almost dawn. The sky had grown a shade brighter, and low-flying clouds scudded past like oily rags. Leaning forward, he cooled his forehead on the glass. He wanted to talk to someone, but the only thing he could

232

have said was how much he missed Elaine, and the only person he could have told was Elaine herself.

Within minutes the nurse returned, rubber soles squeaking, and extended her hand. "Congratulations, Mr. White. You have a daughter. A big one. Eight pounds and three ounces."

"Great." His voice was hurried. "Is everything all right?"

"Yes. They're both fine, although your wife may be sore for a few days. She's had a rough night."

"Can I see her?"

"Not for a while. But the baby's ready, if you'll follow me."

"Pardon me. I . . . " He hung back, unsure of himself.

"Is anything wrong?"

"No. Nothing."

Chattering about what a wonderful job Elaine had done, she led him down the hall, through a pair of swinging doors, and into an alcove next to the nursery. A Negro aide wheeled out a plastic crib, no larger than a grocery cart, labeled *Girl White*. In it the baby cried galvanically, oaring her arms and legs back and forth. Her skin was a reddish purple, and a glinting safety pin had been stuck through the bud of her navel. Carter marveled that anything so small could survive.

"Is the pin necessary?" he asked.

"Yes. Always." Laughing, the nurse put her hands into the crib. They looked large, threatening, and crude as she removed the diaper to show him tiny buttocks and pads of flesh between the trembling bowlegs. Then she smoothed the damp hair at the back of the baby's head. "Beautiful, isn't she?"

"Yes," he murmured, and though tempted to pick her up, hesitated to touch another person he couldn't hold.

As the aid rolled the crib away, the last glimpse Carter had was of the delicate birdlike limbs beating the air.

"Now after you've signed this statement that the baby was delivered in good health"—she directed him to a desk—"you can see your wife."

"I'm not the father."

"Pardon?"

"I'm not the baby's father."

'You're not Mr. White?"

"Yes, but I'm not the father."

"As long as you're a relative, we'll let you pinch-hit."

"I'm not a relative. I'm just . . ." Just what? Just

here. ". . . a friend. It's an agency case," he repeated the earlier explanation.

"Oh, I didn't know. Excuse me. I'll be right back."

With a hand on the desk for support, he closed his stinging eyes and took on the full weight of this night's fatigue. When the nurse returned, she wasn't smiling. "I'm sorry for the delay, Mr. White. If you wish, you can visit your . . . the mother."

His leg ached, his head ached, and he was as dim and vacant as the corridor. He didn't have to check the chromium clock on the wall to know it was too late to review his strategies for convincing her to come back. Through a door he peered into the gloom. Below a curtained window Elaine was in bed, her body so thin it scarcely wrinkled the covers. She seemed troubled by bad dreams, and her face, flushed with pain, fretted between the pillow and the edge of the sheet, like a tired eye between white lids that would not close. Drawing nearer, he noticed a groove in her lower lip, a perfect imprint of her teeth, which she must have clamped down hard when the doctor told her to push.

He caressed her arm. "Elaine? Elaine, it's me."

Clouded by anesthetic, her eyes opened without focus and filled with tears. "Oh God," she moaned. "What have you done?"

"Nothing. I'll explain." Dizzily he bent over to kiss her forehead.

Suddenly her tone changed, and she slipped her arms around his neck. "Isn't she beautiful?" Hugging his head to her breast for a moment, she rocked him like a child. Then just as suddenly her arms stiffened, broke apart like dry sticks, and she started to cry.

"What's wrong?" On her red cheeks the tears appeared tinged by blood. Carter blotted them with his coat sleeve.

"How did you find me? Why did you do it?" As she lifted herself on an elbow, a look of pure panic spun out of her eyes. "You can't stay here."

"Lie down. I'm not going."

"You've got to." She fell back heavily. "My mother's coming."

"What? When?" He clutched at the bed.

"I called yesterday. She'll be here today."

"Why did you do it?"

"Because I . . . I don't know. I was alone."

234

"You should have called me." Carter was faint, and his stomach twisted into a knot of dread.

"It's no good between us any more. You told."

"No. I didn't. Eddie Brown found out through a private detective. Remember that night I went to Brentwood for an examination? Well it was a polygraph . . ."

She had turned her face to the wall.

"You're not listening."

"It's too late, Carter. My mother will be here any minute."

"It doesn't matter. I . . ."

"Yes, it does. You have to go."

"I won't. I don't care who's coming. Elaine, you can't do this to me."

She grabbed his wrist. "I'll call the nurse."

"Have you gone crazy? I didn't do it. Don't you believe me?"

"There's no time." Her fingernails dug into him.

"Then I'll come back. I'm not going until you promise to let me tell you the truth."

"All right." She nodded. "I promise I'll phone you."

"Do I have your word?"

"Yes. Of course."

"Why couldn't I stay here and help you with your mother?"

"Carter, if you want to help, please go."

"All right. But we'll work this out."

When he leaned down to kiss her, her arms locked around him once more and her lips seized his. Then she whispered, "God, what's wrong with me?"

Slowly Carter backed out the door and lingered a moment in the hall. But he could see only a slight curve in the covers, the pale glow of her forehead, the purple slash of her lips.

Chapter XIV

1

Overhead as the clouds scattered, a summer sun blossomed in the January sky, its rays piercing the smog like klieg lights. It seemed to set the stage for a happy Hollywood ending, but Carter felt worse than ever. Now that Elaine's mother knew, the situation had drifted out of his hands, beyond his control, and the bond between them weakened with each retelling of their secret.

Yet he was too tired to think, and it took two cups of coffee to keep him awake for the drive home. Once in the apartment he couldn't hold his eyes open any longer. Staggering to the bedroom, he flung wide the windows, letting in warm air and light, and sprawled across the single beds, burying his face on Elaine's side. It still carried her scent, which choked him with anguish. He wanted to move, but darkness enfolded him.

Exhausting, disjointed dreams denied him the rest he needed. He saw himself trapped in a sweltering jungle, unable to break free of its lush vegetation. As sharp-leafed plants slashed his arms and face, he felt sweat and blood course over him and gather in soggy patches on his clothing. Choking for air, he was at the edge of consciousness several times, yet miraculously remained under the hood of sleep, laboring like a miner in an endless, unlighted tunnel, determined not to emerge until his time was up or he had found what he was looking for.

When he woke to a more palpable darkness, he had found nothing, but was, in fact, clammy with perspiration and ravenously hungry. His joints ached and his tongue clove to the roof of his mouth. Unable to tell what time of night it was, he decided it didn't matter. To get up, undress, and eat threatened far greater discomfort. Already the hectic repetitions, ill-defined plans, and questions were beating to the surface of his brain. He remembered the baby, and it was as if his arms and legs had been oaring the empty air, anxious to locate a fixed point and hold on. Moving away from the damp spot on the sheet, he turned up the cool side of a pillow and closed his eyes.

He was wakened by a knock at the door. He'd heard it half a dozen times before he recognized what it was. Then, having slept the clock around, he required a few moments to recall how to use his feet. They wouldn't work and kicked awkwardly against one another. He limped toward the door, his left shoe on, the right off. It was too late to repair this. The knocking had gotten louder.

"Morning, Mr. White," said Chuck Regan, who appeared to be suffering a terrible hangover. His wife was beside him. "Haven't seen you lately. How's Mrs. White?"

"She's fine." Carter blocked the doorway.

Tilting his head toward his wife, as if to say I told you so, Regan muttered. "Well, the weather's been nasty, but I . . ."

"Is she here?" asked Mrs. Regan. "I saw her leave a few days ago, carrying a suitcase."

"She's in the hospital." He could think of no reason not to tell them.

"Isn't that what I said?" she demanded of her husband.

"The baby was born yesterday. A girl, eight pounds, three ounces."

"Oh, poor Elaine." She bit her tough knuckles. "I warned her. She must be in agony."

Regan stuck out his hand. "Congratulations! When can we see her?"

"She can't have visitors. The baby and she are under special treatment. It was a very difficult delivery. I'll give her your best." He started to shut the door.

"Is it serious? How is she?" Mrs. Regan asked.

"As well as might be expected."

"So much pain and misery, and for what? Well, I guess you'll be wanting to move now."

"What? Why?"

"You know we don't allow babies. You'll have to sublet."

"Couldn't you wait awhile." He fumbled for an ex-

237

cuse. "It may be weeks before Elaine and the baby can travel."

"You'll have till the end of the month. That should be plenty of time. Be sure to tell me before you go. We don't return your damage deposit until we've inspected the apartment. Careful of the stove," warned Mrs. Regan. "That's where most tenants make their mistake. They think we'll clean up after them for nothing."

As they crossed the courtyard Mr. Regan teetered ponderously, while his wife walked a pace behind, taking springy steps like a terrier.

The morning unwound slowly and in silence, while Carter, groggy from twenty-four hours of sleep, fixed scrambled eggs and coffee, then ate beside the telephone. But it was impossible for him to sit still, and the coffee added to his confusion. His muddled thoughts reminded him of the months at Walter Reed, when at any hour half a dozen drugs warred for his mind. During the day he popped pep pills to ward off depression and boredom, and at night munched Darvon and waited for the nurse to bring a needle and pump him full of sleep. Most of the time he was going the wrong way—up when he wanted to be down, down on days when it would have been a joy to be up.

As he sought a comfortable position on the sofa, his insides coiled tighter. He asked himself why Elaine had called her mother. There was no answer. Or rather there were too many answers, all of them useless unless he intended to forget her and leave now. Yet he had deferred his questions so long, he saw no logic in going before he talked to her.

After breakfast he thought he might as well clean the apartment. He wanted the deposit back, and was also anxious to work off his excess energy. Starting with the stove, he soon had its yellow enamel shining brightly enough to satisfy Mrs. Regan. Then he scrubbed the sink, the refrigerator, and the breakfast bar, and swept away a week's accumulation of dust from the kitchen floor.

That afternoon, while packing, he made it a point to mix their clothing in the suitcases, putting her blouses in with his shirts, his suits with her dresses, her stockings with his socks. He stuffed their underwear so that a pair of his jockey shorts lay atop each pair of her bikini briefs. Then, not wanting to spoil the job he'd done on the stove, he walked up to Ah Fong's, a Chinese restaurant on

Sunset Strip, ate a plate of chop suey, and returned pleasantly tired.

While waiting for sleep to overtake him, he tested himself and thought of Elaine to see what would happen. When nothing did, he sat bolt upright and in deliberate, self-induced spasms attempted to rekindle his agony. Just as he had sometimes squeezed his knee to determine if it still hurt, he made himself remember her face, her body, things they'd done, places they'd gone, for he feared if his pain didn't last, his love wasn't real and wouldn't last either.

Nothing succeeded in reviving his emotions until he imagined what his life would be like without her, not for a week or month or year, but forever. At the word "forever" there was a faint tingling in his extremities, and like a man who has lost a limb, yet swears he can feel it or its phantom, Carter was more aware of Elaine by the ache her absence caused. Satisfied at last, he lay back and slept.

He worked all the next day, and by evening had emptied the closet and the bureau. After stacking a pyramid of boxes and suitcases beside the bed, he stepped into the living room to check what was left to be done. Nothing. The apartment looked desolate, as if no one had ever lived in it. The odor of cleanser and disinfectant had transformed it into a public place, and he couldn't bear to stay any longer than he had to. He wouldn't have minded so much if it had been haunted by memories, but everything had fled along with their belongings, and the whitewashed rooms appeared unused, undented, like plastic containers ready to be discarded. Or to be more precise, since the apartment would have another tenant, Carter was the one to be discarded. The spare part.

Though he knew he wouldn't sleep, he switched out the light, peeled off his clothing, and reclined on the couch. At first the darkness was dense, total. Then the beams slowly separated from their white background, and the red-tile floor formed a random jigsaw puzzle from which the wooden furniture—Spanish Provincial, Elaine had called it—rose like dark roots out of polished ice.

In the beginning, although he hadn't wanted this apartment and hadn't thought they could afford it, he had looked on it as a place to hide from the world. It had been like living safely inside an eggshell—until the cracks and the thinness of the walls had begun to show. Then everything had crashed in upon him. But he hadn't been completely crushed, and realized he wouldn't make the same mistake twice. Nothing was more foolish than refusing to live in the real world, which was less like an eggshell and more like the silver beads he'd seen on the windowpane, each swirling with specks of dust, in a condition of apparent chaos where what was precious couldn't easily be separated from what was base.

The phone rang, and as a test of his nerves, he let it ring three more times before answering.

"It's me," said Elaine. "I promised I'd call."

"I want to see you."

"Yes." She sighed. "But . . ."

"But what? Is anything wrong?" The senselessness of the question stunned them both into silence. "Where are you?" he asked.

"It doesn't matter."

"When can we meet?"

"I'll be at the agency tomorrow."

"Couldn't we make it somewhere else?"

"I don't have a car."

"I'll pick you up."

"All right, pick me up at the agency at ten-thirty. I have to be there. It's important."

"Elaine, there's been a terrible mistake. I should have told you in the beginning . . ." Somehow her silence made him stop. He didn't believe she was listening, and realized, reluctantly, he would have to wait until tomorrow for any true communication. "Are you with your mother?"

"Yes. She's not here now. But she'll be back."

"How is it?"

"Awful."

"Have you told her everything?"

"I don't know. There's so much to tell."

"How's she taking it?"

"Very hard. I don't know who's cried more, she or I."

"Maybe I could help. I miss you, Elaine."

"I miss you, too, but I don't think you could help."

"Well, I'll try. There must be a way to work this out." When she didn't answer, he said, "The Regans informed me we have till the end of the month to move out. Of course, they assume we're bringing the baby . . ."

"Carter, I hear my mother in the hall. I have to hang up. I'll see you tomorrow." There were two clicks—the first a door being shut, the second a circuit being cut.

He lay there a long time before the room returned to focus. Her voice had been worse than perfume, as stirring as the softest touch, and he began to brood over desperate plans. He had to go off with her, talk to her alone. Once they spent a night together, he was sure her mother couldn't separate them. If Elaine wanted proof, he'd take her to Fingerhut, who could swear Carter was telling the truth.

Suddenly he felt queasy, weak. If she wouldn't accept his word, why would she believe Fingerhut? And why should she need proof? His thoughts spurted frantically before backing off from these questions. He was tired of taking refuge in laborious sophistical reasoning. Much as he longed for Elaine, he stopped scheming and drifted into an uneasy sleep.

2

Though he hadn't wound the clock, Carter woke at seven, an ominous hush ringing in his ears. He tried to regain the tepid amnesia of sleep, but couldn't shut out the silence, and the room was already too bright. Sunlight, solid as a brass platter, had pressed against the windows. Rolling back the spread, he got up and filled his lungs to loosen the tense cords in his chest.

With its stacked boxes and suitcases, the bedroom looked like a warehouse. He started to finish the job and strip the beds, but thought they might need a place to sleep tonight. After tucking the covers back in carefully, he laid out the clothing he would wear—everything Elaine had bought him for Christmas—then showered, shaved, and dressed himself with hands so cold and steady they might have belonged to someone else.

The trick again was not to think, to concentrate on sensation to the exclusion of reason. He moved like an automation and ate dry cereal and toast as if he were doing exercises. When he had finished, he began to pace, his footsteps echoing through the empty rooms. For no reason he stopped to pat his pockets. He had everything —keys, cards, wallet, money—and couldn't bear to wait any longer.

He drove first to a carwash on Beverly Boulevard and sent the Thunderbird through the hissing tunnel. It emerged wet and glistening, steamed free of grease and road grime. But it didn't look new. As three black men in sunglasses buffed the enamel, a diagram of scratches was revealed. In another year the car would need paint.

At the cashier's window a clock registered 9:16. After paying a dollar fifty, he stepped into the lavatory to wash his hands, comb his hair, and compose a suitable expression. The one he wore was taut and awkward, his mouth set in an unfamiliar smile. If nothing else, his eyes would have betrayed him. Dark themselves, they were surrounded by shadows that seemed to drain into the hollows of his cheeks.

As he bent over to splash cold water on his face, he was seized by a fit of vomiting and promptly brought up his breakfast. Strangely, he hadn't felt ill before and didn't afterward. In fact, he was calmer now. He cleaned himself, rinsed his mouth, and on the way to the car, bought a pack of chewing gum.

When he reached Crenshaw Boulevard, it was too late for last-minute rehearsals. As he turned through the gates, gravel pinged at the fenders, and he was struck again by how much the Harold Wendell Agency resembled a somnolent estate in the South. The deserted grounds were shaded in pools by tall palms. It might have been a Sunday, with everyone off at church. From behind the hedges in back of the house rose the muffled roar of a power mower, and as Carter got out of the car and crunched over the parking lot, he smelled freshly cut grass.

Elaine was on the porch, wearing a sleeveless white dress with red piping at the V neck. Her arms were folded, her legs were straight in front of her, and she sat at an awkward angle, so that her chignon touched the wall. Her eyes wandered placidly over the lawn.

He wasn't certain where to focus his own, since he didn't want to face Elaine until he was close enough to touch her. As he mounted three wooden steps, he smoothed his palms on the nap of his new suede jacket, then looking up, noticed that her eyes, though still wandering, were far from placid. Dark and flat, they reminded him of his. Yet he said, "You look nice." He had planned to kiss her, but settled for a hand on her bare shoulder.

"Thank you. You're pale. Do you feel well?"

"I'm fine." He lowered his hand along her inner arm. Her pulse beat at his fingertips. "Let's get away from here."

They were off the porch before she asked, "Where?"

"Anywhere." He gestured toward the parking lot. "In the car."

"No." She slipped her wrist free. "I can't leave."

"Why?"

"I have some papers to sign."

"For the adoption?"

She nodded.

"At least let's move away from the building." He steered her down the front lawn, which was springy and damp, the texture of a putting green.

"Not too fast. I'm still sore."

"The nurse said you did very well."

For the first time she smiled, faintly. "It doesn't take too much skill. You look good in that coat. Aren't you glad I made you buy it?" Then she said, "This is far enough. It smells like spring, doesn't it?"

He was surrounded by the perfume that had haunted him for days, and wanted to take her in his arms, though not here, halfway between the house and the wrought-iron fence at the street. She had continued her common-place remarks, and although on its own each might be meaningless, their cumulative effect suggested to Carter that nothing had changed. "I've come to bring you home," he casually interrupted.

"So has my mother."

"You know you'd rather be with me."

"It's no good, Carter. It wouldn't work." She delivered this as offhandedly as her comments about the weather and his coat, but she wouldn't look at him.

He lifted her chin. "That's nonsense. You don't think I told Eddie Brown, do you?"

"I don't know what to think."

"I can explain." All the words and emotions that had welled up in him for a week started to spill over. "Eddie found out on his own after we cheated him. He hired a private detective who has friends in Washington and they . . ." She wasn't listening. "You already know this. Miss Dugan told you."

"Yes. I know you wouldn't hurt me." She said it with tenderness, yet again too calmly to please Carter.

"Then why did you leave?"

"I . . . I don't know."

"You must have had a reason."

"Carter, I don't want to talk about it any more."

"We haven't talked about it at all yet."

"It wouldn't matter how long we talked. You wouldn't understand. I was confused. Frightened. That's the best I can do."

It wasn't good enough, and a long moment passed in silence before he said, "All right, we won't talk about it. It doesn't matter. I want you to come back with me."

"Don't you see, it does matter? It means things would never be the same. Too much has happened."

"Didn't we just agree to forget what's happened?"

"No, we didn't agree, and it wouldn't help if we had. It's not that easy. If we got married, we'd make each other miserable."

"We're miserable now."

"If we stay together, it'll only get worse."

"Don't you love me? Haven't you been happy?"

"Yes, I love you, and I was happy right up until the end, but . . ."

"That's all that counts." He tried to break through her distraction.

"No, it's not. It takes more than love. We have too much going against us. We've ruined everything. Or rather I ruined it. We have nothing left except love."

"That sounds like something your mother or Miss Dugan told you," he said angrily.

"Maybe. I don't remember. They've said so much. But it's true. We have too many raw spots, too many conflicts. You're different from me in every way. That's what I've realized. Or rather, finally admitted to myself."

"What are you talking about? You just said you'd been happy for the last five months."

"Five months aren't a lifetime."

"Okay, but what's a lifetime if not a lot of five months strung together?"

"Carter"—her voice quavered; this was evidently more difficult than she'd expected—"I don't want to argue."

"We're not arguing. I simply don't see any conflicts. None that we couldn't cope with."

"Oh, be reasonable." She glanced over her shoulder at the agency, as if for help. "There would be so many problems. Think what marriage means. Children. A career for you. You haven't even finished college. And when you began to support a family . . ."

"What the hell, I've supported you."

"Yes, of course," she soothed him. "But you don't want to work at Danny Boy's the rest of your life, do you?"

"What? I don't . . . You're the one who said it was a good . . ." He was too angry to go on.

"It's all so obvious. On top of everything else you're a Catholic and . . ."

Something rose in his throat and he had to step back to swallow. He wanted to demand what she meant, yet couldn't speak, and wouldn't deny what Miss Dugan and she had insisted upon. He was a Catholic—which he assumed meant exactly what they had implied. That he was odd and out of it.

"I'm going to sign the papers and leave with my mother," she said. "We have a flight to Costa Rica tonight."

"Look, we could make it. Didn't you always tell me things were easy if you let them be?" He didn't know why he said this. The words were a cold accusation, not an entreaty.

"Yes, I used to say that, Carter. But you taught me that everything is difficult."

"Jesus Christ." He laughed bitterly.

"Please, don't act like that. I don't regret anything we've done. I'm not even sorry I decided to have the baby. I've learned a lot about myself and . . ."

"Stop it! Don't make a philosophy lesson out of this. I don't give a damn what you've learned or I've learned or what Miss Dugan has told you. I'm sick of her penny psychology. Sick of everything."

"Don't shout. Don't be angry." Her eyes were full of tears.

"What the hell do you expect?"

"Carter, please don't. I love you."

"Don't say that! Do you hear me? Don't!"

"All right. I won't say it. I have to go now."

"Wait a minute." He grabbed her arm. "I'd like to know one thing, and I want the truth. I hope that's not too much to ask. Why does the baby have my last name?"

"What do you mean?" She tried to pull back, but he wouldn't let her.

"It's very simple. My name was on the baby's crib. Is it on the birth certificate?"

"I suppose so. It doesn't matter. They make a new one as soon as the baby's adopted. After all, that was the name we gave Miss Dugan."

"Of course. But does your mother know?"

"Know what?"

"Did you tell her everything?"

She flicked her eyes toward the building again, as if she would run for it unless help came soon. "We talked for hours. I don't . . ."

"Don't lie to me. Does she know I'm not the baby's father?"

Something strange happened to Elaine's face. It seemed to come apart. Her mouth opened, her nostrils flared, her eyes turned inward. She resembled the death mask of a woman caught in the final lie that had killed her. Only when she bit hard at her lower lip did her features draw back together.

"Does she?"

"I don't know," she murmured, frightened.

"Of course you know." He shook her roughly. "You and Miss Dugan took care of everything. Your mother thinks I'm the baby's father. That was your way of ensuring that we couldn't stay together. Wasn't it?"

"I've got to go. You're hurting me."

Carter released her, and she ducked beyond his grasp. "You don't hate me, do you?"

"No, I don't hate you." He thought he was bleeding, but couldn't have said where the wound was. "I don't even know you."

"Will you let me kiss you goodbye?"

"No. You want too much."

Bowing her head, she turned and ascended the lawn in short, tentative steps. Then at the porch, she paused to glance over her left shoulder, but couldn't have seen Carter, who had started to the right, toward the parking lot. Halfway there, he hesitated. What would he do with the car and her clothing? Elaine had gone inside the building, and the door banged shut.

He dug the keys from his pocket, unlocked the Thunderbird, and hurled them onto the driver's seat. The ring jangled when he slammed the door. Descending the driveway, he stepped off the gravel onto the grass to stop the crunching in his ears.

Chapter XV

Carter wandered for two hours, with no idea where he was headed or how far he had gone. He remembered nothing he'd seen, and the lone thing he heard was his conversation with Elaine replaying like a faulty tape in his mind. He ran it at slow speed, then double-time, stopped it, rewound, and ran it again, convinced there had been a mistake. She hadn't listened. He hadn't made himself clear. Yet the words were all in order and sounded logical. She had simply chosen not to understand.

This snapped the tape, and Carter walked faster, his footsteps resounding through a squalid neighborhood where Negroes eyed him in mild surprise. Ahead, the street and sidewalk narrowed but never met. They looked like bands of black and white adhesive which wrapped the crumbling disorder of each block in rigid boundaries.

A cab braked at the curb beside him, and the driver said, "Get in."

"What?"

He was a burly fellow with a two-day beard and a blue-flannel shirt. "Get in before you're killed."

Carter obeyed, more out of an aversion for argument than fear, and the man flipped up a red metal flag on the meter. While he discussed crime rates, murder, and rape in "nigger neighborhoods," the meter stuttered madly as a cheap clock. At $1.51 Carter synchronized his wrist-watch, but the numbers mounted higher—$1.98, $1.99, two o'clock. Time faded in and faded out, lost control and regained it, as Carter witnessed the rare spectacle of a cliché meeting its moment of truth. Time was money and didn't matter. Money wasn't real either, as he attempted to prove when the cabbie halted on North Harper and said, "Five eighty-nine." Carter gave him a ten-dollar bill and told him to keep the change.

In the courtyard a rumpled gray shape rested at the

edge of the fountain. It might have been a bag of soiled laundry. Carter paid it little attention until a hand reached up, scratched, and retreated into the rags. Then a bloated white face appeared, like a drowned man rising. "Hey, kid, it's me." In a shabby oversized raincoat, Eddie Brown struggled to his feet. "I been waiting . . ."

Someone screamed. Carter couldn't be sure who. A cold wind whistled up his spine, standing his hair on end. In two quick strides he pounced on Eddie, picked him up by the neck, and bent him back into the fountain.

"You son of a bitch! I'll kill you." The words were wrenched painfully from Carter's throat, and as he started to strangle Eddie, he felt he was choking himself.

Eddie didn't resist. He hadn't even removed his hands from his pockets. Wheezing, he whispered, "Psst, kid, stop it. Watch out," and motioned behind Carter.

Carter couldn't speak, couldn't breathe. Twisting around, he met Mrs. Regan face to face. Her cold sparrow-claw hands grasped at his Adam's apple, her yellow teeth were bared to sever his jugular vein. "You rotten bastard. You selfish son of a bitch," she shrieked, while Mr. Regan plucked futilely at the taut strings of her arms. "Honey, please."

For an instant the four of them were frozen in this fierce tableau—Carter and Mrs. Regan fighting to find an object for their all-encompassing rage, Eddie thrashing about now for escape, Mr. Regan feebly trying to separate them. Then Carter relaxed, and Eddie splashed into the fountain. The noise and cold water brought them to their senses. Yet even as she released her death grip, Mrs. Regan ranted about "sons of bitches" and "bastards."

Eddie clambered out of the pool, shedding water from the filthy raincoat, his hair slicked back and his eyes wide in rodent-like panic. He tugged Carter by the sleeve. "Let's split. This bitch is crazy."

"How dare you come onto my property"—she advanced on Carter, beak first—"after what you've done. I could tell by your eyes you were a cruel, no-account bastard. I tried to warn Elaine. But who would have believed you'd leave her the week after the baby was born?"

"What are you talking about?"

"I spent the morning with Elaine's mother, packing the poor girl's belongings. Mrs. Yost told me everything. How you kicked Elaine out and said you never wanted to see the baby. How . . ."

"You let her into my apartment?"

"*My* apartment. And you have exactly one hour to clear out."

"What about the damage deposit?"

"Don't be ridiculous. The place is a mess."

"I spent days cleaning it."

"So take me to court. The things I could tell about you. When you go, drag this piece of trash along with you." She pointed to Eddie.

"Hey, babe, watch it or I'll bust your skinny ass in two."

"Did you hear that?" she asked her husband, who gave no indication that he had. His hands were deep in his pockets and he squinted up as if following the flight of a golf ball. "I . . . I'll . . ." She whirled on Eddie. "I'll call the police."

Instinctively Eddie stepped back. "Kid, she's serious. Let's get moving."

"We're not going anywhere together." Then to Mrs. Regan, "Are my clothes still here?"

"Yes. You'd better start packing, mister." Tapping her foot, she tolled off the seconds.

Carter had no energy to argue. He headed into the apartment with Eddie dogging his heels.

"Kid, I have to talk to you."

"You'd better beat it while you can."

"I'm in a jam. A bad one. I'm broke."

"Tough. After what you did, you're lucky I don't break your neck."

"Be fair. I helped you when you were down." He dodged into the bedroom ahead of Carter.

The room was stark and blindingly bright. The beds, from which the sheets had been stripped, looked like cold gray slabs in a morgue. Someone had stuffed all Carter's belongings into his battered suitcase, which lay open on the bare mattress. At the sight of how little he had left, he sank onto a stool in front of the bureau.

"What's the matter, kid?"

"Elaine's gone. She ran off right after you threatened her."

"What!" Though he acted incredulous, Eddie edged toward the door. Haggard, red-eyed, dressed in mismatched clothing, he might have been a panhandler on skid row. But he wasn't much different than before. Regardless of what he wore, he had always seemed in disguise and on the lam.

"You didn't keep your word. You tried to blackmail us. Elaine panicked and . . . Oh, hell, what's the use?"

"This is a bum rap."

"Don't bullshit me. It's over anyway."

"I'm not. I swear to you."

"You didn't ask for money?"

"Well . . ." His eyes richocheted around the room. "I did drop by and talk to her, but only about the bread you owed me. She was a little uptight, so I told her her family would never know, if she paid off. That's the truth, kid."

"And that's what did it. But if it hadn't been you, I guess it would have been something else."

"I'm sorry. Honest, I am." He squeezed Carter's shoulder and sat on the bed in front of him. "I know how crummy you must feel. I've had trouble myself—which is the reason I'm here. Remember Ebba Sjostrom?"

Tilting his head against the bureau, Carter didn't bother to answer.

"That sweet little piece busted my ass. Guess how old she is?"

Carter didn't make the effort.

"She said twenty-two, but she's actually sixteen, and what's more, she isn't in the States as an *au pair* girl. She's an exchange student. A high school junior, for Christ's sake. When I heard that, I almost went down for the count. But, kid"—he yanked Carter's arm—"that's not the half of it. She thought I planned to marry her. When I told her how far off base she was, she informed me *I* was. For such a hot bitch, she has ice water in her veins. She threatened to scream rape, which didn't really shake me. I've been through it before." Eddie clamped a hand to the maple-leaf scar on his belly.

"Next thing I knew, there was a lawyer at my apartment asking how I intended to handle it. Did I want to marry Ebba? Can you imagine? A sixteen-year-old girl? I swear, though"—he raised his right hand—"you couldn't tell. She could have taken three of what I got and still had room to spare. But this lawyer said the alternative was a cash settlement or legal action."

"What's the age of consent in California?" asked Carter.

"It doesn't make a damn bit of difference. When they're out to bust you, they'll find a way. There are laws on the books just waiting for guys like me to fuck up. The lawyer laid one of them on me. The Mann Act. Carrying

Ebba across the state line to Vegas. Maybe they couldn't have made it stick, but by the time it was over I wouldn't have had a penny."

"So what did you do? Pay off?"

"Hell no! I went underground. I'm living up in the hills with a bunch of hippies. They don't know who I am and they don't care. But every cop in the city, including Fingerhut, is hot on my ass. He might have tailed me here. That's why I need dough. I'm cutting out for the East Coast. Maybe you'll come along now that your girl has dumped you."

"No, thanks." Carter had slumped lower against the bureau.

"What are you going to do?"

"I don't know."

"Are you still at Danny Boy's?"

"I quit."

"You must be nuts. These are hard times. Why the hell did you do that?"

Carter shrugged. "I was busy trying to find Elaine, and I had a lot of thinking to do. Now if you'll . . ."

"Hey, kid, forget the thinking. Every time you start that, you wind up sitting on your ass, looking like a zombie." Eddie bent forward, elbows on knees. As his hair dried, a new crust of dandruff flaked off his scalp. "Come to New York. I'll knock you into shape and have you on your feet by next week."

"I told you, I'm not interested."

"What the hell are you interested in? You can't stay here. You heard the landlady. In an hour you'll be out on the street alone, lugging this cheap fucking valise." He slapped the suitcase shut. "People love a whipped dog. They'll step right on your face if you keep it hanging down like that."

Carter felt a flash of anger. "Do me a favor. Stuff your advice. I've had one complete treatment and I'm not in the mood for another."

"Oh, no?" Bridling, Eddie bounced to his feet and began to pace. As his leather heels detonated on the tiles, his voice took on its characteristic driving vitality. "You need something, kid, and you need it bad. Or are you going to let this put you down for good? I could see it coming a mile away. You want to give up! What the hell, so you lost your girl. You'll get another one. It all evens out in the long run."

"You don't understand. I loved her."

"What do you think I am, a rookie? Of course you loved her. That's what made it good between you, and that's what's eating out your guts now. But you can't curl up and die. You gotta go on."

"Why? What good is anything if it doesn't last?"

"Oh, Christ, kid, even you aren't that dumb. Nothing lasts! Absolutely nothing! If you started worrying about all the things that are going to end, you wouldn't get out of bed in the morning. But why should you miss your whole goddamn life? I tell you, in a few weeks, maybe a month, you'll find a girl . . ."

"No. Not me. I'd rather . . ."

"Rather what? Die? Commit suicide? Sure you would, kid." Eddie laughed. "The point is, you won't. You'll keep living. But no bullshit, I'd rather see you splash your brains all over the sidewalk than sit at the edge, diddling yourself, too scared to go either way."

At first Eddie rambled on, Carter scarcely listened. He was waiting, convinced he had to stack one hour on top of another and build a barrier between him and what had happened. But then he asked himself—maybe Eddie had demanded again—what he would do when he left the apartment for the last time.

Eddie was right. He wouldn't commit suicide. He missed Elaine, and would soon miss her more, but he wondered at the same time if he didn't miss himself almost as much—that "self" he'd become in Los Angeles. The man who had dealt with Eddie and Fingerhut's deviousness, who had survived the absurdity of Danny Boy's, had loved Elaine, helped her have her baby, and finally had to forsake it all.

"Look at me!" Eddie grabbed his chin. "We're going to gather your duds and blow this place. I refuse to let you fold. Not after all the time and energy I put in on you. On your feet."

"Okay, Coach." Smiling, Carter stood up and buckled his suitcase. "But I'm staying in L.A."

Eddie regarded him warily. "What'll you do for money"

"I'll get a job."

"Without my help? Be serious."

"Yes, without your help." Then, seeing Eddie's injured expression, he added, "After all you've taught me, I shouldn't have any trouble. Ready to go?"

"First, fork over two hundred bucks."

"I thought you'd forgotten that."

"Not on your life. Make it out to E. Durwin Braun."

"Who?"

"It's a name I use for professional reasons."

Carter was handing him the check when someone knocked noisily at the door.

"Who's that?" asked Eddie.

"Maybe the landlady telling us time is up."

"Don't answer till you're sure."

Together they crept into the hall as another knock boomed through the apartment. Wedging his shoulder to the door, Carter slid home the bolt. Outside, Mrs. Regan was talking to a man. It didn't sound like her husband. Then a dog growled and scratched at the door. Dragging Carter by the collar, Eddie dashed back to the bedroom.

"Jesus Christ, it's Fingerhut and that goddamn dog." He gave his head a ferocious scratching. "Is there another way out? The windows!"

Carter caught him before he could dive headfirst through the screen. "Calm down. I'll get rid of him."

"Don't be an asshole. If you open that door, he'll break you in half. I told you, he's after me. I wouldn't put it past him to start shooting."

"There's nothing to worry about," Carter whispered. "I'll tell him you're not here. Close the bedroom door and lock it. I'll call when he's gone."

The door shook steadily now under a hard rain of blows, and as Carter opened it, Fingerhut's fist missed his jaw by a fraction. Wearing wrap-around sunglasses and restraining Patton by a choker leash, he once again looked like a blind beggar. But his arm was out of the sling, and the head bandages had been reduced to one flesh-tinted patch over his right brow. "Let me speak to Eddie Brown." He stepped forward.

"Just a minute. You're not bringing that dog in here."

Fingerhut's mouth curled into a lipless smile. "Okay by me." He looped the leash around the outside doorknob. "That should guarantee us privacy."

He pushed past Carter into the apartment, rotating his head from side to side as if it were set in a greased socket.

"What do you want?" asked Carter, trailing him into the living room.

"I told you. Eddie Brown. Where is he?" After circling cautiously, he turned to Carter.

"Not here."

"The landlady says he is." Unbuttoning his jacket, he spread his legs for balance and stood with hands on hips. The shoulder holster bunched up the material under his armpit.

"She's wrong. He left."

Fingerhut sucked in his breath, blowing himself up as big as he would go. "He's wanted for statutory rape, you know."

"Is that so? I'll call you if I see him."

Expelling his breath, he removed the sunglasses. There was no more expression in his unblinking eyes than there had been in the smoked lenses. "Look, White, I'm a busy man. Tell me where Eddie is or I'll tear this place apart until I find him."

"You're not going to tear anything apart," Carter said flatly.

"Oh, I'm not?" He dipped his eyes down to Carter's bad knee, then raised them slowly in a calculated stare of appraisal. "You have thirty seconds to get out of my way." As he waited, Fingerhut's face became harder, more angular and transparent. With the bald confidence of a big man who'd never had to hide his feelings, he let one raw emotion after another—disdain, anger, and then hatred—swim into his eyes like predatory fish into a trap.

Carter's face might have changed, too, as his anger boiled over and all the rage and resentment he'd suppressed for weeks focused on this man whose cleft chin begged to be split.

"Well, White, time is about . . ." he'd started, when Carter swung and struck him on the point of the jaw. Fingerhut seemed surprised, stunned, not hurt much, until a second, then a third punch hit the same spot, and he toppled straight back, cracking his head on the tile. At the sound, which was like a pistol shot, Patton began barking and Eddie burst out of the bedroom.

"Jesus Christ, kid, is he dead?"

"No, just out cold. Our friend Fingerhut has a glass jaw." Carter felt a great sense of release and elation.

"Jesus Christ," Eddie muttered again, approaching the sprawled body. Even unconscious, Fingerhut had the muscular rigidity of a statue and might have been a brass general who'd been knocked from his pedestal in the park.

"We'd better leave before he revives," Carter warned Eddie, who was kicking Fingerhut in the ribs with the grim determination of a used-car buyer testing tires. "That's enough." He spun him away. "Let's go."

But when he'd retrieved his suitcase from the bedroom, and they had gotten to the door, they heard vicious barking on the other side. Patton was in a frenzy, flinging himself against the dry wood, tearing at it with his lethal claws.

"No chance that way," said Eddie. "The window."

This time Carter couldn't restrain him. Sprinting to the bedroom, Eddie kicked out the screen and leaped without a word or backward glance. Carter hesitated on the ledge.

"Jump, kid," shouted Eddie, scrambling to his feet.

"I can't. My leg. It . . ."

"Forget your leg." He waited beneath the window, as though willing to catch him. "It's not more than eight feet. Fall on your fucking head if it makes you feel better."

There was no time for such strategems. In the living room Fingerhut groaned loudly. Carter tossed his suitcase, then vaulted from the window sill, and after a serene free fall, smacked down on his bad leg, which buckled but held. He stamped once to make sure nothing had broken, tucked the valise under his arm, and raced after Eddie, who was halfway to Sunset. The air rushed in his ears and tore at his lungs, as he drove himself harder until he got a quick second wind and drew abreast of Eddie. In tandem they ran uphill to the intersection. where they crouched to catch their breath. No one was behind them.

"My car's around the corner." Eddie pointed east. "Sure you won't come along?"

"No, I'm headed in the other direction."

"Are you all right?"

"I'm all right."

"Good luck, kid."

After they had shaken hands, Eddie started to run again, and as his stubby legs fired out against the baggy raincoat, he looked like a midget inside a circus tent. Yet he was making good time toward Crescent Heights.

For some reason Carter, too, sprinted a block before

slowing to an easier gait and getting a better grip on the suitcase, which weighed more than he remembered. Then he fell in with the crowd on Sunset Strip, paused a second at Sweetzer Avenue, and crossed toward the light.